Kick HOME

OAKVILLE OBSESSIONS
BOOK THREE

KALLYN JONES

KICK HOME

A LATER IN LIFE ROMANCE

OAKVILLE OBSESSIONS
BOOK THREE

KALLYN JONES

Kick Home

Copyright 2022, 2025 by Kallyn Jones

My Creative Jones Press

This book is a work of fiction. Names, characters, places, and incidents are the product of the author's imagination or are used fictitiously. Possible resemblances to actual events, places, or people, living or dead, is coincidental.

Editor: D.A. Sarac/the Editing Pen

Copy Edit: Taming the Ink

Cover Design: the Jones Design Studio

❀ Formatted with Vellum

For WEJ. My best friend. My boo. With a heart so big it inspired two heroes. Thank you for your unlimited belief in me, for humoring my "what if..." questions, and the tech support.

THE LONGEST TIME

THOMAS

"*D*amn."

Damn. It. All.

I stared at the terrified, naked woman shivering at the opposite corner of my bed. Her eyes wildly darted around the room, avoiding mine, tearing me apart.

My shame and lifelong confusion. *Lifelong*, there's a laugh.

My fear. That was the problem. I couldn't love Kick and hold on to my fear at the same time. I'd laid my cards down, making it too late to fold. Not that I would. Not on her.

Kick's untamed morning curls mimicked the shock in her feral gaze when she braved a glance at me. How I wanted to comfort her but knew better. I let myself get caught up in the rage of a panicked female once—the mama bear who'd thought me a risk to her cubs. Kept the scars on my arm as a reminder to never do it again.

I'd planned to ease Kick into my unique reality. Instead, my secret escaped like a wild horse jumping a low fence.

Finally she slowed her heaving breaths enough to speak. "This is a nightmare, right? I'm still dreaming?" Kick lifted her head. "Please wake me up."

A tear threatened to slide down my cheek. My heart splintered as I looked at her beautiful body huddled in a protective ball. I cleared my throat. "Sorry, darlin'. Don't know how you did it, but you figured out my secret before I could prepare you for it." I chuckled—no, sneered—at my idiocy. "You warned me though. Didn't you?"

Why couldn't I just play it off? Let her think it was a damn dream? Because keeping the truth from Kick had been torture. I longed to share everything with her, even this. To be honest, in the hazy minute after she'd declared that I'd been a veteran of the Revolutionary War, my heart soared. Before I remembered that Kick wasn't ready to hear the truth.

"Jesus fecking Christ!" She leaped from her perch on the bed and paced the floor, fingers dragging through her hair. "This can't be happening. This doesn't happen." Kick let out a spine-chilling cackle. "Of course it happens to me. Why wouldn't it? Is there no end to the weirdness in my life?"

I sighed and shifted her way. "I'm so, so sorry. It is the truth. My truth."

"Stay away from me!" Kick's plea came out as a squeak, but the fury and hysteria in her eyes registered as an all-out scream.

When I'd met Banger and he explained our lives as he understood them, the news came as a welcome relief. Of course, by then I had already passed my two-hundredth birthday. After endless decades of solitude, with only my uncle and grandson for comfort, I embraced every aspect of Banger's life as a breath of fresh air and security. Like I'd been found.

Kick's reaction was everything I feared, what every Felidae member feared.

"When were you born? The real date?"

I pinched the bridge of my nose. "June. Seventeen-fifty."

"JaysusMaryandJoseph." Kick fell into a reading chair and let her head drop into her hands.

I carried a quilt over to her and placed it around her shoulders. When the material touched her skin, she jumped, making me wince too. I cautiously eased into the other chair, picked up the portrait miniatures sitting on the table between the wing-backs, and handed her the first.

"This is me. My mother commissioned it before I went off to fight. I was supposed to be a career soldier, but my older brother enlisted too. Then he died." I held out the other, angled it toward her and cleared my throat. "This is Alicia after our betrothal... uh, engagement. Her mother gave it to me since I traveled a lot."

Staring at the painting in her hand, Kick shook her head like it was full of cobwebs. "This is impossible." Her hands trembled as she traced my features in my portrait. "Who are you?"

After sheltering my heart for centuries, it was suddenly in danger of shattering into a million bits. "I'm the man who loves you," I said, hoping my words sank in. "I've been and done many things, but nothing has meant more than the possibility of loving you. We're just beginning." I cleared my throat to hide a sob. "Please don't take it away."

She placed the portrait back on the table and turned away from me.

Dammit.

"Were you ever going to tell me?" she asked, a harsh bite in her words.

"Yes." I leaned toward her. "I promise. Once I knew for certain we were solid. You must see this isn't something I just tell casual friends. These aren't only my secrets you now possess. I had to be sure of us."

"Hang on." Kick sat up, her posture tight. "Are you saying I can't walk away? That I'm trapped?"

"No, baby. I won't force you to stay. Ever. It would tear me in two if you left, but knowing this won't trap you with me. I trust you'll keep these secrets."

Kick jumped up, swiped her glasses from the nightstand, and stormed into the closet. When she returned, she wore my winter robe. She stood over me, skin flushed, breathing hard like she'd run a marathon.

"Why didn't you trust me before? Hell, I told you things my kids don't know. You were completely in my world and you..." Kick gestured toward the paintings. "You held the biggest part of you back." She jutted out a hip and glowered. "I know about being special, Thomas. About people not understanding, even resenting my reality. How could you trick me—"

"You were in danger!"

Kick jerked as if my bellow had knocked her back, and she fell into the chair. I continued more quietly. "I'm not the only one with this... curse... gift... *affliction*. My existence was lonely, confusing, and filled with constant fear until I found people like me. They call themselves the Felidae Society."

"Liam used to be obsessed with zoology. Isn't Felidae Latin for cats?" Kick scoffed.

"It's said cats have nine lives—"

"Nine?" Her breath caught on the word. She dropped her head, curls flying in all directions as she shook it violently. "This isn't funny. I'm often called dramatic for the odd way I live, but this is downright mean. Cruel. You're not like this. I can't—"

I reached across the chasm between us and turned her chin toward me. "I am *profoundly* sorry that you found out this way. Wish I could have eased you into the truth. But I'm not sorry you know."

Kick's chin quivered. "You're not joking?"

How I wished it was a prank. I closed my eyes and sighed. "No, darlin'."

She blew out a long, wavering breath that I felt on my face and in my soul. "How old are your 'cat people'?"

I paced the room now, unable to keep my panicked energy controlled. My life had been laid bare in a matter of minutes. I couldn't stay still in a damn chair. I stormed into my closet and jammed my legs into a pair of sweatpants, finding a modicum of protection, like Kick had. This cliff dive of an introduction demanded full disclosure.

"Some are over a thousand years old, but it's hard to pinpoint exact dates."

Her jaw fell open.

I dropped to my knees in front of her chair and looked up into her perfect forest eyes clouded with despair and fear. Desperate for her to understand, I said, "Until recently—a few decades, really—someone like a Felidae was eventually murdered. People fear what they can't understand, so we hid in plain sight and moved often."

"Okay." Kick's fingertips blanched as she grasped the armrests. "How does knowing this put me in danger?"

I moved back onto my heels and tried to catch her gaze, silently begging her to see me, to believe me. "When I joined the Felidae, I'd already been with a woman for years." Kick's back stiffened, and I continued quickly. "We weren't close like you and I. Don't know how to explain it, but no one's ever reached me the way you have. Anyway, Vivienne and I lived our lives apart, but also together. Back then, I settled for someone like an anchor, and she needed protection. When she had to flee Paris, I set her up with a boutique in New York."

As if propelled by an invisible force, Kick padded out into the hallway to the gallery of old photographs. I followed, finding her in front of the picture of Viv's grand opening. Kick had noticed it the morning after our first night together.

"Your 'family friend'," she said sarcastically, touching my image in the frame. "I thought this was your grandfather or something."

I scoffed. "Or something. We were close, like I said."

Kick kept staring at the photo. "Not a *bic* then."

I flinched at her words as they hit their target. "No." I had never felt comfortable with Banger's term for his disposable women. Now I despised it, hating that I used to use it too.

She turned toward me and folded her arms. "But you do know how to be casual."

I nodded and shrugged at the same time. "With anyone but you."

"Thomas..." Kick exhaled a frustrated sigh. "You still haven't explained how this puts me in danger."

"I'm trying to." I heaved a breath. "The night before the gala, I found out that the Felidae had Vivienne under surveillance back then. The men watching her were supposed to kill her if they gathered evidence she knew about the Society."

Kick stepped away from the wall. Away from me. She tilted her head as she scrutinized me. "You think they'll kill me now that I know about them?"

"I did in December. It rattled me something fierce. That's why I walked out that night. Hell, baby, here I'd been racking my brain, working with Banger to figure out who wanted to hurt you and your café. Then I find out you were in more danger from me?" I groaned as I shook my head.

"Okay. Then what's changed?"

I stepped up to Kick and took her hands, smiling on the inside when she let me. "Two things changed. First off, Banger reassured me he would do everything in his power to protect us when I saw him in France. Tess was there too, and she declared herself on our side. So you'll have more than me fighting for us." I brought our hands to my heart. "I promise to protect you with my body and anything else in my power. Do you believe me?"

Kick narrowed her gaze, studying me, making seconds seem like hours. Finally, in a quiet, rough voice, she answered, "Shit... I think I do believe you."

"Do you understand why I had to keep my secret now? I swear I—"

"No, I don't." She stepped away again and tracked a circle around me in the hallway. "Even though no one will ever hear about this from me, it feels like you tricked me. You... you drew me in. Made me love you. Why, Thomas? Why?"

"Because I've never loved anyone like I do you. Still, I had to be sure."

"Sure of what?" She threw her arms up. "Do you think this is the first time my weltanschauung flipped on its head in a nanosecond? There have been days where it seemed like my whole life was a matter of learning that left is right and up is down. Aw hell, the genetics research..." Kick grabbed her head, and the robe fell open. She quickly retied it. "You're studying yourself, aren't you?"

"Sort of. My two-times granddaughter is my main subject."

"Your *two...*"

"Toni."

"Her husband has Alzheimer's?"

"That's her."

"Jaysus fecking Christ!" Kick tipped her head back, her lips moving like she was counting her breaths to calm herself. "It's all half-truths, isn't it? I thought you were her younger brother, Thomas. How is this—"

"My neighbors tried to *kill* me!" My bellow echoed through the house and practically blew us apart.

Her accusations had to stop. I ended up sitting on the floor across from the line of old photos, not sure how I got there. "I protect my family, Kick. When we met, you were beautiful... infuriating... intriguing. That said, you weren't family." I looked over at her and spread my hands apart. "You are my family now, and that's why we're here. I'll protect you with everything I have, but I'll be damned if Toni, or anyone else I love, will have to face what I did back then."

"What do you mean, your neighbors tried to kill you?" She settled against the wall across from me.

The memories from that time had faded to the point they were almost gone emotionally. Or I thought they had. Everything flooded back as I spoke. "Ridiculous rumors floated around the village. Some called me a wizard. Others accused me of making a pact with the devil because I didn't appear to age. What hurt the most was… my sons. They grew impatient with me. Their peers inherited lands from their dead fathers, while I showed no signs of slowing down. One night, a group of men made their way to my plantation to put an end to me."

"I thought your family bred horses."

"Kick…" I clipped, too emotional to handle the change in focus. "We did and still do. It was also the eighteen hundreds in Virginia."

She wrapped a hand around her hair and brought it over her shoulder. "Well, shit."

"Yeah." I scrubbed my scruffy face with my hands. "So I visited my daughters, ending up at Alice's—my youngest—in Kentucky. Joe is her son, George Jr."

"Joe is George?"

"Rotating names is part of how we survive… as is the fierce protection of our privacy."

"Jaysus." Kick stood and approached the gallery wall again. She stopped in front of each photo, often touching my image in it. "So it skips a generation? This… thing you have?"

"Depends. Some families skip several generations. Some don't." I wrapped my arms around my knees and let my head settle on them, thoroughly worn out. "Are y'alright?" With each step came a hitch of her breath, so I aurally followed her path to every photo without having to watch her.

"I don't know."

"That's me and my Uncle Theo when we founded a bank in San Francisco. For the longest time, it was just us. There were rumors about his grandfather, but nothing for certain. Disappearing was easier back then."

Step. A low keening sound floated around the hall.

"Uncle Theo, me, and Joe just before boarding the train to join World War I." I scoffed at the thought of those years. "We bought into the idea of ending all wars."

A shuffle. Another hitching breath.

"Joe and me, Paris in the twenties," I murmured. "He had switched back to George then, and I was going by Michael."

"Mic—" Two swishes of the robe and a gasp.

"Banger and me in the fifties. In Australia." I lifted my eyes when I didn't hear any more movement.

Kick tilted her head from side to side as she studied the photos. "I haven't kept up my retouching skills, but back in the day, I could've done a decent job with these." She reached back to the nearest black-and-white picture. "Maybe not the colored ones, but I used to switch heads on images like this. Kids today can do this with color photos. It's a basic skill now."

What I would give for them to be faked. I pinched the bridge of my nose, feeling the start of a headache. Or was it heartache? I couldn't shake the ominous feeling I was about to watch her walk out the door.

Over before we'd begun.

Despair rushed through me as I cleared my throat. "They're not Photoshopped. They're not my ancestors. They're me. My life. Hung there to keep me from losing… myself."

Kick moved to the top of the stairwell. She stood stock-still, buzzing with energy. I braced for her to run. Instead, she placed one hand on the banister and the other on the railing defining the balcony to the guest wing. Then Kick burst out a full-on scream at the top of her lungs. "Fuuuck!"

When she ran out of breath, she dropped down on the steps, her gaze trained on the open space below and nothing at all.

. . .

AGAIN, SECONDS TURNED INTO HOURS. I WANTED TO TURN BACK the clock to the night before, when she rode my cock and we just had beauty and freedom between us. I hung my head in shame, convinced she'd abandon the promises we'd made to each other yesterday. At the same time, I felt an inexplicable relief from bringing her fully into my world. The struggle to maintain my sanity through the loneliness hit me full force, knowing that I was about to lose it.

"Do you want to leave me now?" That waiting tear let loose and dropped onto my knee, sinking into my sweatpants material.

Despite a rasp, Kick's voice sounded angelic to my ears.

"No, Thomas. Heaven help me, but I don't." Her breath hitched again, and I lifted my head when I realized she was crying too. "I don't know why, but I can't walk away." Kick looked over her shoulder at me, her eyes searching. I hoped like hell she still saw me there. "I'm scared."

Each shuddering breath I took felt like a fight for life. "You may not believe this, but I'm more frightened than you."

Kick spun around to face me. She was bright red from screaming. "Are you s-sure you're not a vampire?" she asked through another hitch.

I laughed once, needing the joke, even though it had been a sincere question. "You and your damn fantasy books."

"Paranormal."

"Fine." I flicked a wrist. "Promise… I'm a human man. Just have variances in my DNA."

"What variances?"

"That's what my research is about." Another damn tear slid down my cheek.

Kick covered her mouth. She scooted across the floor and pulled me into a tight embrace.

I lifted her hand and brought her flat palm to my heart, holding it there. "This had been locked up tight for centuries. Do you have any idea what that feels like? I'd grown so used to the cold and loneliness… thought it would always be this way. Damned if you didn't have the key. This"—I tapped her hand over my heart—"is what you need to know about me. You're my locksmith."

I fingered the strung-out curls hanging in her face and tucked them behind her ear. "No matter what happens after today, I'll watch over you—even if it must be from afar. Your safety is more important than mine."

Kick sat back on her heels, let her hands fall into her lap, and stared at me.

Please make the vulnerability worth it. Please don't make me regret my honesty.

She sighed a ragged breath, her beautiful hazel eyes darkened with sorrow. "It would be easy to make you love me from a distance. Life would be much easier. But who says love is easy? If this is what makes you the man I love, then I must accept it, right? You accept my health issues. What's an impossible birthday added to the mix?"

"Come here." I grabbed Kick's wrist with one hand and opened her robe with the other so I could hold her skin to skin. It had been an exhausting morning, and it wasn't even eight o'clock. The way a life could turn on a dime, but Kick had plenty of experience with such things, didn't she? This was what people meant when they said home wasn't a piece of land. It was a woman who could lighten the load and give life meaning with her smile.

Kick shifted to straddle my lap and settled into me, occasionally kissing my jaw. I felt a warm, low hum stir in my limbs—the telltale sign of my aura appearing after a highly emotional experience.

Kick murmured, "Why though?"

I kissed her temple and held my lips there, breathing in the scent of her hair. While tracing light kisses down to her cheek and across to her mouth, something incredible happened as she responded. A literal warmth emanated from us, starting with our hands. I laced our fingers. "Wish I knew. Have to figure out *what* first." She shifted, and I closed my eyes, taking in the feel of her embrace. Hope warred with my hard-earned cynicism.

"I'll grow old and decrepit while you stay young and perfect."

"Don't think you'll have to worry about that."

"Why not?" Kick sounded tired, like the morning had worn her out as much as it had me.

I nudged her, making her sit back. "The second reason I decided it was safe to ask you to come back to me in December…"

"Oh, right." She pushed her hair off her face. "What's that?"

I raised a hand, letting the blue aura I thought I'd lost float above my skin. I flexed my fingers as waves of light rippled around them.

Kick gasped and brought her hands to her face. "You do it too?"

"It disappeared a long time ago. Until you."

With a kind of awe, she whispered, "It started recently for me. I thought it had to do with meditation."

"I know." I grinned and lifted Kick's hand.

The same light washed over and around her, only it was a pastel violet color. Her eyes flashed wide.

Then she fainted.

2

NEVER TEAR US APART

KICK

"I'm sorry I yelled."

It was the first thing out of my mouth after I came to. I didn't scream again after fainting, but the feral bellow played in the back of my mind when I woke. It took a minute to remember everything that came after, including...

"My promise stands. You don't have to stay."

Shit. Thomas's confident, chiseled face had melted into something reflecting heartbreak. I touched his cheek, hoping I could coax the cocky back out of him. "That's not why I screeched like a banshee. It's what I do whenever life goes sideways. Who knew I'd end up with a routine for such things?" My brow furled as I thought about the ridiculousness of it.

Thomas rubbed my arm. We were lying on his bed, his arms around me like a child would hold a teddy bear. He must have picked me up and settled us here, yet this didn't feel like cuddling. His movements were slow, jerky—like he had shut down.

"You don't want this life, do you?" he whispered.

I thought I understood what he wasn't saying, and it scared the hell out of me. "Before I passed out, you and I—"

He raised our hands. What remained of the light still pulsed around our fingers. I couldn't tell if I heard the pleasant hum or felt it in my body. In places, the colors swirled around each other. In others, they blended together, forming a pretty lavender. I stared at the light, stupefied. "What does it mean?"

Thomas sighed, like his thoughts stayed stuck on his last question. Then again, I hadn't eased his worries. "I think you have the variances I have," he said slowly. "Whether it's all of them or some of them, I don't know. I would like to do some tests."

I scratched at my nose. It tingled the way it often did before a cry came on. I sensed Thomas couldn't handle any more freakouts, so I had to keep my shit together. Fortunately, I had a lot of practice there too. "Do you think I'll live as long as you have? You said something about a second reason to get back together. Is that what you meant?"

"That's my hypothesis. Obviously, we need proof."

"Wow. Well, shit." I ducked my head into Thomas's chest, trying to absorb this news with grace, fighting like hell to squash the urge to scream at the top of the stairs again. "If you're right," I said, tipping my head back to meet his gaze. "Your life has me whether I want it. It's best if I get used to it. Like with the autoimmunity—there's no wishing it away."

He squeezed my shoulder. "You don't have to join up with the Felidae. Or me. You can live your life on your own."

"Without you? Sounds like a nightmare." I bit my cheek when Thomas flinched. I'd basically disregarded everything he'd done so far. "I'm sorry. I didn't mean—"

He lifted my hand and kissed my knuckles. "It's alright. At times, it has been a nightmare."

"It's just…" I fussed with my hair, trying to tame the rat's nest as I moved to sit. "My head won't stop spinning. And the questions... Jaysus, they're innumerable."

Oh hell, what about my kids? If I have this, would they grow old without me, like Thomas's children had? It was unthinkable.

"Knowing you? I bet." He jostled me, some mischief returning to his face as he chuckled.

I wanted to laugh but couldn't. While it made me happy to see a shy little grin replace the despair on Thomas's face, I was drowning in my overwhelm.

The realization of how alone Thomas had been for so, so, long had hit me like a Mack truck when I stood in his photo gallery. I ached for all he'd been through. "Anyway... despite the mess in here..." I tapped my temple. "Love is the strongest feeling in here." I rubbed over my heart. "Having you to guide me through this tells me it'll be okay."

"At least one of us is sure."

"I have to be."

People often told me I looked young for my age. Did that mean Thomas was right? Or did some people just age better?

One thing at a time.

It had become one of my mantras through other life upheavals, and it applied here. I couldn't jump ahead months or years to know if Thomas was right, but he'd go into scientist mode soon enough. Hell, his work always simmered on the back burner in his mind. So I knew we could progress one step at a time and not worry about the unknowns. I'd learned to handle all the what-ifs the hard way too. It took a strong focus on what I knew for certain. Ultimately, my heart trusted the gift that was Thomas.

"If you hadn't survived this long, you'd only be a gorgeous man in some old photographs. I wouldn't know you. As delicious as your orgasms are, I can't stand to think about going through my life without my friend. Without you. If what you say is true about me—and that's the biggest head-scratcher of all as far as I'm concerned—I'll need you with me."

Thomas pulled me back against his body and kissed my temple.

I wiggled my arms around his waist, and we snuggled for real for a long while. Eventually I laughed. "A thousand years of your orgasms is quite the bonus." Thomas's startled laugh filled the room as he held me tighter.

AFTER OUR EMOTIONAL RESTART, WE NEEDED SPACE. THOMAS USED his horse as an excuse to leave the house. His attachment to his adopted, formerly wild horse made more sense to me now. I saw it as a way to connect him to the man he used to be. Thomas claimed he and Eddie were getting back into their old routine with him boarded at the neighboring stables. I predicted their ride would end up longer than planned. Much longer.

I didn't mind. It gave me the opportunity to go into the bathroom, shove a small towel in my mouth, and scream again until my vocal cords crapped out. What can I say? It helped. It also left me with a slight sore throat and a grumbling stomach.

Before my hunger could be sated, I had to find a peaceful way to move forward. After I showered and dressed, I sat on the edge of Thomas's bed, staring at his miniature. "What the hell?" I reached for it and looked closer. As if there hadn't been enough revelations already, I would swear this was the face of the man in my dreams for all these years and not just the one from the night before. He was young in this rendering, but there was enough diffusion of his features from the brushstrokes to get the same impression of who'd been in my dreams. Could Thomas have been the one haunting me all this time? I would need to ask him more about his time as a soldier. I thought he'd been a horse breeder in middle-age—or the equivalent if he'd lived a normal life. As the visions in my dreams formed more clearly, the man starring in them had been mature, not a teen.

My hands shook with more possibilities, so I set the miniature back down and went in search of a meditation spot before I broke down for real. This was small compared to everything we'd already been through, but it also felt like it could be the last straw if I didn't settle my mind.

I found the perfect place on a small balcony off a guest bedroom. I grabbed a few pillows and a heavy blanket from the bed and embraced the chilly air. Cool inhales and steamy exhales brought me back to center as I let the morning sun warm my face. I soon walked down the staircase in my mind, then sat on the porch there. I found peace as the smell of the gardenias in my meditation spot blended with the crisp air in the real world. No one visited me in the meditation, but I required solitude. No aura showed up either. I suppose I was too tired. I sat in this reality mash-up and focused on these new possibilities.

What did I really think?

It was banana bonkers. But it also weirdly made sense. More accurately, Thomas made more sense from this perspective. Me though? I couldn't believe I would end up like him. Maybe if I hadn't been a mom. Each time my thoughts turned to them, to the possibility of outliving them, I swore a volt of electricity sliced through me. My brain refused to wrap around a world with me in it but not them. Where they aged and I didn't.

"Fuck it." I threw the blanket on the bed as I ran through the room and into Thomas's. I'd pack my bag and go home to think. Not necessarily leave him outright, but take some time. Hell, we'd just met. Maybe I'd have him run the tests, then decide about us.

As I carried my bag out into the hallway, the gallery of photos caught my eye, making me freeze. Something in the photos had seemed off. I stepped away from the bag and studied his pictures again. There was no denying they were of Thomas, but he looked different in them. It hit me hard enough to take my breath away. There was no spark in his brilliant silver eyes.

I raced through my memories of us—Thomas laughing at me the night we'd met. I'd had the feeling he didn't do it much back then. Dancing in his arms. His enthusiastic interest in my gluten-free and dairy free cooking. His smile when we accidentally admitted we loved each other. The angelic look on his face when he came, and it wasn't his aura. It was him letting go. Deana practically told me from day one that the man lit up when I was around.

The gallery showed me inside Thomas's life without me in it. It broke my heart to think of him so alone, alive but not really living. Whether for one year or a thousand, it didn't matter. Something about me, about us, had given him that spark.

I grasped my arms, wrapping them around my torso to control the shaking that swept over me. My gaze shot between the photos and the stairs. Wondering what to do. Both choices were hard as hell, but which was right? And why did I think loving Thomas would be easy? Oh, it was easy as breathing to fall for him, but the doing of it was the feat of a lifetime with anyone. My ridiculous naivete had me surprised.

I'd known he held a secret this whole time. Instincts had told me it was a doozy too. An impossibility? No, but deep down I knew it would rock me. And still, I trusted Thomas more.

Then the tears flowed.

As I rolled my overnight bag back into his closet and unpacked it a second time, the tears kept coming. Grateful ones and fearful ones alike flowed as they cleansed my soul and steeled my spine. After losing one great love, I knew what a gift it was to find another.

It was a shit choice. At the same time, there wasn't a choice between him and my kids at all. If I had similar DNA variances, then I'd be a fool not to stick close to Thomas, lean on him for support. If I didn't have them? I hoped like hell he'd want to stick by me for the years I would have.

On the way to the shower, his T-shirt caught my eye, laying on top of a dresser in the closet. I picked it up, inhaling his woodsy scent still in the soft cotton, feeling it quiet the roar thundering through me. Still holding the shirt, I grabbed my toiletry bag and padded into the bathroom to wash the morning off.

"THAT SMELLS FANTASTIC."

Thomas cautiously approached me at the stove as I cooked up a pack of Paleo bacon for us. It was noon, but it had taken all morning for me to finally think about food.

"I know, right?" I answered, breathing in the heavy smokiness mixed with salt. "It's not at all like the common brands." Sticking with foods that were organic, grass-fed... yada-yada... was a requirement for remaining in my doctor's practice. At first, the cost difference in the grocery bill had intimidated the hell out of me, especially with growing boys in the house. The improvement in taste ended up being a pleasant surprise. I could get past the sticker shock for amazing flavor.

"Joe makes this with the smoker at home. Nothing has ever smelled as good as his until now."

"Funny. When I first tasted this, it seemed like a new food." And so went another reminder that Thomas was from a different era. Something as simple as bacon probably reminded him of the past.

He touched my shoulder. "I bet."

I snorted softly before jumping away from a spot of airborne grease, sliding a few feet in my thick socks. I also knew that bacon wasn't what was really on his mind. Since he'd showered and we'd avoided each other long enough, I didn't want him treading lightly around me anymore.

"Feel better?" I asked.

He stepped closer. "Do you?"

I bit back the growl threatening to escape my throat. I was in a stages-of-acceptance kind of situation. Caught between my desire to pelt Thomas with questions and wanting to eat our meal in peace. A tentative spark had returned to his blue-gray eyes, and I was afraid of saying something to make it disappear again. I shrugged. "I'm hungry."

He stepped up behind me. "You're wearing my T-shirt. Take this as a good sign?"

"You could say that."

He leaned against the island as I placed cooked strips on a plate lined with a paper towel before adding the last of the package to the pan. The tension between us crackled on my arms. After becoming so close yesterday, I wanted to snap my fingers and make us go right back there. Would all this craziness be worth it to have that connection again? I had to find out. I flipped the bacon and said, "Told you I'd figure it out."

Thomas barked a quick laugh, and the knot in my stomach loosened as his eyes brightened a little more. "Yes, you did. Can you understand my need for secrecy?"

My tongue circled in my cheek while I thought about it. I hated how he kept asking, like his insecurities wouldn't let him move on until we were on the same page. I doubted if he'd ever been so vulnerable with someone before. It helped my answer. "I think so. You have to protect your friends."

"And you."

I looked over my shoulder. "Who protects you?"

"Felidae vows go both ways."

I pressed a freshly formed curl behind my ear as I shook my head. "Do they really? According to you, these people threatened Vivienne and me. How is that protection if you can't be loved? Are they supposed to choose your partner?"

Thomas loosely wrapped his arms around my waist. "People

used to pair off more, but it's been a while." I felt his shoulder rise. "It never appealed to me. And I'm still a kid in their eyes. Women are also rare in the Felidae. It's why there's so much buzz about my work with Toni."

"Okay, fine." I turned the meat strips one last time. After a sharp crackle and snap, a speck of hot grease splashed my skin. I jumped, shaking my hand in annoyance. For my skin or for Thomas, I couldn't say. "You were just supposed to, what? Live like a monk? Be a player like Banger? Either way, it sounds miserable." My mind flashed to the photos upstairs. Proof of that life.

"It didn't matter. I'm used to being alone. This is what's frightening."

"Me? I frighten you?"

Instead of answering directly, he asked, "Are you staying?"

And it hit me. Had anyone ever loved Thomas for himself? I believed Banger did in a brotherly way. I hoped his wife had, but couldn't be certain. I turned off the burner and spun around so I could put my arms around his neck. "I don't know what the future will bring. Autoimmunity broke me of that kind of thinking. But today and tomorrow? You've got me."

Thomas closed his eyes and sighed in relief. "You do get it."

"Not planning ahead because life is too weird and potentially isolating? You bet I get *that*. My best life has to be today no matter how it looks."

Thomas lowered his forehead to mine and clung to me. He whispered, "No one's ever chosen me before."

I chuckled at the absurdity. "Need I remind you that you've been married? Plus there was Vivienne."

He shook his head, letting it rub against mine, then placed a reverent kiss to my temple. "Alicia could have called off the arrangement, but she never would have out of fear of her father's scorn."

"He needed you to take care of his land," I said, understanding.

"Precisely. And Viv? I offered her a way out of a difficult life, along with protection." He swallowed stepping back. "Don't get me wrong, I wasn't miserable. Hell, my peers considered me a lucky son of a bitch. But—"

"But I want you as much as I need you."

Thomas pinched the bridge of his nose before nodding.

I sifted my fingers through his hair, then let my hand settle at his firm jaw. What a gift his vulnerability was. I wondered if the other women had ever seen it. I also didn't care. If they couldn't bring it out of him, that was their loss.

Thomas picked me up and set me on the counter. His body pressed into mine, our embrace physically saying more than words could. Next came the kiss, his tongue sharing his gratitude for the ways we complemented each other.

"Mmm." He growled into my neck. "I do need you. So much."

I hadn't felt Thomas's hands travel up my thighs, though my legs were bare—my compromise, not knowing if we were still doing naked weekend. His needs were obvious as he pulled me forward and rubbed me against his hot arousal. I froze, blinked, and placed my hands over his.

"There's still something wrong." The self-rebuke in his silver-blue stare broke my heart as he stepped back.

"I… yeah, suppose there is." I grabbed his wrist to keep him from leaving the room or worse. "Don't get me wrong, I wouldn't want to go through this with anyone but you. I'm grateful you promise to be there to guide me. It's everything else."

"You can't take it one day at a time after all."

"I've learned to take things one hour at a time, if necessary. It's just"—I pressed my hands into the edge of the counter—"ever since my diagnosis, I've worked my ass off to make my life mean something. I figured that was the reason I ended up with these autoimmune diseases. Then the kids became my sole responsibility, and I had to be there for them."

"None of that has changed, darlin'."

I wished I could believe Thomas, wished he would surround me in his woodsy scent and make my fears go away. "How do I make a difference for others when my life's shrouded in secrets now? Helping people requires openness, putting yourself out there. You're telling me I have to lie to everyone I love now." I fought a tear threatening to drop and could tell Thomas noticed it. "More than that, how do I plan a future where my kids will grow old and I won't, if it skips a generation like your family? What about my babies? How am I supposed to be okay with burying them?"

3

(I GOT A WOMAN CRAZY FOR ME)
SHE'S FUNNY THAT WAY

THOMAS

I pulled Kick into my chest. "I'm such a dumbass."

She tipped her head back, her brow furrowed. "That's not what I meant."

"But I should've factored your kids into this. Of course you're afraid for them and what it means for y'all's relationship." One of the blessings of walking into my life blind had been not knowing I'd bury my children *and* their descendants. Technically, I didn't, but I watched for news of them, and it tore at my heart each time it trickled in.

Kick pulled her hair to one shoulder, twisting the bottom curls around her finger. "We have to lie to them, right?"

We. I closed my eyes at the sound of the word. As hard as this was for Kick, she wanted me to be a part of the solution. I pulled the hand fidgeting with her hair into mine. "Nothing has to change right now. All couples keep things from their kids. This won't affect how we live for a time. Hell, you're still working on your remission. The best thing for the both of us is to do what you said earlier—live in the moment."

She pulled her hand away and touched her heart. "But I'll know in here. What do you say to that? Give me some kind of hope. Please."

"Alright." I took her hand in mine and tentatively squeezed it. "Let's take Banger. He's an example of the variance moving from the parents to their child. In his case, both his parents were already Felidae. I don't know how it works if the parents haven't transitioned yet. Or if it's more important to have the variance from both parents. About the only thing we've figured out before our modern research was the fertility aspect. It lasts longer but eventually wanes. That's why the world isn't full of Felidae children."

"Are you saying there's no way to know about my kids?" Kick bit her lip, the worry written all over her face. I fed her a strawberry from a bowl on the counter, hoping the simple pleasure of the taste would ease her mind.

"You had a DNA test done, right?"

"About a year ago, yes."

I gave her hand a light shake. "We start there. I'll run blood work. Check my hypothesis about you. Then we'll focus on the kids. Test them against you and my database." Excitement filled my voice, the scientist in me coming alive with the prospect of tracking the McKennas, adding more data to my research. *Dammit.* I saw the thought-wrestling match in her worried hazel eyes and cringed at my callousness.

"What does all this mean though? What about my autoimmune diseases? Or aging?"

I tilted my head, searching for the words. "It means evolution's alive and well. Despite our progress, we understand just a small part of how it all works." I scratched at my chin. "The discipline you've practiced putting yourself back into remission could be your catalyst. You've come a long way already. Didn't you also say your aura recently showed up?"

"When I started taking meditation seriously. Yes." Kick bit into another strawberry, licking the dark pink of the berry juice from her bottom lip.

Christ, I wanted to give her a normal life. To tell her I was kidding, then lick the juice off her myself. Get back our naked weekend and worship her the way she deserved. The reality was, that had never been my life and now I'd dragged her into my chaos. Instead, I smiled at the reminder of how she had to be nagged into trying meditation. "Alright. Mine also came back recently while meditating. As to your autoimmunity, it should reverse itself over time. And aging? You already look younger than your years."

Kick huffed. "I feel... stuck." Her hands floated around her head, physically expressing her frustration.

"Do you believe me so far?"

"Honestly? Part of me thinks it's bonkers. That you won't find these variances in me. Another part says why the hell not? We already know I hit the genetic jackpot with not one but two autoimmune diseases. Why shouldn't I go full mutant?"

Even though she was being her snarky self, Kick sparked an idea in me. I clicked my tongue and touched the tip of her nose. "Good point. I should see if your autoimmunity factors in. Might help my overall research."

She sighed and hopped off the counter, moving toward the refrigerator. "You're talking about epigenetics, right? Will you study my telomeres? Ever since I read about them, I wanted to get it done." She grabbed a tomato and sliced it on a cutting board sitting next to the stove. The earthy flavor of the heirloom variety filled my nose. I guessed we were having BLTs for lunch.

I chuckled at her words. I'd forgotten she was a magazine article researcher. "It's part of it." I inhaled deeply, remembering my endless years of confusion. "For the longest time, the only possible explanation I could lean on came from a piece written by Aeschylus. In it, he talked about learning via suffering, but what sustained me most came at the end: '...against our will, comes wisdom to us by the awful grace of God.' It's been equal parts a curse and blessing to live this life, particularly because of the secrecy." My hand reached for hers, my thumb rubbing the top of her knuckles. The quote intensified at the moment. "I find myself more awed by grace now that you're here. I am deeply sorry about burdening you with the secrets."

Kick impressed me further as she accepted my words with no attempt at deflection or her often-used self-deprecation. She just nodded her head and added, "I'd love to see your lab if that's possible. It'll help to see your work, give me some reassurances."

A wide grin spread across my face. "Absolutely."

"You think there'll come a day when I've heard all your stories?"

Christ, I hope so.

I shrugged and grunted a response as I checked in with the lab on my phone. Kick currently tried to commit homicide-by-overquestioning. Two more and I swore I'd die. *Finally.*

After clearing the lunch plates, she changed into a purple satin robe and snuggled into me on the sofa in my sunroom—the toastiest room in the house thanks to the greenhouse wall and ceiling. Surrounded by my small orchid collection and the afternoon sun, she did her best impression of a hardline journalist, pelting me with questions about eighteenth-century life.

One of my deepest fears involved being imprisoned in a government facility if my secret escaped. I'd never contemplated the possibility of a hellish version of a Barbara Walters interview.

I ran my hand through my hair and pressed on tension points at the base of my skull. My foot kept jumping, so I took it as a sign and paced the room.

"Understand something. I hide in plain sight, but so does everyone—Felidae or not." I pulled at the invisible collar at my bare neck, feeling like it wanted to choke me. Kick's questions brought back memories of things I never understood myself. At least I had some answers now.

I should have been preoccupied with the goddess sitting on my sofa—mine. We should've finally been ready for another round of hot-and-heavy heaven, one where we would never sit in this room again without thinking of it and smiling. Instead, I was out of breath from revisiting things best left alone.

But Kick needed this even if we walked through my graveyard of remembrances so painful I avoided them at all costs. It all started with, "How many outfits did you have?" Like I'd ever worn an "outfit" in my entire life.

"This eases out of a man in small bites under normal circumstances, darlin'."

The truth is, neither of us could have prepared for this situation. Kick was the first regular person I'd ever talked to about my life. Joe had first approached Toni about who she was, so I hadn't had to explain anything when we met. I had no manual on how to explain *me*.

"I'm sorry." Kick scrunched her nose as disappointment wrote itself on her face as clearly as the freckles on her nose. Her chin did a little wobble thing, and I sank back down on the cushion next to her.

"Baby." I sighed, feeling like a shit for losing my patience. "I haven't time-traveled. I'm not *Dr. Who.* I've lived every second of my years. Not all of them to the fullest but with all I've been capable of at the time. In my book, that makes me a twenty-first-century man." I dropped my head and kissed her knuckles, silently asking for it to be enough. "I-I'd appreciate it if you'd quit treating me like an alien discovery."

I chortled and finished, "Honestly, it was easier when you thought you'd robbed the cradle." Expecting to see her smile at my joke, I looked up. Instead, her eyes glistened. My shoulders slumped in disappointment. Her jabbering was a defense against her own heady fears. *I'm an idiot.*

I reached for Kick and pulled her into my lap. "Where are you right now?"

She took one long inhale and quietly answered, "This… this has been a lot. I know I've said it before, but that's all I've got."

"Agreed." I rubbed her back with my free hand. "Too much?"

She scoffed and answered, "Does it matter?"

"*You* matter."

"Perhaps." Kick blew a curl off her cheek and smiled, though it didn't reach her eyes. "I'll deal with it." She squeezed my hand. "I already live a strange life by most people's standards. Hell, a lot of folks don't believe I'm sick. My health insurance won't acknowledge my condition, which is why most of my treatments are out of pocket. Plus I keep most of my life under wraps because those who need to know do. The rest can kiss my ass. There's a similarity between us already."

I laughed at her comparison. Plus she was right.

We sat in silence for several minutes, watching some deer pick at the vegetation through my garden fence, then walk away.

"Can I ask one more question?" Kick kept her focus on the backyard. "I promise it'll be the last. For now."

I pulled her hair away from her neck, pressed my lips to the back of her jaw, and growled to make a point. She already had from me everything that mattered. Of course she'd get all the questions. "Hit me."

"When did you figure it out? About yourself, I mean."

I snuck another kiss while considering my answer. Then I lifted our joined hands that were again humming with my blue aura. Kick's slowly buzzed to life, startling her. I pressed her back into me with my other hand so I could answer.

"This happened first. Like you, my instincts led me to keep it to myself."

Kick gasped, her eyes wide in shock. I raised my brows and winked, reminding her that she hadn't hidden it from me. "When Alicia died, I lost myself for a while. I kept seeing her around every corner, you know?"

"I do."

Right. She'd also been a young widow. I continued, "My mother-in-law kept the kids and hired a wet nurse for the baby. I traveled a lot for business, so it wasn't odd to go away. I left to spend a night or two on my favorite peak. Ended up sitting on the damn mountain for a week. Not sure if I even ate anything up there. I was angry with myself for not being home when Alicia passed. For not saying goodbye. Angry with her for leaving us. I yelled until I lost my voice. Then the aura happened."

"Oh cowboy." Kick moved her free hand to my chest and rubbed over my heart.

"The aura was darker back then. No idea why." I lowered our hands and caressed her arm, needing more contact. "When I returned home, I convinced myself it had been a dream and resumed my life. The first real clue came when I stopped getting sick. Smallpox swept through the valley, and many neighbors were lost. We almost lost my oldest daughter, but I didn't get more than a runny nose. Later, people would comment on my lack of wrinkles, gray hair, and such. When my first son and I looked like twins, I had to admit something was different."

"You stopped aging?"

"Yeah. At first, people complimented me. Women tried to match me with their daughters, even women my age wanted me to marry their daughters. Friends of my girls." I shuddered at the memory.

Kick lifted her head off my chest and caught my gaze. "You were never tempted?"

I shook my head vigorously. "They would expect babies from me. As I said before, I refused to risk killing another woman with my seed."

"But Thomas—"

"That was how I thought. No correcting it now. Then the accusations started, followed by rumors and threats. So I left. To save my family and my legacy, I left them." My voice quieted at the memory. "I packed up my horse and headed for my youngest daughter's homestead. It was past the time for my sons to inherit anyway. Most of their peers had been running their estates and businesses for decades. Alice had married and settled in Kentucky. Joseph is her son. Stayed about a year. Then I kept going. I had Alice write to her brothers and tell them I died, to make everything tidy."

"All that time and you never knew why?"

"No." My voice sounded sharp, though I'd forgiven my former friends long ago. This was the first time I truly told my story. Everyone else who knew my truth had been through similar situations. They never needed the details or the emotional consequences. "I knew all the things I wasn't. I just never knew what I was. Not until 1957."

Her head popped up in surprise. "No shit?"

"Not a bit. That's when I met Ranger and the rest of the Felidae Society."

"Oh sweets." Kick wrapped her arms around my waist and held tight. I soaked in every ounce of support she offered, realizing for the first time how much I had needed someone to listen to me.

I lifted my foot out from under her and set it along the length of the couch, placing her between my legs. "Can we be done with questions for now?"

"You're drained."

"Completely."

"Me too." As if on cue, Kick yawned, popping her jaw.

I yanked on the blanket that lay over the sofa and draped it over us as we shifted down. Kick fell asleep instantly while I slowly drifted off with my lips pressed to her temple, relaxing in her vanilla scent mixed with the sweetness of the orchids. Did she have any clue how much her presence meant to me? Changed me? I hoped we could find a normal life soon. Our normal. Without having to hurt anyone to do it. Especially someone in the Felidae. I had to make sure Alaric believed my thoughts about Kick and accepted her.

Then I'd figure out how to incorporate her into my research. I couldn't add it to my grant, so I'd have to find a way to work around my contract.

After our nap, we'd wandered outside to watch the sunset while dinner baked in the oven. We currently snuggled back together in the den, changing channels between the New Year's Eve concerts. The weight of the day had lifted when we agreed to focus on us, on the day-to-day of knowing each other and our inconvenient truths. Nothing pleased me more than returning to the Kick and Thomas we were the day before—just a man and a woman in desperate need to begin again, and grateful for the chance.

Kick's eyes cut to the television screen in the den and lit up. "Ooh, I love this singer."

I tilted my hand back and laughed. "You've loved all of tonight's performers."

"True." Kick bit her lip, then chuckled too. Her pert nose scrunching, urging me to lick it, so I did.

The slightly grumpy normal me would have cringed at each of the pop bands. This new, crazy-gone-for-the-goddess-next-to-me guy that I'd become loved them for the way they lit her up.

I turned up the volume and stood, holding out my hand. "Dance with me."

"Naked?"

This woman. As if we hadn't been running around like Adam and Eve since we returned to the house. "What better way is there?" I moved my hands up and down in her direction. "Why cover up your magnificence?" I spread my arms and shook my hips to some Latin beat. "Let me see it move, baby."

"You're so goofy."

My soul found new freedom as I watched Kick's luscious, swaying body. In a few beats, our hands explored each other, feeling the notes on our skin. Everything disappeared in the moment—the walls I'd built, the loneliness, the push to succeed in my research, worry for Toni, and the underlying hum of fear continuously running through me regarding Kick's safety. She lit the way out of it.

At the commercial break, I dashed to the kitchen for water while she headed for the bathroom. I returned to the den and collapsed into the sectional after slaking my thirst.

Kick appeared in the archway, leaning against the wood trim and staring at me, her eyes hooded with desire.

"What's going on in your head?"

The curve of her hip outlined by the glow from the bathroom light was a sight my cock enjoyed. A lot. My breathing deepened as lust filled my chest and reawakened my cock. I caught the moment Kick noticed. A sly grin spread across her face. My goddess became a predator. *This naked weekend thing was a genius idea.*

Kick dropped to her hands and knees and eased toward me, like a slinky feline. My chin lowered as I watched her cross the room.

"What are you doing?" I rasped out. Despite the long drink from a minute ago, my throat turned to cotton as soon as she began her prowl. Her shoulders, breasts, and hips swayed rhythmically, like she was stalking me.

"When we first met," she answered, reaching forward with a hand like it was a forepaw, "I told you I roar and purr. I also snipped at you and said I wasn't in the habit of prowling like a cougar." Kick paused halfway to me. Her gaze lifted from my dick to my eyes. My hand instinctively followed her cue. I started stroking myself, squeezing, beckoning her closer. She licked her upper lip. "But you... sprawled on the couch like a king. So strong, so serene, so delicious. Then your cock came to life... for me. This prowling business suddenly makes sense." Kick finished her trek across the room, her swaying breasts the sweetest sight. My dick bobbed as if it were begging for her.

She reached for my ankle, ran her nails up my calf, then caressed my leg with her cheek the way a cat would. Her tongue followed, and I swear I heard a purr.

"Kick," I groaned, drawing out her name. I couldn't finish my thought once she began carefully kissing her way up my leg. The pain of reliving my memories peacefully retreated to a new shelter in my soul. No need to lock them up anymore. With Kick for a balm, I wouldn't fear my past again.

She nuzzled... *nuzzled* my damn cock. Her tongue, traveling across my ridged bands, nearly did me in as she lightly pumped the foreskin over my shaft. Her other hand scooted under me to access my balls, and I bit my lip. A moan escaped so loud that I knew I wouldn't last if I let her continue.

Then she looked up and caught my eyes as she descended. Her lips stretched around me did me in. I needed her mouth on mine, or I would bite my bottom lip until it drew blood. She mewled when I lifted her up.

"I'm coming in you," I declared in a rough voice I barely recognized.

"It's okay. I wanted to—"

"Another time. Let me come in you."

"That works too."

I centered her hips over my cock, eager to make her come apart. In my excitement, I grunted and lifted up as I settled her on me, so ready for a rough ride like the night before. That's when I caught her slight wince. I quickly settled her back on my thighs. "You're sore."

"Out of practice," she countered.

I wanted to kick my own ass. "Shit. I'm sorry."

She placed two fingers over my mouth. "Shush." She ran her fingers through my hair and laced them at the back of my neck, encouraging me to continue, but I refused. She needed me to take care of her in every way. I was a damn dog.

"You're taking a break." I stood and paced the room, unsure of what to do next. I considered drawing a bath for her, but my tub was small. On my second trip around the den, I saw a huge grin on her face.

"I could watch you walk all night. You're turning me into a lust-filled harlot."

I took a drink from the glass I'd left on the coffee table. "What're you saying?"

"I could be pissed at you for slowing our roll, but it's super-sweet. I'm also a grown woman who can make my own decisions." She waggled her eyebrows. "Pretty hot though."

Kick might have the variances I did, but she also had an autoimmune condition that demanded respect. Thinking of her genetics gave me an idea. Grasping her hands, I had her pivot and lie down on the sofa so I could begin a light massage. As we both relaxed into the rhythmic movements, our auras released, mixed. As if it sought mine, Kick's violet light reached up to meet my blue when my hands moved over her.

I reached the apex of her thighs and gently worked her folds, creating a warming in her sweet pussy. I shifted and placed my free hand on her abdomen while my fingers moved inside her. The light and warmth intensified as I sat in awe of what my instincts led.

"Mmm," she drawled, her eyes half-mast. "This feels amazing."

"Hell yeah," I answered roughly, just as turned on. "I meant to do a little massage. But this—"

"It's like you're filling me everywhere."

"Me as well." I focused my attention on letting our energy mix and run wild. Seeing what it could do.

I moved up her body, working the light—for lack of a better term—over her breasts. When I eased a nipple into my mouth, the warmth flowed through me, down to my balls. We both moaned low and long, drawing out our pleasure at the new sensation.

"I need you, Thomas. Please fill me." She gasped. "Now."

Our energy alone had worked me up enough to almost come on myself. I carefully slipped inside her, and the vitality consumed me. We set a leisurely pace. Each fraction of an inch was a caress like I'd never known, all the way to my toes.

It didn't take long until her moans shifted into the keening I already knew. "So close."

"Same, baby. Let it go."

The light pulsed in time with our movements. The waves created a tiny wind that blew over us, shuffling Kick's curls as she writhed under me. The way the light mixed around us made her appear more like the goddess I adored.

As her orgasm continued, it grew in intensity and set mine loose. Right there, in my den, as the clock plodded toward midnight, we knitted ourselves back together after having nearly come apart. If this was what we had to look forward to, I would never fear my past or my future again.

"WHERE DID YOU LEARN TO DO *THAT*?" KICK ASKED. SHE BRUSHED some hairs off my forehead, a smile and an expression of wonder on her face. I felt the same, to be honest. "Or do I not want to know?"

I kissed her nose, not wanting to move any other part of my body. I could've stayed buried in her, surrounded by her, through the night. "From you, I guess. It's all new."

Her brows shot up like she doubted my words, so I elaborated. "Remember this morning… I told you how my aura had disappeared until recently?"

"Oh, right."

"Plus I hid it, like you did." I winked at her and watched Kick's skin flush a deeper shade of pink as she bit her lip.

Her scent filled my nose differently. I inhaled the vanilla and tropical floral fragrance that I associated with my woman. This was more intense. What we'd done had amplified it. "You smell like a holiday cookie. Love it." I nipped her shoulder playfully.

Kick laughed and said, "I was thinking how your scent reminds me of standing in the middle of the woods. I mean, you always do, but this is… more."

"Is it a good thing?"

"The best."

I peppered small kisses along her jaw, then finally shifted us so she could lie on top of me, afraid I'd crush her. "Let's practice using our energy together, now that we have each other."

Kick showed her approval by giving me the sweetest smile. Then she kissed my chest.

I pulled the quilt over us as the people on the television shouted, "Happy new year!" A new beginning, indeed. One of our phones dinged with a text. Kick didn't jump for it, so I let it go too. Whatever it was, it could wait.

4

I MELT WITH YOU

KICK

Thomas played with my "pineapple" of curls scattered across the pillow as I lay in his bed. I turned toward him standing at my side of the bed. He kissed my temple. "Be back soon, baby. Snuggle in as long as you need."

Then it hit me. "Your nickname for me... baby. You... It's literal. *You're* the cradle robber."

Thomas froze with his leg bent over his jeans in the middle of stepping into a leg. He had the nerve to smirk.

"Was it a joke?" I fought the temptation to take offense. I dreaded starting another day with drama, and I wanted to give him the benefit of the doubt. Still, I had to ask.

He pulled up his pants and sat next to me while I pulled up to sitting. "You're never a joke." He fingered the tips of my ears, his eyes doing that sparkle thing I was noticing more. The gesture helped me finally make peace with one of my many flaws. Thanks to him, I might grow to actually like them. "To be clear, a grown-up is a grown-up. If I wanted to spend all my time with people my age, I'd live at the vineyard. Now, a woman the age of my students? There's a big no." He leaned over and gave me another kiss. "Not you."

"Okay. It makes sense, I guess." I pulled the scrunchie out of my hair and shook it out. "Sorry. I'm so used to being made fun of—especially for things beyond my control. I had to ask so I wouldn't assume."

"No apology necessary."

I reached for Thomas's hand and squeezed it. "Then it's a vineyard? In Bordeaux?"

"Yep."

"I'd love to see it."

He scratched his nose. "I'll speak to Alaric soon. He owns the estate and oversees the American team of the Felidae." Thomas's strong posture slumped a bit. "That was my last reason for waiting to tell you about everything. Alaric deserved to know my plans. I owe him the courtesy. Also, I had to be certain he didn't hold any negative thoughts toward you."

Jaysus. The reminder of another potential danger to me didn't sit well. Not like it ever would. "And now?" I struggled to understand why Thomas would stay with them after what he'd discovered, but again... I'd learned how the benefit of the doubt, and patience, went a long way.

"Let's talk with Banger. Make us official. Last I spoke to him, we were broken up. We'll go from there." He tapped my knee. "Oh, you should know I told him about seeing your aura too."

I worried my tongue in my cheek, not sure if Thomas was ready for my next request.

"Don't worry about it upsetting him. It had the opposite effect."

Well, that was weird, but I'd think about it later. I bit my lip and rumpled my nose.

His eyebrow lifted. "Spit it out."

"Well... I hoped we could spend tonight at my place. You

know, get you used to it without the kids around. Liam and Macushla won't be back until tomorrow afternoon. It'll give us time to settle things between you and Shane's ghost." I squinted at the startled expression on his face. "Let me rephrase that… You know I've moved on, obviously. I feel there's a need to assure you the house has as well."

Thomas let his head drop. "Damn."

I swiped his hair off his forehead, trying to get him to look at me. We had to get it all out and sorted quickly. "It was hard to miss, but I understand. No judgment from me."

"I'm sorry. Consider it the misplaced emotions of a confused man." He squeezed my hand. "I meant it when I told you it made me happy to know you were loved."

My hand moved to his jaw, and he settled his cheek in my palm. I loved the notion that Thomas needed me as much as I did him. "It makes it easier to recognize this time."

"It does, doesn't it?" Thomas reached across the bed and picked up his phone. "I'll have Banger meet us at your house this afternoon."

"Perfect. Maybe we can watch the Rose Bowl at Finnegan's Wake? It'll make coming back to the empty house all the better when we can celebrate Michigan State's victory."

Thomas pulled his shirt over his head. "Why do I think that means more to you than it does to me?"

I laughed, gesturing around the room. "This is an extremely rare treat, Professor. I hate the idea of bursting our love bubble, but the world—especially my children—won't stay away."

"True. You McKennas are a package deal." Thomas kissed my temple again and grabbed his cowboy boots. "Since you're up, check your texts. Think one of your packages texted last night."

"I saw it when I got up to take my thyroid medicine. Dylan has an issue, but he stressed that they're physically okay and I'm to—and I quote—chill. I'll call him later."

"Good to hear." He stomped into his second boot. "I won't be long. Enjoy your quiet time."

After this glimpse of life with an empty nest, I couldn't wait for the real thing. "Oh I will, believe me. Tell Eddie-the-horse good morning for me, and have a nice ride."

"Won't be as long as yesterday's." Thomas waggled his brows and left.

After washing up, I enjoyed a long meditation session, followed by yoga in his workout room. Thomas's house turned out to be a dream home for me. I loved every room, nook, and cranny. I also noticed the miniatures of him and his late wife had disappeared. While I never would have asked him to remove them, the fact he'd done it meant the world. I figured, like with Shane's photos at my house, they had found a new home in a more neutral place. I just hadn't seen them yet, but I also didn't venture to the third floor. For some reason, it felt off-limits, and I'd ask about it later. My surprise quota still overflowed.

I massaged my muscles after my workout, noting how different they felt. The yoga session had been different too. I went through my standard sequence, but the poses were more comfortable and went farther than normal. My mind still struggled to settle without focusing on my meditation porch, but it felt clear and raring to go once I was done. Was this a sign of the variances Thomas would search for? Who knew?

As I bent forward to stretch my hamstrings, I caught Thomas's reflection in the studio mirror.

"Didn't mean to bother you," he said.

"Please bother me." I jumped to standing. "I've been at this forever. Just when I think all is right with the world, my mind takes off at the speed of light in four directions all over again."

"Don't worry, darlin'. Everything will settle." He wrapped his arms around me and inhaled. "Mmm, you smell like dessert. How can I ever go back to my lab when my body cries out for you after a mere hour apart?"

We ate our breakfast in the nude while watching the Rose Parade. Laziness was becoming a new luxury. Days stuck in bed were a regular part of the autoimmune life, but they were about recovering. This decadence without guilt was a new concept. Not to mention the crazy whirlwind of belonging to someone again. I couldn't help giggling.

Thomas stopped stroking my thigh and raised an eyebrow.

I pressed my lips together to make it stop. "It's like we're elite Romans or something." When had I ever had the freedom simply to be with the man I loved? It made any worries about our future dissipate.

5

IT'S THE END OF THE WORLD AS
WE KNOW IT (AND I FEEL FINE)

KICK

 e drove separately to my house because we each had work the following day. Tension grew during the drive, winding me up tight as a drum by the time I pulled into my garage. My mind kept running scenarios about how Banger would react to my knowing everything Thomas had told me. The man and I had started off terribly back in September. I worried we'd lose the progress we'd made. Since he was Thomas's best friend, I hated the idea of Banger's disapproval.

I missed the extra car in the driveway, not to mention Liam's on the street. It was such a common scenario, the wrongness of it this day slipped by my happy heart. I exited my Camaro and met Thomas in the driveway, my arms filled with grocery bags for dinner. It would take a few trips to bring in everything.

Having missed clue number one when I parked, clue number two danced in circles in front of me. Then she licked my leggings-covered ankle. Macushla met us at the door, her fierce tail-wagging and spinning a canine command for "Rub my butt."

Since this was our usual greeting whenever I returned home, it still took a minute to catch on.

"Hi, Kooshie. Did you miss me?" I set my bags down and squatted to her level as she leaned into my knee for a head rub, taking stock of my travels as she thoroughly sniffed me. When my fingers stayed on her ears, she froze, her soulful brown eyes rolling back as she went into "eargasm" mode, complete with drool from the side of her mouth.

A mental light bulb finally clicked on. "Hang on, what're you doing here?"

I glanced past the mudroom into the kitchen. Dishes were piled high in the sink. If I took a guess, I'd say all my dishes were dirty. Paper plates were stacked on the island because the garbage overflowed too. Used pots filled the stovetop.

My eyes widened as I scanned the rest of the first floor. It looked like Monday morning at a frat house. Chips were scattered across the dining room table and the floor—a generous helping of both the poker and tortilla variety. The anger that comes from total disappointment woke in my belly and rose until the accompanying temper practically shot out my ears.

My first thought turned to harassment at my café. Maybe someone had tossed my sanctuary. But that didn't fit this visual. "What the ever-living hell happened here?"

Macushla dipped her head and sent me a mental message. She moved toward the island with her tail wagging low like she was trying to explain.

"Oh, hey fam." Liam sauntered down the steps and had the nerve to sound chipper.

Hey fam? Was he kidding? Still in pajama pants, his curls stuck out in all directions, like they'd been electrified. "What happened here, Lee? My delightful home looks like you lost a game of Jumanji!" Seriously, artwork hung precariously askew on the walls, and a plant lay overturned in a corner. Then I saw a massive stain on the area rug. My heart fluttered like I was running a race. I pressed my chilled fingers to my face to cool it down. To keep from punching something. Not that the house would've been worse if I had.

Liam laughed nervously at my colorful description while Thomas opened cupboards in the kitchen, searching for heaven-knew-what with diligence.

"Sorry about the little mess. We didn't think you'd be back till tomorrow."

"Little mess?" I asked with incredulity. I spun to Thomas and said, "He thinks this is a *little* mess." A goofy grin spread on my face. I'm sure I appeared half-gone. "Son, this is a desecration. You've defiled my piece of the planet." I pointed a finger at the living room and growled. "Mine. Not yours! You will respect our home, not to mention how hard I've worked to keep it over your head."

Liam swiped a hand in my direction. "It'll be fine. We'll take care of it. Besides, Carmen can fix what we don't get to."

Where to begin with that one? Thomas found the garbage bags, pulled out a few, and flicked one open.

"Please don't," I told him. This was not the way I'd envisioned his day going. Guilt mingled with anger now. I wanted Thomas eased into a new arrangement, not thrown into the fire known as my family. "This is Liam's mess, sweetheart, not ours." I pinned my son with my fiercest glare. "He'll clean it up."

Liam shrugged. "It's not like I'm alone here. So—"

"Why aren't you at Dylan's?" I said over him, the puzzle pieces coming together in my mind. "You and Koosh are supposed to be at your brother's for another day."

Dylan's roommate—who went by Dummy despite my pleas to change his mind—trotted down the steps, yawning, his floppy hair still wet from a shower. "Afternoon, Mrs. Mack. I thought I heard your lovely voice."

"Don't even with me, Henry." I held a hand up to him. "With

all due respect, why are you two here? Where's Dylan?" My questions ended in a screech.

"We're out of coffee," Liam said, as if that answered anything.

I rolled my hand for him to continue, then pressed my fingernails into my palms. The number of hours it would take to set everything right added up in my head. We didn't have time for this. Sure, Carmen was in charge of keeping the house, but that was regular maintenance. We set a schedule for the deep stuff so she could bring in more help.

Thomas opened the door to Macushla's cupboard, who contributed a vigorous bark to the familial cacophony. He found a treat and gave it to Koosh after making her sit. He did seem to fit right in. Then he disappeared into the garage. I assumed to retrieve the rest of our stuff.

"Since we're out of coffee," Liam continued, "Dylan went to the new Starbucks to get us lattes."

My hand flew to my chest as if I was having a heart attack. "What? This house disaster isn't bad enough. You have to secretly plot against my business too? Why?"

My son frowned at me like a disappointed father, like *I* was the source of our current drama and not my offspring. "The Perked Cup is closed today, remember?"

I stomped my foot to get his attention. Okay, maybe I was a tad dramatic. He was on my last nerve, and something needed to get through to the boy. At that moment, I longed for the empty nest everyone had been warning me about. *Syndrome* my ass. I'd call it peace. "You have keys to the coffeehouse." Then I remembered the critical issue and shook my hands in frustration. "Nevermind. My question was why aren't you at Dylan's?"

Henry—aka Dummy—spoke up. "There's a… situation with our condo, so we couldn't stay there."

The partly shy, partly discouraged look on his normally sunny face caught my attention. "What situation?"

Liam jumped in. "Let's say Suzy didn't move out well."

"Go on." *Shit.* I should've frog-marched her by her silky hair right out of Dylan's life.

"Well… she vandalized it before leaving." Henry opened the fridge and removed an empty jug of juice. It was a good thing I'd brought groceries, though there wasn't nearly enough for five.

I sighed and placed my hands on my lower back to massage the tension. "How badly?"

Henry leaned against the counter. "Didn't you get Dylan's text?"

Thomas passed by with our suitcases, heading toward my bedroom. He gave me a small, sympathetic smile but kept on moving. Smart man. *Stay away, Professor. Stay far away.* They were my spawn after all.

"The message said he wanted to talk to me. There was nothing about an emergency, let alone vandalism."

"We hated to disturb you," Liam explained. "Didn't want to worry you either."

My son walked by me to push some of the paper plates off the counter and into a garbage bag. He reeked of alcohol. "Were you drinking? You're underage."

Liam sent me another frustrated glare. *That's my role here, pal.* "I had two and they were an hour apart. *You* let me do that on holidays."

"Two what? Gallons of beer? Vats? You smell like you swam in it."

"You're not far off. A lot landed on me when Dylan flipped over the table." He giggled, like he was contemplating a pleasant memory. "It was big."

I leaned into the counter, dropping my face into my hands. I didn't want to think about which table he meant. Hell, it was probably the source of the rug stain.

"I haven't showered yet." Liam brought his shirt to his nose and flinched. *No shit.* "Being the excellent host you taught me to be, I let Dum have the bathroom first."

"Lee—" I planned to tell him there were two other showers in the house, but Henry brought us back to the topic of the condo. "Speaking of bathrooms... the bulk of our condo damage is in Dylan's suite, although my toilet was stuffed with something that made it overflow into the hallway and down the stairs. Dyl and I turned off the water main because his fixtures were smashed. He called your friend Charley, who sent over a guy. The repairs start tomorrow. So we came here."

I jammed my fingers into my hair, messing up my ponytail as I slowly spun around. "I still can't believe the three of you did this."

"There were other guys here for poker." Henry pressed his lips together a minute then added, "We're sorry."

What could I do? They didn't want to ruin my time with Thomas. Plus calling Charley would've been my advice. "No, no. You boys did good with the condo."

"Louie—that's Charley's guy—said everything's stable. It shouldn't take much to fix since we caught the damage pretty fast. Can you believe Suzy took all the towels? Half of them were mine." Henry shook his head angrily. "Anyway, we had to go out and buy a bunch to soak up the water."

My anger subsided toward the boys and moved toward Dylan's ex-girlfriend. "I'm sorry you had to deal with her rage."

"Yeah, well"—Henry threw his thumb over his shoulder toward the bedrooms—"Dyl drank a lot of beer. I tried to cheer him up, but... you can see things got out of hand. He's struggling, Mrs. Mack."

When I looked around, my anger stirred again, as did my embarrassment. On the one hand, I couldn't believe my boys would treat our home this way. I also knew all about my son's temper when he was hurting. He came by it honestly. I pointed, moving my hand around the entire living space. "You will clean this up. All three of you. It's not my job." I shot a glare at Liam. "And this is *not* what Carmen's hired to do."

"She's our maid. Cleaning our house is her *job*."

"Son…" I swallowed my first thought, then held up a finger. "This kind of mess has always been outside of Carmen's contract. Also, you will not disrespect her again. She's a loyal family friend *first* and an employee second. And third, she doesn't get home from San Juan until tomorrow afternoon. I'm not dropping this on her out of nowhere. There's no way I'm living in this crime scene for another hour, let alone for days."

"Fine, fine," Liam grumbled.

I snapped my fingers in his face. "I'm serious, Liam. Remember this: the blue you were born with lives long in your collar, not in your blood. We will *not* be those kinds of people no matter how you're raised."

He lifted his hands in surrender. "Sorry. I'll get cleaning."

I reached into my purse and pulled out the keys to the Perked Cup. "Go to the coffeehouse first and pick up five pounds of the Breakfast Blend for you fellas and a pound of decaf for me." I swatted his shoulder. "I still can't believe you traitorous boys planned to bring the competition into my home."

"It'd take too long," he whined. "Plus we need *food* food."

"Oi!" I rolled my eyes to the ceiling. I thought I'd taught these boys to think. "That's what the walk-in cooler is for. In fact, bring back lunch and snacks for everyone. Banger will be here in an hour, and you've torn through all my food." After another motherly eye roll, I huffed. What did I expect? Just because I suddenly was involved with a spectacularly secret and exceptional group of people—and I might be one of them—that I would stop being a mother? Leave it to my kids to throw a heavy dose of real world my way. I padded into my bedroom for some peace. Who knew what would happen when Banger arrived?

6

LOVE STRUCK BABY

THOMAS

The doorbell rang while Kick and I were holed up in her office. I studied staff notes from my time off while she finished the scheduling and fussing about still needing another employee. We didn't really need to work. I was sequestering us away from the 'cleaning crew', knowing she'd jump in the minute she stepped out of her office.

"Saved by the bell." I sighed, closed my laptop, and greeted Banger in the entry. "Hey man, we're in here." I smiled when his eyes landed on Kick. They softened ever so slightly—a clear sign of acceptance where my best friend was concerned. It had taken a while for them to warm to each other, but she had his heart now, especially after our talks about her in Bordeaux. It helped to know he had my back with the Felidae. I needed it sooner than planned.

"Look at you two," he practically purred.

"Happy New Year, Banger." Kick gave him a hesitant hug.

I moved to the desk chair, pulled my lady into my lap, then indicated a wingback chair with my hand. "Have a seat."

He plopped down and stretched out his legs. A mischievous grin spread across his face. "So we're lovebirds again? Not so broody today, brother." He crossed his legs at the ankle and folded his arms behind his head, letting the grin grow smug.

"*We* are," I answered. "Not so much you."

Banger chuckled from deep in his belly. It was something he only did around close friends and family, telling me everything I needed to know about his regard for Kick.

She laid her head against mine. "Long time no see. Where'd you disappear to?"

Banger twitched his nose. "You remember my assignment. It's why your daughter watched my fish for me."

"You're a spy, aren't you? Fess up."

He answered her with a lift of his eyebrow.

Kick responded by placing her finger along the side of her nose and winking.

I burst out laughing while Banger shook his head.

"This isn't *The Sting*, darlin'."

"I know." She grinned. "Banger's bona fide. I'm simply letting him know I know without *saying* I know. You know?"

Banger chuckled. "Speaking of my detecting skills…"

I held Kick tighter. I wasn't ready for her to learn about what had gone down in Bordeaux with Taylor Johnson, the guy who had tried to kidnap Kick from Ducky's nightclub in November.

"I have updates. We also need to talk about your protection," Banger continued.

"That's not cryptic at all," she murmured in her native sarcasm. Kick looked at me, and I gave her a reassuring wink. I considered Jonn Graham, his father, and anyone else in the community the least of our worries.

"Before you delve in"—I swallowed and pointed at the door—

"there's something more pressing we need to tell you. Can you close that? Lock it too."

Banger slowly rose and did as requested. "What's more urgent than the goings on in your woman's life?"

I turned Kick's jaw, lining up her mouth to mine, then gave her a slow, deep kiss. I used my other hand to rub circles over her hip.

"Um, thanks for the show? But—"

"Will you stop and look?" I lifted our entwined hands. A tiny light flowed around our fingers, working its way up our arms. It wasn't the full-blown aura show we'd experienced at my house, but it did the job.

"Ho...ly shit." Banger nearly jumped out of the chair. His gaze raced from our hands to our faces and back again. "You were right."

A stupid grin filled my face, as if I were responsible for what was happening to Kick.

"You think she's—"

"Like us? Yeah."

Kick raised her free hand. "Hang on, fellas. I thought we were taking this one step at a time."

"That's the plan." I couldn't hold in my excitement, though, and gave her a squeeze.

"This is a hell of a stroke of luck. What is your next step?" Banger shifted in the chair and leaned forward, elbows on his knees.

"One, I have a new test subject. I'll run her DNA against our samples and go from there." I kissed Kick's cheek. "She's a miracle in multiple ways."

Kick stood and leaned against the windowsill. "Thomas told me both your parents were Felidae too—I hope you don't mind. It's been a lot to take in, and I've had many questions."

I chuckled at her statement, getting a glare in return.

"I bet." Banger laughed too.

"Anyway... Thomas implied there's some tough history there, but what about your sister? I'm asking because I'm concerned about my kids. Is Tess Felidae too? Did it skip anyone?"

Banger coughed as if he'd choked on a drink.

She whispered to me, "Am I not supposed to know about Tess?" Then she turned to Banger. "I swear this stays between us. I get how dangerous it is to know about you. Except... I'm also a mother." Her eyes were shadowed with worry, like she carried a too-heavy weight.

Banger rubbed his jaw. "I believe you." Then he looked at me. "Appreciate you leaving some surprises for me."

"All Kick knows is what she just said. Your story's yours to tell."

Kick's gaze shifted between me and Banger as she studied what he and I silently communicated.

"Tess isn't like you? Does she know? What about your parents?"

I shrugged at him. *May as well tell her.*

Banger held up his hand. "Tess *is* my *maman*, Kick."

Kick's jaw dropped, then closed. Up and down that way a few times. Fearing she'd hit her limit on life-altering surprises, I reached for her hand and brought her back to my lap. Not that this knowledge did a damn thing to Kick's life, but she'd taken in her share of shocks in two days' time.

"Mama? As in Tess is your mother?"

"We say *maman*," Banger clarified as he slumped back. "But that's exactly what I mean."

"JaysusMaryandJoseph." I gave Kick's leg a squeeze as she quietly added, "Tess doesn't just appear young, she acts it too."

"Tell me about it." A distant expression crossed Banger's face. His mouth ticked up at the corner. "She was a fine *maman* when it counted. When my arsehole sire let her be." Then his eyes cleared, and he continued, "She feels most like herself when she projects a young image, so to speak. I believe her happiest memories are from back then."

Kick took a moment and closed her eyes. "Wow." She shook her head. "I can't imagine wanting to be twenty again, let alone for forever. I get it too."

"Get what?" I asked.

"You do?" Banger asked at the same time.

Kick bit her lip. "I was in my late thirties when I was finally diagnosed. I'd dealt with gaslighting for years while knowing in my heart something was wrong. Anyway, once I had the information, I looked back and could see the signs of the autoimmune disease as a teen. So I understand filling in the pieces after the fact."

Banger's head tilted as he studied Kick like he saw something new.

I kissed her cheek, feeling compelled to offer comfort. Hearing about how much she'd already been through and the injustices she'd had to fight against left me uneasy.

Banger shifted, settling back on the chair with an ankle over his knee. "You're handling this better than I would've predicted."

"No way, pal," Kick scoffed. "I'm not handling *anything*. I blew up at my boys earlier when I should've recognized the signs of my oldest son's struggle. Connecting what you have already experienced to what I know gets me to the next minute. That's as far as I can let my mind go for now."

Her eyes settled on me. Kick gave me her smallest smile, the one that didn't reach her eyes but let me know she planned to hang in there. *Damn.* I wished we could send Banger home and let her rest. Only my friend's bouncing foot told me he had more news.

Banger stared at us while rubbing his thumb over his bottom lip, except his eyes weren't focused. Then he burst into a laugh. "Hell, brother, you might be a genius."

I raised my brows to encourage him to get to the point. Like

Kick, I also grew weary, wondering when either of us might hit a wall.

"You might be the ace up our sleeve, Kick. What you just said shows you're able to walk in others' shoes. Maybe you can help solve your own mystery."

"My mystery?" Kick turned to me. "I have a mystery? I'm not keeping secrets."

Banger held up his hand. "All I'm saying is Thomas has me working two problems for him. One is who ordered your attempted kidnapping and why. The other involves the death of his lab assistant."

"Presley? I thought she was hit by a car—an accident."

"Banger suspects it wasn't accidental," I answered, then rolled my neck. Kick stood again and shifted from foot to foot.

Banger filled her in on what he'd told me in Bordeaux about the Ducky's bartender making a call to a number in Oxford. I'd been so caught up in his interrogation of Taylor Johnson that I'd forgotten this detail. It was a mistake I couldn't afford to make anymore. As Banger went on, neither Kick nor I could connect the events.

"Coincidences don't happen in my line of work."

"And you don't trust Nigel," I insisted.

"That too."

"Which reminds me… Any chance you can get Kick's DNA results for me?"

Banger waved his hand, letting me know it wouldn't be a problem.

Kick folded her arms. "You really are a superspy, aren't you?"

Banger cleared his throat. "If the events are connected, we can benefit from Kick's instincts. That means, Kick, you see something or sense something? Let me or Siobhan know. Speaking of, Von told me you won't agree to having a bodyguard. Given all this"—Banger spread his hands apart before pointing them in Kick's direction—"I insist on it. In fact, he's meeting us in—"

Kick vigorously shook her head. "No. Why do I need a body-guard?" She held up our hands. The surrounding light lingered some. "Because of this? I've been experiencing this for weeks, and Thomas is the only person who noticed. I'll keep it under control." She made fists as her emotions made the energy pulse again. "The kids and I were fine over the holiday, and that would've been a perfect time for an unknown bad guy to pounce."

I scratched my neck. "Ah, darlin'—"

"One of my men shadowed your family," Banger interjected.

I braced for the blow. We had to wrap up this meeting. Kick truly was about at her wits' end. She opened her mouth, but Banger spoke first.

"Kick, do you ever check your security footage?"

"Isn't that your job? Or your team's job?"

"That's what I thought."

She turned to me. "I won't live in fear."

I reached for Kick's hand and rubbed my thumb over her knuckles. "I don't want you to either. In fact, that's the point. Hear us out." I pegged Banger with a pointed glare. "Anything else he has to say can wait a day."

Banger closed his eyes and nodded.

"You know how I feel about the damsel in distress business. It's not a good state of existence."

"You also can't reshuffle the cards in the middle of play, baby." I squeezed her hand. "You go with the hand you're dealt."

"A bodyguard in this situation will be an advantage," Banger said. "People will think you're taking charge of your situation because all anyone will know is you hired him."

I hated seeing Kick's shoulders slump as she mulled it over. "Okay, fine. But I still don't see the connection."

"Thomas won't say it, but I will—"

"Banger… it can wait," I protested.

"No, it can't. She needs to know all of it." Banger stood,

offering Kick the wingback chair, then leaned against the windowsill. "Has Thomas told you that Bordeaux isn't the only place where there are people like us?" She nodded. "Within the Felidae Society, there are some that don't like the work Thomas is doing. There are even people who want to see an end to certain family lines."

That last was shocking news to me. I looked up at him. "How do you know this shit?"

Banger rubbed his neck. "Tess. Remember when she warned us to watch our backs? She and I agree that Edmund's death wasn't right. She's heard rumors from the staff. Add in every-thing these past few months—including Kick." He wiggled his fingers. "I've got the tingles. Don't like tingles."

A loud crash came from the other side of the office door, making the dog bark. *Christ.* There were so many new lives on the line now. I leaned onto the desk and held my head. "Banger..."

"I'll let the rest wait since Kick agreed to the bodyguard."

"Thank you."

Kick frowned as she checked the wall clock by the door. "We should get over to Finnegan's Wake. The Rose Bowl kickoff is soon, and tables fill up fast. It also sounds like the fellas could use a break as much as us."

Banger pulled out his phone and sent a text. A minute later he said, "Mateo can meet us at the bar."

"Who's Mateo?"

"Your new bodyguard. He served with Jake in the military and does security work now." As we filed out of the office, Banger patted my shoulder. "He passed my background check with flying colors, brother."

"We'll meet with your mother's new bodyguard soon." All three sets of eyebrows raised as Kick's sons and Dummy registered what I'd told them. They were at a high-top in the bar waiting for the Rose Bowl game to start.

"When did it get bad enough for a bodyguard?" Dylan asked.

"When a mob tried to run y'all out of the store," Liam answered for me.

"No, it was the drugging." Dummy added his two cents.

"That was Aunt Cyndi," Liam argued. "But things are escalating." He ran his hand through his hair. "I haven't told fam about the rumors at school. Figured she was upset enough."

"Rumors about Kick?" I asked him.

Liam peeked over his shoulder at his mother and nodded. "Her. The café. Snow too. It's like one dies and another replaces it. It's tragic. Frustrating."

Now I had to find out what else I didn't know. I pulled up the to-do list on my phone and typed in *have Banger investigate rumors at high school.*

Dylan exhaled hard. "I should put off my thesis."

"No," I nearly shouted, then reined in my tone. This kid took on too much when his father died. It was time for him to learn to live for himself. Kick had told me that's where his temper came from, which made sense. "No need for that. I promise." I'd spent the least amount of time with Dylan and made a note to get to know him better. "We'll fill y'all in soon. For now, know that this is a good thing. It shows everyone Kick's taking charge of the situation."

Liam snorted. "I bet. My dude, we know fam. She agreed to this after much kicking and screaming. Pun intended."

I bit my lip to keep from laughing. "Anyway… order whatever y'all want. As soon as we're ready, I'll bring Mateo over for introductions. Sound good?" I tapped the table, and Dylan grabbed my wrist.

"One thing…" I leaned toward him to hear over the crowd, and he said, "Hey man, I'm sorry about you having to come to the house like it was. I didn't… I didn't know Mom had invited you over."

Oh, the things to unpack there, especially given Dylan's frown.

"First off, you apologized to your mother, so I'm good." I caught Dylan's eyes so he could see that I was sincere. "Truly. I'm sorry for what you're going through. I can relate some, and… well, I don't want to tell you how to move past it. The days do get better." I had been angry on Kick's behalf initially and did everything in my power to keep from butting in with them. However, Dylan had carefully cleaned up his mess. He even scrubbed the carpet stain on his hands and knees. Apparently, after drinking twice his weight in beer, he got into a fight with another guest over a poker hand.

"Second, I thought you were good with your mother dating me. You accepted my apology in the café after Kick and I made up. If you need to talk through anything more in private, say the word." I lifted my head and saw that the patio was empty. "We could go outside now if you want."

"No man, it's my bad. I didn't know Mom was ready for… you know… more." Dylan actually blushed. "Anyway, we're good. Except you have to deal with a house full of McKennas."

What a different day it was shaping into compared to what Kick and I had planned. I chuckled, realizing Dylan was right. "Enjoy the game. We'll talk about our arrangements after. Sound good to y'all?"

All three boys—well, young men—shrugged. It hit me how Kick's dating was as new for her children as it was for her, especially her fully grown son. I asked for Dylan's phone and typed in my number. "Call or text me anytime with any concerns. Got it?"

He nodded slowly and cleared his throat. "Thanks."

When I returned to our table, both Banger and Kick were on their phones. "Everything alright?"

Banger put his down. "Following up with Siobhan."

Kick bit her lip as her brows drew together. "It's my brother Bert." She set her phone down. "Bobby's been *Bobby*, of course. This time it means she's coming home later than planned. She made Bert change the ticket."

"That's good. The woman is responsible for more than half your stress."

Kick scoffed at my words. "When I made the work schedule this morning, it was specifically around her arrival plans. You saw me send it off to my employees." Her phone pinged. "Annnd she's picked a time when I'm scheduled to work. Feckity feck. That b—" Kick bit her lip, shaking her head. Hell, her whole body shuddered. "It's not like she saw the schedule or knows I'm putting in extra hours to make up for time off. Bobby simply never looks beyond her own belly button or thinks to seek advice on anything. I'm just supposed to be eager to serve her above anyone else."

Kick texted back as she said, "She can finally get an introduction to ride-sharing then."

"Kick…" I stretched my arm across the back of our booth, scooching closer. "Let me see the ticket information."

"Why?" She texted another thing with several exclamation points. "Jaysus, she went off on Bert's boys and made his youngest cry. He's precocious, but he's not a wicked child. I mean, his parents recently divorced. What does she expect?"

I tapped on her shoulder to pull her attention from the rant. "I can get your mother. Classes at the university don't start until the third week in January."

Kick's gaze swung toward me, her brows making a little crease that told me I was crazy. Banger snorted. He took a drink of his Scotch to keep from laughing, silently letting me know he found it funny how Kick's family troubles rubbed off on me now that I chose what he called *life in the real world*.

I glared at him. *Zip it. We're fine.*

Then he *did* chuckle.

Kick set down her phone. "Sorry, gentlemen."

"I'll pick up your mother," I said, squeezing her shoulder.

"Thank you, but no." She gave me a small, placating smile. "I won't allow her to torture you."

I tilted my head and stared back. "She doesn't scare me." I peeked at her text thread. "Yeah, see? I'm working overnight in the lab the day before this. I can get her on my way home."

She set the phone down and harrumphed. "Are you sure? According to Bert, our mother's in a rare mood. Since she spoils him, that's saying something."

"Send me the flight information." She kissed me solidly on the lips. I waggled my brows. "If it gets me more of this, it'll be worth it."

"Not if she kills you on the ride home. Or you get wise and decide to move away." Kick bit her lip as Banger burst out laughing. He dipped his head to say *Told you.*

I ignored him and wiggled my finger over Kick's phone. "Tell your brother I've got it. Then send me the flight plan."

Her phone pinged right away and Kick snickered. She spoke as she typed. "Trial by fire, I guess." She added some more words, then set the phone down for good and sighed. "I can't even with her."

"I'm not hiding us, darlin'. We might as well figure out where your mother fits in too." At least Kick's kids were delightful. Even Dylan's grumpiness didn't bother me. At his core, I sensed a tender heart and a young man doing his best for his family.

"You're a glutton for punishment."

Banger smashed his lips between his teeth, but I already knew I'd slay any dragon for this family. *Even a beast in her sixties.*

7

MAYBE I'M AMAZED

THOMAS

*A*fter filling up on wings, meeting with Mateo, and introducing him to Kick's sons, we were ready to leave, but I could tell Banger had more to say.

He kept rubbing his jaw and sipping his drink, each swallow smaller than the last.

I rolled my wrist. "Spit it out, man."

He set his glass down. "For the love of anything holy, don't let people see your auras. I can't stop thinking about it. For Christ's sake, I've never been able to do that."

Kick had been half listening as she followed the football game. She did a double take and pulled a cute face. "You mean it's not a normal thing with you people?"

The corner of my mouth lifted in a smirk. "No darlin'. It's a sign of a deep bond." I leaned in and whispered, "I sure as hell didn't know about… last night."

Kick's blush sprinted up her chest to her hairline, her pointy ears turning a deep cherry color. Banger frowned and rolled his eyes.

He pointed at me. "Anyway… I didn't know this one could flame on until I saw him last."

"Remember how I thought it had gone? I didn't tell anyone about it because I didn't think it mattered."

Kick's eyes widened. "Wow." She leaned in. "So… you have different *abilities*?" She made air quotes with her fingers.

Banger nodded. "It's something we've known for a long time. A matter of trial and error to survive."

She tilted her head. "What can you do?"

"A dot-connector, this one." He grinned before swallowing the last of the amber liquid in his glass. "I blend in."

Kick scoffed. "You? No offense, Mr. McHenry, but you stand out. Between the buzzed blond hair, the nearly white eyes with the"—she circled her eyes with her finger—"navy rim. Hell, you're practically a doppelgänger for Rutger Hauer."

"Standing out at home helps me blend in when I'm on the job. No?" Banger lifted an eyebrow.

Kick sat in stunned silence, her mouth saying "wow" without making a sound.

I fought with myself to keep from calling bullshit. Banger spoke the truth to a degree, but he also enjoyed playing up the drama when the mood struck.

He finally broke and grinned. "This is fun. Coming clean to a civilian has its merits." Banger tossed me a little salute. "Gave you a hard time about pursuing this, but your instincts were spot-on. Once again."

"Ooh, what else has Thomas done? I feel like I know everything and nothing all at the same time."

I turned to her. "Aren't you upset about what he said about us?"

Kick waved her hand. "I could tell he didn't want us together."

Banger shrugged and chuckled again. I'd never heard the

amused sound come out of him so many times in one day. He tipped his head my way. "There are other research facilities besides our Thomas's, but he has the best approach. You prove it."

"Really? Go on," Kick urged. She crossed her arms over the cleared table and leaned forward, settling in for a good story.

"Well." I rubbed my neck and began. "In general, I play a long game with the research, hoping it leads to helping all people, not just the Felidae. The pressure for results that I'm under now is new and damn well better be temporary."

Banger added, "We believe there are many people who have the variances but die before gene expression."

Kick pointed at me. "Epigenetics."

A wide grin spread across my face. "Precisely. If you didn't have the café, I would hire you in the lab." I gave her a squeeze. "So we have to figure out this piece first. Then—"

Banger cut in. "Then he wants to see if our blood can improve the quality of life for everyone. Or some such."

Kick smiled at me with stars in her eyes. "You are a hero."

I dipped my head. "The thing is, other members are dead set against it. They've lived a traumatic life, which makes them generally hate mankind. They want to keep any new knowledge within the Felidae." I tipped my head toward my friend. "He hasn't said it outright, but I think Banger suspects some would love to be the ultimate dictators." I chose to believe he was wrong. Very wrong. "He's watched too many supervillain movies."

Banger spread his hands as if to say *we'll see*.

"What does Tess think?" Kick asked.

"Right." The question perked up Banger, and he cleared his throat. "Speaking of, she'll be here next month. I blame you, brother."

"What'd I do?"

"You showed her your lab. Tess won't stop with your damn mice. Like I pay attention to them."

"I'll send her an update."

"Appreciate it."

Kick's tongue moved around in her cheek. Knowing she was about to ask about the mice, I shook my head, encouraging her to let it rest for now. We'd gone over enough.

She gave me a shy smile while nodding her agreement. Then she shifted her attention back to Banger. "I, for one, can't wait to see Tess. It would be nice to start again with her. I have so many questions." Both my friend and I shook our heads. Kick elbowed my abs. "I want to know what she's good at, what she enjoys."

"Yoga and collecting." Banger lifted a finger. "I'll have her bring some of her jewelry. It's older than dirt. A few pieces were made for the Medici family."

I didn't think Kick's eyes could go wider. Her mouth parted slightly as she stared across the table.

"Oh, she's a brilliant painter too. You'd like that."

"Yup, probably."

The look on Kick's face reminded me of when she'd been drugged—part numb, part ecstasy, completely checked out. I figured her new weltanschauung had reached its limit.

KICK, LIAM, AND I MADE A COFFEE ASSEMBLY LINE IN THE kitchen back at her house. The fellas were wired from the Michigan State win, though not as fired up as Kick. Meeting Mateo had also ticked up everyone's emotions. I wanted a moment to process this new reality together. Everyone but Kick received their espressos, and she shooed us toward the dining table.

"What about you?" I protested.

"I'm making a decaf pour-over," she explained as she dumped the used grounds in the trash. "It'll just take a minute. I can hear you from here."

"Alright." I kissed Kick's cheek and pivoted toward the dining area. Three sets of eyes stared at us like they were watching a zoo display.

Kick pulsed her brows and smiled. "Do I have to give you boys another talk on what people do when they date?"

Dylan and Liam shuddered. "God, no."

"Uh-huh. Thought so," she said as she watched her coffee flow through the cone filter. She added almond milk to her mug, then came and sat next to me. "I figured one birds-and-the-bees talk with your mother is about all the torture a boy can take," she said while blowing over the top of her cup, a cheeky grin on her face. She took a sip, then grabbed my hand, placing it on top of the table for the boys to see. I appreciated the power of a simple display of affection.

"What did y'all think of Mateo?" I asked the group.

"Isn't it up to fam?" Liam asked.

Kick spoke up. "No, Lee. You'll be working with him at the coffeehouse too. I want all of you to have his number"—she dipped her head toward Dummy—"even you, Henry. If you see or hear anything that's relevant to the harassment or the attack on me and Cyndi, you can update Mateo. He'll pass the information on to the team at Angel Security."

"Well, I mean Banger and Jake trust him, so...," Dylan said while shrugging.

"So you won't mind him being around us... a lot?" Kick asked.

"I won't be here with my project ramping up." Dylan ran his hand through his hair. "Guess I like you having some extra muscle. You know if you need it. Unless you need me to postpone my thesis and help out more."

Kick tilted her head as she swallowed her drink. "Why would I want you to do that?" She reached across the table and patted his hand. "I hate that you grew up way too fast. This is your time now. Do what you need to finish your degree and prepare for the investor meetings."

Good to see we were on the same page when it came to

Dylan. I rubbed the top of her hand with my thumb. "As many times as you need me to say it, your mom's my priority. In fact, we're putting her self-defense lessons back on the schedule. We took a break for her recovery, but it's needed." I turned to Kick to make sure she saw I meant my words.

Dylan dropped his head into his hands. "Ugh, I need to get out to your range."

"It's there whenever you have time." I took a sip of my espresso. "Send me a text when you're free."

Kick tapped the table. "As for tonight… I think Thomas and I will go back to his house."

Dylan and Dummy shifted in their seats.

"We can get a hotel for the night, Mom."

"Or stay at the condo." Dummy went over to Kick's carafe of decaf coffee and poured a cup.

"Not when the water's shut off," Kick said. "No, boys, this is your home too. But by the way you reacted to a peck on the cheek, I think you need a little time to get used to Thomas spending the night." She leaned toward me, and I placed my arm around her shoulder. She looked up at me and smiled, then set her eyes back on the fellas. "Get used to him fast. I want Thomas here as much as he wants me at his home. Besides, this may be your home, but my name's on the mortgage."

Dylan raised his hand slightly off the table. "But… what are your long-term plans? I mean, is this a real thing between you two?"

Kick and I nodded as we looked at each other. "As real as it gets," she said.

His eyes narrowed on me. "So you're going to live together? Get married?"

I almost choked on the last of my espresso.

Kick answered for us. "We may live together at some point. It's early, lad."

"You mean fast," he said.

"No," she insisted. "When you know what love looks like, it doesn't take long to recognize it when it shows up again. You know?"

She tilted her head back to meet my gaze and smiled. Then she turned back to her sons. "But I don't think marriage is for me anymore."

My back stiffened at her words. So caught up in the Felidae revelation I'd never considered the idea. How did I feel about it? I rubbed my chin, thinking.

"Why the hell not?" Dylan asked.

Yeah, why not? Leave it to the kids to boil everything down to the equal sign in life's equations.

"Dylan," Kick soothed. "It's not like it was when I met your dad. I have money now. Thomas has his own. So no one needs financial protection." She lifted a shoulder. "We're good like this."

"There's more to it, Mom. There's—"

"Enough," Kick said, gentle yet stern. She patted his hand again. "We're good. I have no desire for a fancy ceremony with a gazillion people in a church again. The relationship is important to me. Be happy for me. For us."

"Dyl, ease off, bro," Dummy cut in.

A loud exhale whooshed from Kick's oldest. "Okay." He held up his hands. "I give. I get you're grown. You know what you want."

"Thank you, lad. You'll have the same support from me when you're ready again. Okay?"

"It's not happening from where I stand," he answered with a heavy sigh.

"Give it time and space. You're too good of a man for it not to."

Dylan's face brightened at her words, I think more from his mother acknowledging his adulthood than his goodness. Pride filled my chest for both of them.

"What about you, Wee Man? Do you have anything to add?"

Liam spread his hands without lifting them off the table. "I'm vibin'."

"What about next of kin?" Dylan asked over his brother.

We shifted back toward him. "You kids will still split what's mine. The will's tight," Kick said.

"Sure." Dylan ran his hand through his hair. "But what about an emergency?"

Kick waved her hand. *"Pffft."*

"But the drugging… What if it had gone south? You designated me to make your hospital decisions when I came of age because you don't trust Grandma. If I'm not around, will Thomas get a say?"

Fuck me, the kid had a point. I wouldn't trust Kick's mother with the life of a toad, let alone any of the McKennas.

"It's one thing to recognize we're already in love. It's another to jump into marriage status after a couple of months," Kick said.

I swallowed, blinked. Both of them were right. A sense of urgency loomed over me, an impression that we didn't have time to develop like a normal relationship. Whatever that was. I spoke to Dylan. "Lack of a government paper will *never* mean your mother isn't protected. You do bring up a good point though. I'll have my lawyer research it."

BACK AT MY HOUSE, KICK SETTLED HER OVERNIGHT BAG ON THE empty bathroom vanity. I hoped she thought of it as hers. Then she sat on the edge of our bed holding her head in her hands.

I settled beside her and rubbed her back. "It was a big weekend."

She turned to me, a feisty smirk on her face. "Liam big?"

I laughed. "You take out all the huge revelations, research, and bodyguard shit. Boil it down to you and me? It was also wonderful in a 'Liam big' way."

She leaned into me but let her gaze drop back to the floor.

The tension rolled off her like her tight muscles were trying to grab it and throw it.

I hugged her tight. "This is why I wanted to ease you into my world." I brushed a curl off her forehead and kissed her temple. "Too much happened all at once."

Kick sighed and shrugged. Her reluctance to share every feeling she carried surprised me. Scared me if I was honest. I couldn't remember her ever being this closed off. It's not like I ever cared about dragging things out of someone. Kick was the mentor in that department.

"You want to go downstairs and watch a movie? I don't have a television in the bedroom like you do."

She shook her head. "It's only there for the days I'm stuck there."

I opened my mouth to repeat the question when she asked one of her own.

"Is your guitar nearby? Could you play for me?"

My lips curved. "My guitar's always nearby. Do you want to go down to the music room, or should I bring it here?" Hell, I'd have driven to the music store and demanded they open if I didn't have something handy.

"In here please." She lifted her face and gave me a small smile. I gladly took it.

When I returned with my favorite Gibson guitar, I sat in the wingback chair next to her. As I settled the strap around my neck, she pointed to the space on the table between us.

"You moved the miniatures."

I closed my eyes and strummed the strings to make sure they were tuned. "They're not right for here anymore." I plucked my tricky string and adjusted the tuning peg. "They're in a better spot."

Kick bit her lip as I moved to the last string. "Because of me? Thomas I don't want to impede your memories. I'm okay with—"

I stopped tuning and turned to her. "Did you move Shane's photos because of me?"

"No," she said. "It was for me. Moving them to a neutral space helped me move on."

"Neutral. Exactly. They're in my third-floor office if you're wondering." I brought her hand to my lips and kissed her fingers. "Is that what's bothering you? I want you to think of this space as yours as much as it's mine. In fact, I'd love it if you brought bathroom supplies and clothes so you don't have to live out of a suitcase when you're here."

Kick closed her eyes and sighed. "Sounds great, sweetheart. I'll work on it this week. Thank you."

"No, thank *you*. Ready for your song?"

With her eyes still closed, Kick nodded as she settled back into the chair. I played the opening bars to the acoustic version of "Maybe I'm Amazed." She swayed her body to the song as if she were hypnotized by the notes. Though her eyelids stayed down, Kick smiled, her breaths lengthening as she relaxed.

I paused after the second verse. "Good choice?"

Kick shifted forward. "This is the version Jem sings. It's one of my favorites. Did you know?"

I lifted an eyebrow, and she guessed it with a sly smile on her face.

"The playlist?"

I nodded and laughed, falling more for her as the tension she'd been projecting transformed into something like excitement.

"I'd forgotten about the thrill of being thoroughly pursued. Thank you, cowboy."

I cleared my throat. Kick was my woman. I'd do anything to put a smile on her face. "Feel like singing along?" My singing voice would have ruined the mood, for sure.

She leaned in. "I'd love to sing with you."

I restarted the song, and Kick sang it with the word *girl*

instead of the original *man*. We sounded amazing. My fears about whether I could help her dissipated with each note.

When I finished playing, Kick walked to me, cradled my jaw with both her hands, and kissed me. "Thank you for making old thought patterns fade."

"Old thought patterns? Are you upset about Bobby?" To me, the text exchange with Kick's brother had been a minor bump compared to everything else this weekend. "Put those negative feelings away."

Kick sat across from me on the foot of the bed. "I'm trying to, but it's kind of an addiction." She tapped the side of her head. "They won't move out of here."

"Acknowledging it is progress. Judging the thought keeps it tied to you. Did recognizing it let you step away?"

"I suppose. Singing with you—remembering who you really are to me—helped more."

"Who I really am? What does that mean?"

Kick shrugged. "She'll rub your supposed age—what everyone thinks is our age difference—in my face." Her body shook as she exhaled slowly. "You reminded me that it doesn't matter."

"Damn right it doesn't matter." I leaned the guitar against the chair and pulled Kick up for a hug. Embracing her full body, I said, "No way in hell am I letting your mother or anyone else come between us."

8

I LOVE YOU ALWAYS FOREVER

KICK

I went into Thomas's bathroom—I couldn't think of it as mine yet—naked and wondering where my nightshirt had landed. The navy walls made it difficult to find anything without turning on the lights, and I wasn't ready for the brightness.

Fortunately, Thomas had raised the heat for me when he left to visit with his horse, Eddie. I stretched, testing my body to see if anything was sore or different. The notion of having a life like Thomas and his family, let alone Banger and the others—*Jaysus*, how old was Tess? Would it be rude to ask her?

Memories of specialists gaslighting me—telling me I'd been too young to have the symptoms I did—rushed through my mind. *No shit. That's why I made an appointment.* My spirit might have been resilient, but my body never had been. I walked a tightrope where it was concerned. Clearly I couldn't wrap my head around Thomas's belief that I was graced with a special genetic profile.

I bent forward and touched my toes. Did I just imagine better flexibility? I tried it again, and my nose touched my knees. That never happened before. Could it be attributed to more recent exercise or was it another sign of Thomas's suspicions being right?

After he had played his guitar for me, we'd snuggled in bed and talked until we didn't. Afraid of pushing my body more than it could take, he'd gone slow and easy. I didn't know which side of Thomas the lover I liked more. Hell, I had to admit, when it came to sex with the man, I wanted a Thomas smorgasbord.

It wasn't a shower day plus I ran a little late. So I washed from head to toe at the sink, humming "Something Stupid"—the jazz song from our date to the Italian restaurant back in October. It felt like a lifetime ago. I propped my foot on the side of his bathtub as I dragged the washcloth up my leg.

"What are you doing?" Thomas's rough voice made him sound like he had laryngitis, but he'd already told me he didn't get sick. He stood gloriously naked behind me, his stare unwavering as he held his shirt in midair.

"Morning, cowboy. I'm almost done." I glanced over my shoulder. Wow, he was beautiful. Dust particles floated around me from the morning sun's rays, making it difficult to see him clearly. Still, I bit my lip to keep from drooling. We didn't have time for pleasure. "Would you like me to pour you a coffee to go?"

No response came from his mouth, only a swallow and a stare. He stepped into the sunbeams, letting them caress his skin.

"No hurry." He really sounded like he struggled to speak. "Please don't stop."

"Okay… just doing a quick birdbath." I straightened, my head tilting, eyes sweeping him from top to toe and back. Something was off. Could he have been on the verge of crying? "You okay, sweetheart?"

"I…" He finally dropped the shirt and scrubbed his face with both hands. "Everyone I know takes daily showers…"

"Not everyone, obviously." I took a step toward him and touched my hair. It was still in the pineapple style I wore at night. "My hair gets weird from too much washing."

"No. I… Christ, I'd forgotten how"—Thomas made a groan that convinced me tears were eminent—"sexy it is to watch." As much as his words lit my fire, his body language puzzled me. He tensed, muscles locked as if ready for a fight. His face paled, like he'd seen a ghost, like he couldn't decide between fight or flight. From me.

I took another step and reached for him. Thomas began babbling things I didn't understand, and his accent thickened. Whatever was happening, I instinctively knew he needed me. Not just my support or my opinion. Something told me he required my body. *Now.*

To hell with schedules and responsibilities. Thomas said I was his priority now, well, he'd become mine too. I turned toward Thomas fully, my arms extended, offering myself.

As if fired from a gun, he put me on the counter, entered me, and began kissing my neck in desperation. With each thrust, his lips traveled farther down, settling on my breasts, worshipping and punishing each one. Sudden as it was, I was wet and ready and it didn't take long for me to let go. For him. For us.

Thomas groaned like he was falling apart emotionally. Our auras flared into a flame of brilliant color.

"Ohmygod… ohmygod…," I chanted as he set a brutal pace. What had come over me, and when had I become so wanton? Life had flipped in more ways than one.

On the verge of climax, tears gliding down Thomas's cheeks, my head smacked the mirror frame, causing it to crash behind me onto the counter. We froze from shock, then I laughed. I felt nothing but surprise. Thomas jumped back, pulling me into him, lifting me away from any glass. He felt around my head for any sign of a bump. I winced at a tiny, tender spot. "Dammit. Sorry, Kick. I'm a selfish asshole."

I touched his face. "Stop. If you can be my refuge, I can be yours. I barely noticed."

He clung to me, burying his head in my neck, and squeezed me like his life depended on it. "Been alone so long. It's hard to believe we're real. Forgive my irrational nonsense."

"Shh…," I soothed. "You're not alone anymore. I'm happy to fuck your ghosts away for you. Anytime you need it."

He pulled back, peering into my eyes. "How'd you know?"

"The emotions on your face felt familiar, I guess." I ran my fingers through Thomas's hair, brushing it off his forehead. "Want to talk about it?"

We clung to each other after we ended up on the edge of the tub. In the bright light, Thomas blushed. "I've been haunted by a woman for years. She's in my dreams—or she has been. They started as nightmares about the war when my uncle died. Then this angel would show up." He leaned back and stared like he saw me for the first time.

That's what had been familiar about him earlier—he looked like how I'd felt when I saw his miniature.

"Just now I realized…" Thomas's voice caught. "It's been you this whole time."

I pulled him against me as a sorrowful groan escaped him. It only took a moment for me to fall apart with him. Unlike my fear of falling apart in the past, I knew we would knit each other back together. Apparently we had been doing that already. For years, it seemed. I encouraged Thomas to tell me about this angel from his dreams. He let everything out as I held on. The parallels were ridiculously similar to mine—especially the emotions we'd been left with afterward.

When Thomas quieted, I leaned back and played with the hair at his temples. "Have you ever had gray hair here?"

A wrinkle formed between his brows, then he nodded. "I

usually do. I feel the most myself that way, but I use meditation to keep it at bay for now. To stay on the younger side for the professorship." Right. He couldn't just show up with credentials and teach, he had to go through the steps to get where he was. That meant appearing a certain age—midthirties at the moment. "Why do you ask?"

"I recognized something in your miniature." I filled him in on the details of my dream man. The gray temples had been the last mystery, and Thomas explained it easily. He'd fought in the War of 1812. When he described his uniform from back then, I knew it had been him all along.

We had haunted and encouraged each other for years without knowing it.

I wiped the tears from my eyes as we settled down from our revelations. "You know, most of my male friends saw their temples turn gray in their thirties. Some even earlier."

He laughed against me, and I sighed in relief. My Thomas was back. He even leaned back and flashed me his cocky smirk. "You like it."

I grabbed his chin as I studied his face despite knowing it by heart already. "You'd wear the hell out of the silver fox look." Then I jabbed him in the abs with my elbow. "You shit."

He chuckled as he stood. "What'd I do now?"

"You tortured me."

The laugh deepened into his diaphragm. "You damn well tortured me too."

THE PERKED CUP'S BELL CHIME TATTLED ON ME AS I FLEW through the door thirty minutes late. Cyndi stuck her hand out palm up and wiggled her fingers to Deana. Dee clicked her tongue and handed my closest friend some money. A ten, I thought.

I stopped behind Cyndi's stool. "What's going on?"

"I bet Deana here you'd be thirty minutes late this morning."

I looked at Dee. "What'd you bet?"

She folded her arms and tipped her head up to the ceiling. "I said an hour." She pointed at me and raised her brows. "You've been an hour late the past three days."

My face heated. "I'm sorry, Dee. Thomas and I are trying to figure out a schedule."

"Don't apologize. I know exactly what you're figuring." Dee shrugged. "Sounds like you wasted thirty possible minutes of man meat to me."

I lowered my head as the corner of my mouth lifted. "Wasted nothing."

They "oohed" and stared me down as I strutted to my office to settle my bag. Their eyes continued to follow me when I glided behind the counter. Freshly brewed coffee lingered in the air, and I moved some used cups to the washer.

"There's a lull, so spill, Kicky," Cyndi demanded.

I wiped the counter, glancing around at the mostly empty café, thanks to snow in the forecast. The mother and baby story time had been canceled. Of course, the way North Carolina snow-forecasting juju went, it was currently sunny and dry outside. Midmorning sun streamed through the windows, bouncing off the warm wood tabletops. They reminded me of my morning.

"You're bossy for someone who waited days to ask me about my new beau. Where have you been?" I asked Cyndi.

She waved. "Hellooo? Tax season. My early clients are already booking. It's been busy. Besides, I left messages. Why didn't you return any?" Cyndi's "disappointed mama" face rivaled Deana's.

I gave her a salute and shrugged to say *back at you*. Then I played coy with my bestie as I wiped down the bar. "But do *I* come to *your* business and bother you?"

"If I made the best coffee in town and had recently landed the hottest professor? You bet your ass you would." She waved Deana over for support. "Don't be so tight-lipped."

I hadn't planned to, but messing with Cyndi lightened my mood, not that it was bad. There'd just been so much going on. I kept finding myself fighting for every ounce of energy and relying on meditation like it was a double shot of espresso.

I turned to Deana. "Will you give Cyn one of your mama stares and keep her in line like you do the kids?"

"Naw," Dee answered with a snicker. "I've been trying to get you to talk since you came back, but you keep deflecting." She looked at Cyndi. "Kick's only bored me with the basics."

"I don't kiss and tell." I fussed back while pouring myself a decaf coffee. I couldn't wait for my appointment with Dr. Chaddha next week. Hopefully, I would have my beloved Americano in my hands in a few short days. It was another reason I relied heavily on my "Om time." I didn't want anything to ruin the appointment.

"Yes, you do. You just won't make the opportunity."

"You better." Dee pressed in unison with Cyn.

Cyndi plopped her chin onto upturned hands. "Was it still magical? Or is the tin roof rusted already?" She waggled her eyebrows at the B-52's reference.

I blushed. *Fecking hell.* "No rust chica." I tried to keep a straight face, but it wouldn't behave. "You could say the roof sparkles—it's even shiny." They made gasping and squealing sounds as I raised my wrist and showed Cyndi the bracelet Thomas gave me.

Deana jumped in and played Vanna White, glorifying her role in Thomas's purchase of it.

I told them it represented our promise to give each other the next day. We didn't need to define ourselves beyond that.

Cyndi swooned but Deana gave me her best side-eye and shook her head. What did she want? A proposal already? Like

Dylan? Was a line forming somewhere? The thought made me squirm. Then it warmed me somewhat. Maybe marriage could be an option eventually. Definitely not now.

According to Thomas, his mentor Alaric and a woman named Ellie had been together in different capacities for centuries, though they'd never married. I could never imagine diluting our relationship into a business partnership. That much was certain.

"Does it feel weird to be with someone else?" Cyndi asked out of the blue. She took a sip of her latte.

I thought about her question while absent-mindedly wiping the counter down. "It did at first. By the time I'd made it to Thomas's house last week, I'd missed him so much. The first time had been amazing, but this... with the commitment part settled..." I shook my head, searching my brain for words to explain and settled on, "It's spectacular." Images flashed through my mind—Thomas kissing me on the kitchen counter, the after-noon in his bedroom, meeting Eddie, the fun parts of our naked weekend. The frenzy over finding out Thomas's age and how I might be like him had overshadowed those fantastic memories. It was nice to have amazing ones balancing out the shock of every-thing else.

Cyndi's eyes shimmered with tears before her expression changed. Her face filled with mischief as she asked, "Are you sore?"

I barked a laugh, causing my lone customer to start. I flashed him an all's well smile, then leaned down toward her. "You're such a teenage boy. You only care about the sex."

"Stop stalling."

"Fine." I flicked my wrist. "At first, sure. The man can give a *massage* though." I thought about the way our combined energy healed my muscle pains and nearly swooned. "I feel great now."

She reached for my hand and smiled. "I'm thrilled for you, chica. Somewhat jealous too, but it's all good."

"Jealous? Didn't you and Manu go away to an exotic island or something over the holidays?" I gestured toward her. "I'd kill for your tan, not that I'd ever have your warm glow. I just get weird, red patches everywhere."

Cyndi sighed. "He's great, but I don't know."

"One of these days you're going to have to trust a man again." This time I held her hand. "If Manu's a good one—and it sounds like he is—then it's not fair to expect him to do what Joel did."

"Maybe that's the problem," she muttered, looking away.

I tried to catch her gaze but let it go when she persisted in staring the other way. Did she still pine for her ex?

"How is it you struck gold twice, and I haven't hit it once?" Cyndi asked sadly.

Deana caught my eye and winked. I squeezed Cyndi's hand tighter. "You *had* gold with Joel, but the dumbass pawned it. He's never going to find something as precious as you. It's his loss." I gave her a moment to consider that, then continued, "Sounds like you're afraid this time." Did she not see her worth? "Thanks to Shane, I know all about that gold. I also know love and fear can't exist in the same place. Your heart can only live by one or the other."

I glanced up and saw Deana's satisfied smile. "It wasn't easy for me to jump again," I said.

"You can say that three times." Dee chuckled her deep, bubbly, I-told-you-so-you-dummy laugh. "You and I saw it before Kick did." Closing the space between the three of us, she added, "You gave her solid advice, shug. Take some of it for yourself and let the baggage go."

The phone rang and Deana danced over to it, swaying her hips to the beat of Donna Lewis's "I love you always forever."

"You should listen to her," I quietly told Cyn, moved by how much our roles had flipped. In the past, it had always been my bestie gauging whether I was ready to find another love. My answer always was *not yet*. "I bet you'll find a true love when you least expect it, like I did."

"I suppose. Can I have a refill?" Cyndi handed off her cup as I blew her a kiss. She took her life advice in small doses, especially during tax season.

Deana returned with a frown on her face.

"Who was on the phone?" I asked.

"The bank that holds the line of credit."

Shit. My blood went cold. "What'd they say?"

With a straight face, she said, "Nothing. Just one of those bugle things playing taps." Then her face broke into a grin.

"Seriously? You stinker." I shook my head as she belly-laughed at my expense. Like I needed more to deal with, but Dee couldn't ever know the total story. I ended up laughing too. "So who actually called?"

She gestured behind her with her thumb. "Hugh from across the way. He has a letter from the tobacco board about complaints from the citizenry."

Double shit. A wheezing sound like a balloon deflating whizzed between my lips. "Of course he does."

"What's going on with the tobacco board?" Cyndi asked.

A familiar-looking woman entered the coffeehouse, her demeanor shouting "nervous to be here." At the moment, I agreed. I'd forgotten the harassment hadn't been resolved. It had simply stalled out for the holidays, like a temporary cease-fire.

I answered Cyndi while the woman scanned the menu board. "It has to be over the hullabaloo from last month. The paper's coverage of it was so one-sided my lawyer's talking about suing them. The governing body may claim it's for the common good, but it's all really an old boys club. I hate that Hugh's caught up in it though. If my dad were still alive, they'd have no problem securing a cannabis license."

"Nonsense." Cyndi tapped the counter. "That whack-job crowd would've still gone after you and thrown Mr. Mickey into it for good measure." She winked at me. "You have a secret weapon though."

"I do?" I glanced around. *Mateo?* Probably not. "Who? Banger?" The man scared me sometimes. He seemed like the kind of person who had no problems going to the dark side to protect his own.

"Me, silly." She pointed at herself with both index fingers. "Most of the board is local. It's a pain in the ass to drive across the state for the meetings, and these guys are shit with videoconferencing."

I rolled my hand. "So…"

"Over half of them are my clients." Cyndi's face filled with a wide grin as she spread her arms wide. "You triple a man's tax return, word spreads among his buddies. Like you said, it's a club."

"You can put in a good word." My fingers tapped an excited rhythm along my chin. "Oh. You. Are. Brilliant, Ms. Sendaydiego."

She shimmied on her stool. "That's what I keep telling you."

Deana filled the order for the familiar auburn-haired woman. A vision flashed through my memory as she handed off the cup.

I leaned toward the counter when she neared me. "Batman's mama."

The gaunt young woman jolted and dropped her cup. Her shoulders drooped like that had been her last straw.

I raised my hands to keep her from crying. "No worries, sweetheart. I'll fix a new one. What was it?"

Her chin wobbled as she stepped back to the counter. "It's just… your coffee doesn't upset my stomach."

I tilted my head. "I hear you." Deana mopped up the spill while I tossed the used cup in the trash. "You were here on Halloween." Jade green eyes risked a glance my way then turned back down as she nodded.

"I'm so sorry you went through that nightmare." I tentatively touched her hand, and she met my eyes again.

She quietly answered, "I was mad at you. The paper said horrible things." She ran her hand over her ponytail. "But… I don't know anymore."

I huffed. "Most times, I don't either lately." I remade her drink and handed it over. "I'm Kick, by the way."

She took her latte, in both hands this time. "Faye. Nice to meet you."

I pointed to the new surveillance screens. "If it helps, we updated the security system." I gestured toward Mateo. "I hired security too. Until everything is settled."

Faye nodded and gave me a small smile.

I tucked a curl behind my ear and leaned in. "You know, I've been having dreams about that day."

She blew into the cup. "So has Nox. My son."

"I'm truly sorry, Faye." My shoulders dropped along with my head. "Tell him the police are working on getting justice. I have a private firm on it too. Okay?"

"I will. Thank you."

She smiled, and I gave her one back. "Come by anytime. Please. Nox can get a new snack, on the house, okay?"

"Thanks, Kick."

Faye walked out with a lighter gait, making my day brighter too. Conversation quickly turned back to me. I told the girls about meeting Eddie the horse and Thomas exercising him in the corral as the sun set. They both swooned, sighing in sync as their eyes glazed over.

Deana said, "Thomas reminds me of my favorite musical."

I paused midwipe in my counter-restoration ritual. "Oklahoma?" It was the first one I could think of with a cowboy.

"No." She sighed again. "Thomas is 'practically perfect in every way.'"

I puffed a little laugh at Dee's reference to "Mary Poppins."

"Ooh." Cyndi clapped. "Let's call him Marty Poppins from now on."

My eyebrows raised. "At your own risk."

The door chime rang again. It made a crisp sound, more like a warning than its usual warm welcome. *It knew.*

My mother had crossed over the threshold.

9

TAINTED LOVE

KICK

If it were possible for smoke to spew from Bobby's ears, she would have been covered in soot. The glare from her narrowed eyes set off warning bells, telling me to throw the shields up. At least Thomas didn't look physically harmed. That wasn't nothing.

Well, screw it. I couldn't help the smile spreading on my face when my gaze met my man's as he entered behind the dragon lady.

Bobby settled onto a stool two down from Cyndi and nodded to her, a phony smile in place. She tossed me a disapproving eye roll.

"Good morning, Mother." I greeted her with a tight kiss to the cheek. "Your flight good? Want some coffee?" I bit my lip. Why did my heart race? *Was my face warm?* Clearly the shield wasn't secured as tightly as I'd hoped.

Thomas gave me a quick squeeze, pressing a warm kiss on my temple. Bobby clucked her tongue disapprovingly. Her gold drop earrings swayed as she snapped her fingers for Deana's attention.

"Morning, Kick." It was clear Thomas had stayed calm and clearheaded on the drive from the airport. I wondered if that was another one of his magical skills.

"Thank you," I said under my breath.

"Anytime."

"You don't want to mean that." I chuckled.

"But I do." He turned to Cyndi and Deana. "Morning, ladies."

"Hey, Dr. Harrison. You're looking fine as always," Cyn drawled.

"Thank you, Cyndi. Please call me Thomas. We're friends after all, right?"

"I don't know." She smirked, her eyes darting between us. I flinched, preparing for however Cyndi planned to embarrass me. "According to Kicky, we should call you Dr. Feelgood."

I rolled my eyes while Thomas and Deana laughed. "That so?" He looked to me for an answer.

I played it off with a shrug. "It is appropriate."

"Good to know." He leaned in for another quick peck. "Mind if I work in your office?" Then he yawned. "Plan to ride Eddie soon and don't want to risk falling asleep at the house."

Deana and Cyndi sighed again as I said, "Help yourself."

Dee handed Thomas his usual, and he headed into the back with purpose and ease. I noticed her watching his retreat as intently as I did. "Hey!"

"What can I say? He's fiiine." She drawled the word out before giving me her warm chuckle.

"Mm-hmm," Cyndi agreed.

"You too?" We all laughed then.

Bobby snapped me out of my cozy spell when she spat out, "It's disgusting." Her face pinched like she smelled a fart. I scanned the dining room. The one customer with the laptop stayed focused on his work. My bodyguard, Mateo, sat in another corner. I supposed I could take her bait. Thomas and my friends had given me a shot of strength.

"Okay, Mother, I'll bite. What's got your underwear in a bundle? According to Bert, you were miserable at his house. I figured you'd be happy to be back."

Something about my words acted like lighter fluid for her heated mood. "Well, I need a coffee for one. Really, Kathleen, how long can you keep running this place with such lousy service?"

When I set Bobby's latte down, Cyndi gulped the last of her refill and stood. "I'd best be getting to the office. Those taxes don't file themselves."

I leaned over and hugged my bestie. Who could blame her? Not me.

"I'm truly happy for you," she whispered in my ear.

"Thanks, chica."

As Cyndi left, my mother jumped back in. "A lady doesn't show affection in public. It's indecent."

"We weren't sucking tongues, Bobby." It pissed her off when I used her given name, and I used the little dig to tell her I wouldn't be controlled. Not anymore.

"Don't be crass." She began a slow cackle, one that sounded like it had been fermenting for days. "You turned out just like me after all. What would Mick say?" She popped her eyebrows for effect.

I sighed and jammed a hand onto my hip. "Never." I was the anti-Bobby to a fault.

"*Pffft.*" She flicked her wrist, bracelets jangling along her arm. "Can't hide from it, girly. I caught a younger man. So did you." She leaned on her elbow like she truly cared about her next words. "I thought you might end up a dried-up old maid like your mother-in-law Anna. Except she's not your mother-in-law anymore, is she? Has that Tom introduced you to his parents yet? Or are you just *temporary?*"

"His—" *What the hell happened in Michigan?*

"I'm back with Juan," Bobby blurted out, a grin reaching her still-high cheekbones. "I ran into him at Royal Oak Market while shopping for Christmas dinner." She sighed like a Disney princess.

I stared back, blank-faced, like a helpless prey watching a pounce play out in slow-mo because of my denial.

"Anyway, as I waited for Gino to wrap my lamb—the same Gino by the way." *Yes, that's how owning a business works, Mother.* I tapped my nails on the countertop, wishing she'd just get this over with. "Juan bumped my shoulder with his." *Annd pounce.*

She placed her hand on said shoulder, a dreamy visage in place. "He said I look more beautiful now than I had when we were—you know." Bobby scrunched her nose to look cute. "Together."

"It's called an *affair*." I hissed.

She spoke over me, a sick light twinkling in her eye. "We had lunch the day after Christmas. Dinner too... Breakfast the next morning." Her head bobbed on her shoulder as if she were dancing to her own song.

"Jaysus—" I ran my hands through my hair.

"Juan asked about you. How you were. We talked about what a beautiful dancer you were."

"Don't." My spine froze, stock-still as I silently willed her to stop talking.

"He asked if you had found someone new," she sang, a malicious grin spreading her lips thin.

My hand slammed on the cold, smooth counter. "I. Said. Don't."

"I told him you had, and a dancer at that." Bobby ignored me, delighting in my discomfort. "I also told him how your husband made you stop. I mean, money can't buy *everything*, can it? But now..." She lifted her eyebrows, as if it were a big secret that Thomas and I liked to dance. Rachel had probably brought it up in passing. Leave it to Bobby to use it against me. She could turn anything into a weapon.

"Stop!" My hands shook. Hell, she'd blasted through my shield with awful reminders of Juan. My embarrassment. My insides thrashed around under my skin, like a helpless animal fighting for its last breath.

Bobby stared out the window behind me as she gloated. My angst fed her, letting her know she'd won this round. So this was why she'd had Thomas bring her here instead of going to the condo. "Juan still has amazing moves. In many ways." She gave a lusty sigh so there was no doubt what she meant. "It was the best trip."

The woman must have been shaking with anticipation the whole ride home. She couldn't wait to brag. No one would have cared as much about her hookup as me because no one else knew the whole truth. Years of putting up with this shit, stuffing it down and packing it tight. It all burst. "Seriously? Then why didn't you stay up there?"

Bobby leaned in, a Cheshire grin in place, like she one-upped me. "Juan had to leave town. He judges ballroom competitions now." She repeated, "He said it was such a shame you quit."

"Enough!" My hand trembled as it flew to my mouth. My customer glanced up from his work and frowned. I gave him an apology and offered a refill for disturbing him.

When I returned to the counter, Bobby jumped back in, her words like blades slicing me open. "You spoiled brat." She seethed through her teeth. "Everyone takes care of their *precious Katie.*" She pointed at her chest. "While *I* gave up *everything.* And you… you always get *your* fairy tale. You always ends up smelling like a rose, don't you? But what do I get for my sacrifice? When do I get to be happy? Huh? I wasted my best years on *you.*" Bobby's light blue eyes narrowed to dark slits as she quietly added, "You little *bitch.*"

It wasn't a tiny word in my book, especially coming from her. In this context, I considered it violent.

Turning on my heel, I pulled a to-go cup from the dispenser, taking care to fill it exactly the way she liked it. Handing it to her, I answered coldly, "I told you long ago to never bring up that man's name. But you couldn't wait to rub my nose in it. Tell you what, you withering ball of bitterness, you think you have a major scoop on Thomas and me? What we have is nothing like you and that deceitful asshole you cheated on my father with. Now take your cup and get the hell out of my coffeehouse."

"Your boy toy gave me a ride here, remember?" Bobby rolled her eyes, certain she had me beat.

I threw my hands in the air. "For fuck's sake. You're a grown-ass woman. Figure it out yourself."

"Don't you swear at me." Bobby's voice climbed into a higher register with her anger. Her eyes darted to each person in the coffeehouse, like she was making sure they were paying attention to her.

"You rub my nose all up in your *pussy exploits*, think you can call me anything you want to my face, *then* have a problem with me saying *fuck* to the universe? Get over it," I scoffed, laying on the sarcasm as thick as I could muster.

"You really are a *bitch*."

Thank God Deana jumped in because my arm was cocking back. Mateo scrambled over too. Bobby and I had our fists clenched tight, ready for action. Dee stopped me with a hand on my shoulder, a calming voice in my ear. "How about I take her home?"

"Oh, the help can drive me, but my family won't give me a minute?"

"Not even a second," I snapped back, then held my hand out to Dee to keep her from going for her purse. "Make sure you thank *my friend* for offering. As far as I'm concerned, you can walk home now."

Bobby gasped, her eyes wide with fake hurt as she reached down her leg. "But my knee."

"You don't disrespect the people I care about and expect me to keep catering to your whims. You've been—"

Deana placed her free hand on my jaw and turned my head. Her empathetic eyes defused my fury. "Go to the back. I'll handle this."

"No," I insisted, not wanting anyone else to be dragged into our mess. *Maybe I should just take her.*

"I can't leave the café, but I can sit with her and call a cab. Will that do?" Mateo quietly asked.

Deana nodded, deciding for me since all I could hear was the buzzing of emotions in my head. "I'll call for the ride," she said.

"I won't sit in some immigrant's car," Bobby snapped.

Deana folded her arms. "Would you rather hobble home on that knee?"

"A taxi was good enough when I auditioned for the Rockettes in New York. I guess it'll have to do now," Bobby snipped with an exasperated sigh.

Dee shook her head as she worked her phone, then looked up at Mateo. "The woman's yours. You're earning your money today, son."

Mateo pointed at his table. "Can you tell me about your trip over here, ma'am?"

"I don't need a babysitter—"

"The hell you don't—"

Deana touched my arm, then tipped her head toward the back. Great, we required two referees. What the hell had happened? I walked away in a daze, fighting for breath and filled with shame over taking her bait. Bobby had dug her claws into a scar and ripped it open where the original wound had formed a hardened seam, toughened by years of purposeful forgetting. A tear rolled down my cheek when I entered the back hallway.

The tears were flowing fast as I turned in to my office. I

halted at the sight of Thomas behind my desk. I'd forgotten about him working there. My only plan had been to make it to the office before falling apart in peace.

Now I needed to keep it together. If anyone saw me fall apart, she'd know. That couldn't happen. I spun in circles, searching for somewhere to escape. Nothing came to mind even though there were other rooms in the back. Strong, loving arms circled me, spinning me into Thomas's solid chest as I cried.

"Easy," he soothed.

I shook my head. "No. I'm weak and stupid… should've known better."

Thomas's hands moved up my arms in a gentle caress. "You're the strongest woman I know. Come on, tell me. I saw the camera feed. Only your mother can get you this worked up."

I stepped away from the safety of his body. I didn't deserve it. "We have enough on our plates. I won't put this on you too."

"You'll never be a burden." He jammed his hands on his hips and looked up, muttering, "Dammit. Should've taken her straight home." He sat in a club chair and pulled the other close so our knees touched when he had me sit in it. "Is this why you were upset on New Year's night?"

I filled in the details of the fight for Thomas, including how my mother had apparently rekindled her affair with the man who broke my father. Correction, *his wife* did that—I couldn't think of her as my anything at the moment. I also filled Thomas in on the key aspect, mainly, Bobby's pity punch about having to marry my father because she was pregnant and how that ruined her life. Oh, the many times I had heard from her, and all the other Sullivans, how much Bobby wanted to be a Rockette and would have been one if it wasn't for me.

Well, I'd had plenty of dreams change over the years. Hell, by my estimate, I was working on plan G at the moment. That's why I "smelled like a rose," as she liked to put it. Dreams shift. You adjust or you crumble to pieces.

Thomas rubbed his jaw after I finished spewing my word volcano at him. "You told me about the affair before, but I don't understand what has you so far gone today. After everything we've been through in the past week, why is this triggering you?"

I sat back and adjusted my glasses. "You want to know about Juan and *me*?"

"Think so, yeah." Thomas leaned forward and took my hands.

I blew the curls off my face, an attempt at drying my wet cheeks, as I decided on where to begin.

"When I was in high school, interest in Irish dance was waning in our area, so Bobby added ballroom to her school's schedule. Juan taught the Latin classes while Bobby was in charge of the rest. I took to Latin immediately. It came to me easier than what I'd been doing since toddlerhood."

I let my head fall to gather the words and give myself a moment to deal with the embarrassment of what came next. "The summer before my senior year, Juan asked me to be his assistant instructor. He called me his 'special instructor.' I spent the afternoons teaching beginners step and the evenings teaching Salsa. I was in heaven."

"Let me guess… you developed a crush." Thomas fingered a stray curl before placing it behind my ear, his voice full of understanding.

"Juan was a huge flirt, and I didn't know anything about romance. So I fell hard." I blushed from the shame and residual anger. "Hell, I didn't know what love looked like thanks to living with my parents. I convinced myself there were deep feelings between us." I blew out a long cleansing breath. "My girlfriends helped me plan a full-scale seduction—teen style—including giving him my virginity." I let out a shuddery little laugh.

"That came to a screeching halt when I walked in on them."

"Oh, baby." Thomas pulled my hands to his lips, kissing them, letting me know he was on my side. It gave me the courage and energy to stay with one of my worst memories.

I rubbed my nose and sniffed. I had to be a puffy mess. "What's almost laughable is that at first I thought Bobby was hurt —like there was an emergency hurt. I dropped my stuff by the door and bolted up the stairs, following the shrieks and moans. They were so into the act I could've been an elephant and they wouldn't have noticed." A terse laugh exploded from my lips. "So there they were, on the piano bench in Juan's room." A tear dropped again. Thomas reached up to wipe them, but I shook my head. I craved the cleansing. I tilted my head. "Know what hurt most?"

"Did they play it off, like a misunderstanding?"

I shook my head. "No. I stood in the shadows, stunned and slightly fascinated, if I'm honest. I mean…" I tipped my gaze up to the ceiling and snickered. "Now that I know what I do… Bobby put a porn star to shame that afternoon."

I pulled Thomas's hand to my heart, seeking strength from his touch. "What hurt most was Dad's reaction. It broke him, Thomas. If I'd just kept my mouth shut—"

"Kick… no."

I shook my head. "How did it help Dad to know?" I told Thomas about the fallout. I raised my hand toward the dining room. "Now she gets her wish. In Bobby's world, you and I together justify her actions, past and present."

Thomas shook his head. "How?"

I shrugged. "I'm with a younger man now. It doesn't matter that Juan was closer to my sixteen than he was to Bobby's thirty-six."

Thomas wrapped his hand behind his neck. "For fuck's sake." His eyes glistened in sympathy, which made my tears fall in earnest. Thomas pulled me off the chair and into his lap. The love and safety there let me finish the last bit.

"Dad looked like you just did… his eyes shimmering. Not for me, for him. See, I had no idea how sex worked, so when he pulled it out of me, I told him everything. The vocalization, the carrying on. I certainly didn't know about orgasms. Thinking on it… remembering my father's reaction… I'd bet he hadn't seen that from her in ages, if ever." I tucked my head into Thomas's neck. "Bobby broke me but she shattered Dad, then blamed him for it."

"Christ."

"When will the drama end?" I hiccupped my question.

"It will, baby. Promise." Thomas swiped a hand over his face. "Remember what I said about your mother's gaslighting?"

I growled down to my toes. There's *being* gaslit. There's *knowing* you're gaslit. Then there's *immunity* to it. Like an autoimmune disease of the mind. "I remember."

"Your father was wrong to drop the burden of her happiness on you. It wasn't his responsibility, and it's not yours."

The accuracy of his words surprised me. "Dad told me the same thing last month."

"He…" Thomas's eyes flashed with surprise. "What?"

I clarified. "He came to me in a dream."

He chuckled into his belly. "Of course he did." Thomas's face steeled with seriousness as he inhaled. "Let me fix this."

I rolled my eyes at him, but Thomas raised his hand. "If you don't want to see your mother again, I can make her go away."

This time my brows climbed into my hairline in surprise. I opened my mouth to protest anything close to murder, but Thomas placed his finger across my lips.

"It's nothing nefarious." He nodded his head along with each point he made. "I'll set her up wherever she wants to be. Give her staff to take care of any need. She won't go without, Kick. Except for going without *you*. If your brother wants to visit, that's up to him. Same with the kids, but you won't be responsible for her ever again. I have the means to make it happen. If you want me to."

I jumped up and walked over to the clerestory windows in my office. The glass figurines Thomas had given me when he asked for my forgiveness refracted tiny rainbows of light. Could it be that easy?

"She'll have the best care."

I giggled at the prospect. Hell, I'd mourned the lack of a real mother for as long as I could remember. What would life be like without Bobby in it? Despite her complaints, the woman was healthy. I imagined myself saddled with her for decades more. My giggle grew into a laugh. "You'd do it, wouldn't you?"

"In a heartbeat."

I paced the space behind my chair, starting sentences only to have them stop after a simple squeak. Finally I stretched my back, easing the tension I'd been holding for over an hour. "I asked you to stand by my side as I fight my battles though, not to battle them for me."

Thomas came to me, placing his hands on my shoulders. "Kick darlin'"—he bent his knees to level his gaze with mine—"I'll be whatever you need. Your best friend." He kissed my forehead. "Your mentor. Your student." He kissed my nose. "Your lover." He cocked an eyebrow, making me laugh, releasing more emotional tension. "Baby, you've fought this dragon your whole life." Thomas tilted his head as the corner of his mouth lifted. "Perhaps this challenge requires a champion."

10

OUR HOUSE

KICK

"Please tell me you're on your way here. The roads are getting worse. We just heard an accident in the shopping center driveway. It's fishtail city out there. So Dee and I are closing up."

"Almost reached the parking deck. Don't worry, darlin'." Thomas's calm voice soothed me through the phone.

The first snow forecast had been a dud, but January decided to leave behind a direct-hitting bomb cyclone. Department of Transportation trucks had brined the roads for days in preparation, then the initial wave of sleet washed most of it away. To make matters worse, the storm had sped up overnight. Schools and businesses that had planned to release early were scrambling to get everyone home even earlier. By noon, we had the gridlock usually found in a hurricane evacuation. The news called it a "Snowmageddon" even though there seemed to be one a year lately.

"Deana's husband's been on the road for an hour, and he's still not here. It could take you all day in the Camaro, not to mention sliding from the rear-wheel drive."

"That's why I switched to my Range Rover after checking on Eddie yesterday."

I froze midwipe on the back counter. "You have an SUV?"

"Yes, baby. Comes in handy on occasion. It's been in the little barn while I fixed the brakes."

"Your brakes are bad?" The question came out more like a panicked screech, and I envisioned Thomas holding the phone away from his head.

"No. They're perfect now." I held my racing heart, like that would force the beats to slow. Apparently, I had PTSD when it came to the men I loved and their vehicles. Thomas's tone lowered into soothing-the-horse mode as he continued. Funny how it worked on me too. "Should I remind you of my vast snow-driving experience? I'll be fine, Kick. Promise."

I blinked several times as I stared out the window, watching the snow pile up. Right. Vast experience and Thomas covered many things. I blew out a steadying breath. "Okay, cowboy, I'll calm down. Just get here as soon as you can. Without rushing, of course."

Thomas chuckled into his phone, further settling my nerves. They wouldn't truly stop until I knew every one of my people were safely secured. It didn't help that I hadn't heard from Dylan or Rachel yet. They were terrible about returning messages— voice mail or text. "More speed, less hurry. Got it."

"Thank you," I whispered back.

As if he could read my mind, Thomas closed our call with, "We'll all be fine."

Our last customer walked out as Liam walked in from school. "You-ready-to-leave?" He asked at his typical 10x speaking speed.

Pointing to the customer climbing into her car while dodging sleet, I said, "She was the last one. Help me transfer as many of the perishables as we can from the cooler to our cars in case the power goes. Then we're free to go." Our neighborhood utilities ran underground, so we never lost electricity at the house. As I was about to insert the key to lock the front and turn off the OPEN sign, Deana ran back inside.

"Of all the times to go diva on me. My car won't start."

"Gave up on Gordon picking you up?"

"Had to." She sighed. "Several lights went out on G's route. The police are directing traffic where they can, but it's a mess."

"I'll drive you," Liam offered.

"That would be sweet, sugar," Deana answered. "Thank you."

I pegged him with my laser-eyed mom stare, silently asking *are you sure about this?* Liam was a novice on snowy roads, but he also had four-wheel drive. "We could swap cars and I could drive Dee in the Jeep."

"Naw, fam. We got it," he said with his top-of-the-world confidence.

I blew a curl out of my eyes. "Okay. Just remember a Jeep has its limitations, ice being a major one."

He flashed me the dimples. "I'll be a good boy with my special cargo." He wrapped an arm around Deana.

"Even after you've dropped her off and are by yourself."

"Yes, fam. Then too," he drawled. I sent some good juju their way as they rolled out of the parking lot, the back filled with food for Dee to take home and a bag of salt to weigh it down. I had no idea if it would keep my boy from a vicious slide, but my dad had always put a few in my trunk when I started driving.

Dylan's BMW greeted me when I pulled into my driveway. His roommate's presence in front of the flat-screen television, even more so. There was one text I didn't have to send again.

"What are you two doing here?" I called out. "Don't you know there's a storm outside? How're you planning to get home?"

"Not too bright there, Ma," Dylan answered, taking the bags from my hands. "You've got us for the storm."

"Why?" I asked, my brow furling as I calculated the state of our groceries. Store shelves emptied days ago.

"We're out of food." He raised a shoulder. "The grocery stores near the warehouse district are bone dry."

"Yeah, emp-tee," Henry-slash-Dummy added. Maybe this was the time to finally speak with him about his name.

"Well shit." I ran my hand over my damp curls from the snow, starting to plan. "Let's get cooking, boys. Our numbers may add up to five, but y'all eat like ten people."

"Aw, Mrs. Mack," Dylan's roommate swooned. "I love it when you talk Southern."

"Is that so?" I laughed, relieving my stress. I smiled at the thought of my adopted hometown rubbing off on me.

"Wait, are you still Mrs. Mack?" he asked.

I paused in my unpacking of supplies. "It's been my name most of my life."

Dylan took the bag of beans from his roommate. "I'll make the espresso, Dumb. Yours is awful."

"You complete me, bro." Henry leaned in and stage-whispered near my ear, "I knew if I picked up the bag of good beans, he'd freak and make some."

"You are a genius, Henry," I said. "A devilish one, but a genius nonetheless."

He rocked his head. "Please, Mrs. Mack, not Henry. Dummy. Or Dumb."

I thought about it and shook mine vigorously back at him. "Sorry. No can do, sweetheart." Maybe the time was now. "What about Harry?"

"That was my name until middle school. Then I became"—he switched to a bad British accent—"'Arry Potta."

"Aside from glasses, you two look nothing alike."

Dummy pouted like he might cry. "Tell that to the masses."

I handed him clamshells of premade sandwich wraps,

wondering how long they'd last now. "Load these into the fridge for me."

As we worked, I suggested, "What about Hal? You don't hear that much in the States."

"Hal was my great-grandfather. He went to jail for having two families. It's... a taboo name in the fam you might say."

Jaysus. This was harder than I thought. Too bad he wasn't a William. We currently had a dozen variations on the name in our family. "Well, what's wrong with Henry? It's a wonderful name. Regal, even."

"God no." He sighed, then explained, "Henry is my old man. I have to stand on my own, you know?"

Right. His parents had been awful to him for the years I'd known him. I snapped my fingers. "What about Hank?" I handed over the salads. "It's a good romance hero name," I encouraged. The boy was a hopeless skirt-chaser.

Henry shook his mop of dirty-blond curls and blushed. He reminded me of Liam in that regard, only light hair instead of dark. "Cute, Mrs. Mack." He rubbed his chin, a sweet, slightly sad smirk on his face. "My grandfather went by Hank."

"Then it's perfect." The boy obviously loved his grandfather. "It would be a beautiful tribute to him."

Henry's face grew wistful. He moved to the sink, so I handed him a bag of potatoes and slid the peeler over too. Without a word, he began washing and peeling, the skins piling up in the sink. "It would be a hell of a lot to live up to."

"Were you close?"

"Yeah." A sad smile stretched across his lips. "Gramps understood."

"I'd bet he'd love it." I tilted my head at him. "It fits you. Can I be your beta-tester, perhaps? You can see how it feels."

He nodded shyly.

"Think about it... Hank." I smiled, nudging his shoulder.

"I don't know. He was so... good." He sniffled, his nose

twitching. "It's easier to surpass expectations when they're nothing."

I wished I could punch his parents. "You underestimate yourself, sweetheart."

"Who's your sweetheart?" The front door burst open letting in a whistle of wind.

"Thomas!" I strode over and kissed him as he removed his soaking-wet jacket. "Thank God."

He flashed me a brilliant smile, his cheeks and nose rosy. "Took longer than expected, but at least I'm not still stuck on I-540. There are cars in the ditch left and right out there."

I grabbed a freshly dried towel from the laundry room and handed it to him. "Did you see the car fires on Glenwood from the freeway? We heard about it on the news."

Thomas nodded and shivered. "Mostly the smoke and a ridiculous backup."

I gave him a hug, grateful he missed the danger. "Go change into dry clothes. Dylan's making espresso, and there's enough for you."

"Perfect." He dipped his head toward my ear. "There a reason the boys are here? Something happen to the condo again?"

I tucked my hair back and whispered, "They surprised me when I arrived home. Apparently, they're riding out the storm where the food is."

"And it's alright for me to be here?"

I shrugged. "It better be by now." Thomas had spent several nights at my house already, but he and Lee had already spent the most time together. Being a teenage boy, my son basically ignored me anyway. Not only did Thomas have a second set of essentials at my house and me at his, Liam had taken extra clothes and spent a night in the farmhouse's guest room the previous weekend.

Thomas nodded and padded down the hall toward the bedroom.

I had just set up the slow cooker when the garage door opener went off. Liam had finally made it. I breathed a tremendous sigh of relief. *One more baby bird to check on.* I'd text Rachel again in a minute.

Liam shook out his jacket and called out, "I've been good, I swear. It took forever because of an accident on Roland Dairy Road."

"Jaysus." I gave him a quick hug. "Glad you're safe. Go change. You can help me with lunch as soon as I get the stew going."

He started when he saw our guests. "What are Dylan and Dummy doing here?"

"Seeking appropriate shelter, pretty boy," Dylan answered over his shoulder.

Liam nodded slowly. "Big. Did you get the sleds down?"

"Not yet." Dylan turned back to the espresso machine and made another.

"Hel...lo fa...mi...ly." The singsong soprano of my daughter's voice surprised me. I almost bumped my head on the refrigerator as I pulled out an appropriate number of wrap sandwiches. Rachel carried three massive travel bags too. I was about to scold her for leaving the front door open when her roommate, Isabella, entered with her own weekender case. The girl promptly closed the door. She even noticed the draft dodger on the floor and shuffled it into place with her foot. I made a note to make sure she had extra blankets at bedtime. *What the hell is happening to my space?* I pivoted back to the fridge and grabbed more sandwiches.

The girls didn't appear overly soaked. In fact, their jackets looked dry and toasty.

"How were the roads?"

Bella sighed dramatically and answered, "Took almost two hours. Capital Boulevard is a mess."

"Yeah," Rachel cut in. "It was so icy my back end fished three times."

Bella flicked her wrist. "Don't listen to Rach. She drives like a stuntwoman."

My heart raced and palms sweat as I pictured the girls nearly dying in Rachel's Honda, cold and scared. Did these children have any regard for my car-crash triggers?

"Who's a stuntwoman?" Dylan asked, jogging down the stairs. "Ah, Snow. Thought I heard your screeching."

"Yo, butthead." Rachel glared at her brother. "What the hell are you doing here?"

"Same as you, apparently."

Then it hit me. This was New Year's weekend on steroids. When I twisted around to check on Thomas, I was dumbstruck by his shit-eating grin. We were invaded by overgrown teenagers, for who knew how long, but it didn't appear to faze him. I guess he'd taken my encouragement from earlier and ran with it. Me, on the other hand… a twinge of fatigue made me pause, roll my neck.

After Rachel and Bella went upstairs to settle in, I walked back to Thomas and whispered in his ear, "Is it too late to escape to the farmhouse?"

He pulled me into a hug, rubbing my back. "This is about me, because like you said—"

"It's the crowd," I answered, a bit curt. "I mean, no one called. I texted them several times to see if they were set up for the storm. Why didn't they send one back?"

"I shouldn't be the one to talk to them about it." Thomas took a step back and scratched his head.

"No, no. I didn't mean for you to fix it, just to listen to me vent."

"Ah. Gotcha." He turned me toward our bedroom. "Why don't you escape to the suite and recharge? Now that everyone's safe, take a minute for you. I can monitor supper, and the others can fend for themselves until then."

"If you insist." Easing up onto my tiptoes, I kissed him gently and left him in the kitchen, lifting the slow cooker lid to sniff the stew.

The front door opened, which meant Liam and the dog had returned from a quick walk, only my son's face appeared pinched and strained. He nearly stumbled into the mudroom, wincing as he kicked off wet shoes and socks—Lee's clues for a migraine. My heart sank.

"How bad is it?" I asked. Seemingly unable to remove the rest of his stuff, I unzipped Liam's jacket like I did when he was little and carefully pulled it off.

"Bad and quick."

The storm made the barometric pressure drop fast. Liam had an app to alert him of barometer drops. Then he was supposed to take his medicine and make use of special earplugs. It had been an issue for him for a few years. He let out a shaky breath and closed his eyes.

"Pain level?" I asked.

"Nine going on a hundred," he said, his lids still down. I sifted through his coat pockets for sunglasses and settled them on Lee's face.

Sighing as I gently pushed his curls out of his eyes, I murmured, "Mister learn-the-hard-way." I waved to Thomas for help. "Let's get you to the sofa, Wee Man. I'll grab your medicine and the ice hat."

"Thanks, Mama."

Thomas placed Liam's arm around his shoulder and walked with both their weight.

"My leg's not broken, fam," he said to Thomas. "I'm only a bit woozy."

I gasped at the use of "fam" for Thomas—the goofy endearment he said to all his relations—and smiled slightly. Thomas backed off on the support, still making sure that Liam arrived at the sectional couch safe and sound.

I brought over the migraine medicine, a glass of water, and a cold wrap we called his ice hat. "Do you want me to make the migraine tea?"

Liam's face soured even more. "That stuff's so nasty. The pain goes away out of spite so I don't have to drink anymore."

"Bone broth?"

Liam shook his head. "Mmm." He shuddered from the pain. "Not now. Too nauseated."

I popped up from my squatting position in front of him. "I'll get a bucket, just in case."

"Thanks."

Rachel yelled at Dylan about something nonsensical in the kitchen, and Liam's hands flew over his ears as his whole body jerked.

I ran to the kitchen, grabbed a towel, and snapped at them both. "If you can't be respectful of your brother's pain, get the hell upstairs." My stress over seeing my kid's pain and annoyance at their assumption to just come by converged.

"Sorry," they mumbled.

Rachel added, "But—"

"No." I cut her off. "You don't get to show up unannounced and act like you're both preteens anymore. Liam's got a migraine, and you two will grow the hell up for once."

"Fine," she snipped.

"I'll see if Dum wants to play Smash," Dylan said. He glanced at his brother and turned back. "We'll mute it."

"Oh sure, leave the cooking to the womenfolk—" Rachel turned to me and jumped at my glare.

"Whiny womenfolk aren't needed here. Seriously, Snow. If you can't control your mouth, go upstairs too."

"Why don't you send Liam upstairs where it's quiet? Public areas are supposed to be noisier."

"I want to keep an eye on him." I gritted through my teeth. "Anything else you can criticize regarding the way I run this house?"

"No." She dropped her head and resumed slicing mushrooms.

"Where's Bella? She could help you make quick work of this."

"She's not much of a chef."

"I'll help," Thomas said. He reached out and squeezed my shoulder. "How about you stretch out on the other side of the sectional? Pull up a book on your e-reader."

"Thank you." I kissed him lightly on the cheek. "Can you make rice too, to stretch the stew now that we are seven?"

"Sure, baby."

I walked away with a big pot and placed it on the floor by Liam.

"Baby?" I heard Rachel ask. "That's your thing? Baby?"

"It is," Thomas said with confidence. I turned toward him and saw a corner of his mouth lift as he winked at me.

"Ironic, isn't it?" she prodded.

"You have no idea."

I snickered quietly and lifted Lee's head and pillow so I could rest his head in my lap to massage his temples. Removing the ice hat, I rolled it and placed it under his neck. I lightly rubbed his head until the deep crease between his brows eased.

Macushla—an expert at sensing when we needed her—appeared at the side of the sofa, nudging his hand with her nose. "Thanks, girl," Liam said.

She carefully jumped up on the couch, stretched out her body like a Slinky, and belly-scooted alongside him, ending with her head resting on his stomach. Liam's breathing quickly deepened and slowed as I continued to massage his head and neck. He fell asleep soon after.

For all the years that I dealt with my often debilitating health issues, watching my baby struggle with his pain was worse by far even if he was technically larger than me. I mumbled over his head, "We need to get you back to the doctor. It's time for you to seriously consider a Celiac diagnosis." He didn't hear me though.

I allowed my head to rest against the back of the sofa and fell asleep too.

By the time the evening news aired with footage of a thirty-car pileup and two on fire, my attitude about the day had changed. With my family safe around me, I sent out thankful thoughts to the universe.

I padded into my bedroom to change out of my jeans and into sweats. The soft gray joggers were on my right leg, and I bent over with my left leg ready, when I glanced out my window—movement had caught my eye. A man stood on the frozen sidewalk. Despite the maelstrom swirling around him, I could tell he was staring through the open blinds. At me.

I dropped to the floor, my heart pounding against my ribs.

"Thomas…" Fear mixed with anger made my voice choke in my throat.

MY BABE

THOMAS

"Kick... everything alright in here?" I knocked lightly on the bedroom door while entering the darkened bedroom. She'd taken longer than expected to change her work clothes. Usually those things flew off as fast as her fingers could fly—especially the bra—when Kick had declared her day's end.

"Shh..." She waved at me as she leaned around the drapes at one window from a kneeling position. She was filming something with her phone. "Get down. And shut the door."

The door closed with a soft snick. "Are you recording the snow?"

"No. A person," Kick murmured while studying the fuzzy image. "A peeper, really."

I quickly crept over to her position and squatted behind her. "What the fuck?" I said, peering over her shoulder. A young man paced the sidewalk across from her side yard. Every minute or so, he'd stop and glare. I ducked, though I figured couldn't see us in the dark. "The son of a bitch is staring this way."

"I know," Kick answered. "The little shit watched me undress."

An icy chill tap-danced up my spine. "What? Why didn't you say something?"

She cleared her throat. Come to think of it, her voice sounded wrong. Scratched. "I tried, but nothing came out. My vocal cords locked up, probably from shock. Anyway, when my heartbeat settled down, I figured I'd spy back on him." She adjusted the image. "He can't keep at it much longer. If it hadn't been for the storm, a neighbor would've noticed him by now."

The peeper stopped pacing and stared up at the second floor. Kick gasped. "Do you think he can see into Rachel's room?"

"Maybe." It was a good guess, actually, but I didn't want to stir her more. I started hashing out a plan in my head.

Kick adjusted her glasses and squinted. "It can't be Cody wanting her back. He's too lazy to go out in this weather. You think it's whoever's been harassing Snow?"

Anger spiked over these two women I cared about being violated this way. I pulled my phone out of my pocket and brought up the Angel Security app. I told it to play the video feed at the house for the past thirty minutes. The system Banger had installed operated like any voice-assistant service, except it ran on a private network. Kick let me monitor her properties along with mine and vice versa.

"Why didn't I think of that?" she said as she shook her head.

"I've had Angel for years," I said absently as I studied the footage. "It's new to you." I saw the figure—dressed head to toe in black winter gear—move past the front of the house, then disappear as if he were a regular neighbor passing by.

Shit. "Bet he knows how to spot the cameras. He found a hole in the coverage." The question was how?

Kick glanced at me over her shoulder. "I thought he ran away after I caught him, but something told me to wait a bit in case he came back. When he showed up across the street and just stood there, my alarm bells really rang. I mean, if he was a regular peeper, wouldn't he just move on to another house? Or maybe I'm still on edge after Halloween and everything. Anyway, that's why I started filming. I should've texted you though. Sorry, cowboy. My brain kind of shorted."

I kissed her head and stood while texting Banger. Maybe he could see something in the footage.

"You think it's Jonn?" Kick asked as she fussed with her glasses again.

"Isn't he on an ankle monitor?" I tried to get a better view over her. From this distance, with the snow falling, it could have been any young man.

"Right. Plus he was mad about the business. It was the café he tried to hurt."

That's what I had thought until the kidnapping attempt, but again, I didn't want to stress her further. I simply had to get to the bottom of this. I shifted back to stand. "I'll gather Dylan and Dummy and see if we can flank this guy—"

"Hank," Kick said.

I pointed out the window. "Do you recognize him?"

She shook her head. "Not the peeping twerp. We're calling Dummy Hank now. Well, I talked him into beta testing it with me, but you should be on the team too. You know, so he can see how it sounds from a masculine voice."

Not for the first time, I wondered how the hell Kick kept all her thoughts spinning simultaneously without driving herself mad. "Will you focus on yourself and the kids for a damn minute?"

"I can walk and chew gum. Or in this case, film and think about the family. Besides, Hank needs someone to protect his future. He's been so beat up by his family; he won't do it."

I gripped the back of my neck, taking in everything as I crossed the room. "Fine… Hank." With that settled, my mind ran through potential scenarios to handle the guy outside. I called over my shoulder, "Oh, and keep the dog in the house." Couldn't have any barks give us away and spoil my plans. *Plans that might involve fists and threats.* My patience had run out with this shit.

Kick stood and followed me. "No problem. I'll quickly close her dog door before I grab my coat."

"Your coat?" *Oh shit.* I didn't like where this was headed. No way would I let her near this guy. My shoulders moved back as if with their own resoluteness as my arms folded across my chest. "You need to gather the girls and the dog. Stay in the loft out of sight."

Kick approached and placed her hand over my heart. "Remember our promises to each other at the oak tree?"

"No." Of course I did, but this was different. My promises to keep Kick and her family safe came first.

"Yes, you do." She went up on her tiptoes and kissed the underside of my jaw. It was this weird yet cute thing she'd started doing. Probably had to do with the way my jaw flexed when I stressed about something. Like most things Kick did, I liked it. It settled me.

"I know you can fight this battle for me, but what if we did it together? Back-to-back, like we talked about when you gave me the bracelet."

I closed my eyes and silently counted.

"Have you reached ten yet?" she asked.

I opened an eyelid and saw her brow raised.

"Nine… ten."

"Good." She squeezed each of my shoulders. "You can still wear your shining armor. Just let me wear my own." The corner of her mouth ticked up. "Think of it as the kind the female characters wear in video games."

Then my brow lifted, envisioning Kick as an elvish wet dream.

She didn't give me a chance to respond. "I want to ask my own questions, get answers firsthand. With you at my side, I'll feel safe enough to do it. Please don't turn it into a fight between us."

"Aw hell." I pinched the bridge of my nose and growled. What did she plan to do after this? Walk into a tiger's den and make it purr?

"I'll take that as a yes. It's not like he's going to hurt me with you three there."

I exhaled a weary breath. "Meet me in the garage. I'll send Dylan and Hank-or-whomever out the screen porch. We'll take the side door. But stay behind me and promise you'll do everything I tell you to."

"Got it, cowboy."

"I mean it. You're. My. Shadow."

She made a crisscross over her heart with her pinkie finger. "Promise. Besides, it's not like we're going to hurt him. We need answers. Right?"

I growled again as I held the bedroom door open for her.

The operation started out as planned, but our timing was off. When Kick and I emerged from the hedges at the side of her house, the peeper had disappeared from his spot across the street. We moved into the front yard and saw him several houses down, jumping into the passenger side of a bright red BMW. It fishtailed several times as the driver sped out of the neighborhood. The boys took off after it, but it was futile on foot.

"Damn it all."

FLUFFY SNOWFLAKES STILL FELL THE FOLLOWING MORNING. I watched them through a crack in the drapes at the window. Kick turned and snuggled into me as I listened for any indications of life outside our sanctuary.

"Good morning, handsome," she said, her eyes still closed as she clung to me. She yawned and rubbed her eyes. "Did you sleep?"

"Not much."

Banger beat the police to the house, thanks to multiple accidents tying up the Oakville PD. We found plenty of tracks in the snow near Kick's bedroom window. A few of them were good enough to tell they came from a high-end men's basketball shoe. Not that it meant much in suburbia. Banger did his Banger thing, though, and sent the information off to his right hand, Siobhan. It was a good thing he had. By the time the police were free enough to send an officer over, the footprints were almost covered in new snow. The whole thing left me with a headache. Nothing like Liam's, but it was a rare occurrence for me. Made me grumpy.

Watching an action movie had helped ease the group tension last night. The boys were as ready to pound flesh as I had been. None of us could figure out what the hell the peeper wanted. What it meant. What he—or they—had planned. One thing was certain—that kid didn't come out in a veritable blizzard for shits and giggles. Was it because everyone had gathered together? Or was that what kept him from doing more?

The questions spinning through my head kept me up most of the night.

Kick stretched and flexed her legs like a cat before draping one over my thigh. "I didn't sleep much either."

I pushed a loose curl behind her ear and rubbed the cartilage at the tip. "I noticed." Her sleep had been fitful at best.

"If it wasn't Jonn Graham out there, do you think it was someone related to the kidnapping attempt?" she asked, picking up where last night's conversation had left off.

That had been the thought playing on a loop in my head,

keeping me up. "Doubt they're separate things. We know the guy who tried to take you was a part of the attack on your squawk box. We just don't know who ordered it."

"Well, it couldn't have been Jonn doing *that*. Attacking my business is one thing. Why try to take me? And for what? He worries me more when it comes to Rachel." She fluffed out her hair. "Honestly, I'm afraid he's obsessed with her." Kick shook her head, making the loose morning curls stand out in all directions, like they were waking up along with her. "I can't make the dots connect."

Hell, I couldn't either. I slid my free hand into her tumble of soft brown curls and massaged the back of her head. I loved watching them fluff out, then settle before she went through her morning routine refreshing them. "Most criminals don't make sense, baby." Taylor Johnson had vehemently stuck to his story about not knowing who had hired him. The arrangements had been made through texts via the bartender. I thought he'd been too spooked to speculate but had my suspicions.

"Argh." Kick grumbled despite the massage that should have settled her. My sentiments exactly.

I pulled her closer. "What can I do in the meantime?"

"Just a minute." Kick sighed as she moved the covers back to leave the bed. Then she shivered. "Jaysus it's freezing." She returned to my side and pulled the quilt higher than it had been. "You know, every winter I swear to myself that I'll upgrade the insulation come spring. Then the weather warms, I get busy, and I forget all about it."

I waggled my eyebrows. "How about I warm you from the inside?" A little nookie could take both our minds off the night before.

A slow, sexy smirk spread across Kick's face. "Yes please." As I slid under the covers, kissing my way down her neck to her belly, she added, "Just… no screaming Os, okay?"

"I'll bite my lip." I teased her with a smirk and demonstration for effect.

Kick rewarded me with her sultry, exasperated schoolteacher glare. "I know you love to hear me holler and all, but the boys are early risers. That little hobby of yours is fine when we're alone—"

I inhaled the vanilla scent from her lotion before looking up and teasing her with a pout. "But it's always been just us when you get your freak on."

"All I'm saying is"—Kick's head fell back on the pillow—"there's value in a quiet freak too."

I focused more on the value in seeing that crease between her brows relax. Or watching her hazel eyes sparkle again, but I could abide. I already knew how to make her orgasms detonate. I liked the idea of experimenting with making them creep up and linger.

"However you want it, baby. I'm your man. Get ready for a low and slow moan." *Christ*, I couldn't wait. I ducked my head back under the quilt, moving down her body with open-mouth kisses, touching her skin with the tip of my tongue until finally tasting the fruity sweetness of her magic spot. Low and slow. Hot as hell. My new favorite way to wake up.

After several minutes of postcoital cuddling, Kick darted into the bathroom like a water sprite running from Jack Frost. I typed a note on my phone to consult with the insulation guy who'd done my house, then leaned back against the pillows, ruminating on the odd direction my life had taken. The privilege of making love in a house filled with children—even grown ones—was a cherry on my ice cream dish called contentment and newfound purpose. It was both new and pleasantly familiar at the same time —waking up memories that had long passed.

DYLAN MEANDERED DOWN THE STAIRS AS I HELPED KICK WITH breakfast. He spotted us and scowled, taking me by surprise. I distinctly remembered him saying he was fine with my staying over. He'd also mentioned being relieved I could take charge of last night's incident.

"I get you're the queen of the house and all, Mom, but it was pretty rude to keep me up most of the night with your"—his face scrunched up as if he'd taken a body blow—"noises and shit."

Damn. I was certain we'd kept our recent playtime quiet.

Dylan's eyes narrowed at Kick. "Aren't you a little old to go all night? I mean three in the morning. Come on." He made the same disappointed face his mother was so good at. "I need a triple shot in my latte."

Kick blushed red, then her brow pinched together as confusion replaced embarrassment. "Son, in the immortal words of Shaggy… It wasn't me. Last night's excitement wiped me out. I slept fitfully, but uh… my mind was on other things…" She glanced at me and bit her lip. My eyebrow raised in anticipation of what would stream next from her lovely lips. "Last night."

"Then who the hell was squealing with"—Dylan swallowed hard—"*ecstasy* in the middle of the night? I swear I didn't imagine it since it continued after I woke up." Dylan yawned, his jaw popping, then he took a long pull from his mug, made a face, and emptied the rest of the contents down the sink. "Don't you have real milk?"

Kick folded her arms. "No. We're out. I wasn't expecting to be snowed in with a crowd." She stepped toward the sink and picked up the cup. "Want me to make you a bulletproof one?"

Dylan thought for a moment and nodded. "Sure. Thanks."

"Pay attention so you can do it yourself next time." As she demonstrated the process, I turned the oven on and placed a dozen gluten-free scones on a cookie sheet to warm.

Rachel and Bella bounced down the stairs in matching Pierce University T-shirts and joggers. Bella stopped at the large window in the living area and squealed. "Look at all that snow! Can we go sledding soon?"

"After breakfast," Rachel grumped. Her hair and face were perfectly coiffed and composed, but her demeanor said she wanted to be back in her bed.

Dylan winced at Bella's high-pitched noise. Both his eyebrows and Kick's rose in unison, equal parts recognition and disbelief. After glancing from her son to me and back, she mouthed a silent *You think?* I shrugged and laughed. My sense of humor was easier to find given my relative distance to the kids. Rachel had been dating a boy when we first met, but it ended with a load of drama. Maybe she decided to try something new.

"Morning all," Liam chimed as he sauntered in. He grabbed a mug from the cabinet and prepped his own pour-over. "What'd I miss?"

Kick, Dylan, and I exchanged glances before laughing.

"What?"

The three of us took turns getting Liam up to speed on the peeping incident.

Liam propped his elbow on the counter and dropped his head in his hand. "Can't believe I was out for all that."

"At least you look well rested," Dylan said.

Liam sighed. "I'm spicy, bro." He pointed to his ears. "Used my earplugs and fam refroze my ice hat. Your snoring couldn't even keep me up."

"I don't snore," Dylan grumbled.

Kick held out Dylan's mug, then pulled it back. "Maybe you should go back upstairs and try to sleep some more. We can always make another one of these later."

"Dum and I plan to snowboard after breakfast."

A flash of a memory raced through my mind. The face of my eldest son when he had been equally exhausted. I hadn't thought of Young Tom in a long time. Those memories were more like a hot coal to my heart—touch them and get burned by grief. This time the sorrow didn't come. I tested it again, allowing myself to remember something else about him. The day Tom married came to mind for a second, not long. I turned toward the window over the sink and let a smile spread across my face, delighted to remember my children with happiness again. It had been so long since I had let myself go back there.

Kick interrupted my thoughts. "The snow's not going anywhere today. An extra hour or two of sleep will probably keep you from hurting yourself out there."

The moment was over, but it stayed with me the rest of the day. I decided to explore more areas of my closed-off heart when I managed some alone time. As it was, I felt lighter and taller all at once. I had planned to work in Kick's office for the day but figured I'd use the bonus holiday and go snowboarding with the boys instead.

"Fine then. I'll go. Thanks, Mom." Dylan bowed his head slightly to both of us and asked, "Can you say something to them?"

Kick patted his shoulder and murmured, "I'll take care of it."

The girls had perched on stools by then while Liam filled a large thermos with coffee and ground more beans.

"Should you be drinking that after yesterday?" I inquired. "Not to lecture but—"

"Naw. We good," he said. "Caffeine's not a trigger."

"It's nice to see the migraines are getting shorter," Kick added, then handed Dylan's abandoned cup of bulletproof coffee to Rachel.

"Ew no." She waved it off. "My body is a temple. I don't drink that swill anymore."

Kick jumped like she'd been slapped. I pitied anyone who insulted her coffee. "They're locally roasted, organic, fair trade beans. Even tested for mold. What more could you want?"

"An herbal blend with chicory," Rachel answered smugly. "No coffee beans at all."

"You're shitting me? That stuff tastes like bark and dirt if you're lucky."

"Not this one. I found an amazing blend online." Rachel added water to the kettle and set it to a low boil. "It gives me energy without any nasty toxicity. Then my body performs the way it should."

"So I've heard," Kick quipped under her breath.

Isabella reached across the counter and drew in the orphaned mug, taking a sip. "Tastes great, Mrs. Mack."

"Thank you, sweets." Kick turned to me and sighed. She shot me a *what do I do now?* look.

Maybe they needed me after all. I leaned down and whispered in her ear, "Talk to them. Ask questions. Do you want me to go to another room? Give you privacy?"

She grabbed my arm. "Would it be wrong for you to stay? I'm so tired of doing these things on my own."

I patted her hand and tipped my head toward her second son.

Fortunately, Kick caught on to my signal. "Hey, Lee... take your coffee into the living room and check on the forecast, will you?"

Liam frowned, his eyes darting around the four of us. When they landed on me, I tipped my head toward the television and mouthed, *please.* "Okaay." He cautiously made his way across the area and settled on the sofa.

"So... girls." Kick squeezed my hand as she swallowed hard. "Is there something you need to tell me? Or us? You know... any big news?"

Rachel said a quick no through a yawn, but Isabella froze with her cup in the air.

"Nothing's different between you two?" Kick leaned forward. "You can tell us."

"Rach...," Isabella started.

Rachel picked up her cup of chicory and blew on it. "What?"

"I think they know."

Rachel scoffed and took a sip while I sent the girls my best supportive look. Hell, I rocked that thing around the entire room.

Had I really signed up for this? Yeah, I had. Honestly, this was the aspect of teaching that I liked best too. Not just the passing of information but helping kids with life.

"Well shit." Rachel set her cup down and folded her arms. "How? We were planning to talk to you later."

Kick worried her tongue in her cheek. "So you're... like together?"

Isabella beamed as Rachel sighed. "Yeah, we're trying it out."

Rachel smiled at her roommate, but it didn't make it all the way to her eyes. She patted Isabella's hand as the girl preened.

Kick sent me another questioning look, which had me returning an encouraging nod and smile. Again. My way of telling her, *you're doing fine, keep going.*

She moved between the girls and hugged each one. "Okay then."

And really, that was all there was to say except for the part about Dylan.

"How the hell did you find out?" Isabella asked.

"Told you she figures shit out," Rachel answered. "Mama has superpowers."

"Not quite," Kick said while chuckling. Considering what had happened on New Year's Eve, I sided with Rachel.

Kick put on a stern face and said, "You practically announced it to the house when you kept Dylan up last night with your"—she waved her hands while turning beet red—"noises and such. That's why I told your brother to get more sleep. Snow, that was fecking rude. Especially after what you went through with Cody. You should know better than to come back here and carry on."

Isabella turned a deep shade of pink while Rachel kept a stone face. My instincts told me something wasn't right with Kick's daughter, but this wasn't the time to pull it out of her. Her roommate, or new girlfriend, seemed to be on cloud nine, however.

"Way to embarrass my new girlfriend, Mama," Rachel grumbled.

"You did it yourselves last night." Kick came over to me and squeezed my side. "Believe me, I'm glad you're moving on, but your brother's pretty sensitive right now." She looked up at me and smiled. "New love is amazing. I'll vouch for that. All I'm saying is, it doesn't give you license to throw consideration for others out the door."

Rachel's shoulders dropped at the word *love*. Maybe that was the issue. Were the feelings lopsided? The girls would have to work that out for themselves. For the time being, I let my pride for Kick and happiness that Rachel could at least move on show on my face. I turned around and pulled the scones out of the oven.

"Fine. Sorry, Mama." Rachel kissed Kick on the cheek. "I didn't think you'd freak out, but thank you anyway." She turned to Isabella. "Come on, Bella, let's shower and get ready for sledding."

Isabella gazed longing at the tray, so I wrapped a scone in a paper towel and held it out to her. She smiled, took it, and followed Rachel up the stairs.

Kick called after them. "Alone. Shower alone."

Liam slinked back to the kitchen and picked up a scone for himself. He grinned at me. "Did I hear that right? They..." He waved his finger between the two girls and waggled his eyebrows as they padded up the steps.

Kick blew on her own pastry. "You were supposed to be minding your own business, Mr. Big Ears."

I answered him with a quick nod. The boy whistled, his eyes as wide as an owl's.

"So Snow White wasn't waiting for Prince Charming after all." A quiet chuckle emitted from him, the kind that I already knew meant Liam thought more of his joke than the rest of us would. "Turns out she wanted *Cinder* Bella."

Kick shoved his arm. "Don't tease."

He took a bite and swallowed slowly. "All night?"

"They woke your brother up at three. Beyond that?" She lifted a shoulder.

Liam's whole body shuddered. "Glad I had my earplugs in." His face morphed again with realization. "That's the reason for all the grumpy faces when I came down."

Kick touched the tip of her nose as if they were playing charades.

1 2

UNDER PRESSURE

KICK

The snow stopped falling after breakfast to be replaced with the bright blue, cloudless sky that followed every major storm in North Carolina. It was the kind of sky that put a smile on my face. After the drama of the past twenty-four hours, we were ready to play.

We found enough snow toys in the garage for each person to take something to the neighborhood hill. One side of it was perfect for sledding. The other, a tad steeper, attracted kids with snowboards. Everyone took turns doing both except for me. I stuck with sledding since I never could get the hang of a snowboard and didn't want to risk an injury. Technically, I was still recovering from my flare and the drugging in November.

It lifted my spirit further to play with the kids. They were still young enough to consider themselves invincible and attempt stupid stunts. I marveled at how easily they shook off their crashes and walked back up the hill to do it again. One incident in particular, Hank—the name fit him perfectly—and Rachel collided midhill and rolled the rest of the way down. They ended up in a heap, laughing so hard it took several minutes for them to stand again.

In the midst of all of it was Thomas. His eyes lit as bright as the sky each time he met me at the bottom of the hill. He would pick me up, dust me off, and then throw snowballs at each of us as we trekked back up. He became the same, easy Thomas I saw when he was with his horse or when making love. That, added to his willingness to let me join the reconnaissance party last night, made me love him more. Even when a snowball splatted on my back.

In time, the crew became too soggy and too hungry for another round. We headed back home to enjoy the rest of our bonus holiday inside. Macushla and I led the pack back to my house as I mentally inventoried the groceries. A chorus of masculine whooping behind me stopped my trek. I turned around and saw all four fellas lined up on the snowboards in the middle of our frozen street. They stood in the crossroad, which plateaued the hill my neighborhood had been built upon. The last section, which went past my house, made the steepest part of the incline. It prevented any flooding during hurricanes but made the road downright deadly after an ice storm. Especially when adventurous SUV owners ended up carving tracks into the road ice. Liam had learned that the hard way a few years ago when his sled caught in a rut that dumped him into the storm drain at the bottom of the street.

"Countdown from three," Liam called out.

"Guys, hold up. Stop!" I yelled. When they ignored me, I added, "Come on, you know better!"

Thomas, of all people, egged the boys on. "Hear that? She said go…"

It happened all at once. A second of hesitation from either party and no one would have been wiser.

I waved my hands in a futile attempt to make the man-children kill their bad idea before it killed them. At the same time, Macushla spotted a rabbit with a death wish of its own. She bolted and the leash loop slid off my splayed thumb. Once the chase began, no one involved heard or saw anything other than their prize. The adrenaline-junkie hare shot across the street halfway down the block.

"Ma-cush-la!" I bellowed to no effect.

Dylan caught a superslick rut and pulled in front of the group, his competitive focus homed on the finish line. Koosh had the same focus on the rabbit as she darted in front of all the racers except for Dylan. She took him out at the knees with the same tackling skill she displayed when I went down at her expense last fall. Both of them rolled and hollered. After a few flips, Koosh found her legs on the neighbor's lawn and limped home.

My mountain of a son fell on his back like a mythical giant crashing to the ground. Still in the frozen rut, Dylan flew down the road thanks to his slick snow gear. We all winced when he crashed into the same storm drain Liam had hit those few years prior.

"HOW'S YOUR BACK, LAD?"

Dylan stood in the living room, rubbing his sacrum, looking too skittish to navigate the long drop to a sofa cushion. "It'll be fine," he gritted out through his teeth.

Thomas helped situate him, and I settled ice packs on my son's back and shoulder. "You take the painkillers I gave you?"

He nodded, his eyes glazing over, and he turned his gaze down toward the floor. I recognized it as him retreating inside to deal, breathe through the pain.

"Ice now. Soak in my tub after lunch," I ordered.

"I remember the drill from football days. Thanks, Mom."

I ruffled his recently cut hair, turned on cable news, and handed him the remote, adding, "I bestow the power upon thee."

I walked to the kitchen window to check on the rest of the crew, who were shoveling the drive and sidewalk. I turned to Thomas. "With seven in the house, we did well with one casualty." Macushla had stopped limping as soon as she saw her brother walking so gingerly. Her Nurse Nightingale instincts kicked in. She currently lay on the sofa near Dylan's hand.

Then I swatted his shoulder. "What was the big deal egging them on?"

"What can I say?" Thomas ducked his chin. "The promise of victory and male posturing lured me in."

"I told you guys to keep the boards off the road for a reason."

Thomas shrugged and gave me his middle school half smile.

When I glared back, he kissed my forehead and sheepishly said, "Sorry about breaking your boy. *And* for not noticing the dog on the loose."

What could I say to that? Dylan was grown now after all. I sighed hard, admitting the obvious. "Nobody talks the lad into doing anything he doesn't want to do." I went up on my toes and added, "I'll gladly forgive you for a massage later."

"I'd love a massage. Thanks, baby." Thomas winked as I slapped his ass.

We heard a scraping noise in the garage, and I checked the front again. "The crew's finished. Can you oversee the requisite cocoa-making while I figure out lunch?"

"My pleasure."

Hank came in, removed his gear, and checked on Dylan. Isabella was second, beelining for the kitchen and helping Thomas set up the mugs while he heated the cocoa. Rachel and Liam finally entered together. He bolted for the stairs, and she joined us in the kitchen, a mischievous grin on her face.

I watched Liam with interest, then turned a narrow glare on my daughter. "What did you do?"

Rachel kept her grin. "I don't know what you're talking about."

"Sure you don't. Come cut these quesadillas."

She scrunched her face and shuddered at my food. Again. I pulled in a deep inhale. Again. Whatever was going on in my daughter's head, I didn't like it.

Rachel pulled items from the fridge, the freezer, and even stepped into the pantry. Eventually she had a decent pile of ingredients on the counter, along with the food processor.

I surveyed the haul. "You're making a hash? Chopped almonds will go nicely with that." I didn't like deferring my plans to hers, but my daughter gave off an air that I wasn't of a mind to mess with. My spine prickled with the telltale sign of my temper beginning to climb. I struggled for deep, even breaths, had to purposely tell myself to take them. *When this was over, the older two and I needed to talk.*

"No, thanks," she answered.

I checked on the progress with the hot chocolate and turned back to Rachel. "Do you want ice in your cocoa?"

"Nope. None for me."

Oh, hell no. I leaned into her space and planted my hand on the counter. "No coffee, no grains, no nuts... Rachel, are you doing the AIP?" The autoimmune protocol was a diet most newly diagnosed patients went through to check for food issues. Some stayed on it longer than others. While it was a lifesaver for most patients, *autoimmune* was the operative word in the plan. Like going gluten-free, it wasn't meant to be a fad diet.

With a set jaw and practically gunning for a fight, she answered. "As a matter-of-fact, I am."

I scanned her from head to toe, wondering what I'd missed. Had falling in love narrowed my vision so much? "What's wrong? What are your symptoms? Do you want to see someone at the clinic?"

"Nothing's wrong." She shrugged me off and turned back to the food processor. "I told you, my body is a temple."

"That's not what AIP's for, Snow. Food restriction isn't something you do for the hell of it."

"What are you getting your underwear twisted for, Mother? I thought you, of all people, would support me."

"Fresh, quality food? Absolutely. But this is the kind of behavior that gives elimination protocols a bad rap. People who turned gluten-free eating into a fad, or worse, a nutrient-vacant cash cow, have also turned it into a punch line."

"This isn't a whim," Rachel bit out through gritted teeth, her eyes narrowed, reminding me too much of the Sullivan side of my family.

"If it's not needed, it's a whim," I retorted. "Unless you have autoimmune issues, you're not worshipping your system, you're depriving it."

"Annd once again… I'm not supported." She had some kind of silent conversation with Isabella. Then she blurted, "I do have symptoms."

"Oh." I looked at Thomas, who was watching me with silent support as I inhaled and exhaled slowly, counting to ten. Heaven help me calm my last nerve. "That's what I asked. What are they, sweetheart?"

She murmured, "I'm fat."

"Where? In your big toe?"

"Mother!"

Our volume had ratcheted up with each exchange to the point where Dylan lifted onto an elbow and bellowed, "Hey!"

Was this fear for my daughter's health, my default jump to defensiveness in matters of all things autoimmunity, or leftover tension from last night? I didn't know. But I didn't like it one bit. My head spun with it all.

Thomas stepped between us, picked up the platter of finished quesadillas with one hand and backed me out of the kitchen with the other. "Your lunch looks delicious, Rachel. If you have any leftovers, I'd love a taste."

Tension eased off her shoulders. "Thanks, Thomas. I'll be sure to save you some."

He leaned toward my ear and whispered, "This is getting nowhere. Let her be for now."

"But—"

"Sit. Relax."

My shoulders threw back like I was a soldier. "Are you handling me?"

Thomas's hands went to my back. His thumb immediately found a giant knot. "Consider it pressing the pause button and trust me." He stood back and called out, "Lunch is ready, everyone."

Isabella set a salad on the table but went straight back to the kitchen, fussing with the mugs of cocoa. I had the feeling she didn't want to leave Rachel.

Thomas walked over to her and whispered something. Bella nodded, answering in a muffled voice. I heard the word "Cody" and made a rumble low in my throat. They spoke some more until Thomas finally said, "Come on then."

He and Bella carried the mugs to the table, distributing them to the six of us. By the time Rachel sat down, we'd both cooled enough to eat a quick but pleasant meal. She'd made enough sweet potato hash for everyone too.

When I finished, I was so tired my head wanted to drop right onto the table. A loud yawn made my jaw pop. Maybe that's where my ire had come from. I carried a load of dishes to the dishwasher and caught sight of the rest of the gang sitting around the table doing much of nothing. The ridiculousness of it impressed upon me.

I adjusted my glasses before stretching. "Hey gang, it appears I'm plumb out of spoons. Y'all are definitely big enough to clean up. Can one of you roast a few dozen chicken thighs for later too?" Roasting chicken thighs in large quantities saved my hide when I opened the coffeehouse and the kids each had their own after-school activities. They were easy, tasty, and convenient. They also fit the Paleo protocol.

"There you go again, Ms. M—"

I raised my hand as I crossed the space, heading toward my room. "Not now, Hank. My tank's on fumes."

Rachel scratched her head as she rose from the table. "Who the hell's Hank?"

"Your mom's beta testing a new name for me," Dylan's roommate answered her.

My daughter shook her head. "Because why wouldn't she?"

I stopped to explain but couldn't. I remembered the food though. "Oh, can someone be in charge of saffron rice?"

"Show me where the spices are and I'm in, Ms. M," Hank said.

"We've got it," Dylan added.

"And steam up something green."

"Dum and I have that too."

"Thanks guys. Really. I-I need a bath and... something. I don't know." Brain fog and guilt overtook my senses. It shouldn't have been a surprise.

"We're good. Go ahead," Liam said.

Thomas opened the silverware drawer. "What do you mean, you're out of spoons? There are plenty in here."

I turned around to clarify, but the connection between my brain and my mouth still short-circuited. Rachel waved me on. "I'll explain spoon theory to him."

Despite the sudden onslaught of soul-deep fatigue, I padded the rest of the way to my bath with gratitude in my heart. Our conflict hadn't gone off the rails the way everything between Bobby and me always did. Thankfully, the power had held at her condo. I didn't know what I would've done if we had to bring my mother over too.

I stood in my room, eyeing my bed, the meditation area, and my bathtub. Even though speech eluded me, my head spun with images. Flashes of the events of the past two days bombarded my brain and prevented it from shutting down.

A bath it is.

I settled into the balmy water, salts efficiently dissolved, the oils effectively scenting the air and coating my skin. I turned on the jets and the chroma-therapy lights, then reached for my e-reader. Then I noticed I'd left my glasses on the counter. Well, shit. I stood and stepped over the tub, carefully crossing the tile floor to retrieve them. I was certain one chapter of my book would quiet my brain and allow it to rest. Grabbing them, I turned back, took a step, and went down with a crash.

13

OH GIRL

THOMAS

Rachel brought her laptop to the counter and pulled up a website called ButYouDontLookSick. An article there told the story of a woman who used spoons as a metaphor to describe life with a chronic illness. She also clicked traditional medical websites that embraced the concept as a tool for patients and their loved ones. With what I'd learned from Kick, it all made sense. In the middle of reading the article, an echoing thump coming from the primary bedroom made my heart stop.

Thankfully, the bathroom door hadn't been locked when I burst through it. After hearing the loud bang that sounded like a death tumble, panic ensued. We were lucky I turned the handle instead of crashing through the door.

"Are y'alright? What happened?" I grabbed the back of my neck as I assessed the bathroom. Too much water on the floor. Some jars overturned. Kick winced and blew out a long breath through tight lips as she eased herself into the water.

"I'll have a nice hip bruise." She looked down and raised her arm. "One here from smacking it on the counter too. Otherwise, I'm hunky-dory." Kick settled into the water and closed her eyes. "It's what I get for forgetting my glasses."

I eased over to the side of the tub and sat on the edge. "You didn't hit your head?"

"Naw." She kept her lids shut as she smiled. "Any future stupidity is just the brain fog waiting to clear."

My shoulders dropped in relief. "Christ, darlin'. You scared the shit out of me. The street's not fit for an ambulance yet."

Kick opened an eye. "It wasn't fit for your snowboards either, but it didn't stop you lot."

I took her hand and checked the darkening red mark. "Are you mad about that?"

"No." She adjusted her scrunchie, making a top knot. "It comes with the boy-mom territory. I'm simply pointing out I'm not the only one prone to accidents."

That was a relief. I pulled a towel off the warming bar, spread it over the wet floor, and wiped up the puddles with my feet. Then I began to strip.

Kick pushed her glasses up her button nose. "What are you doing?"

"Relaxing with you." I breathed in the floral scent hanging in the humid air. "It's already working."

I took a step forward and held out my hands. "Stand please. Reassurance me your bruises are as minor as you claim."

Kick pushed a button on the light panel. The cycling colors became a solid warm white. "The colors will make it appear worse than it is." She took my hands and stood. As I carefully turned her, checking for signs of something needing a doctor, Kick's hooded gaze told me she was checking me back. Water droplets meandered down her skin, making my mouth water.

The corner of my mouth ticked up. "Like what you see?"

"Always. Can't get enough."

The possessive, heady looks passing between us proved our

like-mindedness. I stepped in opposite Kick and lowered us into the steaming water. I lifted one of her feet and ran my thumb along the sole. I felt her muscles relax and heard her breaths lengthen.

I'd always been a shower guy, or variations of it. Between the scented oils, the relaxing water, and the woman I loved, I could get used to this. The extralong tub helped.

Kick settled her head against the bath pillow. "I'm a terrible mother."

Well, that took a turn. "The stuff with Rachel bothering you?"

"Yes, but there's more."

My ministrations moved up her calf, rewarding me with a moan. "Tell me."

"My body hates the cold. And any other year, I would've taken it easy outside. Gone home earlier. I guess I thought this talk of me being like you… you know, the Felidae stuff. Well, I thought it meant I could have all the energy again."

"I see." I took my time on Kick's calf, digging into the muscle there. "I need to be more sensitive to your limits. It's not like flipping a switch, you know. The first time I noticed something was different was ten years after Alicia died. Remember how my aura appeared when I spent a week on the mountain? It didn't come out again until much later. During the time between, I wrote it off as grief."

Kick turned the chroma lights back on, and it amused me how they created an effect similar to our own energies.

"What happened ten years later?"

"Aside from my peers going gray or dying early, a terrible virus spread across the valley. It almost killed my son and my mother-in-law. Many families were devastated, but all were touched by it to a degree. Everyone but me. I didn't catch a sniffle."

Kick flexed her now-relaxed foot as I switched to the other

one. "So it could take a while until I see a total remission, or will it always be an issue, you think?"

I focused on a tight knot below the ball of her foot. "Keep up with your doctor's advice. But there's old folklore specific to the Felidae, or those like us. The elders have been around long enough to make long-term observations." My thumbs dug into the length of her sole. "They say healing works in reverse for us. In other words, a recent issue resolves first. Older ones take longer." I lifted a shoulder. "Of course, when you have all the time in the world, it's still a short time. What's interesting to me is I've observed similar things on a cellular level in the lab. Guess they have a point."

"You're saying be patient and watch."

I chuckled at her summation. "Spoken like a scientist."

"Hopefully it won't take so long to help my temper. Thank you, cowboy." Kick sighed and settled into the massage as my hands moved up her second leg.

"You've called me cowboy on and off since New Year's. Is this a thing now?"

Kick smiled like she was visiting a memory. "There was something about the time you took me to meet Eddie."

"It's the damn coat, isn't it?"

She laughed and brushed the damp hairs off her face. "The coat leaves a fantastic image in the mind, for sure. It was also like you were telling me something without words. Considering everything I know now, you probably were. It suits your soul, I guess."

"It would be nice if cowboying could combine with healing mankind."

"You really want to end diseases like Banger suggested?"

"I want answers to my existence first." I stretched my neck, letting the water loosen my own tension. "Why not take it as far as it'll go? I have all the time in the world." We sat with the words, and I listened to the tub motor hum as the tub jets pushed against my back.

Kick's free foot eased up my thigh. I closed my eyes for a moment, absorbing the contact. Thoughts circled back to her reason for my new nickname. "I like the way you look when you call me cowboy. It's possessive. Zings straight to my cock." I sank down in the water, let my legs fall some so her foot could travel. We still had things to talk about. Items on my agenda. We had to get through hers first. Back to her lack of patience and time to test mine.

"Do you want me to talk to Dylan and Rachel about their rudeness by not calling first?"

"It's okay." She sighed. "They didn't mean it."

"They're old enough to infer it, darlin'. They have their own households and understand the amount of work to keep one. Or they should." I squeezed her calf to get her full attention and winked. "As much as I love your elven ears, you're not magical. Evidenced by how run-down you are now. That's also why your temper appeared."

"I suppose. If you think it'll help." Kick propped her elbow on the edge of the tub and held her head like her tiredness wore out her neck muscles. The kids and I were definitely having words. "I think I'm actually ready for the nest to be empty. Their bickering gets to me, along with the constant need to think several steps ahead of them. I love them to the moon and back, but they can drain me."

I kissed the top of Kick's foot, then took her hand and spun her around, sliding her back against my front, and scooped water up over her body.

"What are you doing now?"

"Drain in to me. I'll talk to them." I kissed her temple. Now for my agenda. "Speaking of talking to people, you never gave me an answer about your mother." Kick's back tightened, and I coaxed her back. "Why is this so hard for you? Since you're working on self-care, this would be a giant step toward it. After all she's done. Help me understand."

Kick turned and wrapped her arms around my waist while I continued lapping water over her. "It's stupid… I keep hoping she'll apologize. That one day we'll have one of those big reconciliation moments like in the movies and books and such."

"She'll never do that."

"I know. She can't."

"Exactly."

"I'm not sure I can take another stressor right now either. What with the investigations, the kids' problems, the peeper last night. Blending you into everything. My stomach does this coiling thing when I get anxious, which often leads to a panic attack. I'm working hard with meditation to change it, but I swear it's creeping up on me again. Another person to battle is too much."

"That's the point of the offer—to relieve your stress." Damn her stubbornness. "Let me take care of it."

"And what? Ghost her without an explanation? Any other tack invites World War Three. No, Bobby talks to Juan every day, according to her text messages. Heaven help me, but they may have something real. If I can keep her at arm's length, she'll probably move away on her own."

"Alright." I tipped her chin up and kissed her soft lips until they swelled with proof of my love for her. "Let me know if you change your mind." I set my head on top of hers. "You're not alone anymore."

"I know." She squeezed me and added, "Even though it's fast, and we've made a big deal about going slow more than once, what would you say to officially sharing our places?"

I shifted to catch her gaze. "You mean moving in together for real?"

"I do. I also want to work my schedule around yours to free up more time together. My doctor's appointments are winding down. I could work longer hours when you're at the university, less when you're here. You know, use our time strategically. What do you think?"

"I think you're brilliant. Since you're reworking your schedule, let's be serious about your self-defense training."

She tipped her head back and pulled her brows together. "Why'd you go and ruin the smarmy mood?"

My head dropped as I sighed through the frustration, determined to stay firm without starting a fight. Kick made a joke, but this was important to me and should have been to her. "After last night, *you* should be asking me to make time. The faster you can add to your skill set, the better I'll feel. Oh, and Mateo is with you anytime I'm not, Kick. Any. Time."

She surprised me by tightening her hold around my waist instead of storming out of the tub. I feared my bossy lecture would amp up her stress, but it had to be said. I shook her shoulder. "Are you listening?"

"I am," she whispered. "Thanks for having my back."

I tucked Kick into bed for a nap after promising to wake her for supper. Then I put on fresh sweats and a Lord U T-shirt. I headed to the living room in search of my e-reader. Liam, Rachel, and Isabella were in the kitchen finishing the trays of chicken.

"Are y'all opening a restaurant?" I asked, stepping around the island.

Rachel brushed her hair back in a way that reminded me of her mother. "The boys could each eat a tray full. Mama used to say she felt like she was cooking for a fraternity."

"She still says that," Liam said as he washed his hands.

"When do these go in?"

Rachel checked the clock on the microwave. "About an hour and a half. We're going upstairs to do homework. I'll come back down when it's time to turn the oven on."

Bella stacked the trays in the fridge, then washed her hands while Liam put the spices away. It was nice to see the kids working together. Gave me confidence that I could talk to them about being more respectful of Kick.

"Write down what's left to do—what temperature and when? I'll finish up. That'll give y'all more time to work, as long as we can have a chat before I wake your mom."

"Thanks, fam."

Not going to lie, hearing that from Liam helped my mood as much as, if not more than, horsing around outside earlier had. The whole day assured me I was on the right path. It was time to make that call to *Grand-père*. Tomorrow. I needed to do it from my secure line at home. It gave me a hell of a boost to know I'd done the right thing by bringing Kick into my world even if she'd been the one to barge her way through.

I checked each window for signs of another intruder before settling down in a lounger and reading a science article. According to Rachel's notes, Dylan and Hank would work on their dishes once the chicken went in the oven. So, after sliding the trays into the heat, I jogged upstairs and gathered the kids in the loft.

"We need to talk about showing up here unannounced. As much as your mom loves you, it's taken a lot out of her to host four extra people during a snowstorm. Especially with everything else going on."

"We didn't know there would be four," Rachel said.

"Yeah, and we don't exactly know what's *going on* either." Dylan used finger quotes for emphasis.

Alright, man, take care of this right or Kick won't let you intervene again. I focused on Dylan first. "Y'all know what we know. Banger talked with the suspect who tried to take Kick from the club. He was moderately helpful. The one who knows the most —the bartender—is in the wind. Jonn Graham is supposed to be on an ankle monitor, but after last night, I'm not sure.

Banger talked about keeping a better eye on the Graham house.

"We have a good print of a men's size 11 basketball shoe from near Kick's bedroom window. The fact he got so close pisses me off. I'm sure she's trying to play off how upset she is about it. When the weather gets back to normal, you can bet the Angel Security team will come in and adjust the system. Also, Kick asked me to move in officially. I hope you don't mind me saying it and not her. She just... she needs a break, y'all."

Dylan nodded along with each point I made.

"Rachel... if you had called or texted before coming up... any of you, there could have been coordination. Hell, at this stage in your life, it wouldn't hurt to ask Kick for permission to spend the night, any time. You never know how she's feeling."

Rachel shrugged. "It's fine. We're used to her disappearing to lie down or fending for ourselves."

Liam cleared his throat, catching our attention. "The prof's trying to say y'all were damn rude assuming we could handle it. Have you seen the refrigerator, Snow? It's wiped. Fam had planned to use the potatoes you cooked earlier for tomorrow's dinner."

"Oh." Rachel hung her head. "But we were out of food."

Liam scoffed. "There's a pizza place and a grocery store around the corner from your apartment. Ours is a mile walk. Sure it's out of bread and milk, but you don't eat that stuff anyway."

"I hadn't realized you'd cottoned on to her stress," I said to Liam. Guess it was hard not to when you were raised in it.

He lifted a shoulder like it was no big deal. "Since it's just been us, we kind of made our own language about how we're doing. I can tell if she's off by looking at her. Mom's the same with me."

Ah, these kids. I saw the reason for Liam's reluctance to pick a college in that moment. The fear of leaving in the way his cocky grin disappeared. The way he nervously fingered imaginary chords against his thigh. I'd do something about it later.

I clapped my hands and rubbed them together to get back on track. "Do y'all understand where I'm coming from? No hard feelings for being here on my part, or on Kick's. You should know that. I'm impressed with you. All of you. Just… understand your mom means a lot to me. You might think it's fast, but we're in it nonetheless. And I admit to being overprotective right now. It still pisses me off that she could've been seriously hurt right under my nose. Twice." My fists flexed with unspent anger. I craved a sparring session at the gym as much as I did answers from any damn person in the investigation.

Dylan rubbed his new beard during my speech. He cleared his throat. "I hear you." His eyes moved over his brother and sister. "We all do. Thank you for what you're doing for our mom. Snow and I will apologize for not calling her. I knew better but was in a hurry to get ahead of traffic."

We all bumped fists before heading down to the kitchen to finish prepping dinner. I considered it a mission accomplished and hoped it would sell Kick on letting me handle Bobby even if she were the human equivalent of rescuing a village from a dragon.

AFTER DINNER AND APOLOGIES, THE OLDER KIDS AGREED TO HEAD back to their respective apartments the following afternoon. Icy morning roads kept the schools closed for at least another day, but Kick was set on opening the Perked Cup.

The best part of what Kick kept calling our "bonus holiday" came in the evening. We gathered around the big television for a movie, but nothing caught our attention.

"I know." Liam jumped up off the sofa. "We'll have a jam sesh."

In a matter of minutes, we were gathered back together. Lee and I had practiced together in the past, so one of my guitars was already at the house. Dylan kept a bass guitar in Liam's room since his old sanctuary was now a workout room. Kick rigged up drums for Hank from cookware, a cookie tin, and wooden spoons. The girls dug out kiddie tambourines from Rachel's room.

After tuning our instruments, I turned toward Liam. "Want to work on the song?" His eyes darted to Kick as a sheepish look crossed his face.

"What's wrong, Wee Man?" In typical Kick fashion, she caught it straightaway.

He studied his fingers and strummed a chord. "It's one of Dad's songs. You probably don't want to hear it."

He hadn't told me that when he asked about it. Hell, it was a song that often hit too close to home for me, not something I imagined touching Shane.

Kick moved to the sofa, next to where Liam and I perched on the fireplace hearth. "Journey? As long as it's not—"

"No. You know... 'Desperado' by the Eagles."

Kick leaned forward and chuckled. "I love it. The song was special to Dad because Granddad sang it all the time. Hell, he could whistle it like a bird." She reached out and shuffled the flop of curls off his forehead. "Dad would be thrilled to hear you play it. He's so proud of you. All of you."

Is? The use of present tense startled me, but I didn't have time to dig into it. Liam grabbed my attention when he played a chord. "G, right?"

I nodded, and we began.

Kick harmonized easily with her son, reminding me of her stories of singing with him in the car, Liam strapped into a car seat as they ran errands. Pride and peace shone in her eyes as everyone else joined in where they felt appropriate.

As for me, the song that haunted me in the past—an indictment of the prison of my lonely existence—now cleansed my soul. The queen of my heart found me, forced her way into my prison, and gave me all this. Damned if I'd take it for granted.

We progressed through several more classic songs with Liam and Rachel taking turns singing lead. Kick and Bella sang backup and shook their moneymakers with the tambourines. We turned it into an old-fashioned hootenanny, playing and dancing the night away.

When Kick drifted off to sleep later, I slipped out of bed to check the perimeter of the house, trusting my eyes more than what the camera feeds showed. I owed it to them to protect Kick and her family with everything I had.

14

JUST CAN'T GET ENOUGH

KICK

Cyndi took a large pull from her latte and sighed. I could practically see the stress float off her. She'd entered the coffeehouse thoroughly wound up, but who could blame her? I saw footage of the multicar pileup she'd been in on the news.

"Thank you for the use of your man, chica. He saved my hiney."

"Anytime. You helped him scratch his itchy hero complex." I held my glasses up to the light and rubbed the lenses. They'd been blurry all morning, but the lenses looked clean. "Guess the helping thing went both ways."

"Where is Dr. Feelgood anyway?" Cyndi's nickname for Thomas had occasionally popped up during the past month. It always made Thomas shake his head, but I thought it beat Marty Poppins and left it alone. She craned her neck to case the café's dining room. "I want to thank him with a coffee and muffin."

I stopped filling the napkin dispenser in front of me and clicked my tongue. "You know he eats for free, like you."

"Exactly."

Cyndi's Cheshire cat grin made me shake my head. Then I tipped it toward the back. "He's tinkering with the HVAC system. The offices are ice cold, and the maintenance company said it wasn't an emergency."

"Is there anything your man doesn't do?" If I could live as long as Thomas, I supposed I would be a Jack—Jacqueline?—of all trades too. Not like I could tell Cyndi though. I lifted a shoulder. "He grew up on a farm. They're a resourceful bunch." I hoped my explanation would suffice. I patted her hand. "Can't believe you were caught in the middle of our Snowmageddon."

She shuddered at the memory. "I'm at the top left of the photo from the News website." Her mouth lifted into another grin. "The officer who rescued me gave me his number. A young buck at that. I'm taking a play from your book, Kicky."

I put the lid back on the dispenser and reached for the next one while biting my tongue. I didn't want to ask what happened with Manu. Silly me thought he might finally be the one to repair the heart her ex-husband had shattered.

"An...y...waay..." She nervously tapped on her cheek.

Oh hell. We'd fought over her playing the field in the past. She must have interpreted my silence as a judgment. My guilt over having to keep this huge secret from her probably looked the same. I gave her my best smile. Now I just wanted to see her happy, however it looked.

"The roads were fine once Thomas made my little car drivable again, which is a good thing since I have a tax appointment in an hour."

"Cyn, I—"

"Speaking of, when will you have your shit together?"

I laughed, breaking the tension, knowing she meant my paperwork to do my taxes and not my life. "My shit's all good. I'll send it over tonight. Oh snap." I stopped my chores and actually snapped my fingers. "I better check in with Uncle Hugh. This is his first year doing taxes on his own."

"Tell him to call me if he needs anything. He won't have to wait for an appointment."

"I will. Thanks, chica."

The bell chimed and Jake walked in, two hours early for his shift. "Well, hey, mister. Did I call a meeting and forget about it?" I reached for my phone in my back pocket to check the calendar.

"No, Mrs. Mack." He grabbed a pastry and took a bite. His eyes shifted around the dining room, then he pointed toward the back. "I'm uh… catching up on my paperwork."

Jake's steps slowed when Banger's second-in-command turned the corner from the back hallway. "Hey Siobhan," he said, dipping his chin to the side.

The spiky-haired redhead gave him a coy smile. "Hey yourself."

My eyebrows rose up my forehead, and I turned to Cyndi. "Paperwork my ass. Someone has a crush."

The attraction made sense. I never saw Jake with a "little woman" type. Siobhan gave off serious Lara Croft-meets-Tolkien vibes. And people said *I* looked like an elf.

Jake pointed over his shoulder with his thumb. "Can I talk to you when you're done out here? In my office?"

Cyndi and I made faces at each other while Siobhan smiled back. "Sure. Give me a minute."

We still snickered like proud aunties when Siobhan approached us. "Your update's all set. Again, my deepest apologies for the gap in your coverage. Let me know if you need anything else."

"Thank you, Von. I appreciate your hard work. If you have any insight into how this guy found the hole, can you speak with Thomas? He's not sleeping well over it." Cyndi opened her mouth, but I raised a finger to ask her to wait. I hadn't mentioned the peeping incident yet. I wanted to forget about it and let Angel Security handle it all.

Siobhan grimaced at my words, then bit her lip. "I'll be sure to do that." She turned and disappeared into the back offices.

"What's wrong with your security system, Kick?"

Before I could answer Cyndi, Deana, and Thomas emerged from the hallway, both moving in our direction. Dee vigorously rubbed her arms and poured herself a cup of coffee. "Not used to it being so cold." She took a quick sip and sighed. "I sorted the new shipment and couldn't tell the difference between the walk-in, the hallway, or the outside."

"Won't be long." Thomas stepped near me and moved my ponytail aside to kiss my neck. He pulled harder than I expected and made me shiver. I wasn't sure if it was from surprise or something else.

"Interesting." His quiet rumble reached only my ear.

I smiled at him over my shoulder. "What?"

He winked. "Making a mental note for later."

I raised an eyebrow, but Thomas moved away before I could say anything. "Getting my other toolbox from the SUV."

I watched him walk out, admiring the way his worn jeans fit his ass. He wore a sweatshirt without a coat and walked with sure-footed confidence as he navigated the icy patches in the parking lot. When he rounded the Land Rover, I turned around to find both of my friends ogling him too. "Ladies?"

Deana graced me with her warm chuckle. "You can't blame me for admiring God's handiwork, can you?"

My lips pressed into a smile as I looked at Cyndi expectantly.

"What she said." Cyn tipped her head like she was studying something—the something being me. "That little hair-pull business tells me you like a little 'funky bump bump'." She shimmied her shoulders with the words. "I learned something new today." Both women fell apart, giggling.

I folded my arms, struggling to keep from laughing too. I

opened my mouth to say something sarcastic, but Cyndi put her hand up to stop me.

"It's all good, Kicky. You're just fun to tease." She sighed, the action leaving an introspective expression on her face. Or was it sadness?

"Want to do a girls' night tomorrow?" I asked. "Not like last time with the dance club. We can stay in, drink wine, eat cashew cream. There's a new rom-com I want to stream." I turned to Deana. "You too, Dee. Please."

Cyndi tapped her lower lip. "Let me guess, the professor's out all night and you don't know how to be alone anymore."

"Well—"

"What's Lee up to?"

I shrugged. "Band stuff. Friend stuff. He's hardly home anymore."

"You're afraid you'll sit around all horny and moping for your man." She pretended to pout and Deana belly-laughed. Apparently, I was an absolute hoot to tease.

I dipped my chin and glared. "I thought we could use some catch-up time together. All of us. There's also a new shipment of gummies coming in for Hugh's place. We could test them out. Take notes."

Cyndi finished her latte and slid the cup to me. "Sorry, chica. I have a date with Officer Hotpants. But let's sync our calendars and find something." We hugged and said goodbyes before Cyn left for her appointment.

I placed her mug on the dish tray, then asked Deana, "What about you? No obligations on the gummies." Deana hadn't come around to the possibilities of cannabis. To her, it remained an evil drug. "Hanging is plenty. In fact, Carmen brought over more of the empanadas you love this morning."

"It sounds exactly like what I need, but I can't either," Deana said while flushing and wiping down the dispersion screen on the espresso machine. "I'm babysitting Dex's boy. We hope they can smooth out this rough patch." She began scrubbing the rest of the machine, getting heavier handed than usual. She quietly added, "Something has to help."

I felt the pang of her worry deep in my gut. It still grumbled over the near fight with Rachel, wondering if she'd be okay. Deana's son's marriage had been rocky from the get-go. Watching her struggles over it had been part of the reason for my relief at Dylan's breakup. It could have been so much worse. "It's wonderful how you and Gordon support him."

Deana sighed. "Sometimes we're not sure Charice's fire-cracker ways are worth the trouble, but Dex loves her." She wrung out the dishcloth an extra time. "For the sake of that angel boy, I hope they figure it out."

Dee emerged from the restroom area, drying her hands and mumbling about the convoluted things people did to public bathrooms. The word *wrapper* caught my attention. I looked up from my work.

"What's wrong?" she asked.

It was then I recognized how much I'd missed her. Between time off for my health and Thomas, our interactions had become sparse. I sat on a barstool, working on my laptop, since my office was still too cold for more than a couple of minutes. I was setting up new ads to counteract the harassment efforts. Business had improved but was pitiful compared to the previous year.

"What makes you think anything's wrong?"

"Puh-lease." Dee stood in her trademarked fist-on-her-hip stance, not taking guff from anyone, including me. "You showed up this morning like you were walking on air. Now I find you staring at the coffee grinder like you're about to burst into tears. Is it your mother? Usually you get this way when you regret calling her."

I let my vision soften as I stood in front of the window,

thoughts tossing in my head like decision salad. "Huh…? Oh. It's not her, thankfully. By some miracle, she started texting me instead of chewing me out when I can't answer her calls immediately. She still implies that she and Juan had crazy monkey sex, but it's easier to read than listen to. At least she sounds happy *and* she's leaving soon." Juan needed hip surgery, so my mother planned to fly up to his bedside.

"So—"

"I don't think I can partner with Hugh in this cannabis venture, and I don't know what to do," I blurted.

"What the—?" She shook her head. "Why?"

While running a hand over my curls, I blew out a shuddering breath. "Business may be on the mend here, but the campaign to ruin my character has worked with the tobacco board. The good old boys' club."

"You're saying all this…" She circled her hand in the air, what she did when desperately trying not to swear. "All this *crap* has been over Mick & Hugh's?"

"No, but it overlaps. Cyndi talked to some board members for me, and even she can't convince them I'm a good bet. The smear campaign has quieted, but it was successful." I rubbed my cheeks and forced my hands to stay out of my hair. Nothing said *out-of-control Kick* like sudden disco hair. It was the last thing my precarious reputation needed. "I've enjoyed learning about a new product and business model, but after everything else… I'm tired, Dee. Cyndi and I dodged a huge fecking bullet at the nightclub. I don't want to let Hugh down, but I can only fight on so many fronts, you know?"

Deana reached across the counter and had me in a hug before I registered the movement. Her breath at my neck, the beat of her heart against my ear, and shea butter lotion in my nose allowed me to take my first deep breath in what felt like hours. Her beautiful, sincere face that refused to show her age had grounded me long before Thomas came along. She was there for me first, and I would never forget it.

"So you want to what? Give up?"

I grinned into her shoulder. *Here comes her tough love.* I leaned back to answer. "I'm trying to figure out if it's worth the fight." My fingers pressed into the base of my neck, seeking relief from the tension knotting my muscles. "Now that I have Thomas, I want years with him. If someone's trying to hurt me or one of mine… It doesn't do Hugh any favors to pretend he has my focus. Or am I simply a stubborn fool who can't say no?"

"Of course." Dee smiled. "But it's also who you are. It's why you've come so far."

I knocked her arm lightly and chuckled. Leave it to Deana—the consummate optimist—to turn a character flaw into a strength. She helped though, except… "What about the near misses? Here. You and the rest of the staff. Customers—*children*—who hang out after school. I mean, there's bravery and female empowerment, and then there's stupidity."

She nearly snapped her own neck, recoiling in shock. "Female empower— Are you saying someone's after you because you're a woman in business?"

"The board members believed those articles about my 'moral failings.' One of them brought up Thomas to Cyndi, as if being with a younger man makes me a harlot."

"Didn't Hugh ask you in order to diversify the next set of licenses?"

"That's right. Hugh wants me to consult too from a health angle. That's why I've been researching pain relief and cancer patients."

"Then go behind the scenes and put someone else up front." I half expected her to finish the order with a *duh.*

"It's not a bad idea. But who? Jake? Play the veteran card?" My shoulders dropped. "He and I are working on a way for him to open another Perked Cup location when he graduates. The coffee business suits him."

"It does." Deana leaned down, placing her elbows on the counter. "Will this cannabis thing be profitable?"

I barked a laugh. "Ridiculously so."

Deana straightened her tiny spine with the majesty of a queen. She almost appeared taller than me when she declared, "We've come too far, earned too much with our blood, sweat, and tears to be chased away from what we've worked so hard for. Remember what I told you last fall—we don't let our ancestors down."

"There's an Oprah speech if I ever heard one."

This time she swatted me. "You can't let these people run you off, a'ight? Promise me. I have an idea too."

"What's that?"

"Well, would Hugh work with Dexter? He's perfect for it."

A smile bloomed across my face. I couldn't love the idea more. Deana's son was a hard worker, so charismatic. He held a degree in entrepreneurial business or some such. Hugh would adore him. I tapped my bottom lip. "I could stay involved as a consultant. Does Dex need a job?"

"It's a big part of this round of problems with Charice."

My heart broke for Dee and her son but lifted at the possibilities for all of us. "You might be a genius, my friend."

She pierced me with her fiercest gaze. "Now go surround yourself with your army of fine men and run your damn empire like the queen bitch you are."

My brows spiked in amusement, my smile even bigger. "Deana Douglas, did you swear? Twice?"

She pursed her lips and dipped her chin hard. "Sure did." Following her naughty words with her bright smile set my mood to rights again. The ton of weight that had pressed my shoulders down lifted off like it was a feather.

I called Mateo over, then touched Dee's shoulder. "I'll go talk to Hugh."

15

MILESTONES

THOMAS

*M*orning arrived too fast. Kick and I had accidentally slept in, creating a frenzied rush to meet the day. Blending our lives together was another level of joy that also came with its own road bumps.

I slid into the bathroom in my socks, my eyes darting around the space in annoyance. I stopped for a moment to watch Kick shake out her curls as she readied herself. It was the only thing that could make me pause. She caught my reflection in the mirror.

"What's wrong?"

"Can't find my watch and keys." At the farmhouse, everything went in a bowl near the coffee station on the way to the mudroom. The layout here was different, and I hadn't figured out my routine.

She paused with the stuff she called a finishing serum. "Are you serious? You're a grown man."

Instead of arguing, I kept staring. I didn't have time to debate.

Shit happened, and we'd been distracted last night. Hence, our lateness.

"For Pete's sake." Kick lifted her eyes to the ceiling. I couldn't tell if she was thinking or praying. "Are they all the same? This one's almost three hundred years old and still can't keep track of his shit." She looked over her shoulder at me. "They're in the kitchen by the coffee station."

Well, damn. I kissed her check. "Thanks, baby. Love you." Then I shot out of the bathroom.

As I wrapped the watch around my wrist, Kick called out as she entered the living room, clipping her earrings in, "You know... you should research the finding-things gene on the Y chromosome. You'd transform humanity. Or at least improve life for my side of the gender pool."

I laughed and slid my feet into my shoes. How she handled this new reality of hers with such grace and now humor, I couldn't figure out. It did lift my mood. But the keys hadn't been what flustered me. A looming phone call did. "I'll put it on my to-do list. For you."

She stopped in front of me and nodded at a corner of the mudroom. "What if we put a small catch area there?"

I slipped my jacket on and pulled her in for a proper kiss. "I have a small table that'll work. I'll bring it after I see Eddie. Thank you, darlin'. You blow my mind."

She stroked the dent in my chin with her finger. "There's something else, isn't there?"

"Today's the day to call *Grand-père*," I confessed. I had hoped to give him solid proof that Kick was in transition but hadn't found it yet. We were coming up on a month since our commitment to each other. It felt disrespectful to both Kick and Alaric to keep our relationship quiet.

"He'll listen to you. From what you've told me, I can tell he loves you."

I squeezed her again, felt her heart beating against my chest, absorbed her optimism. "Hope so."

Kick turned me and gave me a gentle push toward the door. "You've got this. Are you still working with Liam this evening?"

He had scheduled one last SAT test and asked me for help with his weak spots. "Wouldn't miss it."

"Thanks, cowboy."

It had been easy enough to make the plans with Liam. I cared about the boy and loved teaching. Seeing Kick's eyes shine like I was her hero was another reminder of how much she'd been carrying. I cleared my throat. "He'll do great this time. Don't worry."

I left her with a sweet smile on her face, one that didn't come from an orgasm, yet I still felt like a king. Yeah, I could make this call.

I PACED THE SPACE IN FRONT OF MY OFFICE WINDOW, WATCHING students rush across the quad on paved walkways crisscrossing campus. Coeds had worn the grass down first before the university made the paths permanent, safer. Wasn't that what I was about to do? Break the rules and carve a fresh path out of necessity. I dialed *Grand-père.*

"Allo." The unexpected feminine voice of Ellie came through the line.

"Um… hello *Grand-mère.* My apologies. Did I dial the wrong number?" I checked my phone screen.

"Thomas? No, my dear. You reached Alaric's office. You called him, yes?"

"I did. Good to know nothing's wrong with my phone." I hoped she didn't catch my nervous chuckle, except the woman missed nothing. "It's nice to hear your voice. I just don't understand. You've never answered this line before."

She made an annoyed, growly *"rohhh"* sound. "Something

broke at his distillery while we were looking at the finances. I stayed to finish them."

"Well, uh…" Damn all the cross-continent tension making me tongue-tied. "*Grand-père* is proud of his brandy. More so than the wine. Hope it's fixed soon."

"*Bof.* Can I help?"

I'd never known Ellie to be annoyed by anything. She'd always been the epitome of dignity and poise. The definition of ladylike. Between her responses and my anxiety before the call, I was in a veritable tailspin. "I'll call his cell phone."

"He left it here so he wouldn't be disturbed."

"Can you tell him I need to talk? It's urgent."

Had they been fighting? Alaric and Ellie hadn't been involved for a long time. They were more like business partners now. These hints of tension, mixed with Banger's concerns, suggested bigger problems than I thought at the top of the Society. It didn't bode well for what I needed to add.

"Let me guess, you're not allowed to speak business with me."

Hell. I pinched the bridge of my nose. "It's not business, I mean my research." It would be doubly rude if Alaric felt like the last to know. I'd already be on thin ice with him as it was with this news. "I should speak with him first."

She sighed an exasperated "*oui*" down the line. "I will leave a note. He should be available after dinner. If you don't hear soon, call him then."

"I will. Thank you, *Grand-mère.*"

"A pleasure, my dear."

Despite Ellie's plausible explanation, I spent the rest of the morning with the same question rolling around in my head. "Why the hell was she in Alaric's office?"

16

THE GOOD LIFE

THOMAS

*K*ick stepped up to me and pulled my right hand to her lips. It had a significant cut from fixing the Perked Cup's HVAC system.

"Ugh, God," Dylan complained.

I smiled at the idea of an eight-year-old's reaction coming from the mouth of a twenty-four-year-old. *Might as well get used to it.*

"Come here, lad," Kick ordered. Dylan took a step toward us.

She planted a sweet kiss on my lips. "Get used to it, because I'm keeping him."

"Thomas isn't a new puppy." Dylan rolled his eyes as I laughed.

She tapped my cheek. "No kidding. He's housebroken." I raised my eyebrow at her tease. "Definitely a plus."

From the corner of my eye, I caught Dylan shaking his head at us and wondered if the hesitancy I felt from him came from our perceived age difference. I was aware of the various "oohs and aahs," as well as blatant snickering around the coffeehouse over her dating a younger man. Hell, it had been part of why Kick kept me at arm's length in the beginning. Now we loved our inside joke regarding the truth.

Did these murmurings bother Dylan? At least I had an opportunity to find out later. We were about to play poker at Mick and Hugh's. This game was set up by Dylan himself and featured his friends instead of Hugh's senior crowd.

Speaking of Dylan's friends, his roommate had entered the smoke shop during our exchange. "You go, Ms. Mack."

"Not helping, Dum." Dylan groaned.

Hank lifted his shoulder. "I'm happy for her." He knocked my shoulder with his fist. "You found a treasure, Professor."

"Don't I know it," I said.

Kick swooned. "You're very kind, Hank, sweetie."

The young man blushed. He leaned toward us and whispered, "It's not you. Suzy called earlier."

"Should I..." Kick pivoted toward the office, where her son had just gone.

"Let me," Hank said. "I swear, he's happy for you. Given everything else, it might be hard for Dyl to let go of his protectiveness."

Kick worried the inside of her cheek with her tongue. "He better learn fast. I never wanted him to be anything other than my son anyway."

"What can I say?" Hank raised his hands. "He's a reluctant alpha."

What the hell did that mean? Kick laughed at his words.

"Are you sticking around? I heard you host these things," he asked her.

"No," Kick answered. "I just do that for Hugh. I came by to sign out a product to test and say hello. I'll head back to the coffeehouse now."

"I'll pop over after I go out. I always lose my shirt at these things." Hank nodded slowly, like he was thinking and speaking at the same time. "Imma head back to the office and make the roomie laugh before we get started." He waved at Kick. "See you later, Mrs. Mack."

I worked hard to keep from frowning. The term *Mrs. Mack* rankled my possessiveness despite Kick having been a McKenna most of her life. It made no sense for her to go back to her maiden name. I liked where we were at, what we had. Blending our schedules had helped us become more comfortable as a couple. Why blow that up by pushing to take our relationship to another level? Nevertheless, the desire to be more had sparked in me.

I threaded my fingers with Kick's. As she tipped her head back, I saw the shadows under her eyes. "You're tired."

She gave me a small smile. "I'm fine."

"If we're still here when you close, don't come over. Go home and sleep."

Kick wrinkled her nose. "What about Mateo? Is he supposed to watch television while I snooze, like a babysitter?"

As much as Kick liked her bodyguard, she still wasn't comfortable with the day-to-day reality of him. "Tell you what… Have him do a thorough sweep and text me. Or I could just come get you when you're ready to close."

"And make you leave early?"

"I'll be fine. Your safety is more important." I touched my forehead to Kick's as she grumbled. "I could give you a massage… help you relax before you sleep."

The corner of her mouth ticked up. "That sounds like you're offering me some vitamin O, Professor."

"Yeah? You want another piece of me?"

She kissed my chin. "Always." She stepped around me and slapped my ass. "See what you've done to me?"

I waggled my brows. "Love what I see."

Kick opened the door and waited for Mateo to lead. Her bright grin threatened to stop my heart. "Go fill up on cigars, lewd jokes, farting, and chips. I'll call you when I'm ready... Oh, hey Banger."

I was laughing at her words when my friend walked in. As if the description of our poker night motivated me to stay away from her.

Banger and I grabbed arms in greeting. He tilted his head as he studied me. "Yep. Still googly-eyed and shit."

"What can I say? When you find your goddess, you hold tight and worship her."

Banger spread his hands out to his side. "All I know is... 'no woman, no cry.'"

I shook my head, knowing where the sentiment came from. I wasn't around to see his heartbreak but had known all about the tragic story.

He patted my back before I thought of a defense. "Seriously, brother. I'm happy for you. It looks good on you."

I grinned like a kid on Christmas morning on the inside, but kept my visage tight on the outside. Banger would've just given me more shit.

We wandered into the game room where Dylan sorted poker chips.

"How's your project coming?" Banger asked him.

"The pretend one or the surprise for Mom?"

Banger turned to me with an expectant eyebrow raised. I lifted a shoulder and lightly shook my head. "Maybe you should start from the beginning."

"Oh. Sure. See, Mom thinks my final project is a game because my team has focused on that until now. In fact, we plan to keep the game development side going since it's lucrative. It'll help with research and development for what else we want to do. Anyway, my final project is inspired by her."

"Go on," Banger encouraged as he took a seat next to him.

Dylan finished the last stack of chips and stretched his back. "You're familiar with the functional medicine clinic we help support?"

"Yes."

"I'm working with Dr. Drummond at the clinic to create an app doctors and patients can use together. It'll let them keep in touch between appointments. It's basically a symptom journal, a food and medicine diary, and workout tracker, all in one. It'll analyze what's input, detect any trends, and send reports to both the office and the patient. In addition, certain things will flag and send alerts to the doctor, who can then post a prescriptive message right away."

"Sounds brilliant."

"Yeah," Dylan sighed. "The functionality developed as expected. The problem came when we took it to the clinic for beta testing. We tightened up HIPAA compliance but hit a roadblock with hacker-proofing it in the cloud. You see, insurance companies can be hostile toward this type of patient. I've heard many stories from Mom—hers included—about how hard it was to get a diagnosis because the insurance wouldn't cover the tests." Dylan shook his head in disgust. "It's why a lot of these treatments end up out of pocket. That's why my dad started the foundation. It's one thing to know criminals are poking at apps to steal from regular people, but the board members are more afraid of big, domestic entities who'd want access to highly personal information. If you know what I mean."

"Whoa," Banger said. I could see the wheels turning in his mind.

I rubbed my chin. "Thought insurance companies couldn't deny coverage anymore."

Dylan's eyes darkened. Made me wonder how much he'd watched of Kick's experience. Did she even know? There were deep waters in this young man. "Plenty of politicians openly admit they want to revoke that part of the law. So many families would end up screwed. Doctor-patient confidentiality is a joke from what I've heard. I don't want to put in all this work and have it blow up the career of a good doctor, or the life of the patient."

"Well?" Banger turned, his attention on Dylan. "Did you figure it out?"

A wide grin spread across Dylan's face. "I did. I've developed a new security login system. The clinic received it at the beginning of the month. Initial feedback is encouraging."

Banger leaned in and quietly asked, "Can your security system be used in other applications? On other platforms?" He bubbled with an enthusiasm I hadn't seen in a while, like Dylan had just given my friend proof of Santa's existence.

Dylan's grin stayed put while he made a deliberate nod.

"Hot damn." Banger gasped. "My team's been working on something like this for six months for the Angel System. Could you adapt it for me?"

Dylan steepled his fingers and tapped them with a cockiness that made me laugh. "I think so. Sure."

"If it can, kid, it could mean millions."

The hands stilled. "Come again?"

Banger laughed, letting his head fall back. "You do not know. I have high-value clients who'd give a firstborn for better security." His gaze lifted. "What are you planning on doing with it after this?"

"As long as it stays on course, the gang and I have two venture funding meetings set up this spring. We're working on two more."

"Cancel them." Banger knocked his knuckles on the table.

"Really? Why? I haven't told you who they are."

Banger waved a hand. "Then don't cancel, but give us first crack at it. I think you have something we need. I want to help you finish it and grow it right here. In Raleigh."

"Who's us?" I asked.

Banger sat back and glared at me. "You and me, numpty."

"Why do I need—"

"Your research. We've danced around the idea of taking it into the private sector. Thanks to the developments with Ki—ah… your new subject—security will be your first concern."

I ran my hand through my hair, catching up to his train of thought. "Christ, you're right."

"You two have the capital my team needs?" Dylan asked, his tone doubtful. He looked at us like we were investment amateurs. The kid knew nothing.

Banger clapped his hand on my shoulder. "Son, your mama's new beau is a gazillionaire. And I'm a bigger one. Trust me, we have your capital."

"True?" Dylan's eyes shifted to me, studying me like he was searching for typical signs of wealth.

My brows narrowed in a tight grimace. I kept a lock on my funds and an even bigger lock on who knew about them. It wasn't that I didn't trust Dylan, but I'd learned the hard way to trust no one.

Keeping this project in the family, so to speak, had its appeal. Kick would be thrilled if her son could stay close. Raleigh would be the perfect place to launch both aspects of Dylan's future enterprise. "Banger's right. We could be equally beneficial."

"Wow," Dylan whispered.

"Moreover, your mom's going to be thrilled you did this."

He answered quietly, "Her first remission took forever. If this can shorten the time it takes to sift through tests and symptoms… do you know how many supplements made her worse before they figured out the right combination? It could save so much heartache and money."

I patted him on the back. "Let me know how I can help."

The rest of the guys walked into the game room with Hank making introductions. Banger stretched his arms and cracked his knuckles. "Let's whoop these punk kids and take their candy."

. . .

AT THE BREAK, BANGER AND HANK WERE IN THE LEAD. THE GAME had grown so intense that we needed a release valve. While everyone else filled up on junk food, I pulled Dylan into the humidor. "Are we alright?" The tension I'd felt when I arrived hadn't lightened despite the easy conversation at the table. "Hank mentioned you had a rough day, but I want to make sure it's not something else. For Kick's sake as much as mine."

Dylan scrubbed a hand over his cheek. The few day's growth he had during the storm was turning into an actual beard. "You're going with the Hank thing too?"

"Your mother has a point." I lifted a shoulder. "Can't put *Dummy* on a résumé."

"He won't have to. Dum will head up my marketing team."

I'd already heard about Hank's branding talents, which made me question his choice of nickname all the more. "You want a C-level executive with the name *Dummy?*"

Dylan folded his arms across his chest and set his feet like he'd become a wall. Something did bother him. Instead, he deflected. "You know he has a crush on your girlfriend, right?" He grimaced at his own words.

"Why don't we go with my 'partner?' Kick doesn't like the 'girl' reference anyway."

"Partner, huh?" Dylan's face scrunched before he nodded. "That works."

"Regardless, she told me enough that I know Hank's parents don't support him. I think he's smitten with her as a mother figure. Seeks her approval."

"She mothers everyone my age."

"Exactly. Like I said, is there something else?"

"You didn't know about Spoon Theory," Dylan blurted.

"Pardon?" *This conversation just took a turn.*

"Yeah. Rachel had to explain it to you." He ran a hand through his hair. "Guess it worries me."

At least he was talking, though I had nothing but questions swirling around in my brain. "I don't understand why that of all things—"

"All three of us… hell, Gran knows about the spoons. She sneers at it, but she knows the concept."

"Go on."

Dylan's fingers laced at the back of his head as he pivoted away from me. "Mom will go to the very last drop of her energy. She'll be like a car sputtering on fumes. We never paid attention when Dad was alive because he'd step in. When it was just us, running out of spoons meant we had the house to ourselves until she was back on her feet. I-I didn't mind doing it, except it scared the shit out of me. It always came with this…" He made a fist in front of his waist.

"Anxiety?" I guessed.

His eyes pressed shut as he sighed. "Yeah. I hate when it happens. Feels like I fucked up, made her push too hard."

"Are you afraid I'll push Kick?"

Dylan paced away from me and spoke while staring at the back wall. "I need to know you protect her. Not just this bullshit with the investigation, but her health too." He turned around but spoke to the cigar boxes on the shelves. "This is new to me, man."

I stepped closer but studied the boxes too. I doubted Dylan had ever shared anything like this before. The weight of it hit me hard. "From what Kick's told me, she didn't want you to step in as the man of the house. She'd rather you stayed her kid."

Dylan dropped his head as his shoulders fell. I watched the facade crack. How much had the responsibility crushed him all these years?

"I've got her. You too if you need it." I reached out and touched his shoulder. "Focus on finishing school. On your future. On *you*, Dylan."

"Thanks." When he lifted his head, Dylan gave me a tight grin, but it was enough. His demeanor brightened with my promise. We could build on that.

I picked a cigar from the shelf. "I don't know about you, but I could use another beer."

He chuckled as he opened the door to the muggy room. "Same."

"Too rich for my blood. I fold." Dylan was the last man to toss his cards to the dealer, leaving the pot to me.

Damnit. I'd bluffed—went all in on a pair of threes because I wanted to go to the Perked Cup before it closed. What Dylan had said about protecting Kick's health—her energy—had stuck with me all evening. And damn if she hadn't looked spent when she left here. Except the kid had chicken-shitted on me. I'd been certain he had a pair of Jacks, thanks to the river.

Our night dragged on, with the table evenly matched. It had been entertaining too. Dylan's friends were mature for men with whole lives ahead of them. By the end of the evening, Banger and I concluded that Hank's "Dummy" schtick was just that.

Between the cigars, the drinks, and decent winnings, I was in the middle of a successful guy's night—an important thing when the host is your new love's son. Then I received a text from her bodyguard.

MATEO

Someone on your "no fly" list walked in.

I checked my watch as more text bubbles bounced. Ten minutes to closing.

MATEO

That Jonn Graham guy.

Damn.

ME

The kid??

MATEO

The dad.

Fuck.

IT'S MY LIFE

KICK

A familiar woman with a boy stepped up to the counter. Well, she did. He sat on the floor, kicking his feet. I wasn't a newbie to sleepy-time fits though. I snapped my fingers when her name matched up to her face in my mind's contact list. "Faye, right?"

"Hi, Mrs. Mack."

"Call me Kick please."

She dipped her chin. "Hi." The little boy howled.

I bent over the counter. "I remember you. You're Batman."

He tipped his head back and scowled at me. Faye grabbed his fist and shook it. "Nox, stop. We won't be long."

"Wanna. Go. Home." His lip stuck out in a pout that reminded me of little Liam.

I bit my lip to keep from laughing. "It's Nox, huh? What a cool name." He growled, and I bent farther over the counter. "Am I not supposed to say anything? You know because Batman's name is a secret."

Nox rolled his eyes at me. "That's Bawoos Wayne. I was pwee-tending."

"I see. Thank you for clearing that up." I smiled at his mom before glancing back down. As she swayed on her feet, I swear I felt her fatigue more than mine. It had been a while since I'd worked so late.

Jake walked over to us, and Faye's face lit up like a romance cover model had walked in. Then she turned bright red. He had that effect on a lot of our female customers.

Nox kicked the floor again, and Faye appeared ready to cry. She bit her lip, I presumed to keep from doing just that.

This time Jake peeked over the counter at him. "Hey, buddy. Can I get you something?"

"Not talking to strangers," Nox said to the floor tiles.

"That's enough, Mr. Man," Faye scolded. "When you're with me, it's okay to answer a question. No matter how tired we are, we can be polite. Besides, I'm almost done. Fall asleep in the car after this for all I care."

"What are you getting at this hour?" I asked Faye, afraid she needed dinner for them. We didn't have much left, but there might be something in the cooler for the next day. I raised my hand to clarify. "I didn't mean to sound judgy. Just being nosy. It's unusual to be graced with a mom and her handsome son at this hour. Do you work nights?" *Jayz*, I hoped she didn't have to. Faye appeared ready to drop.

Her hands fluttered around, like she'd forgotten why they'd entered. "Right. I'm out of beans for tomorrow morning and… it's a big day. I can't risk an upset stomach."

"I hear you," Jake said. "What size bag?"

"A pound. Ground please." She blushed again.

"On it."

I rang up her order and quietly asked, "You think Nox might like a chamomile tea with a touch of honey? It used to help my youngest when he was overtired."

His grumpy, high voice floated up from the floor. "No hot stuff."

I leaned over again. This kid's surliness cracked me up. "What if it came with milk in it?"

He blew a raspberry. "Boo cow milk."

"Allergy?" I asked Faye. She blew out a long breath and nodded. "You like almond milk?" I asked.

I waited for the answer and heard nothing.

Faye looked down. "She can't hear your head bobbing, son. Please stand up and use your words. One more time."

He slowly obeyed. "Yes, pweese."

I winked at him. "Coming right up, Mr. Man."

His mouth dropped open. "How did you know?"

This time I did laugh—a big, energy-building belly laugh. It was what I needed. "A birdie told me."

Faye smiled too.

"How about one for you? It helps after a long day."

"Sure. Thanks."

"My pleasure."

Nox crossed his arms on the counter and laid his head on them. As I worked on their to-go cups, I couldn't help noticing what a tight unit they were. Faye obviously made sure her son had as much as she could give him. Nothing expensive or flashy. But they were both dressed cute and trendy. Her floral puffer vest over a soft pink sweater was just the kind of funky and artsy that I liked. A part of me was proud of her for doing as well as she was.

However, the tiredness in Faye's eyes wouldn't let me go. Or maybe the memory of my years like that was too familiar.

I handed her the teas. "They're on the house."

"Again? Mrs.—Kick... you can't keep giving me drinks."

"I can, and I will. Have you called the functional medicine practice I told you about last time? It could really help."

Faye lifted her cup and stared at it a minute before blowing on the lid. "No. I'm sorry. I can barely afford an in-network doctor, not to mention a sitter for Nox."

I kept a stash of McKenna Family Foundation cards in a corner by the window for when I ran across customers like her. I quickly passed one over. "Call this place. They'll take care of the bills. You can even get a voucher for the drop-in daycare around the corner from the clinic. Please check it out. I swear, I know how you feel."

"McKenna Family Foundation? Aren't you a McKenna?"

"My late husband started the endowment after I met a woman with my same illness, only she couldn't afford the out-of-pocket treatments. She was a single mom, like you." I patted Faye's hand. "They'll take care of you."

She shrugged but pocketed the card. "The doctor said I'm just stressed."

"Of course you are. You don't feel well." I tapped the counter indignantly. Whether you called it a brush-off or gaslighting, it pissed me off. Jake passed her the bag of ground coffee. "Think about it. If you have questions, you know where I am. Or call the foundation. The staff is eager to help."

She gave Nox his tea, who took a sip through the straw. His eyes flashed wide with enthusiasm as he gave me a thumbs-up. The three of us laughed in relief at pleasing our tiny dictator.

"Thank you, Kick. I'll… be back if nothing else."

Jake waved at them. "Bye Nox and his pretty mama."

Faye blushed as they waved back at us.

"Look at you dancing and stuff at this late hour," Jake said.

I checked the clock over the door. It was late. I'd found a second wind from serving Faye. And from working with Jake. I'd forgotten how his enthusiasm to learn from me boosted my energy.

The door chime announced a new customer, and I adjusted

my glasses. What the hell was wrong with them? They had helped my fuzzy vision for a month or two, but I kept getting days where nothing seemed to work.

As the man approached the counter, my brows climbed onto my forehead. I took a step toward the emergency button as I tried to keep my poor poker face. "Hello, Big Jonn. Wh-what brings you in tonight?"

I glanced at Mateo. As usual, he tracked the three of us, me especially. It made me feel safe enough to hear the man out.

Jake moved to step between us even though a hefty counter already did the job. Mateo must have read Jake right because he moved from his perch in the corner of the dining room too.

"Hello, Mrs. McKenna." Big Jonn checked over his shoulder. "What's with the muscle?"

I wrinkled my nose. *Be honest, Kick. Be brave. No fear.* I nodded toward Mateo. "Thanks to men in your employ, I have a body-guard." I pointed to Jake. "My assistant here apprehended your son when he terrorized us. You'll have to forgive the fellas for being protective."

"Men in my employ? I don't understand." Big Jonn's hand moved over his bald head.

"Your nephew and one of your crewmen plotted to kidnap me two months ago." He had to know about this considering his nephew had lawyered-up with the Graham family's personal firm. My palms began to sweat even though they were suddenly ice cold.

He dropped his gaze contritely and slid a newspaper across the counter. "A peace offering."

The three of us examined the headline for tomorrow's edition of the *Oakville Weekly*. It read, LOCAL BUSINESSWOMAN REDEEMED. I scanned the article and looked up at him. "You vouched for me?"

"In the beginning, I thought the articles were filler for a slow news time." Big Jonn shoved his hands in the pockets of a company jacket. He gave off the impression of being just like any one of his guys until your eyes traveled down to the Ferragamo shoes. "That scene in December went way out of hand. So I asked around."

I tucked a curl behind my ear. My overwhelming need for answers made me take the bait. "What did you find out?"

He raised his shoulders without moving his hands. "Nothing. Whoever's behind it is good." He dipped his chin toward the paper. "This is my backup plan. Like I said before, we single-parent entrepreneurs should help each other out."

"Thank you, Big Jonn." I followed the caption to a photo with my finger. It was from the near riot at my café and Hugh's. It got me thinking. "Aren't you friends with tobacco board members?"

The corner of his mouth quirked. I wondered if he'd already caught on to my meaning. "Two members are my oldest friends, actually. I heard about your venture with Hugh Reynolds."

I closed my eyes and inhaled slowly. Hugh hadn't told me if he'd passed on the revised application yet. "Can you let them know they won? I pulled out as Hugh's partner."

"But Kick… I thought you were in the deal to fulfill a diversity request." He acted like I'd disappointed him.

"Hugh's new partner still meets their goal. Plus he's lined up a proper budtender once the license is approved. She'll oversee product acquisition and education while Hugh's new partner will run the business." Summer, the budtender, came courtesy of Thomas's vast connections. Both Hugh and I had conferenced with her. She'd spent years in the industry on the West Coast and was searching for more responsibility.

"I see." Big Jonn nodded as he scoffed. "And you're just, what… stepping out of it?"

"I am." For now. Big Jonn didn't need to know everything. "As long as Hugh gets to see his vision come to light, I don't mind that your misogynist friends won."

Big Jonn faked a head snap, as if my words had hit him. "That's harsh for a simple business policy."

I scoffed. "Is it *not* a boy's club over there?"

"The whole government complex is a boy's club, Mrs. McKenna. That's my point," he said with a sly smile.

I raised an eyebrow in question, and Big Jonn tapped the newspaper. "If you need a bailout from a small group of loud-mouths, how will you run with the big boys?"

I adjusted my glasses, wondering if my temper was fogging them. Then again, Big Jonn had a point. "Anybody can be targeted and accused of things they didn't do. If any board member had come to me, I would've eagerly cleared up their questions." I waved my hand to keep him from saying something worse. "No matter. It's done, and Hugh has a fine arrangement. That's what matters."

"You're truly altruistic," Big Jonn said, but he made it sound like a character flaw instead of a compliment.

"Thank you," I answered with a grin.

Jake sighed loudly. "Alright, Mr. Graham. You've made your hero play."

"Jake…" I elbowed him. To me Graham was neither fully dirty nor fully pure. But Oakville was my home. If his help made it possible to regain my status in the community, I'd take it. With a tight smile.

Big Jonn leaned toward me, and both my guards stepped closer. "The loyalty you inspire is admirable." He tapped the counter and turned to go.

Then I remembered the peeper again. "One more thing—"

Thomas burst through the door with Banger and Dylan on his heels.

Big Jonn stumbled backward like he'd been pushed. "What are y'all doing? Running in here like there's a fire."

Thomas glared as he answered. "I'm Kick's." Steam practically rushed out his nose. The protectiveness in his dark expression turned me on. Made my grin wider.

Big Jonn pointed two fingers at Thomas. "The cigar-smoking ex."

"Yes. And not anymore," Thomas answered with a steely coldness. He'd been serious when he said he'd "had enough of this shit."

"I see." Big Jonn's eyes traveled up and down Thomas, assessing. Then they shifted to me. "Interesting." He raised a hand and waved. "Nice talking to you, *Mrs. McKenna*." He stared straight at Thomas as he drew out my name, making my man's head snap back. Then they both glared. I wondered if they would grow horns and headbutt each other. Or maybe just piss on each other's nice shoes.

To break the tension and get an answer to my current burning question, I blurted out, "Is Young Jonn on his ankle monitor?"

Big Jonn's head whipped around to me, his brows cutting into a deep crease. "It's a condition of his parole."

The nonanswer didn't help, but something told me it was futile to press. "Your kind gesture regarding the article is much appreciated. One last thing… will you get your son some therapy?"

Instead of answering my plea, he rubbed his head and said, "You should mind your daughter. Teach her not to mess with a young boy's mind."

"That's it." Banger stepped forward, but Big Jonn sauntered around him.

He opened the door and said, "My kindness only goes so far, y'all." Then he winked at me and left.

"Why the hell didn't you throw him out? What were you thinking?" Dylan yelled, pitching a fit in my direction.

Since he came by his temper honestly, I didn't take it personally. What did surprise me was he'd turned to both Mateo and Jake, expecting answers from them too.

We'd closed up the coffeehouse, but all five men stood guard over the dining room as I quickly cleaned. Thomas stayed near me, helping with the machinery. He cleared his throat and did his jaw flexing thing, but I placed my hand on his chest to hold him back.

"Mateo and Jake did their jobs exactly as we required. You could tell Big Jonn knew better than to pull anything in their presence." I nodded toward Mateo. "Hell, he was the one packing."

Banger grunted. "Guys like him... it's not their character to get their hands dirty anyway."

"See?" I pointed at Banger with both my hands. "I still want those questions I have for his family answered. I had the advantage. So you bet your ass I took it."

Dylan stared at me, both his fists planted on his hips. Thomas cleared his throat again, this time annoying me.

I turned toward him. "I know how this goes. I've got it."

Thomas leaned down and whispered, "You don't know as much as you think. Give him a break."

My eyes swept back over my son. I saw his worried stress—from the planted feet to his quick breaths. *Shit*. Thomas understood my kid better than me. What the hell was that about? "Dylan...," I started. "The plan worked." I turned to my employees. "I assume one of you texted these guys."

Mateo nodded.

"See, lad? I was fine the whole time. In fact, it's been a good night overall." I showed him the newspaper. "Whatever his reasons for helping, Big Jonn seems confident his 'magic mojo' made the deranged articles and rumors go away. I call it a win."

Dylan ran his hand through his hair as his posture relaxed. "You're sure?"

"Some help here, someone?"

Mateo spoke up. "She wasn't in any danger. I bet he won't be back again."

I moved around the counter and stood in front of my son, looking up at his stubborn face. Jayz, I missed the days when I could pick him up and reassure him. "See? All this will end."

"Fuck all, Mom." He bent over me as I hugged my ornery son. He sniffed and said, "I can't be an orphan, okay?"

I answered, "Everyone is eventually."

At the same time, Thomas said, "You won't be."

His tone—and the jaw flex when his head turned my way— told me I'd be in more trouble when we were alone.

18

NEED YOU TONIGHT

KICK

I padded out of my bathroom, wearing only my robe as it floated around my legs. Thomas had already been in bed working on his laptop when I entered, heading straight to the bathroom. Already the key differences in our houses were making themselves clear. The biggest one being a need for him to have his own office space.

Our drive home had been tense. Being in no mood to fight, I walked straight to my office and finished the paperwork I'd planned to do at the coffeehouse after closing. Between Dylan and Thomas, I'd been eager to get out of there once we cleaned up.

I sat on the edge of my side of the bed, finally calm enough to listen. "Okay, let me have it."

Thomas shook his head without looking up, but he wasn't on his laptop anymore. Instead, he read a book, his hair falling enough to shade his eyes. I did a double take at the cover. He was reading a romance novel Cyndi had recently returned. I had left it on my nightstand instead of reshelving it in the bookcase.

I froze as a broad grin painted Thomas's face. It put me off since I expected a grumpy look. This was his middle school mischievous smirk.

"You think a man should act like this?" he asked.

My spine straightened in defense, knowing what he insinuated. "He's what some call an alpha male," I answered, biting my lip. Did he think I wanted him to behave like that character? *Jaysus*, I hoped not.

Thomas held up the book with his finger in his stopping spot. His eyes shone with incredulity. "You call *me* a man-child? This punk's temper is off the charts. He refuses to listen and... Christ, he takes her any and everywhere and lets his spunk just... what? Run down her leg in the middle of a cocktail party?" He pulled a face of disgust.

My head tipped back, laughing, as I thanked the universe we were, once again, on the same page. "Caught that, did you?"

"How could I not?"

"That's the fantasy part of the story."

He "pfffted" at my answer as I slid under the covers, chuckling.

Thomas rubbed his chin a moment. "Would you want me to handcuff you to the bed like he did? Because there are moments..."

Since my new bed was a sleigh bed style, the current chances were slim to none. I gave him my best innocent look, hoping to take his mind off our not-finished argument. "Silk ties sound comfier—"

He lifted a hand. "No, no. Handcuff you and leave you there while I run out to catch a bad guy."

I remembered the scene he referred to and raised an eyebrow. "I wasn't in danger tonight. If Jake and Mateo hadn't been there, I would've pressed the emergency button. Even though Big Jonn doesn't have a restraining order against him, I know he's on your 'bad man' list."

Thomas narrowed his eyes and flexed his jaw, letting me know he doubted my logic. To be honest, he was right, but I wouldn't admit it. Big Jonn ended up doing me a favor. Two, actually. Whatever his reason, I'd take them.

"Need I remind you that the heroine was thoroughly pissed, *and* the hero promised not to do it again."

Thomas folded his arms across his chest. "Still reads like he's measuring his dick to prove his manhood. That's a little-boy ego there."

"Alpha's not a real thing anyway." I leaned into him and brushed his hair off his forehead, treasuring the silky feel as it sifted through my fingers. "You missed the most important part of the story."

"What's that?"

"Our heroine owns her sexuality without apologies. You know, the earliest romances were influenced by society's rule that good girls don't and bad girls do. In the books, if a woman had sex outside of marriage, she was essentially date-raped and shocked when she discovered she liked it."

"You're kidding?"

"I wish. For way too many, it's true."

Thomas's eyes squeezed shut. "I hate that I ever bought into the patriarchy."

He'd never acted that way with me. Then again... Oh. "Did you?" I couldn't imagine him being violent with a woman.

His face crumpled like he might cry, but that wasn't Thomas's way. He owned all the parts of himself, even what he regretted. "I coerced Alicia after we were engaged." He sighed deep and sad. "She asked me not to, but the men in my life had told me the refusal was part of the game. They gave me ideas on what to say to convince her to give in."

I adjusted my glasses. "How long have you felt this way?"

He blushed like he was reliving intimate memories he didn't want to share. "There were clues while Alicia lived, but I didn't truly understand until I befriended a sex worker years later. In my second life."

I raised an eyebrow, intrigued. Thomas laughed at the face I made. He brought my hand to his lips and kissed my knuckles. "You know I said I'd never risk another woman's life." He shrugged, as if the gesture explained everything while it created a dozen more questions from me.

"Thomas…" I laced my fingers with his. "Alicia had to operate under the same idiocy as you, except in the opposite way. For all you know, she wanted to be with you but was brainwashed into thinking it would make her dishonorable. Lord knows I lived under a similar cloud, and it was the twentieth century."

His moue stayed grim, so I leaned over and kissed him. "I forgive you on Alicia's behalf." As weird as it sounded, it also felt like we were talking about a different person. Now I understood why Thomas and the Felidae people referred to having different lifetimes. He had been another kind of man back then.

Thomas pulled me into a hug and held on tight. "Thank you."

When we finally let go, I sighed and pointed to the book. "Anyhoo, this one is signed. It is nice to see the heroine's growth across the series. If you want to read about my favorite hero, I can lend you that one."

Thomas returned the paperback to the nightstand, slid down to rest his elbow on his pillow, and propped his head in his hand. I grabbed my e-reader, brought up the regency story, and slid it in front of him. Then I joined him, matching Thomas's position and tracing circles on his broad shoulders with my free hand.

"Tell me about it," he said, his voice like smooth whiskey to my ears.

"It flips tropes. The heroine's father beat her and the hero had to sell his body when he was young. Of course, they start their journey with a misunderstanding or two, but how else would they grow? Anyway, it was a beautiful navigation of the period, as far as I can guess. Not like I was there."

"What period is this?"

"It's regency, so… Georgian." I started, then it dawned on me. Thomas lived this time. I blushed as my fingers went to my mouth. "Whoa, shit."

His smile morphed from cocky to sadness. He cleared his throat. "Let me guess… the hero was the youngest son."

My eyebrow raised. "Yes. How did you know?"

Thomas shrugged. "As the third son, I was meant for the military from the time I was little. My second brother was supposed to inherit Mother's land. Then the war happened and my brother enlisted too. He was killed instead of me." He shook his head. "Since I became the second son, the land went to me after the war."

"I'd read that story," I said in awe. I could listen to him talk about his life for hours.

He absently stroked the tip of my ear as he pressed his lips together. "It didn't end well, Kick. The heroine died and left the hero bitter for a long damn time. Until you."

"Well, shit."

Thomas chuckled as he connected the dots running through my mind. This was worse than his masked iciness from our early days. I'd do anything for this Thomas, who was brave enough now to be vulnerable.

"My blood pressure spikes every time something happens to you. I'm terrified I can't protect you. That it's all wishful thinking."

I closed my eyes and let my forehead fall against his. "I should've texted you as soon as Graham arrived, especially since you were only across the parking lot. We could've worked through his 'peace offering' together. It was probably scarier coming from Mateo."

"Probably." He kissed my temple, letting me know we were

good. "There's more to it than tonight. As we do this day-to-day thing, I see farther down the road. I want you there with me."

"Me too," I breathed through a smile.

His expression turned to business, like it did each time we met with Banger to go over the investigation. "Something about the laws here have been niggling in the back of my mind since I had to take you to the emergency department. The hurdles I had to jump through then were hard enough, but what if you'd needed surgery?"

I opened my mouth to speak, but Thomas's warm hand settled on my shoulder to stop me.

"I want my attorney to draw up papers of Healthcare Power of Attorney for each of us."

I winced at the formality and shook my head.

"Without a marriage contract, if something happens, I have no say in your care and vice versa."

"Dylan has that now, to keep Bobby and her moods away from anything regarding my healthcare."

"Should he though?" Thomas asked. "I won't breach his confidence, but he needs this to help him let go too. You're mine, Kick. And I'm yours. What if it's me? Do you want to wait for Joe to drive down from Virginia?"

"It doesn't work that way... does it?" Did it? Hell, I didn't know. All I knew was how nice it had been to take each day as it came. I hoped we could do that... well, forever. "I'm in no hurry for any of this."

"Under normal circumstances, I'd say we have time." Thomas winked as his fingers wrapped around a curl. "Literally. But every time I get a text about you, my heart drops into my stomach. I can't keep my head when it happens."

I cupped his jaw with my hand and slid my thumb over the stubble. "Okay, I give." As hard as it had been for me to lose Shane, when the time came for us to part, I hoped Thomas would go first. I never wanted him to be left alone again.

19

FOREVER MAN

THOMAS

The following afternoon, I finally reached Alaric.

"*Allo,* Thomas. Everything alright with you?" The hesitancy in his voice told me Ellie had passed on my message, yet I wondered why he hadn't called back.

"*Oui, Grand-père.*" To keep my wits, I switched to English. "I'm fine. But there's important news."

"Oh? Have you found your mystery genes?"

I laughed at his simplification of my work since Alaric understood the intricacies of what I did. "It's coming along. No, I have a new test subject. She's younger than Toni, and the work pairs well. I only wish I could match this person's ancestry against the Felidae records. I haven't found anything in my files."

"Another woman?" he asked excitedly. "She's not from your family?"

It had been the first test I'd run. We all ended up cousins if we went back far enough. Kick's family history had been different from mine, but it would've been irresponsible to not verify it.

"No, although her ancestry's European. You still don't want me to consult with Nigel right? It's also why I didn't speak about it to Ellie first."

He gave me a firm French, *"Non."*

"Alright. Banger's running her background for me. It will take more time, but it's doable."

Grand-père chuckled. "You two picked well with your friendship. Like brothers."

I took a deep breath. *"Grand-père—"*

"Who is she?"

"Her name's Kick—"

"Keek?"

"Well, Kathleen McKenna. Kick is a nickname everyone uses. It fits her."

"I see."

"We're together. I couldn't be casual with her. You should know... we're living together. Blending our lives."

"You didn't think to say something?" I could picture the offended curiosity on *Grand-père's* face.

"She can manifest her aura. In fact, we can blend ours together, do... remarkable things with them."

There was a significant pause before he quietly said, "Edmund could do that."

Edmund had been Alaric's best friend, although the term didn't do their relationship justice. They'd been partners, brothers—even more—for centuries. Ellie had spent time as a wife to both men. Edmund had mysteriously died right after I joined the Felidae, so I hadn't known him well.

I swallowed hard, wondering if I'd just found Kick's connection. "I'll let Banger know." Edmund came from a Saxon kingdom, so I saw the possibilities.

"Sorry, my boy, Edmund's line died with him."

Damn. I still planned to tell Banger about it. Maybe it would give him ideas of where to look. My big fear had been finding out

Kick was descended from Nigel. Since Banger had mentioned a connection to the bartender and a phone number in Oxford, I'd wondered if Nigel had wanted to end his line. He wanted Felidae abilities kept to as few people as possible.

"To be clear, she knows about the Felidae. Banger and I have promised to protect her, including from any of us." I closed my eyes and braced.

"Why would you do this without consulting me first? I told you to find a companion. Have a good time. Not to tell a girl our secrets! What about your vows?" His words tumbled over each other angrily. A series of French curses followed, some of them old ones.

"My deepest apologies." What else could I say? There was a reason Kick and I had found each other. There had to be. The line went quiet, as if Alaric waited on my explanation.

"Like attracts like," I said. It was the most succinct explanation I knew.

He scoffed at my description, but I pushed on. "I didn't betray the Felidae, *Grand-père*. I wanted to tell you about her and seek your permission, but here we are. See, Kick's had abilities for years—sight is one of them, from what I can tell. Also... she figured it out. It took me by surprise."

Alaric grumbled over the line.

I changed tack. "What do you think will happen when my research produces real-world results? Unless you are like the others, the day is coming when we won't be able to keep our people a secret. Banger's work gets harder every year."

"So better to beg forgiveness than seek my permission. Is that it?" His petulant tone ground at my nerves.

"I told you I'd planned to tell you about Kick." Damn him. Was he even listening? Hell, it had taken several days to reach him.

"You were here last month. You could have said something then."

"She and I had problems then. We..." I sighed, remembering

why I'd broken it off with Kick, more like what had scared me enough to do so. "Before I left North Carolina, Joe finally told me why he left the Felidae. You hired him to assassinate Vivienne. That scared me shitless. How could you? I broke it off with Kick to protect her. She and I were over when I arrived last month." I absently rubbed my chest to calm my racing heart, lost in my thoughts, wondering how he could justify his past actions.

"I'll do anything to guard our secrets. Without each other, we'd be extinct. Don't you see that?" Alaric tried for a mollifying tone, but his anger seeped through.

"Don't you see how the world has changed?" I shot back. "What about the fact that Kick is probably one of us? Would you rather she walk around for years questioning her own existence like we did? Terrified of her life? Her friends and family?"

"The Felidae take priority over potential family, even blood," Alaric steadfastly insisted. "That's why we wait before considering someone new."

"We don't need to anymore. You're excited about my work with Toni, and she's not a hundred years old. If I can interpret her physiology, I can track Kick's. If we don't evolve our attitudes, we'll drive ourselves to extinction."

How I wished to be in his office. Having this conversation over the phone added another layer of frustration. "She won't betray us, Alaric. Are you so removed from your first life that you've lost hope? Because if you don't have hope, why am I doing this research? I reinvented my life for this, not only to answer all our whys but to make a difference for every person." I drew in a long breath to slow my heartbeat.

Alaric groaned in his own way. His voice dropped like he was also forcing himself to calm down. "Perhaps it's time to get away from the vineyard," he murmured.

"What do you mean?"

"Oh my boy." I heard squeaking and shuffling, like he was walking around his large office now. "Ellie and her people hold the opposite opinion. It's why I want you to send updates to me alone, instead of conferring with Nigel's team."

I ran a hand over my chin, watched a cardinal settle on a branch outside my window. "Then what's the point of Nigel's work? I don't understand this thinking."

He clicked his tongue and made a gallic grunt. "You're young in our world, but I didn't think you were naive. Knowledge is power. Eleanor has always been made to rule. She'd like to do it again."

"You know how futile that sounds, right?"

"Not to her and Nigel. You're a son of revolution, a man of the Enlightenment. In Ellie's first life? Science was *alchemy*."

The phone calls to Oxford poked at another question. "Did you know about Kick? Is someone tracking her? There's been—"

"You just mentioned her." Alaric scoffed. "I work fast but not *that* fast."

I told him of Banger's suspicions, just enough to feel out the situation for myself, but he insisted Kick's identity was new to him. "What about Nigel? Could he have someone on her? Like you did with Vivienne."

"I told you—"

"I know. You protect the family. Understand that my family has expanded. I'll protect them with everything *I* have."

The old man growled—a warning for me to remember my place.

The cardinal sang to its mate, sitting a few branches lower. I thought about the indigenous legend of the cardinals and the maiden and wondered what force on earth had brought me to my lonely woman. If only handsome birds had led me to her. *Like attracts like.* Could it be that simple?

I didn't want to trade thinly veiled threats and barbs with Alaric. I still loved and respected him even if I didn't approve of all his ways. He'd been family when I was lost. I'd never forget that.

He finally spoke. "My world was a dark and dangerous place. Life crushed the weak for the good of the village, whether it be a runt or a wayward son."

"My world was like that too, *Grand-père*. It's why I lost the mother of my children."

"Ach. *Oui*." Emotion filled Alaric's acknowledgment.

"We don't have to be so brutal anymore. We can be patient. Give a little extra to the weak until they stand on their own. You'd be shocked by how much they'll contribute. Especially when it comes to compassion."

"I hope you're right, Thomas."

2 0

JUST LIKE HEAVEN

KICK

"This last test isn't just improved, it's in ideal range. Excellent work." Dr. Chaddha shuffled her set of my lab work papers. "Congratulations, Kick. You're officially back in remission. Keep it up."

Thank the heavens. My last IV appointment had been four weeks prior. The food reintroduction was chugging along too. I still had problems with raw vegetables, so I took that category slowly.

I smiled at my video camera. "Thank you." My smile faded when she had no answers for why my glasses didn't want to work anymore. She told me to go back to the optometrist, but I doubted the prescription was the problem.

"Anything else?" she asked. Her eyes darted to the lower right-hand corner of her screen—the clock. We had ten minutes left, which included speaking with the lifestyle coach and ordering my supplements.

"As a matter of fact..." Thinking about supplements reminded me of a question I'd forgotten to write down. "Can you recommend a sleeping remedy… for nightmares? My dreams have become quite violent lately. Is there a mineral, herbal combination, or cannabis strain that helps with it?"

Dreams about my mystery man used to be my nighttime concern. Now that I knew I'd been channeling Thomas somehow, I thought the overnight upsets would go away. They had only morphed into another thing.

Dr. Chaddha recommended a mineral and an herbal remedy, but her philosophy had always been to take as little as possible. I appreciated that, given how much I still took to make it through a day.

"Meditation should have helped this too." She paged through her notes. "In our last appointment, you mentioned meditating daily. Are you still doing this?"

I sighed. "I am." And I was, though I had needed to shorten some sessions to keep up with my schedule. Self-care sometimes ran short to make time for Thomas, but that was self-care too.

"Try lengthening your sessions. Or try a different focus. I'll have Audra go over the clinic's recommendations."

It was like she read my mind and gently chastised me. "Okay. Thank you."

As I finished the tele-session and filed my papers, Thomas walked into my home office. I had taken the call at home to keep from causing a fuss about turning off the surveillance in my space at the Perked Cup. Some days it seemed like everyone I knew was waiting around for me to get shot. Hmm. Maybe their stress showed up in my dreams?

"You're having nightmares," he stated.

Well, hell. I bit my lip. "I am."

"You have Friday clear?"

This time his tone lifted like it was a question. "I do. To match your day off, in fact."

Thomas shoved his hands in his pockets. "We'll spend the

weekend at the farm. The fence should be finished for Macushla. Liam can drive over after school."

"Okay, but—"

"We're having a training session." He cut me off in a voice that brooked no argument. "See if Dylan's free too, though he mentioned working with a trainer at school."

Dylan had been. Working out helped him release pent-up emotions from his breakup. It also counteracted those long hours in front of his computer.

I blew out a breath and made a rumbling sound of frustration.

Thomas chuckled as he rounded my desk. "So stubborn." He bent down and kissed my temple. "Self-defense skills will clear your mind. That'll help your dreams more than any supplement."

I turned my head and glared, making that chuckle drop farther down into his belly. "You going to pout now?"

If that was all I had to do to feel that resonance, I'd glare at the man all day long. As it was, I'd probably end up frowning at him all weekend. At least his rumblings did fun things to my lady parts.

He took my hands and pulled me into a full-body embrace, making me relax faster than anything I'd learned on my call. "Congratulations on your remission. Let's celebrate tonight." He tilted his head and sighed. "Christ, woman, don't look at me like that right now."

I didn't realize I wore any particular expression. I blamed the chuckling and the thought of celebrating. I felt his reaction against my waist.

"Not until we have time to do something about it. We both have places to be," he murmured in my ear. "Dinner first. An actual date. Where do you want to go?"

How wonderful to focus on normal things.

. . .

THOMAS WHISTLED AT ME, THE SAME WAY HE HAD WHEN HE accompanied me to the holiday gala for Lord University. I entered the living room from my bedroom, wearing a dusty rose-colored velvet wrap dress that fell just below my knees. It paired perfectly with block-heeled Mary-Jane's in cognac. I hoped the color complemented the maroon lowlights my hair still rocked from the holidays. I had also found an online tutorial and learned how to put my hair in an easy, twisty updo. According to his face, I'd done well.

Thomas though… as much as I still loved his old-school suits, he rocked the hell out of the sexy professor image. He wore black flat-front trousers, a gray grandfather shirt, a black vest, and a gray tweed sport coat. We were doing a fancy date—for a provincial town anyway.

Thomas took my hand and had me do a spot turn. Then he dipped me and kissed the open space on my chest created by the V from the wrap.

"Damn, it's pinned," he whined.

I righted myself and laughed. "You're lucky I didn't tape it. No unwrapping until we get home. No flashing the restaurant staff either."

"KEEP IT UP AND THERE'LL BE NO WAITING TILL WE GET HOME," Thomas said in his delicious baritone, as we entered the restaurant and he removed my cape, his eyelids heavy with lust.

I didn't realize I had hummed when we entered the elegantly restored nineteenth-century mansion. It had been so long since I'd done something like this—usually for one of the kids' accomplishments—I'd forgotten how much fun each moment of the experience would be. The staff was especially good at creating a luxurious yet attentive atmosphere. I took mental notes on how we could adopt something similar at the Perked Cup.

When the host found our reservation, he gave me a soft smile. "I see madam has food allergies."

"That's right." I bit my lip and looked at Thomas.

"They asked when I made the reservation." He shrugged. "Figured you knew about the chef since you seem to know all the others."

"Uh—"

"No worries tonight, Mrs. Harrison," the host interjected. "Chef transformed the kitchen after his Celiac diagnosis. We've got you."

No shit? I let out the breath I didn't know I'd been holding. Could I actually relax in a high-end setting? Eat something more than a salad?

At the same time, I smirked at the name the host used and caught Thomas's stuttered step from the corner of my eye. I could swear he walked taller the rest of the way to our table.

"You haven't stopped smiling since we walked in," Thomas said as I bit into a delectable almond and date bread-ish appetizer that I'd received instead of the homemade country breads the other patrons received.

"It's nice to be seen instead of feeling like a pain in the ass." Seriously. Our server took the initiative and asked about my diet. After taking notes, he spoke to the chef and came back with a marked-up menu. The kitchen even offered to make a butter sauce to substitute for the spicy one they served with the filet. It sounded so amazing I went for it.

I closed my eyes as I swallowed the last bite of almond bread. "I feel like I'm floating." Why did so many other places make it so hard? *Because they were more interested in their recognition for unique recipes than service.* I answered my own question and vowed to do better with the coffeehouse.

Thomas pushed the basket holding his rolls aside. "You sure you're ready for a cocktail?"

"I am." I wiped a bit of honey butter off my fingers. "You're also usually better at the covert eye-dart-around-the-room thing."

He gave me a guilty smirk.

"What's riled you up?"

"New questions keep piling on before the old ones have answers." He brought my fingers to his lips and pressed a kiss to them. "I'm impatient."

I thought about his description of the hypothetical romance and understood. I also didn't have the heart to remind him my drugged drink had been nonalcoholic, and we were already drinking water. "As far as the cocktail goes, I'm sticking to one, and you're with me." I leaned in and said, "You can go upstairs with me to the bathroom when the time comes. If it'll make you feel better."

"Can I unpin your dress?"

I rolled my eyes. "Are you telling me all I need to do is flash my boobs at you and you'll relax?"

Thomas shot me his middle school smile.

I was still laughing when our drinks arrived.

A talented mixologist is a god in the hospitality industry. I stuck to one drink but was determined to make it count. I saw absinthe listed in the Elixir Alpestre on the cocktail menu and knew it was for me, although I requested a swap of one ingredient for a local gin that I knew for certain was gluten-free.

I took a sip of the delightfully tart art in liquid form and sighed. Thomas raised an eyebrow, making me laugh again. "Isn't it wonderful to feel normal?"

I held my glass to his for a toast, surprised when he said "*sláinte*" along with me—the Irish toast my family used. I tipped my head toward his drink. "Nice to see you keeping with your brand." Thomas chuckled from deep in his belly as he sipped his Old Fashioned. Anything to keep him at ease. Hell, I purposefully leaned toward him several times just to give him an eyeful. Anything for this man.

We were coming to the end of one of the best meals I'd ever enjoyed when both our phones pinged with a text. Then Thomas's rang.

"It's Banger." He put the phone to his ear. "What's happening?"

I swiped my phone and read the text. Someone had tried to break into Rachel and Isabella's apartment.

HAVE A LITTLE FAITH IN ME

THOMAS

"**K**ick with you?" Banger asked.

My gaze swept over her as she read her text. "Yep."

"Need you two to get to my condo ASAP. I'm driving Rachel and her roommate there now." His voice rasped like he was out of breath. "We're shutting this shit down."

I pictured spit flying out of Banger's mouth as he bit out his words. The unexplained tingle that kept dancing along my spine all evening now made sense, except the wrong McKenna had been in danger.

"On our way."

WHEN KICK STEPPED OUT OF MY CAMARO, RACHEL BOLTED straight into her arms. "I've got you. Mama's here," Kick murmured softly as she rubbed her daughter's back like she was an infant. Isabella stood to the side until Kick opened an arm and drew her in too.

Banger stalked over to me, reminding me of a blond version of the Hulk. If the women in front of us didn't motivate him, nothing would. I was ready to spit nails and struggling to keep my breathing smooth.

"I want you to tell me this was a college apartment prank, but you wouldn't have brought the girls here over a coincidence."

Banger pointed with his thumb toward his condo. "Inside."

Kick walked the girls into the house after kissing each one on top of her head—a feat for Rachel, given their height differences. That was the thing with my lady. The more the weight of the world pressed on her, the higher she rose to the occasion.

We hadn't even finished celebrating her new remission. Seeing her ease those girls simply by being there pissed me off to no end. Beneath her steely grace, Kick wasn't giving a thought to her own needs.

Banger addressed us as he walked toward his bar. "First off, it could've been worse. The girls handled the situation exactly as they should've. Be proud of them." He raised a glass. "I was pouring us each a tipple when you arrived. Should I add two more?"

Kick did a double take at Banger's use of Scot's slang. Tess was French, but Banger's father had been a notorious Scottish laird of old. After his father's death, my friend traveled the world for a century—a surefire way to stifle someone's original dialect. Like me, he held on to a precious few words connecting him to his roots. He only let them out in safe company.

She shook her head at the offer. "Water would be great though. Thank you."

I squeezed her knee, encouraged to hear her recovery had stayed on her mind. "I'll take whatever you're pouring. Thanks, man."

Everyone stayed quiet until Banger finished playing host. He sat on the end of a large, circular leather sofa filling most of his den. Rachel and Isabella were together in the middle, blindly staring at a muted Seinfeld rerun while Kick and I sat opposite Banger. I stretched my arm across the low back and tried to gather her into me to no avail. She gave me a small smile over her shoulder and shook her head. As cool as she played it, Kick's stiff posture told me she wanted to hurt someone too. I acquiesced by lightly rubbing her back, finding some way to remind her that she wasn't alone in this anymore.

Banger turned off the television and zeroed in on the girls. "Who wants to begin?" Both shook their heads. He sighed. "Fine. Jump in if you need to correct anything." They nodded. "Around eight o'clock this evening, Rachel and Bella were disturbed by a loud pounding on their door."

Kick opened her mouth, but Isabella spoke first. "A neighbor had let them in when he went out."

"Right," Banger continued. "My team found that point on our camera." He took a sip of Scotch. "We're looking for three young men."

"Jonn's friends," Rachel said, her voice hitching on an inhale. She took a long pull of her wine.

"Those geniuses did nothing to hide their identities." Banger pointed in Rachel's direction. "So Rachel gave a solid statement to the police."

"I didn't open the door," she clarified. "I saw them through the peephole, then called Angel Security and the police."

"They kept screaming at us, demanding we open the door… said horrible things to Rachel… threatened to take her to Jonn… other things too," Isabella told us in a faraway voice, her eyes focused on the television like she still watched the comedy in her mind.

"Bottom line… they took off when the sirens grew loud. Rachel and Bella are shaken but physically fine." He leveled the girls with a stern look. "They're staying here for the time being."

Banger raised his hand as they both shifted from their trancelike states. "No isn't an acceptable answer."

"You should move back home," Kick said. "Bella can come too."

"Mama—"

Banger smirked at me. It was small, so the women didn't catch it. It took me back to our predawn breakfast a few weeks ago when he told me to cut ties with Kick. I patted her shoulder. If it kept everyone safe to bring all the McKennas under one roof, I'd do it. But I'd take them to the farmhouse. My friend briefly rolled his gaze up to the ceiling.

I shrugged. *Yeah, I'm a goner. So what?* My eyes challenged back.

Banger's plans ended up making more sense. "Ladies... You still have school, and my condo is much closer. Why interrupt your routine more than necessary?" He addressed Kick. "We're just making them more secure. Besides, we don't want Rachel any closer to Jonn Graham."

Kick scrunched her nose. "Hmm. Good point." She finished her water, set the glass on a coaster, and finally settled into me.

"On that note," Banger added, "I'm also putting guards on Rachel and Bella."

Kick and I nodded as the girls exploded from their seats. They spoke over each other, complaining about privacy and inconvenience. Isabella, especially, didn't understand why she needed one.

"*Enough.* Sit down, girls." I jerked when Kick brought out her mom voice. "You know how I fought working with a bodyguard." She looked at me. "Having Mateo around has eased everyone's tension. The mood in the coffeehouse is even more relaxed. Plus there was an incident the other night that I *know* went in my favor because Mateo and Jake were there to back me up."

"But—"

Banger went over to Rachel, crouched in front of her, and

grabbed her hands. "Hear me on this… you've done nothing wrong."

"But—"

"Why won't the police do anything?" Isabella burst out. "One of those assholes waved a gun in front of the peephole and threatened to use it!"

The answer pained and frustrated me. I gnashed my teeth at the helpless feeling. It's why I was determined to make sure Kick could hold her own long enough to get away if she was ever attacked again.

Banger's eyes swept from me back to the girls. "Laws suck, little one." He squeezed Rachel's hands. "You've been doxxed." He turned his head toward us and said, "Jonn Graham's behind the online bullying. The proof's in my office."

Kick's body stiffened as she growled low in her throat. "Son of a bitch."

"Agreed." Banger continued speaking to Rachel. "You did everything right, but *no* isn't a word in that little fucker's vocabulary."

Rachel tucked her hair behind her ear, reminding me of her mother. "Maybe I should call him. Talk some sense into him."

"Absolutely not," both Kick and Banger said with equal authority.

My friend softened his voice and added, "Don't let him mess with your head. My people will keep you safe so you can finish the year. We'll snare the bastard before then."

Isabella crossed her arms, making white marks where her fingers clutched her biceps. "I don't know if you're the nicest, most protective guy on earth. Or the most terrifying."

"Good." Banger let the word hang in the air without explanation. His posture tightened as his gaze shifted between the girls.

Isabella flipped her bangs off her forehead. "I still don't understand why *I* need a guard."

"Once the bastards realize Rachel's untouchable, you'd be the easiest way to get to her."

Rachel smiled at the word *untouchable*, and Banger gave her the sweetest grin back. It took me by surprise. Guess he had a weakness in the McKenna family too.

"We don't want to intrude on your privacy though, Rafa." She patted his clasped hands, then laced her fingers in her lap.

I stared at Banger, trying not to show my surprise. Rachel knew about his real name? Tess probably told her about it when she'd visited, considering how quickly the two women had hit it off. *Except Banger didn't flinch or growl when she said it.* Then again, she hadn't called him Rafael.

"No worries." Banger moved to sit at Rachel's free side. "I'm leaving tomorrow, so you ladies won't invade anything."

"And you'll be gone until May? Come on." She rolled her eyes at him.

He rubbed his stubble as he laughed. "I have other places to stay when I'm in town." He spoke to me. "I'll be in Orlando for a few days first."

"Again?"

He went down there about once a quarter, but he'd already been last month. Banger nodded his head stoically, and I knew. I pressed my lips together and tried to express my sympathy without giving anything away.

Banger turned back to Rachel. "The guards assigned to you are good men. You'll have Siobhan at your beck and call as well. You won't miss me."

"Oh…" Rachel finished her wine and stared into the glass.

"I can still check on you when I'm in town, yeah?"

She nodded, then blushed as Banger laughed. "Come on, Bella. Let's get settled." Rachel stood, lacing her finger with Isabella's. "Mama, can you come up before you leave?"

"Sure, sweetheart," Kick said while texting someone.

"Who are you messaging?" I asked.

"Cyndi. I need her to set aside funds for the guards." She turned her head toward Banger. "You're billing the business, right?"

He and I both shook our heads in objection. Then a three-way stare-down ensued, each of us angling to foot the added expenses. I didn't know why Banger wanted to comp it. I was currently covering everything. Or I thought I had been.

He leaned toward us. "Need I remind you? Compounded interest. In case you didn't catch it the first time, it means more money than I can spend."

"We," I pressed.

Kick tapped her chest. "My. Daughter."

Banger made mistake number one and spoke to Kick as softly as he'd just been speaking to Rachel. "You have money, but you don't have our bank accounts. I know things have been tight."

She moved to stand, but I held her to me. "Come on, man." He was right but didn't understand her pride. It wasn't that bad either. Kick did fabulously with her finances, considering.

He raised his hand in surrender. "We'll do a three-way split."

When Kick went upstairs to help the girls settle in, Banger pulled me into his office. The dark, woody space reminded me of the one on the third floor of my house. The air was thick with the scent of old books, thanks to two walls of floor-to-ceiling shelves filled with first editions—and lightly of cigars. I did a double take at the bookcases. They were newly crammed full with volumes from his collection in France. *He'd moved everything out of the vineyard then.* This was the only room in Banger's home that didn't smell like the lemon cleaner his service used. We didn't allow just anybody into our sanctums, which said a lot about him having the girls use the condo as a safe house.

"Did you get through to him yet?"

There was no other him he could mean besides Alaric. "Yep.

He gave me a lead for you." My gaze traveled the room as I listened for the sound of feet prematurely padding down the stairs though this wouldn't take long. "The old man's alright. He was pissed but intrigued by Kick." I sighed heavily before dropping my notes onto his desk.

"We need to get to the bottom of this shit."

"Here's his take on both the Oxford team and Edmund's abilities." I pointed to the last bullet point. "Tell me you can get his DNA." The dark Chesterfield behind me beckoned, but I wouldn't get back up if I did. My head was tired of spinning so many damn plates.

Grand-père had said Edmund's descendants were gone, yet Banger had his own special detective skills. He tucked the folder into his bag on the floor. "I have an idea but need to speak with Tess first."

My shoulders dropped as I exhaled a tight breath. I jammed my fingers into my hips. "Can't tell you how much it'll help."

"No need. I see it." Banger handed me a folder in return. I didn't see him pull it out of the bag. "Kick's good for you, but worry isn't."

"Tell me about it." I perused the papers in my hands—bios of the new bodyguards for Rachel and Isabella.

"These fellas know the girls are together? They won't give them a hard time? It already happened to them on campus and just walking to a damn coffeehouse." I couldn't believe how horrible men had been to them when Kick relayed the events. Then I remembered some of the men I'd known over the years and wasn't surprised in the least.

"They're professionals." Banger folded his arms over his chest and leaned back in his chair, glaring up at me. "Don't act like I started this work yesterday."

"Shit." I hung my head and closed the folder. Part of me worried these men were like that alpha bastard from Kick's book. But this guy was also a security expert. "Can't help being protective." I held out my hand and squeezed it shut. "I hate the worried V Kick gets between her eyebrows. Had her relaxed and laughing all evening at the restaurant. It showed up again as soon as she received that text. She's more scared for Rachel than herself."

"Look at you in daddy mode." Banger teased me, though he kept his wry face.

"Whatever."

"Naw, brother." Banger waved his finger up and down in my direction. "This is a new visual. Told you they were sticky."

"Let it go, man…" My brows lowered. "Or we'll pivot to Rachel calling you Rafa."

EVERYWHERE

THOMAS

"*Y*ou have an excellent memory, Professor. Thanks to the state's Marriage Amendment, the rights for unmarried couples do 'suck,' as you say. For hetero couples too."

Dammit. I sat in my office at the farmhouse, speaking with my lawyer. "What should I do, Penn?"

His chuckle mocked me as it came through the line. "Either move or put a ring on it."

"What about the Healthcare Power of Attorney?"

"It'll help, but your lady, in particular, is vulnerable in other ways. A significant number of politicians in our general assembly don't like their neighbors living in sin, sir. I read the articles you mentioned too."

"Can't they just… mind their own business?"

The laugh grew louder. "Not when they have the power. You know how it is."

Unfortunately, I did.

"You've given me a lot to think about. Put a rush on those papers please. Thanks, Penn."

"My pleasure, Professor."

I ended the call and rubbed the back of my neck, trying to loosen it. *What did I want?*

I wanted—no needed—Kick by my side, whether I was right about her genes.

Was it too soon to ask her for more? We had been together officially for a little more than a month. I thought back to the morning. I had stayed up late working with Liam and turned off my alarm while still asleep. Then I found myself buried inside Kick before either of us had fully awakened.

"You sure you don't mind?" I'd asked her.

"Mm-hmm," Kick said in a sexy, sleepy tone. "I don't know why, but when you want, I want. There's no question, only instinct. And trust. It's never been this intense before. Of course, I've been alone a long fecking time."

Her words made me gasp. I'd known exactly what she'd meant. We'd been alone for so long, and yet we'd bonded very fast. After she'd been worried about whether I'd judge her body for what Kick viewed as flaws... I hadn't seen her doubt herself, or me, since. Getting to be the recipient of her ownership of her sexuality was a privilege that left me speechless. In awe. Kick told me she admired the one heroine for the character's growth, but I'd witnessed no one taking their life by the reins like Kick. The defamation campaign against her had always been personal, still she stood up to the ridiculousness, especially with our relationship.

How I desired to be a better man. It was a gift to unwrap her every night and make her smile. Watch her come undone for me alone. I adjusted my pants as I thought back to her giggle afterward and how she sang to me, changing the words to the Beatles' "Norwegian Wood" into "Mmm, morning wood."

I knew what I needed to do.

Before I could take the first step, Banger's voice boomed through my house. "Hey brother! You home?"

"Third floor," I yelled back. "You're back fast."

He sauntered up the last few stairs. "Private jet," he answered, beelining for the bar on the far wall. He surprised me by bending down to the little fridge and grabbing a water instead of pouring himself a whiskey.

He plopped into the corner chair, his face drawn, contemplative.

"The other night…," I started, "sounded like you're losing another girl."

Banger twisted the top off and chugged half the bottle. "She was in hospice."

"Weren't you there last month? Seems quick."

He set his ankle on his knee, like the relaxed posture meant he wasn't hurting. "It was nice to comfort her through it, yeah? Everyone she's ever had passed first. Was an honor to be there for her."

"Wow."

Even a man like Banger, who put solitude before emotions, needed connection every so often. He made peace with the fact he would always outlive his special companions centuries ago, like all the Felidae did. Usually he gave them a few months, occasionally a year, then he'd disappear.

Lately, he'd find one here or there, in her old age, thanks to the population living longer and better. The way memory played with their advanced minds, the former girlfriends often recognized him since Banger's features stayed the same as when they'd been together. He found a certain peace in being able to say goodbye in his own way. My hard-as-nails best friend had a soft center, though I'd never tell.

"I'm sorry, man."

Banger swiped his hand across his body. "Don't care if I sound like a heartless bastard in this. She had a beautiful life, brother. A lot of love and living. In my book, that's cause for gratitude, not sorrow. I just brought her some comfort at the end."

While stewing in the meaning of his words, Banger stood and handed me a folder. "Tess turned out to be a gold mine for Edmund's DNA samples."

I slid out the paperwork detailing his profile. I couldn't wait to run it against Kick's after hours. Gautam would have no problem putting in the extra time. He loved this stuff too. Plus he'd signed a nondisclosure agreement. After the near debacle with Presley, we had them all updated. Gautam would swoon over these profiles. In fact, it wouldn't hurt to also run it against my cache of current Felidae members to study how much had changed since Edmund's time. I jotted down a quick note to the effect.

"How'd Tess manage it?"

Banger pulled a chair closer to me and sat. He ran a hand over his cropped hair. "He'd been like a father to her, yeah? A thousand times better than the trash who raised her."

I nodded along since I knew this.

"Plus she loves her memories. Tess had hats, gloves, a hairbrush, even a razor of Edmund's, for Pete's sake. She kept envelopes from letters he'd written to her." He groaned and slumped in the chair. "She loved playing spy for me. Even paid off the lab like I told her to. Now I think she misses us again. Thanks for that."

"Stop it. It was your suggestion. You know she's searching for a purpose. Maybe she's trying to fit into your life. Better late than never."

Banger clicked his tongue. "For how long?"

"As long as she can handle it, I guess," I answered with a shrug. It was harsh but true. No sense sprinkling sugar on it when Banger would've called me on the bullshit.

"Precisely." Banger hated how Tess had been an inconsistent presence. In fact, this was one of the rare times she'd come through for her son when he'd asked for a favor. It usually went the other way around.

I leveled him with a sly smirk. "You know, she could stay with the girls."

He pointed at me, grinning. "Now there's some good news."

23

DREAMS

KICK

February flew by. There's no other way to put it, other than life became sort of normal. Big Jonn Graham came through with his article in the town paper. The opinion pieces and social media slander stopped. Business picked up. More high school kids studied at the Perked Cup in the afternoons.

More importantly, putting guards on Rachel and Isabella relieved the pressure on them and me. I felt terrible for Bella taking on more than most would for a budding relationship, but she handled it like a champ. The girls also loved playing house in Banger's condo. It might have been the consummate bachelor pad, but it also oozed luxury and came with a cleaning service.

I hadn't seen or heard from Banger since the night he'd installed my daughter in his home, but I could tell Thomas spoke with him regularly. However, my man had been spending many late nights working in his lab. When we did find precious time together, we didn't talk about his friend or whether he'd made progress. I figured if Banger wanted me to know something, he'd make sure Thomas passed it on.

As March approached, I planned a romantic surprise for Thomas. We'd made our commitment to each other two months ago, but it seemed like much longer. I blamed some of that on how crazy life had been. Mostly, I think it came down to how well we clicked once we let ourselves get over our baggage.

The open-mic night would be the perfect time to do something romantic for Thomas. Liam's band planned a short set at the end. The kids were graciously going to let me jump on stage and sing one of my favorite songs to Thomas.

A smile burst across my face as I double-checked every corner of the coffeehouse. It looked perfect. Setup had been a breeze. The crew all showed and pitched in. In fact, I'd been waiting for the other shoe to drop, as it usually did. I guessed life could go your way sometimes.

There was one small snafu. Jacklyn, one of Liam's best friends and a bandmate, arrived late, making it hard for Metaphorical Chemistry to get in a warm-up. Her deep frown and the way she kept biting her lip were familiar for the girl I'd known since she'd been four. For most of their lives, Lee and Jax had been each other's person. After Shane died, I learned her father had allowed their mixed-gender friendship because of my late husband. Alton Moore enjoyed being able to rub elbows with a football Hall of Fame player. Ever the patient celebrity, Shane accommodated the man as much as he could. Plus our whole family adored Jax.

In Alton's eyes, Liam became a bad influence overnight when Shane died and our family was a single-parent household. Over the years, I'd bent over backward to appease the Moores, but nothing helped. Then my father opened a smoke shop with Hugh. I supposed rumors about my family's morals were floating around all the way back then.

"What's the matter, sweetie?" My instincts had me moving out from behind the counter to fix what I presumed had been another fight with her parents over the band.

Liam intercepted her before I could round the snack display, and I made myself stop. Jacklyn would turn eighteen in the spring, and Lee already was. They needed room to sort this out on their own. After five minutes of animated conversation near the walk-in cooler, he stormed over to me anyway, his face beet red.

"What happened?" I asked.

Liam did his best to keep his voice down and ended up growling in my ear. "Mrs. Moore saw the sheet music for our opening song. She forbids Jax from singing it."

I ran through the song list in my head. "She has a problem with 'Keep on Loving You'?" If anyone should appreciate that song, it was her, considering how many times she took back her philandering husband.

Liam scoffed. "It's because we're doing the arrangement by Cigarettes After Sex. Their name was at the top of the note sheet."

"JaysusMaryandJoseph." I lifted my eyes up to the ceiling. "When will that woman learn there's never been a way to make someone sin-proof?"

"Sounded like she's afraid of Mr. Moore finding out." He threw his hands in the air. Liam knew better than to run them through his hair. It turned into a wild, fuzzy mop when he did, thanks to inheriting my curls. "At first we planned to do 'Apologize.' You remember the arrangement you showed me by Kacey Musgraves?"

I nodded. "And…"

"Mr. Moore said it's never too late to apologize. Our harmony was big too."

"Why am I not surprised?" I muttered. I'd tried my best not to speak badly of the Moores. The couple seemed perfectly qualified to dig their own graves where the kids were concerned. This night, I neared my breaking point with their ways.

"I don't know what to do now. Jax is depressed, and we don't have an extensive list for her."

I adjusted my glasses and leaned closer. "Actually depressed? Or is this another of your Liam-isms? Because if she needs to talk with someone—"

Liam made to stick his hands in his hair, but I tapped them away. The kid was truly upset. "She's fine, fam."

To be extra certain, I said, "Like *big* fine?"

He rolled his eyes. "Sure." Then he cracked a smile while shaking his head.

I snapped my fingers. "I know, why don't you do 'Maybe I'm Amazed'? She sounded just like Jem when I heard you practice. It was beautiful."

"Well… I don't know." He bobbed his head once in decision and pecked my cheek before I could argue my case. "Thanks. We got it."

"Oh, okay." I forced a quick hug on him. I couldn't help it. It was one of those moments of parental pride where you pause and notice your kid's growing up. "When you get home, print out the REO Speedwagon arrangement—or at least cut and paste it. They're just notes for Pete's sake."

He laughed back. "No kidding. You still have the third song?"

"Yup. Can't wait."

"Me either." He gave me a cheesy grin, an echo of his little-boy self, then bounded off to confer with the band.

As I prepped a tray of drinks for Thomas to take to the band, my friend—and go-to for any construction needs—Charley Rodriguez stepped up to the counter. "You made it." This would be her first time hearing Metaphorical Chemistry. "Give me a minute to finish, and I'll hug you."

"I've got this," Thomas said in his sexy baritone, taking the last cup from my hand. "Go catch up. Good to see you, Charley." He slapped me on my ass, and I gave him some side-eye, along with a smirk. Then I reached across the bar to hug Charley.

"Glad you could get away. I've missed you."

"Yeah," she sighed. "Work's been centered on Durham, thanks to the growth in restaurants. Two extensive projects out this way will start in the spring. Hopefully I'll be able to stop by more often."

"Your usual?"

Her head shook a crisp no. "Decaf, hon. I'm still wired from the day."

"Sure thing." I made her drink and set it on the counter. "I can tell your team's been jumping. Three different groups have come by since the New Year to see your handiwork in person."

Charley scrunched her face. "I hope you don't mind."

"Not at all. They obviously like seeing two different projects in the same shopping center." After she'd done a fantastic job on the Perked Cup, my dad and Hugh had hired Charley to remodel the smoke shop.

She let out an exhale of relief. "Probably. Thanks anyway."

"Anytime. Are you staying long?"

"Not sure. Like I said, it was a long day."

Deana cut off our conversation when she stepped on stage and introduced the first act. I don't know why she'd insisted on coming back for this open-mic night, but she had. Then she wanted to emcee the thing and reminded me how I promised to delegate responsibilities. Her version of an "offer I couldn't refuse," I suppose.

The night's sign-up sheet was short, so it didn't take long before it was time for Metaphorical Chemistry to play. Their first two songs were fantastic. They improved every time they played. Jax was featured in the first song. Then she and Liam performed an original duet for the second. My heart pounded when Lee called me up for the third song.

"You're singing?" Thomas asked. He stood with me at the counter, talking to Charley and listening to Liam's band.

"Surprise! It's kind of a present to mark two months together."

"Lucky me." He kissed me hard for luck and patted my ass again. "Break a leg, baby."

I sang "Dreams" by the Cranberries. The only one surprised was Thomas. I'd been listening to the song at least once a day since we'd decided to be more. It even became an earworm for Liam, who practiced it to appease me. To me, it summed up how my heart had changed since meeting Thomas.

After the song, I gave hugs around the band for letting me crash their gig. The kids were improving so quickly my heart swelled with pride for each of them. Thomas greeted me at the bottom of the stage step. He kissed me on the cheek, then hopped up on the platform himself.

"Where are you going?" I'd expected more emotion after pouring my heart out in a song.

The jerk winked at me. "I have a surprise back."

"You're not... Oh good Lord." It took restraint not to make the sign of the cross. Thomas was amazing at many, many things, but his beautiful speaking voice disappeared when he tried to sing. The man couldn't carry a tune in a basket. Shaking my head as I backed up, I quipped, "Please tell me you're using Autotune."

"Faith, lady." Thomas put his hands to his heart, feigning offense. Then he high-fived the band while Liam introduced their new guest. My eyes watered when Lee introduced him as his new fam.

Jacklyn opened the song with a perfect Jamaican accent. Though she'd occasionally say things with her grandmother's inflections, it took me by surprise. It was good to see her enjoy herself after starting the night frustrated. I should've recognized the song immediately. We played it in the café enough. Shock was my only defense.

Then Thomas broke out in a spirited—if not-quite-on-key—rendition of "Say Hey (I Love You)." The music flowed through me more than it had when I sang my song. I stayed up front, dancing for my man as he spoke-sang about his love for me. His handsome face kept blurring, and it had nothing to do with my glasses. It was a fearless declaration of his love for me and the life we were making. He knew exactly what would get me.

His hand suddenly took up my field of vision. I put mine into it, and Thomas pulled me up on stage with him. I let loose and shook my arse for him like a go-go dancer. A few taps on my shoulder and his eyebrow lifted as he sang. I remembered the song was essentially a duet. The stinker wanted me to join in. Jax fed me the first couple of words, clearing my head. Then she shoved her phone in my hand, open to an app with the words and music. My part was a mix of call and echo. We shared the mic, dancing and pseudo-singing like a funky reggae version of Sonny and Cher but with height and curls.

Under the lights, the audience fell away, and we were just jamming with the band. Thomas spun me into a dip and planted a deep kiss on my mouth. A dull roar filled my ears, but the audience didn't become a reality until I heard, "Eww gross! Kissing is yucky!" I knew that voice anywhere, except the last time he'd said those words it was several octaves higher.

Thomas stood me up, and my eyes found Dylan. He'd brought his poker crowd with him. In fact, the place was now packed to standing-room only. My first thought went to fire codes, but it was a moment to celebrate love. Thomas and I had given each other the same surprise. How cool was that? Most of the audience would probably grab a drink and take off in a few minutes anyway.

I turned around and found that the band had rearranged itself around two chairs in the middle of the stage. Each chair had a low mic stand. Thomas took one and waved me over to sit in the other. He grabbed his guitar, and I couldn't believe he'd snuck that in too. Seriously. I was supposed to be the woman who noticed everything.

I sat as Thomas strummed the opening chords to the song he played for me over New Year's and many times since. It was the acoustic version of "Maybe I'm Amazed." So this was why Liam looked at me funny when I suggested it. I waited for him and Jax to start after Thomas's intro, but no one did. After swiveling my head around, I saw the whole band had left the stage. It was just Thomas, me, and his guitar. He stopped and gave me one of his smoldering eyebrow raises.

I pointed to my chest. "Me?"

He nodded.

"Like Jem?" I mouthed.

He nodded again, with a little, impatient smirk. He dramatically restarted the song. His face told the audience I needed to get with the program. The guests up front laughed.

I heard an encouraging, feminine "You've got this, Mama" from the back.

Was Rachel here?

I searched for her but couldn't see past the first tables with the lights fixed on us. This time I caught my cue and started the song. It meant a lot when we'd discovered we both loved this version over that weekend. Since then so much had happened, it was easy to forget how romantic it all had been.

Like before, I sang the song as if it was written for a female. So, when I got the part where I would replace *man* with *girl*, Thomas stopped and shook his head. It was my turn for the eyebrow raise, trying to communicate my question telepathically. He huffed and pointed to himself. *Oh.* He didn't want his voice to flatten the song, but he wanted me to understand the song was coming from him. I nodded my understanding, and he resumed.

A single tear teetered on the edge of my lower lid as the

words filled me like they truly were the words of his heart, telling me how much it meant for him to find me after being alone for so long. I knew what he meant.

The interruption.

The angst.

The fear.

The awe.

Joy.

As soon as he finished, Thomas quickly returned the guitar to its stand and dropped to one knee in front of me. The gasp from the crowd filled my ears before I registered what he was doing. Deana let out a shriek, but I couldn't see her. It was like a weird dream where I could hear my loved ones but I could only see Thomas.

He took my hand to bring my focus back to him. Thomas had a velvet box in his free hand.

I leaned into him, out of range of the mic I'd sung into, my performance smile plastered on my face. "What the hell are you doing?"

"What the hell does it look like I'm doing?" he answered, his wide grin a challenge to my dumb question.

"Something I thought you didn't want," I snipped back through a frozen smile, my eyes wide. The last thing I wanted to do was to embarrass him before the crowd.

"Do you trust me?"

"What?"

"Answer the question. Do you trust me?"

"With every fiber of me."

"Then trust me now."

"Louder!" A discombobulated voice cried out.

"Yeah, we can't hear!"

"The crowd's getting restless," I said while doing my best impersonation of a ventriloquist.

"Then dial back the sarcasm and listen."

I shimmied my shoulders and settled into the chair to give Thomas my attention. The struggle was real. A proposal was the last thing I expected from him, given we'd already said we'd take things one day at a time. How could I not give him my full attention, though, when his navy eyes filled with emotion? His cheek twitched slightly from nerves.

This man, in a fitted, overdyed navy button-down and ass-hugging black denim jeans. This man with his statuesque face and body. This man who could do anything with competence—he'd even won over the crowd with his awful singing voice because it was all heart. This man had become my world. Thomas made it okay for me to let go of my baby birds.

And he loved me.

"Kathleen McKenna, in the briefest of time, you've become my heart and soul."

A collective "Awe" filled the room.

"The afternoon at the oak tree, I vowed to be your Atlas, and you promised to be my home."

I opened my mouth to tell Thomas I remembered it all, which was why this seemed so redundant. His mastery of a professor-ly glare reared its head. I clamped my jaw shut, put the smile back on and waited for him to continue.

"You're already my wife in my heart. You've done that for me and much more these past weeks. Nothing about our pledge has lessened. It's only grown." He looked up at the ceiling, a shaky breath filling his lungs. "You told me once you needed an extraordinary, transforming love. My lady, you have transformed me. You're *my* extraordinary. Trust me, Kick, and take this last leap with me. Let's make our day-to-day official. Let's take it all the way."

"You really want this?" I asked, bending to his ear again.

"I do."

What do you say when the man of your dreams just told you he remembers the deepest desires of your soul, and he treasures them? You give him whatever he wants. A peace swept through me, and I knew if Thomas thought it was best, I could trust it.

"Can we keep it a small ceremony?"

"Anything for you."

My frozen grin became real and spread across my face. "Yes, Thomas. I've pledged myself to you already, why not make it official? Now show me this ring."

The crowd roared, and Thomas flipped the top on the ring box. He'd been so nervous he'd forgotten to open it.

"Ho…ly shit!" I bellowed at first sight of the work of art. The cheers turned to laughter. Thomas placed the most beautiful symbol of our commitment on my finger. The word *ring* didn't do it justice.

A rose-gold setting was sculpted into tiny vines circling my finger. At the top, a purple stone sat in what looked like a bed of leaves. Smaller leaves peaked around the vines at the sides, without poking into my skin. Sapphires were set in the center vine, in varying shades of blue. I stared at it as Thomas gently took my hand and slid the ring on my finger. The huge gem shifted color as I moved my hand. Something about it seemed familiar, like it was me in ring form or his vision of me. Then it hit me… it was us.

I gasped. "It's our—"

He leaned toward my ear and said "Energy. Yes, baby. It's my forever attraction to you, wrapping myself around you as you glow."

At a loss for words, I cradled his jaw in my hands. I pulled him in for a kiss. He tasted faintly of cigar, making me wonder if he'd needed it earlier to settle his nerves. This had been a ballsy risk, considering I'd said I was done with the marriage label.

Our kiss deepened into one so big, so hard it was a miracle our auras didn't release. Boy, did it try. It prickled until we pulled away before we had serious explaining to do. Thomas's hands fell to the seat on either side of my thighs, his forehead landing on mine, as he laughed. Take that back, he roared with joy. Then came more cheers, whistles, and catcalls from the crowd, our extended family. Then he stood and lifted me up and off my feet in a bear hug.

"Office. Now," Thomas growled. He grabbed my hand and dashed us off the stage.

24

THE NEARNESS OF YOU

THOMAS

I'd done the right thing. A pressure valve that had begun building in me over Kick's safety was released when she accepted my proposal. It turned out I wasn't the modern man I thought I was. I needed Kick to be my legal kin, and it had to happen before I found the results of her DNA analysis. For my sake more than hers. If I had to take care of her fragile, aging body the way Banger occasionally did for his former girlfriends, I'd do it with joy. It would be an honor.

We were swarmed by the crowd in the Perked Cup, small as it was. It took ten minutes to make our way from the stage to the counter to get drinks. Loved ones and strangers alike—who came for the Open Mic Night—stood in a reception line to give us hugs and congratulations.

When an opening to the back hall was made, I took advantage, pulling my new fiancée with me. Banger's profile caught my eye as he spoke to Deana and her husband. Damn him for arriving so late he almost missed it. Despite his recent travels, he'd promised to be here for the proposal. Securing his support in all of this had meant more than I could express.

The part I hadn't considered? The downside to a public proposal? The part that was drastically different from the first time we promised to be together?

I didn't factor in how horny I'd be.

We were real, not a fling or a hidden affair.

Real.

Kick.

My woman.

She wore my fucking ring. I needed to celebrate inside her. I had to unwrap her, tear away her pretty, satin-and-lace bra—knowing she'd fuss at the waste—and make her orgasm all night. I hoped the office cameras were off. I opened the door, spun us around, and lifted her up against the wall. The slit to her skirt fell away for me, rising to her waist, letting me rub against the satin of her underwear. My hand holding her steady touched the wetness in the material, causing a growl of desire from us both.

Kick batted at my hands, but her eyes held no anger, only teasing. "I should stop you. Make you suffer." She panted.

"Me? For what? Outside of blowing your mind with a fabulous proposal?" I asked between kisses I peppered down her neck.

"You stole my thunder. I poured my heart out in song, and you upstaged me." Her writhing in my hands told me I wasn't in trouble. Yet I felt bad. *A little.*

I smiled against her neck. "The ring makes up for it, doesn't it?"

She gasped as my fingers found her sweet spot, letting me know I was right.

My free hand sought the bow of her sweater. I needed more arms, dammit. With my present unwrapped, I kissed Kick down her chest. My free hand reached around to her bra hooks. There were too many. Damn, these long-line things.

"I loved your song," I said as I worked the tormenting clasps. "Especially the banshee notes in the middle. Sounded beautiful. You should do it again, in fact. Encourage my efforts."

She let go of my shoulder to slap it, both mischief and lust filling her woodland eyes. "Nitwit."

Giving up on the hooks, I lifted a breast from its cup. My lips ached to suckle it, but I paused and teased. "Are you saying you didn't like my surprise? Do we need to talk more?"

Kick nearly wiggled out of my hands from her writhing. I pressed my hips and thighs into her, making sure she didn't slip. Her groan grew louder with the friction. "You know you won the night. Shut up and kiss me."

My primal brain became a caveman who needed to conquer. "Where?"

"Ahem-mm." The clearing of Banger's throat jolted me back to reality. I righted Kick and shielded her body from our intruder.

"What the hell, man?" I growled. "You almost caught us *in flagrante*."

"You were *in flagrante*, my dear," a familiar feminine voice said from behind Banger. I caught the smile in her inflection. "Fortunately, you were not *delicto*. Not yet." Tess stepped out from around her son, her arms wide. "Congratulations, kids."

"We knocked." Banger had the decency to appear repentant as he rubbed his jaw. "Guess you didn't hear it."

"Tess," I said, more in shock than greeting. Kick's frantic movements to turn and fix herself while squeaking at being caught snapped me out of my stupor. I stepped toward our visitors and hugged Tess, keeping my body between our company and my fiancée. "Heard you were thinking about visiting again."

"Surprise." Banger spread his hands wide like it answered everything. Considering he had Tess with him, it did.

"Tess texted me just before she boarded the plane. We came straight from the airport."

"Hel-lo-o." Tess flicked her hand. "Stop talking about me as if

I'm not in the room. You boys know it's a pet peeve." Her French accent on that last word made it sound like *piv*. Like a pin bursting my pent-up energy, I snickered. Then I bent over and dissolved into an uncontrollable fit as my emotions crashed in the ridiculousness of the moment.

Banger and Tess stared at me like I was an unruly child. Kick's hand ran down my back, soothing the last of my nerves as the laughter settled down. I threw my arm around her, pulled her in, and kissed her temple.

She looked up at me, blinking. "Did you get it all out, cowboy?"

I nodded, not trusting myself to speak yet.

"Cowboy?" Tess asked. A gleam in her eye said *aren't you two cute* as she studied us.

I grunted as Kick scoffed and stepped toward them. She gave Tess a warm hug, saying, "A lot's happened since we met."

"So I've heard." Tess kissed Kick's cheeks in greeting, then held her at arm's length, her eyes traveling over every inch like a new mother making sure their newborn was healthy. "Rafa tells me you're one of us."

"The fuck, Tess?" Banger rubbed the top of his head. "I told you—"

"Thomas is running tests. I know." She tilted her head and smiled. "He's right."

Tess hugged Kick again and whispered something in her ear that elicited a smile.

Since the celebration time with my lady had been crashed, I turned on the desk lamp. We needed more light than the streetlight shining in through the windows could supply.

"So everyone is telling everyone everything." Tess glanced over her shoulder at her son. "How efficient," she added with a devious smile in place.

"The secrets need to stop," Banger said, his words tinged with a defensive tone.

I moved to shut the door and almost bumped into Charley.

"Sorry, guys. I've been waiting out front with Deana, but she thought it would be alright since you weren't alone." Charley turned to Kick, who had crossed the space to greet her. "I have to leave. Early morning and all."

"Absolutely. Thanks so much for coming," Kick said while giving Charley a hug. She laughed and pulled back. "Who knew it would be so exciting?"

As Charley laughed in agreement, Tess stepped from Banger's shadow and made one of her distinctive French sounds.

"Teresa?" Charley's face twisted with confusion. "Is that you?"

Tess paled as she breathed, "Carlotta?" Her eyes widened like she'd seen a ghost.

These women knew each other? The tension in Kick's office thickened like an epoxy had filled the space. Tess and Charley practically vibrated with emotion.

"It's Charley now." Kick's friend's demeanor shifted before our eyes. The warm smile she'd given us transformed into the cold steel of the construction worker I'd first met. Now I wondered if there were other reasons she possessed this ability.

Tess's delicate, charming manner crumbled before my eyes. "But of course," she stammered. "I-I didn't know..." Her gaze darted around the room as if trying to figure out where Charley fit in.

We all ended up staring at Banger.

I cleared my throat. "You mentioned investigating..." I tipped my head toward Charley.

He moved to Tess and put his arm around her shoulders, causing me to do a double take. "Yeah. I uh... wanted to speak with Tess first."

Shit. My eyes couldn't stop shifting between the two women. They were in pain. Old pain... which would mean Charley...

"You know each other?" Kick put her arm around her friend.

"We *used* to," Charley said. An awkward hush fell across the room. The two women shifted like they wanted to bolt.

Kick being Kick went into fix-it mode. Her face brightened with the smile she gave a customer on a bad day. "That's wonderful!"

Charley must have noticed it. She spoke to Tess. "I didn't mean to intrude. I-I just wanted to give my congratulations. I-it was a... lovely night."

Kick gave her a tight embrace. "It means the world you were here for us." She glanced over her shoulder and frowned at the room before turning back. "Let's talk soon, okay?"

Charley nodded. "Alright, my friend." She waved at me and dipped her chin to Banger. "Gentlemen. Teresa. Good night." She left the office, then we heard the thump of the back door closing.

"Whoa." Kick's eyes moved from Banger to me like she didn't know where to begin. Not sure about him, but I couldn't take my thoughts from the implications for Charley.

I kept going back to our conversation over Thanksgiving dinner. She and her brother had been born in New Mexico. When though? Her gray eyes... just like... I shook my head, forcing the thought away. I'd think about it another time. Soon.

Kick crouched in front of Tess, who had dropped into a club chair. "Are you okay?"

Tess's hand shook as her fingers covered her mouth. "Fine, my dear. Just give me a minute, yes." She giggled in a way that reminded me of my earlier hysterics. "There goes the reason I'm an official yogini."

The pain in her voice sparked me out of my selfish state. Tess needed us. I squatted down by Kick while Banger took the other chair.

His fingers dug into his forehead. "Sorry, Tess. If I'd known she'd be here, I'd have told you Charley lives here now."

"Carlotta," Tess snapped back.

Banger nodded once, showing an unusual patience for Tess. "I thought you deserved to hear it in person, but…" He grunted with derision. "We've been busy."

Tess waved him off, her brows pinched like she was in physical pain.

"She looked familiar," Banger muttered. He rubbed his knee as it bounced. *The son who felt he had once again let down his fragile mother.* "Her background search didn't add up. Dug into it personally. Then I saw the photo of her in your room when you were out of town."

"Well, you don't forget a face, Rafael. Do you? You also won't let a puzzle go until you solve it." Tess scoffed. "You never asked about that photo either."

Banger flinched like he'd been punched. I didn't know whether to defend him or let him take it. Moments like this reminded me how new I still was to the family.

"Maybe Kick and I should go," I offered, attempting to defuse the tension.

Tess put her hand on my shoulder. "Stay please." She stared straight at Banger. "I feel the need to speak now."

"Of course." I moved to lean against the desk and pulled Kick in front of me, wanting to support and be supported by her. This felt like some deep shit, but maybe it was what Banger and Tess needed to break through the walls they'd erected.

"Rafael and I were in one of our distant times when I was with Carlotta… pardon, Charley." She growled, her eyes spiked with anger as she stared at her son. "You were off earning your *disgusting* name."

The misunderstanding between them didn't need rehashing on top of all this. "You two were… friends?" I jumped in to keep the conversation from rocketing down its usual dark tunnel.

Tess tipped her head back at me, her brow drawn in disappointment. "Foolishness doesn't become you, Thomas. Would I react thus if we were just acquaintances? It's been decades since I've seen Charley. Still, no one compares." A tear slid down her cheek as she added softly, "She was the love of my life, and the Felidae put a stop to us." Her hands shook more violently. "I chose their security over her."

So that's why she'd been adamant about me pursuing Kick. I grabbed Tess's hand and squeezed. "I'm so sorry."

"Hang on," Kick interjected. "Does that mean Charley is—"

"A lesbian? *Oui*—"

Kick waved off Tess's words. "That I knew. I mean she's—"

"Like us?" Tess answered again. "Also yes. Carlotta's younger than the boys here, but much older than she appears."

"You were together in Spain, weren't you?" Banger asked.

"Very good, Rafa. Yes. She and her brother... we fought against Franco. We thought we'd get a chance to do something big with our useless lives." Tess released a sarcastic laugh full of self-disdain and regret.

I turned to Kick. "Did Charley mention her brother's name at Thanksgiving?"

Tess answered instead, a faraway expression on her face. "Teodoro. Theo."

Fuck. I looked to the heavens and muttered, "You old bastard." Then I squeezed the back of my neck to relieve the pain. What my uncle had said to me in my dream... *Your work... your cousins can help.*

"What's wrong, cowboy?" Kick ran her hand up and down my arm, melding herself closer to me.

I swallowed, blinked, tamped down my temper before I spoke. "I think they're my uncle's children."

NUTTIN' BUT LOVE

KICK

I slid onto a stool next to Cyndi. "Hey chica. What brings you in at this hour?" Afternoon visits from her were highly unusual during tax time.

Cyndi tossed me some side-eye. "Are you some kind of Vegas boss now, monitoring your empire from the back?"

"Jake said you'd come in." Then I checked the monitors in my office. Her slumped posture worried me. From the tone of Cyndi's voice, I had reason to worry. I wrapped an arm around her shoulders. "Something wrong?"

"Aside from exhaustion and needing a pick-me-up?" She took a drink of her latte. "I'd bug you about being the caffeine police, but we just know each other too well, don't we?"

"We do. You go for cola in the afternoon, which means you came by for a dose of 'Kicky,' so spill."

"Fine." Cyndi put her drink down, her shoulders drooping. "The cop didn't work out."

"Oh, honey, I'm sorry." I gave her a squeeze. "I thought you wanted him to be a quick fling anyway. I didn't know you'd hoped for more."

She shrugged. "Maybe it's you too." Cyndi pointed at my engagement ring. "I'm still wandering around in the dating thrift store, and you hit pay dirt the first time you go shopping."

"Thrift store?" I raised an eyebrow. *Cyndi abhorred thrifting.* Jake caught my attention and pointed at the tea carafe, silently asking me if I wanted some. Thankfully, he knew I took it iced and unsweet with lemon. I nodded, thanking him when he brought it over.

He slid the iced goodness to me. "No problem."

"Dating over forty is like trying to find the least damaged merchandise at a thrift store." Cyndi sighed.

"Oh." *Oh.* During all the times Cyndi had bugged me about getting back into the dating game, her analogy had been my biggest fear. I had been terrified of digging through the options, trying to find someone normal without any more baggage than I had myself. I hated finding out that was her reality. I gently turned her chin to me. "Yet you came here anyway. You want me to tell you how badass you are? Because it's true."

Cyndi lifted a shoulder and smirked. "Maybe I just wanted to stare at Jake's butt for a while."

There's my bestie. Not that I always appreciated her antics. In this case, it beat seeing her so down.

Jake glanced our way and shook his head.

I grimaced. Jake received a fair share of comments on his looks at the café, just like the girls and I did. I'd never be comfortable with it though. "Don't ogle my staff, Cyn. You know they're family."

She cocked a brow at me. "There's *no* scenario where that man will be like a godson to me."

"Fine." I rolled my eyes. "Just do it in silence." I could tell she was deflecting anyway. "Want to tell me what happened with the cop? I didn't even get to meet him."

Cyndi waved off my words. "Consider yourself lucky." She drummed her fingernails on her coffee cup, considering. "Ever meet someone who's built like a god, then you have time alone and find out that when he's turned on he kind of brays like a donkey?"

"So you didn't make it past dinner?" I gave her a sympathy pout and patted her arm.

"Oh no." Cyndi took another sip. "I wasn't wasting *that* body. It's just… I ended up semipolitely asking him to shut the hell up in the middle of sexytime."

I had taken a sip from my iced tea, laughed at her words, and began choking. It was worth it to see her amusement. "That would"—I tapped on my chest a few more times—"suck." I hoped a subject change would settle my lungs. "How's work going?" She always had terrific stories.

"Busy." She dropped her head in her hand.

While pointing at her, I circled my finger. "I figured, given your roots situation. I can't remember the last time they were this deep." She hadn't used hair makeup either. Man, the dating situation really had her bummed. "Wait… is your stylist sick again?" I rubbed her arm. "Shoot, Cyn."

She shook her head. "It's nothing like that, thank gawd." She sat a little taller and shimmied. "I'm growing them out on purpose. A couple more months and I'll get a major trans-formation."

I fought like hell to keep from choking at another surprise and slid the glass of tea away. "What do you mean? You're like… going silver? Before fifty? *You?*"

She slapped the counter. "Damn straight, chica. I've had it with the patriarchy." She played with her front part a bit, moving pieces to the side. "See how white the front is? I think I'll like the contrast with the dark in the back." She dipped her head so I could see the roots on top. "It goes all the way down."

I rolled my eyes again. "Do you know how much shorter you are than me? I always see the top of your head."

"True." She sat up straight and shrugged.

"Doesn't it take years to grow?" My bestie wasn't the patient type. Not anymore.

Cyndi brought her hands together and tapped her fingers like she had a diabolical plan. "That's the best part. My stylist has trained under this master stylist who taught her how to use the new growth to blend it into the old color. The samples are gorgeous." She pulled up photos from her phone and slid it over to me.

"Wow." I scrolled through a half dozen pictures. None of the women seemed dowdy. Or old. "It's like the opposite of covering your roots. They're a feature."

"I know. Can't wait."

As I kept scrolling, I gasped at how much the women sparkled. One photo had LIFE GOALS written across the bottom of it. The silver-haired model stood in a spring forest, dressed like a goddess, her still-toned arms firmly planted on her hips.

I pulled my hair over my shoulder. "Life goals for sure."

"No kidding. Why can't we be silver foxes too?" Cyndi asked. She had a point. I loved the idea of aging like this… proudly.

Plus Cyndi's mood had lifted, so I asked, "What does this have to do with the patriarchy?"

"Have you ever noticed how men our age and older get rude when you have an inch or more of roots showing?"

I scratched at my head, probably from all this talk of root growth. "You know, my curls kind of hide them. I'd have to wait as long as you have for them to show." I lifted the front of my hair. "It's just a little right in front." Come to think of it, I should have had my touch-up appointment already. *Maybe the remission brought some color back.*

"Trust me." Cyndi finished her latte and slid the cup to back of the counter. "It's all about fuckability. For so many of these over-aged boys, as soon as they see your sparkle hairs, their faces shift from flirty to asshole mode. As if I'd been trying to trick them into thinking I was as fresh as Rachel." She shuddered, then tucked part of her still-gorgeously-sleek bob behind her ear. As if *I'd* ever fuck *them*." Even with the long, silver roots, I considered her exotic and stunning. I could see her vision in my mind. She would look like that model in the forest.

"Anyway," Cyn continued, "those misogynists can suck it with their rudeness. Of course, it helps that I work for myself. No boss can tell me what to do. And if a client doesn't like it, they can find someone else."

I scrunched my face. "Are you saying—"

She nodded, "I have a friend who was given an ultimatum—dye her hair again or quit. Her much older boss didn't want to have to endure an 'old bitty' all day."

"Isn't that illegal?"

Cyndi shrugged. "Does it matter? She didn't have the money for a lawsuit. Besides, this was a few years back, and her boss was from the *Mad Men* generation. Hell, it took her six months of threats to get the man to stop slapping her ass. They got away with that shit when they were young, and the women bought into it because… bills."

I slid my tea toward me and took a long pull through the straw. It seemed safe to do so again. "They were gaslit."

"Whatever." She waved me off again. "Just saying we don't have to take that shit anymore. Especially not from some wrinkled-in-his-own-right stranger at the hardware store. If I can go there for parts to fix my own sink, I can wear my hair however I freaking choose."

I smiled at her righteousness. "You can hire a plumber and still decide how you want to appear before the world."

She nodded her head briskly. "Damn straight."

Oh, how I wished Deana were here. She'd get a laugh out of all this. I didn't know how she felt about color, but Dee supported the natural hair movement when it came to curls and texture. I bet she'd enthusiastically back Cyndi.

Cyn leaned in for a hug. "Thanks for the ear, chica."

We kissed each other's cheek. "Anytime. You want something to go?"

She slid off her stool. "No, thanks. I had my pick-me-up." Cyndi waved at Jake and bounced to the beat of the music as she made her way to the door.

As the afternoon moved into evening, my thoughts kept going back to the visit with Cyndi. I imagined letting my little streak of white grow out. Would it stand out? Or would it just disappear inside the coils around it? What would Thomas say?

When I was little, Grannie Allen had told me folktales about women growing into their power as their hair grew whiter. At the time, I thought she'd been trying to convince me of her awesomeness, as if she needed the help. The stories were about healers who grew more connected to the earth as they aged. What would that be like? It sounded incredibly powerful.

Then my speculations landed on what Bobby's reaction might be if I did what Cyndi was planning. I was sitting in my office when I thought about it, and my desk rumbled from the violent shudder that rolled through me. She'd probably try to pull out my hair.

"Here you are. What are you doing?" About an hour after dinner that evening, Thomas found me in our closet at my place, surrounded by multiple boxes of clothes. Skirts, pants, and jeans, in particular, had been spewed all over the space. He was in his boxer briefs, ready for bed or some reading before turning in. I didn't take the time to admire his fine form standing there. Not that I took it for granted. His ass was always a topic of appreciation to me, but I was too upset to focus.

"Thought you were in the bedroom relaxing," Thomas said. The crease in his chin deepened as he grimaced at the mess.

"I can't relax when my pants keep sliding down." As I fussed with my ponytail, I barely glanced his way. "I'm searching for my smallest-sized things." I pointed at one stack of boxes. "Those are the big sizes, from the early days of the flare. Then I dropped into my regular size." I shifted my hand to two boxes behind me. "But they're…" I held on to the waist of my jeans and pulled my pants up and down without unbuttoning. "So I'm taking an inventory of what's buried in these boxes." I gestured to those in front of me. "If I lose any more weight, I'll have to go shopping again."

Thomas's head tilted from side to side, like my dog did when she looked at me like I was a bit kooky. "Thought women enjoyed shopping."

I bit my tongue to keep from complaining. Ultimately, this was a good problem. Many would consider it a blessing. My BMI had dropped from too high to acceptable, and now it was optimal. But I'd been burned by my metabolism before.

I sighed. "I don't trust it." I carefully tried to un-pretzel myself and stand within the tiny space of floor I'd left for myself. Thomas reached across the boxes and helped me up. I pointed to the entire collection of plastic tubs. "I could open a boutique with all this, but I don't dare send anything away. What if my weight swings back again? It would be a waste to buy an entire wardrobe every time my size changed."

Thomas rubbed his chin. "You know, between the two of us, there's enough money to keep you clothed no matter your situation."

"Sure, but our money's better spent on other things."

"True." His hands landed on his hips as his gaze swept over me. "It's not a temporary swing. But if you want to hold on to these boxes to be sure, works for me. If you don't have room here, I can take them to the farmhouse."

The thing was, I didn't want logical Thomas in fix-it mode. I was in a bad mood about several things. I wanted him to grump with me. I didn't have the heart to tell him though. When I'd grabbed at my hair, I'd committed frizzy hair crime number one. So I gathered it into a scrunchie I kept on my wrist.

Thomas folded his arms over his chest. "Alright, what's really going on?"

I gestured toward the bathroom and stepped around the boxes. Thomas followed me and stopped behind me as I leaned into the mirror. "My roots don't show."

He pinched the bridge of his nose. "Darlin'..."

I started separating little sections in the front, the way I had when I'd washed my face about forty-five minutes earlier. "I'd forgotten my hair appointment is next week." He sighed, but I pressed on. "Before you get sarcastic, let me finish. I should have to touch up this area with hair makeup by now. But it's as brown as the rest of the new growth. In fact, I could reschedule the whole appointment."

"Still not comprehending."

I gave him points for risking my sarcasm at this point. "Something's happening to me that's not normal. There should be a bright patch of white right here." I touched the front of my hairline.

He rubbed his jaw. "So... you're prickly because your clothes are too big and your silver hairs have disappeared. Am I following?"

"Prickly?" He had best watch it, or I'd give him prickly. "As a matter-of-fact... My glasses have been acting up for weeks as well. They're blurry no matter what I do to fix them. For the hell of it, I took them off this afternoon and looks like I have my distance sight again. I went back to using the old readers for small print stuff." I turned around and folded my arms. "Is this some kind of remission side effect? Because no one ever mentioned it to me."

Thomas drew close and spun me back around. He pulled my

T-shirt over my head and slid my jeans down without unbuttoning or unzipping them. It left me in my underwear. His hands moved up and down my arms. "Remember me telling you about the body healing itself in reverse order? How the last symptoms to occur heal first and so on?"

"Um, maybe," I said as I watched him assess me in the mirror. "Do… do you think this is hap… happening to me?" I closed my eyes and focused on his soft touch.

His fingers traveled up my neck. Then he rubbed the tips of my ears and smiled. "I do." He kissed my jaw and nearly short-circuited my brain. It certainly stopped the spiral of upset I'd been in. "I remember the first time I finally had gray hairs. After so long, I was thrilled. Disappointed when I had to make them go away to get my degree."

"Wh-when did it happen?" My words grew breathy as Thomas's fingers brushed over my stomach. I sank into the front of him.

"Around the time I found the Felidae."

I gasped at his answer.

"The point is… you can have whatever hair you want. Hell, dye it white if you want."

"You wouldn't mind?"

Thomas chuckled in my ear, and it rolled through me. "I just told you how much I liked it when I had them."

I found his eyes in the mirror. "Why don't we both work on it then? Thirty-six isn't too young to go gray. That's the age your license reads, right?"

He cupped my ass and gently squeezed. "Good plan."

I shut my eyes and let myself feel, then opened them when his hands came back around. "Never will forget the first time I saw you naked. Such a gift." He stilled his hands over my navel. "From the beginning, every inch of your body has been a feast for my eyes." His hands moved to my hips. "Some parts are smaller, tighter. I adore it now and did then because it's you."

Had he noticed my changes before me? I paid more attention to how my clothes fit than what I looked like. No one enjoys staring at themselves in a mirror.

Thomas growled near my ear. "Don't ever think your body doesn't do it for me. I have a theory based on my observations."

"What's that?" I gasped as his fingers undid my bra, exposing my breasts until his hands covered them, massaging.

"Most Felidae members learn to control their energy little by little, over decades and by accident. But you've already been practicing intention, thanks to your autoimmune issues. I think your body's already responding to what you want it to do." One of Thomas's hands drifted back down until it glided into my underwear. "I wonder how much you'll be able to influence since you're getting a head start."

My knees buckled some when his fingers slipped inside me. "Focus on what you really want, not how you think it *should* be." He peppered kisses along my jaw, then tugged lightly on my ear lobe. "Silence that critical voice in your head—the one that made you run away from me. A certain someone planted it in there when you were a little girl. I could hurt her for that, Kick."

My hips found a rhythm of pleasure, instinctively helping his fingers spark our flame.

"For your sake, I'll leave her be until you tell me otherwise. But you have to kill the critical discord living in your mind."

"I will." I hummed. "Promise."

"This is changing too, you know."

My brows pulled together as I watched Thomas pull my bikini pants down my legs until I stepped out of them. "What do you mean?"

He spread my lips apart in front of the mirror—a shocking move, but I trusted him. "Look at it. Feel it."

My breath caught at the first light brushes of my fingertips. I didn't like touching that specific area. It made me feel damaged.

Wrong. The scars were still there, but he was right. The jagged edges had smoothed. Would it change any more?

"Such a pretty orchid." He growled against my neck. "Don't ever think you have to change for me." His hands disappeared from where I needed them, and he placed them on my shoulders, spinning me around. "Set your intentions for you. Got it?"

I didn't care about any fecking intentions or energy or healing. I wanted Thomas's hands back on me. I frowned and almost pouted.

He kissed my mouth. "I've got nothing but love for you baby. Never forget."

I pulled back from his lips and raised an eyebrow. "Did you just quote Heavy D and the Boyz?"

"Sort of." He had the nerve to grin and boop my nose with his finger. The one I wanted back on my body, along with the other nine.

I pointed at him. "You've been listening to my '90s playlist."

"How do you think I found the song for your surprise?"

The mood in the room shifted from lust-filled to looney. Thomas's grin turned into his middle school smirk as he jumped his feet apart and started singing Heavy D's "Nuttin' But Love," his hands on his knees as he twerked. In his black Calvin skivvies.

I couldn't believe him. My eyes narrowed, but my smile betrayed me. "Stop listening to my music."

Thomas just sang louder, grinding harder as he jumped around the bathroom, gyrating to one of my favorite hip-hop songs. He bumped my hip, making me stutter-step to keep standing. "Come on, sing and dance with me."

"You're only saying the hook. Over and over." That egged him on. I gestured to where we'd been standing. "Seriously? You're shutting us down like that?"

He grabbed my hand and rubbed it up and down his erection as he shifted into *Dirty Dancing* mode. Thomas bit his lip like he was enjoying a moment of bliss. Is that what this was? "It's not going anywhere. Now..." He spun me around and shook his hips against my back. "Let loose and dance with me."

I had to admit, I loved it and couldn't help but laugh. He'd pulled me out of my grump.

I shimmied against Thomas and added in the female backup lines to the song as he kept repeating the hook.

"Dancing is like making love standing up," he said with a lusty lick of his upper lip. The ham.

If we had unlimited time together, like he claimed, at least I'd laugh my ass off.

He stopped when a giggling fit overtook me. He stepped around me, pulling me in for an embrace. "Did it work?"

"I suppose." I pretended to push him away but actually took a moment to breathe him in. "Except for the part where you worked me up and left me horny."

Thomas stood tall and drew a finger down my face as he backed me into the counter, pressing into me. "Just know how much you love edging."

"Jaysus." I chuckled and gestured to where we'd just been dancing. "Whatever that was, it had nothing to do with edging."

"Mmm." Thomas waggled his brows and pressed his erection into my belly. "Beg to differ."

I swallowed hard. The temperature in the bathroom suddenly went tropical again. I gave him a small push. "You think you can, what? Snap your fingers and turn me on?"

"What was it you told me?" *Curse that smirk of his.* Thomas put it to full effect as his fingers rubbed the tip of my ear. He had me. "That's right..." His voice rose in an imitation of mine. "Oh, Thomas... 'when you want, I want... It's never been this intense before.'"

I pressed my lips together as I folded my arms. "Touché."

"I know." He leaned in and lightly licked along the edge of my ear. "Also know precisely what I'd find if I dipped my fingers into those satiny folds of yours."

The frustrations from the day that had built until I was in a closet surrounded by plastic boxes fell away. It's what Thomas did. He made the nonsense disappear and showed me what was possible. I dropped my forehead onto his shoulder and whispered, "Thank you."

He pulled me close until I felt our heartbeats sync. We did that for each other. "I didn't mind, baby. For you, I'll never mind." He lifted a shoulder. "Delayed gratification, makes the finish line that much sweeter." He pulled me toward the door to the bedroom, and I swung my ass as I passed him, getting me a crisp slap there. I winked at him, egging him on.

"Just want to cross the line in the sheets"—he bit his lip—"with you making those banshee noises again."

SOMETHING TO BELIEVE IN

THOMAS

I cracked Kick's office door while knocking and heard Charley on the phone. She waved us in, then raised a finger to let us know she was almost finished. When done, Charley walked out from behind the desk and sat in a club chair. I took the other and Kick settled in behind her desk. "Thank you for taking some time to come in," Kick began.

"Is this about Tess, because—"

"No." I waved my hands. "That's y'all's business—"

"If you want to talk to me though," Kick said. "I'm here."

Charley tipped her head up to the ceiling. "I really don't." She turned to me. "What's going on?"

Now for the hard part. If there were ever an etiquette for this kind of thing, I'd yet to figure it out. "Charley, have you… do you know—?"

"You know Tess's secrets, don't you?" she asked.

I clamped my hands on my knees, wishing Kick was sitting in my lap so I could draw strength from her. It's not that I wasn't excited to give Charley this information, but I feared that she wouldn't receive it well. "I do. I'm a member of the Felidae Society too. That's how I know her."

Charley sat stick-straight in her chair, but she gave me the feeling she wanted to bolt. Not that I could blame her. "So you've made the vows of secrecy."

"Yes."

Charley's hand moved in Kick's direction. "Then why is she in this meeting?"

"She's one too. Unofficially."

Charley's head swiveled like a flash between Kick and me. "How? She's not old enough."

That vow of secrecy still had its hold on me. I gave Charley the bare facts. "She's transitioning."

Her brows lifted to her forehead. "You're kidding?"

Kick shrugged. "Thomas's tests kind of confirm his suspicions."

"Wow." Charley popped forward and pointed at me. "First off, I won't be one of you people, so don't even try to recruit me. I don't trust those sons of bitches."

I raised my hands. "Promise, it's not why I asked you here." I tried a different tack. "Let me start by telling you about my Uncle Theo." She lifted an eyebrow. If I was right, her brother was named after him.

"Uncle Theo and I founded a bank in San Francisco in the late nineteenth century. First we'd found an abundant line of gold in a creek feeding the American River in California. As rich as we became, he hated the business. Adventure was his first love. Even overseeing our mining efforts in the mountains and traveling the barely-there trails to the city didn't satisfy him."

"Why are you telling me this?" Charley asked. Her hands shook as her knees bounced a staccato.

"Bear with me." I rubbed my jaw and prepared for the worst.

"He took off for several years. When a letter reached me, Theo was helping a rancher in New Mexico, named Carlos."

Charley's head snapped up. One knee practically bounced a foot off the floor.

"Carlos had a widowed daughter."

Distraught, her eyes shimmered. "Stop."

I rubbed my temples. "Most of us can control our bodies, especially in areas of fertility."

"Stop please," she squeaked.

"Uncle Theo didn't believe in it. He—"

"No," she whispered.

My shoulders collapsed. This should be happy news, but I knew my uncle never went back to them. He broke their hearts. He did that to anyone foolish enough to love him. Even me.

I lifted my head and just spilled the rest. "I think you and your brother are my cousins. I promise not to press you about the Felidae Society if you don't want it. That's not why I bring it up. But I'd like to run a few tests in my lab to confirm my suspicions. I won't share the results with anyone outside this room, not even Tess. However, she knows about my theory. I figured it out the other night when we were all together. In my shock, I let it slip."

"Well, shit." Charley dropped her head in her hand.

"She and Banger already knew the important stuff, and they support your decision to live apart from the Felidae and the other groups," I said.

"Other groups?" Kick asked with alarm.

"We focus on Europe and the Americas. Others like us gravitated to each other elsewhere." I didn't have time to go into detail. My focus stayed on convincing Charley that I wouldn't hurt her. With that in mind, I told her, "I have a grandson who took the vows, then revoked them a decade later. He's now helping his granddaughter through her transition. They live in Virginia. Haven't told them about this, but I think they'd like to know about you."

Kick came out from behind her desk and sat on the arm of Charley's chair. She hugged her friend and said to me, "You're dumping a lot on her today, sweetheart."

"Right. I'm sorry." I made a fist, letting the edges of my nails dig into my palms. New bloodlines meant a lot to the research, but it represented more to me as the head of my family. I'd been piecing together the tracks of my broken lineage for over a hundred years. At first I wanted to know they were alright, to help them out secretly if needed. In the end, they were my motivation for taking on this work. What if one of them were on the verge of transitioning and it never happened? They should be able to have the choice.

In a soft voice, Charley said, "It's alright. I think I understand."

"Tell me one more thing. Was your mother's name Magdalena?"

Kick hugged her tighter as another tear fell. "The bastard told you about us?"

"Well..." I didn't have the heart to say he only mentioned Magdalena. If I'd known about the children, I would've made him go back for them. "He spoke about... her. Did he know about you two? Knowing Theo, he ran when his feelings became too much."

"We were six when he left us."

My eyes squeezed shut as if from pain. Then again, my heart ached for her. I couldn't explain Theo's behavior to myself, let alone his own child.

I leaned on my knees and nudged once more. "Don't you want to know where you came from? Let me at least find some way to make this right. The test is simple. You'll be in and out quicker than a lunch break. I'll do the analysis myself."

Charley moved her gaze to Kick, who gave her a sweet, sympathetic smile.

"You have the same eyes as him," I said. "That bright silver. Some memories have faded since he died in World War I, but his eyes were burnished in my mind."

Her hand dropped to her heart. "He's dead?"

My shoulders fell again. "He took a direct hit, right in front of me. There was no healing that kind of destruction. It threw me for a loop for a long time."

She sank into the chair. "Yeah."

"Theo was a strange paradox, Charley. He hoped he could be something like a genetic Johnny Appleseed, but he refused to watch another loved one die. He was a coward who only spoke about his love for Magdalena when he drank enough to let his defenses down." I scoffed at the memory flashing through my mind. "That required a lot of booze."

"*Dios mio.*" Charley covered her eyes with her hand, and I knew she believed me. "I'll do it."

"Thank you." I reached across the gap between us and grabbed her hand. "If I'm wrong, we're still friends. I can study your ancestry line if you'll let me, but no matter what, you have my confidence. I'll do everything to keep it."

Kick took Charley's free hand, then reached for mine. She winked at me before turning back to her friend. "I wouldn't love him if he wasn't an honorable man."

She gave us a small smile. We stayed like that, holding hands. Lost family found.

THE WAY I AM

KICK

"Nice. Remember... toes face me. Pivot... good. Now your combo... Shit." I'd nicked Thomas's nose with my jab. He grinned at me. "Well done. Keep your back heel up."

It was our day off, and Thomas had me spar with him in the back by the firing range at the farmhouse. I'd taken defense classes before, so I already knew some of the concepts he taught me. Still, I struggled to keep my shoulder hidden as I struck him, which was why he insisted I use my full force. He wanted my muscle memory to be as real as possible.

Normally, we trained in Thomas's workout room. Today he said he wanted to add more reality to our efforts. He briskly rubbed his hands, then pointed at the table set up. "Now to the guns."

I was puffing steam out my nose, trying to catch my breath on this chilly March day. "You've got to be kidding." I took a pull from my favorite water bottle—pink with a pen drawing of Tinker Bell. It was the only one Liam didn't steal, then lose.

"No baby." Thomas tapped the table with his hand. "This is self-defense. Brawling, shooting, quickly finding another weapon. Fighting to live another day. It happens all at once." He waved me over. "Come on. Give yourself one deep breath to center and go."

I reached for the Sig—the one I felt most comfortable with—stood in mountain pose, and sighted the target. *Breath in for four, hold for four.* I squeezed on the exhale.

Thomas's head tilted to the side. "Not bad. Do it again and empty it this time. Focus on where you need those shots to land to keep yourself alive."

My curls had gone crazy in our workout, coming out of my ponytail. Thomas made me keep it loose, since there was no way of predicting my hairdo in an actual fight. I tucked what I could behind my ear. "Okay, boss."

"Hey." He rubbed my ear to get my attention. "You still struggling with imagining a person?"

"Honestly?" I swiped some hair behind my other ear. "Knowing what I do about Jonn Graham, it would probably be easier if his face was on the target."

Thomas laughed as he checked his Glock. "Except it's not a given that it'll come up in the moment. Getting away and surviving will matter most. If you have to kill to do it, you go for it. Then deal with the aftereffects."

"But… in the scenario you see in your head… isn't the weapon used to manipulate? You know, make me obey or whatever?"

"Never assume that." With a deep frown on his face, Thomas lifted his piece and emptied the weapon like the expert he was. Talk about muscle memory. He'd been around countless types of arms and munitions since he was a boy. I bet he could target and fire in his sleep. Or at least half-asleep. "Always… always assume a weapon pointed at you is intended for use. If you raise a weapon… Don't care if it's the wasp spray you keep by your bed. Use it, dammit."

"Gotcha." From my perspective, the best part about this scenario was me no longer flinching when I fired or any of the times Thomas had. As much as I still hated this talk—barely believed any of it, to be honest—I was becoming accustomed to it. I took it as a win. Then I sighted the Sig Sauer again and made a better pattern on my target. The small victories. Did I wish this came more naturally to me? For Thomas's sake, hell yes. Maybe it would in time.

I actually liked the physicality of fighting. There was a connection to the past, not just to making my body move better but to the history of how people have been defending and protecting their own... since the cave times, I guessed.

As for our daily life, except for lectures and exercises like this, it was downright peaceful. Most weeknights it was Thomas, Liam, and me. Lee had received his latest SAT score. He'd come downstairs with a smile on his face, so Thomas and I were happy. The boy had been so excited that I let him take my Camaro to band practice.

Last Sunday, we finally arranged a family dinner at Thomas's. Nailing down Rachel in her tight schedule had been the victory, and she only stayed for the meal. It did my heart good to have the kids together. Hosting it at Thomas's farmhouse made our situation that much more real. Lee already had some things in the main guest room. He'd made it clear, though, that he didn't want to move in officially, like I had with a duplicate of anything I'd need. Still, we called the room Liam's now.

"How's it going at Banger's condo with Tess there?" I'd asked Rachel as she plated sweet potatoes and I carved the roasted chickens. From the way they'd hit it off the first time they'd met, I hoped their friendship had grown. I couldn't tell her the truth about Tess's age and all, but I thought they could help each other through their current hurts and stresses.

"Good. We know about Charley," Rachel said.

My eyebrows instantly rose to hairline heights. "Really?" How much could she disclose? Tess was as secretive as the rest of the mysterious Felidae. "What'd she say?"

"That they're exes." Rachel stopped mashing as she sighed. "Isn't it romantic?"

I put my knife down and turned around. "Snow, they'd seen neither hide nor hair of each other for… a while. What I saw looked tragically painful, not romantic. Trust me, no one smiled in the moment." *My daughter and her desire to tell a story.*

"Exactly, Mama. They still love each other."

I laughed through my incredulity. "How the hell did you conclude that? From the little I know, they came to a massive impasse and called it quits. I think for the better."

She resumed mashing. "Still, Charley's the love of Tess's life."

Jaysus, she told the girls that? With my knife, I dug into the stubborn hip joint. I'd never liked this part of cooking chicken, but the memory of Charley's despairing visage gave me the mojo to push through. "I don't think Charley feels the same."

Rachel rinsed the masher in the sink and placed it in the dishwasher. "Bella and I plan to get them talking again."

Oh hell. "Snow, let them be. Please. They're not like you and Bella."

Rachel started to pick up the bowl but folded her arms instead. "What's that mean?"

"Uh…" How do I explain the Felidae without explaining it? "You and Isabella are in a rush. To finish school. To start your life. To live. Remember when you cried last fall about not yet being engaged to Cody?"

She clicked her tongue. "Of course. Thank God though."

"I know, right?" Macushla had been waiting at my feet, so I dropped a small piece of meat to my sweet pup. "You've been in a hurry to grow up pretty much since the day you were born. I'm telling you, some people aren't like that. Give Tess and Charley time. Their own time."

Rachel picked up the bowl and hip-checked me. "Sometimes people need a gentle push."

I shook my head as I watched her leave the kitchen, the dog tight to her heels. *Heaven help those two women.*

Thinking back to that conversation with Rachel reminded me of something Thomas had needed for his research. As we carried our gear back to the house, I cleared my throat. "Hey cowboy…"

He turned to me and smiled.

"I can't believe I forgot to tell you… my brother, Bert, agreed to do the DNA tests for us. Well, for me. I told him it'll help with my diagnosis, like you suggested. He's all set at your friend's lab at Wayne State tomorrow."

Thomas blew out a long breath. "Excellent news."

I moved the bag I carried to my other shoulder. "Will you check him for variances?"

"Absolutely. We've moved into the phase where Gautam's algorithm is pulling most of the workload, looking for patterns and anomalies. So, yeah… the more information we get, the better."

We moved past the narrow trail through the woods and into Thomas's backyard. He opened his arm and pulled me in. "You think you could get Bobby to test? She could use the same lab in Detroit. They're sending it straight to me without registering it."

I lifted my gaze, my brows raised. "This might come as a shock, but my mother's a bit of a conspiracy theorist. She thinks DNA tests are for suckers."

Thomas tipped his head back and laughed.

My fingers moved to adjust my glasses, but they weren't there anymore. Funny how quickly the gesture had become an unconscious thing. I ended up rubbing my eye. Considering pollen had irritated it a little, it helped. "I could pop over to her townhouse if you tell me what to look for. Or you can come with me."

"Well…" Thomas rubbed the cleft in his chin. "I've never run a panel without consent before. It's technically illegal. Immoral. Would you have a problem with that?"

If it helped me or, more importantly, my kids? Nope. When it came to her, something about the wrongness of it added to the appeal. Immature, I know, but I didn't care. "You promise it's staying in your database and no one else will have the information?"

Thomas crossed his heart with his pinkie finger.

I shrugged. "I'm good."

He squeezed me into his side. "Now you're thinking like a Felidae member."

"Naw…" I gave up the hair fight and pulled my scrunchie out of it with my free hand, letting the curls fly free. "I'm thinking like Banger."

LOVE ME TENDER

THOMAS

Hugh joined me in the humidor in his shop. I'd distracted myself with cigar shopping while he finished a call.

"Thanks for coming in."

I held up four perfectos. "Not a problem."

Hugh took them and led the way to his office.

I cleared my throat. "You're not ringing me up?"

"Hell no. You saved my keister."

Aside from the day we'd met, Kick hadn't let me pay for anything at her coffeehouse. Not that it mattered. Deana would have snuck stuff to me, regardless. This was different. "So a guy can't spend his money anymore?"

Hugh chuckled. "Don't act like you're not about to drop a cool chunk of change on my desk, Professor." He gestured to the chair beside him. "Sit please."

Before doing so, I reached across the other desk—the one that had been Mickey Allen's now faced Hugh's. According to Kick, this was the setup the men used while her father had been Hugh's partner. I shook hands with the man sitting there—the new manager, who would oversee the cannabis expansion. "Dexter Douglas, I presume?"

He gave my hand a solid, confident shake. "That's right. Call me Dex though." The handshake fit him. Dex took after his father in size, though not as broad. His facial features reminded me of an edgier version of his mother. Or he'd just inherited Deana's cordial smile.

"Thomas Harrison. Feels like I already know you."

"Same, man. I've heard all about the 'mighty fine professor'." The corner of his mouth lifted. "My moms has a crush on you."

Hugh and I laughed. "Spent enough time with your parents to know your father has nothing to worry about. What's that my students say?" I snapped my fingers. "Right. Hashtag, life goals."

Dex blew out a hard breath. It puffed out his cheeks, but he didn't say anything.

"I didn't realize you two hadn't met," Hugh said.

"Not officially." I shrugged. "Between Kick and Deana, it just seems that way."

"Exactly," Dex said with a nod.

Hugh's mouth twisted as his brow furrowed. "Why would you go to bat for an unvetted stranger?"

"Wouldn't call Dex, here, unvetted." I brought my ankle over my knee and settled in the chair. "Kick went to bat for him first. I trust my fiancée's judgment." I looked straight at Dex. "My team did do a background check. You found a good one, Hugh."

"I agree," he said. "Can't thank you enough for also recommending your lawyer. You were right about the one who'd been working on our license. The man turned out to be a big conflict of interest." He leaned back in his chair and folded his hands behind his head. "You wouldn't believe the flak I received from the board for replacing Katie with Dex on the licensing petition."

Oh, I'm sure I would. "Let me guess… the racism is as strong as their misogyny."

Dex pressed his lips together as he rolled his eyes.

"That first lawyer would've let them veto us without a fight. Roly-poly bastard. Then my contact calls… tells me they just wanted Katie to sweat a little… make her more *grateful* for her opportunity. Pliable is what he meant. They didn't want her showing up with any feminist ideas."

I scoffed at the comment. If you claimed to want progress, then do it, dammit. It didn't matter if it was a local government or the Felidae Society.

Hugh misunderstood my outburst and said, "Your guy made the difference, Professor—"

"Thomas please. Since we're partners now."

"Yes, well. The new lawyer reminded them of the suits in other states where black entrepreneurs weren't given equal access to the licensing process. He convinced them we had the bankroll to take them on."

There was an understatement. Whether it was Kick or Dex being hassled, I'd go all in. I would shake up the whole system if needed.

I turned to Dex. "You good with this?"

"It's nothing new." He slid his tortoise-framed glasses up his nose. "Fuck 'em. Let's do this."

I shifted my gaze back to Hugh. "Dex has full powers as manager? He has oversight of the remodel and set up of the new store?"

"Katie wasn't lying about your protective side." Hugh raised his hands. "Our new partner has an MBA. He's more than capable, and I can't wait to step back some." I knew this, but I liked hearing the praise in Hugh's tone. The man sounded equal parts grateful and relieved.

"Damn straight." I rubbed my hands together. "What do y'all have for me?"

Hugh slid some papers my way, and I leaned forward to read them. "Walt left these for you to sign."

"Yeah." I uncapped my Mont Blanc. "His partner, Penn, mentioned the family emergency. I hope everything's alright."

"Me too. Hang on a moment..." Hugh pressed the intercom. "Liz... can you come on back now?"

"Sure, Mr. Reynolds."

Hugh explained, "Liz is a notary."

When we took care of Hugh's stack of papers, making me their silent partner, Dex cleared his throat. "Hang on, Liz." He placed a smaller set on the edge of his desk.

I lifted an eyebrow as I read the first lines. "Right. The loan." Dex nodded. "You know this is just a formality?" I reminded him.

With Dex's finances tied up because of his pending divorce, he needed a quick loan in order to buy into the partnership. "Would've cut you a check from my personal account."

He shook his head. "I wouldn't have taken it. This protects us both."

"True." I signed and initialed the highlighted areas. Then Liz made everything official.

I reached into my briefcase and produced two new Mont Blanc pens. I handed them to Dex and Hugh. "Will these buy your silence, gentlemen?" The silent part of our deal included Kick and Deana. I didn't want to risk anyone thinking I was throwing money around for the hell of it. Or worse... to prove something. As Banger liked to say, compounded interest ensured that I had enough to help when I saw an opportunity. But I didn't want to have to explain it to Deana or put Kick in the situation of hiding more from the people she loved. She knew I had enough to live on. She didn't know exactly how much. Not yet.

Dex whistled at his gift. "You never have to worry about me. The silence is written into our deal though I appreciate this kind of bribery." The men laughed.

"What Dex said," Hugh added.

"I started the deal to see Kick smile." Her smile motivated so much lately. I also believed these were men who wouldn't ask many questions. I liked that about them, especially Dex. If he did as well as I thought we would, I had plans for him.

"Oh." Hugh raised the new pen like he was pointing with a finger. "Thought you should know… Kick told me about asking Big Jonn to pull whatever strings he thought he could with the tobacco fellas. From what I can tell, he followed through." He dropped my cigars into a bag and handed them over. "One of the board members was furious over some conversation his wife had with Kick."

I slid the bag into my case. "Do I want to know?"

Hugh grinned. "This woman treated herself to a weekly outing at the Perked Cup when she was going through chemotherapy. Katie noticed her, as she does. They talked. The treatments caused some kind of… you know… vaginal dryness or some such. Katie recommended some kind of cannabis remedy to fix it, and it worked."

"Christ." I tapped my pen on the desk, not liking where this story might be heading. "This was a problem because…?"

Hugh swallowed hard before turning a bright red. "According to Big Jonn, it put her… uh… in the mood."

What was wrong with men? I wrapped my hand around my neck. Could've howled at the stupidity, but Dexter barked a laugh instead.

Hugh giggled as he added, "The guy claimed it drugged her or something."

I moved toward the door, but his words struck a chord as I reached for it. I turned around. "Are you saying this is the reason for the whole 'immoral whore campaign' against my fiancée? Some idiot's wife got her mojo back because a caring barista gave her *advice*?" My nostrils flared from the effort to contain a roar. My new partners didn't deserve it.

If only Hugh had seen the pain and confusion on Kick's face

when she saw the graffiti on her café wall. I don't think he would have stayed so calm. Not to mention how tortured she'd been over what Big Jonn's son did on Halloween. I'd still throw the kid out of either store if I saw him again. Hell, I'd never trust either of the Grahams.

Hugh sighed, adjusted his cap. "I don't know. Just wanted to tell you about Big Jonn, is all. I know there's bad blood between you. He's always been supportive of me. Plus he helped with the board."

"I hear you. I do. I also believe Kick and Rachel. Then there's what I've personally witnessed." Thanks to the men connected to Big Jonn, I could've lost Kick before I had her officially. I'd never forget it. I gave Hugh and Dex a chin tip and opened the door. "Gentlemen… pleasure doing business with y'all. Let me or my team know what else we can do to help."

WITH OUR FINGERS LACED TOGETHER, I PULLED KICK THROUGH the door to my lab. My heart raced faster than when I showed Tess around. To be swift and efficient, I'd drawn Kick's blood at home, so this was her first time in my lab. My space. As I tried to see it through Kick's eyes, a vision formed in my head regarding what changes could improve workflow in the new lab.

It hit me for the first time how, in my heart, I'd already left the university. *Damn.* I'd miss the lectures. When I pursued this new life, I never expected to fall in love with it or with teaching the next generation. But it was best for the work, and I'd bring over my postgrad students in partnership with the university. It was the compromise I made to get out of my contract, though I'd planned to take them anyway.

For added moral support for Kick, Tess came with us. The information I was sitting on might thrill her the most. Besides, she'd been asking about the mice. I had a feeling they'd have names by the end of this. Either way, both women were about to be floored.

Kick's bright face fell when I had her sit around Gautam's computer setup—what he called "the *Enterprise*"—because we were going "where no one else had gone before."

Tess had talked up the mice on the drive over, and Kick was more eager to see them than she was to learn about her results. It's possible my face already gave it away. I had lost my practiced poker face in matters related to her.

I made the introductions between Gautam and the women. Tess stayed true to form and remembered him. She asked about his classes with the interest of a mother.

"Tess please." I gestured for Gautam to bring up the report. It contained numerical data, along with graphs and pie charts for readability. We'd based the output on reports that other DNA services provided. "Give us about twenty minutes," I told him once everything was ready. Nondisclosure agreement or not, it had been hard enough to explain this new project to my assistant. He already knew the details but not the personal significance of it.

"No problem, Professor H. Anyone want a coffee?"

Kick smiled at him, then said, "No, thank you." I'd only known her to drink coffee from another café once.

"I'm fine too. Thank you, dear," Tess said.

He gave her a double take before heading for the door.

I moved into Gautam's chair, feeling the grin form on my face as I turned to Kick. "According to this, you're officially related to a Felidae member."

"Thank God we didn't have to search outside the Society," Tess said while squeezing my fiancée's shoulders.

No kidding. Kick's extraordinary amount of European ancestry had been a big clue. The frown on her face surprised me.

"Are you not happy about this?" I thought for sure she would be.

She rubbed her palms on her thighs. "Is it you?"

I grimaced at the thought. It melted fast as I logged myself onto the computer. I couldn't wait to show her the good news. Then I pointed to the smile on my face. "Would this be here if we were related?"

"I don't know. Your uncle was apparently prolific." She shoved her hands between her knees. "We could be cousins."

"True." I ran my hand through my hair. "Go back far enough and we're all cousins eventually. But not in this case. You're from another bloodline. We'll have to take it all the way back to find our genetic crossing." I kissed her temple and felt her tension fade.

"Anyway…" I clicked on the screen, and Tess's hand shot to her mouth. Kick's gaze darted between us. "Meet Edmund Stanton. Well, it's the name he used last."

Kick stared, speechless, at the screen, like she was looking in a mirror for the first time.

"Don't search for a resemblance, darlin'. You're too distant to worry about such things."

She turned to Tess, who shrugged. "I only gave birth to Rafael. What do I know?"

"Here." I clicked on a chart. "We connected you through your brother's Y-DNA, so Edmund's line runs through your father."

That put a smile on my lady's face. *Just wait, my love.* Before I moved on, I thought she deserved to know about her ancestor. It's why I'd asked Tess to join us.

"So… Edmund was a founding member of the Felidae Society. He oversaw the European operation before Ellie. It focused on protection and politics back then. He was also Alaric's closest friend and spent many years as Ellie's partner, which is why she took over Europe when he died."

Kick's head tilted to the side. "He's dead? I thought you didn't die."

"We age extremely slow, and we are hard to kill. But we are not immortal," Tess said.

"Remember, my uncle died in World War I."

"Right." She tapped her chin. "Alaric is the one you call *Grand-père*, correct?"

Tess scoffed, but I smiled at her. "He is. I can't wait to tell him about this." I frowned at Tess. We didn't need her old wounds influencing Kick. I wanted her to make up her own mind about the Felidae and its issues. I told Tess, "Alaric knows about Kick. He promised to leave us alone. He'll be thrilled with this news."

Tess leaned toward Kick and placed a hand on her knee. "We thought Edmund's line had died out, yeah?"

"It happens easier than you'd think. Through the ages, it's been harder to keep health and wealth than it's been to lose it," I explained.

Kick blinked at me, like she was struggling to keep up. I clicked on more photos that Tess had sent of Edmund. In one, he and Ellie stood together in the manicured garden at the chateau. They made a regal image, even centuries after their first lives. It was the characteristic I saw echoing the most in my lady.

Tess squeezed Kick's hand and smiled as her eyes moved over the photos. "Ask me any questions you have. There's so much to share, and everyone I know already has the same stories." She seemed downright giddy to pass on the information.

Kick opened her mouth, but I raised a hand to keep her from asking. They had all the time for sharing memories. I was still on the clock and only half-done. "Before you go off on a tangent, there's more."

I closed the files on Edmund and opened another set. "You have another Felidae ancestor from your mother's side." I clicked on the link and pulled up Ellie's information. The irony of a match to these two had struck me right away. By the way Tess's features twisted, she shared a similar opinion. "Your *mtDNA* is traced through mothers and evolves the slowest of any DNA."

"Is this woman as bitchy as Bobby?" Kick asked.

Tess broke into a hard cackle as I shook my head at her. "We're not researching those traits."

"I must disagree with you." Tess wiped away her tears from laughing.

"More stories?" Kick asked.

"It seems," I answered. "Again, you two will have to catch up another time." I clicked on my photos of Ellie. I was in many of them, as well as Alaric. Banger was even in a recent one. Since he'd been able to develop a secure system for the Society, we'd loosened our rules on the sharing of videos and photos for documentation.

"As you can see, these are fairly recent. Since I've mentioned her before, you also know that Ellie's alive and well. She's another Felidae elder."

Tess's eyes narrowed as I spoke until I added, "You two aren't ready for introductions."

"Why not?" Kick asked.

"Let me tell you what I know," I started. "Ellie is short for Eleanor. She was a queen in her first life. She was denounced for having her own mind in a time when royal women were no more than brood mares and prizes to form alliances."

"Then she was ahead of her time?"

"You can say that. This blending of two powerful lines, so to speak, points to why you've already shown abilities."

Tess scoffed and stood, moving to the work area where the mice lived.

"She and this Ellie have issues, don't they?"

I pulled Kick closer and kissed her temple, pausing for a moment to appreciate this news. I understood Kick's reluctance to believe my theories about her, but I buzzed with the implications of this news. I'd found a true life partner.

"The vibe in Bordeaux has been changing for months. I didn't know it had spread to Tess until recently, but yes, there's a particular iciness between the women. You can trust Tess's instincts."

Kick folded her hands in her lap. "Okay."

"There's a discord between the American and European teams that's new. That said, Ellie's always been supportive of my work. So I don't have all the answers. We just need to keep this information quiet for now." To lighten the mood, I added, "We also brought in a genealogy specialist with a team of her own. She also found your connection to Ellie. They're working on an ancestry tree for you."

"Okay." The little V formed between Kick's brow as she studied the photos. She had so much catching up to do. And I couldn't stop my smile. *Like attracts like.*

"What about my kids?"

I sighed deep. "This tangent has taken me away from Toni, my grant work. Since there are only two months left in the semester and four for the academic year, I need to pivot back to her. I can't take on anymore diversions until I'm out on my own. I'm sorry, darlin'." I raised her hand to my mouth and kissed her knuckles, wishing for all the world I could work faster. "As soon as I can, I'll study them. We'll watch them the way I keep tabs on my descendants."

"Except they're direct from me, and I have two lines of influence."

I grinned at her. "True."

LATER THAT NIGHT, AS I SAT IN MY OFFICE ON THE THIRD FLOOR OF my house, I dialed Alaric. It was just past breakfast time in Bordeaux. This time he stayed true to his routine and was in his office. Something told me Ellie wouldn't like hearing about Kick. At least Alaric could decide how to broach it to her.

He picked up on the first ring.

"*Allo, Grand-père.* Are you sitting down?"

MORE THAN THIS

KICK

"**I**s it safe?" Charley asked while conspicuously scoping out the Perked Cup's dining area.

"If you mean is Tess here? She's at a yoga studio. You should know she plans to teach there soon."

"Then she is sticking around." In the years I'd known Charley, she'd been certain of her path, even cocky about it as she bulldozed her way through a man's industry. It unnerved me to see her deep brown eyes so lost and confused. "What about your daughter? I-is she here?"

I dropped my rag onto the counter. "Well, hell. You're getting it from all sides, aren't you? No, she's not in yet." I expected Rachel soon. She always worked on Saint Patrick's Day, though I used the term *work* loosely for her once the partying started. I gestured toward a stool, and Charley sat. "Your usual is on the house."

She patted the counter. "No, Kick. We pay each other."

I called over my shoulder as I made her latte. "Humor me today." I set the mug in front of her grimacing face. "I feel partially responsible for your troubles. For what it's worth, I tried to call off Snow and Bella. But they're rooming with Tess. I believe they're using her happiness as a diversion from their own stresses."

Charley stared into her drink, blinked, and sighed. "When I left Spain, I told Teresa I didn't want to ever see her again. That hasn't changed. *Those people* don't change."

I knew she referred to the Felidae, except... "I don't want to meddle, but Tess has been great to me. It doesn't make me love you less..." I smiled at her, but Charley stubbornly held on to her frown. "Listen... she's helping me through some hard information—"

She threw out a hand. "Yada, yada... you can't talk about it. Believe me. I know. Teresa always chooses them. Now you're doing it too."

Right. For a minute, I'd forgotten Charley knew about the Felidae. For all intents and purposes, she was the one without the protection they offered. What the hell. I leaned in. "It turns out I'm descended from someone who had been like a father to Tess. She's been sharing memories of him with me. I think it helps her to have someone to pass the information along to, you know?" I chose my next words carefully, wanting her to really listen. "From what I've heard, she's been a fan of Thomas and me since the beginning. He risked his status with those Felidae people to be with me. In a huge part, it was because of a push from Tess. She and Banger both had his back." I lifted a shoulder. "Can't help wondering if that isn't because of you."

"No shit?" Charley said. She picked up her cup but set it back down without drinking. She dropped her head into her hand.

"Total honesty, my friend, I haven't asked her or anything." I didn't want to interfere beyond this little pep talk. "The impression I get from hanging around Tess suggests she's not the blindly obedient woman you used to know." I wiped the counter as I sorted through my thoughts. "They are a ridiculously secretive bunch. You're right about that. And I don't think it's easy to let it go."

"They have reason to be. My brother and I have barely escaped death multiple times, and it wasn't because of anything we'd done. It was over who we are."

I froze in the middle of my chores. "That sounds a lot like an incident Thomas shared with me."

"If he only had one, he's damn lucky."

"Careful…" I adjusted my ponytail. "Sounds like you're defending your ex now."

She finished her latte and stretched her back. "I understand the appeal of safety. It's the way they protect it I can't abide."

Did these women have any clue how closely they aligned? "I swore I heard Tess say pretty much the same thing the other day."

Charley scoffed at my words, but her shoulders relaxed some.

"Are you sticking around for the bands?" I changed the subject to give her room to think.

"Maybe one. I have a meeting nearby this afternoon."

"Refill?"

She nodded. "If you charge me for it. Along with a chicken wrap." Charley's phone rang, and she grimaced again. "This can't be good. It's my new site supervisor."

I tipped my head toward the back. "Take it in my office. I'll bring your stuff back."

"Thanks, my friend." Right before turning down the back hall, Charley called out, "If she comes in, don't tell her I'm here."

I brushed my pinky finger over my heart. "Promise." I didn't know if she referred to Tess or Rachel. I bit my tongue and reminded myself to let it go. As tempting as it was to want to spread the relationship bliss around, not everyone was ready for it. Heaven knew I hadn't been for a long time. Meeting Thomas didn't equal readiness either. It forced me to face what held me back, but I had to knock down the walls I'd built up on my own. Maybe it was the same for my two friends.

"Yo Mama!" The bell announced Rachel before she called out. Seeing her brightened my mostly happy day even more. Our Saint Patrick's Day party was always a highlight of the year.

"Are you ready to dance, sweetheart?"

"Fired up for it. Do you want help setting up or serving right now?"

"Serving would be fantastic. Your brothers will be here soon with the equipment."

Growing up, we celebrated Saint Patrick's Day as a holy day. My dad hated the revelry associated with it. I still cringed at memories of dancing on the sticky bar stages. The coffeehouse provided the perfect compromise. All the culture without the hangover. It was our tagline for the party ads too.

This year, four bands were lined up to play from lunch to closing. Popular bands used the café as a warm-up, then moved to one of the Irish pubs in the area during prime party hours. We ended our celebration with older folk groups who didn't like the rowdy scene either.

The bell chimed and in walked Big Jonn Graham. It was nice to see him enter without the vision blurriness I'd experienced in the autumn. That didn't stop my spine from tightening as he approached. My gaze swept toward Mateo. Like the good guard he was, he caught it and nodded. His head shifted to the other two guards stationed in their corners of the dining room. I watched their silent exchanges. Except for the Open Mic Night, when Thomas proposed, this would be the biggest party the Perked Cup would throw since the Halloween fiasco.

I had to admit, Big Jonn's gesture of good faith helped us. I was back in good standing with the community, and Hugh was moving forward with Dex Douglas. Still, I didn't like the possible omen that the presence of a Graham might mean.

A cold chill whispered along my neck. I plastered on my service smile anyway. "Hello, Big Jonn. What can I make for you today?"

He sent me a seriously flirty grin. I'd watched it fall upon so many women in the community that I knew it meant nothing. He showed me his phone. It displayed an ad for the festivities, along with our tagline for the day: ALL THE CULTURE. NO HANGOVER. "I took the day off since it's raining cats and dogs outside. Got to say, your ad intrigued me. Can't tell you how many of my boys will show up at a jobsite still drunk tomorrow morning."

"I bet." I cringed at the thought of someone operating heavy machinery under those conditions.

"Exactly." He shifted the display to a barcode. "How does this thing work?"

"I'll scan it. It gives you half off a latte or cappuccino with a four-leaf clover in the foam."

"Well, isn't that cute?" Big Jonn ran a hand over his chin. "I'll take a cappuccino if you don't mind. When does the music start?"

"Soon." I gestured toward the stage. "The fellas are almost ready. The kids from the dance school will perform for an hour first."

"How sweet. Everyone loves a neighborhood pub, but I hate how it can get debaucherous on this day."

After scanning the barcode, I lifted my shoulder. "I've never known Finnegan's Wake to get too bad. It probably depends on the management." He ordered a pastry to go with the drink. "If you want a seat, maybe grab one now? The full crew of dancers and their families will be here any minute. We fill up fast."

"I think I will. Thank you, Mrs. McKenna."

I rolled my eyes at his use of my married name, wondering if it was some kind of dig at Thomas. Surely he'd noticed the engagement ring. I'd shifted the three-stone mother's ring I wore for years to my right hand. The center diamond on that one—for Rachel's April birthday—had often fooled customers into thinking I was married. It had even confused Thomas the day we met.

Despite the harassment campaign dissipating, rumors occasionally floated to me and the staff about Thomas living at the house without us being married. Some people just refused to let go of the immoral mother box they'd tried to cage me in. I wondered if Big Jonn followed that same train of thought or if he just pretended to. Pretending could take someone a long way in our area. I thought many of the disturbances against me related back to my refusal to play along.

I wouldn't engage this time either. "And thank you again for putting in a good word for Hugh. It's made a big difference. I think his expansion will be good for the community."

Graham's face twisted before he found his smile again. "It was my pleasure. Reynolds is a good man."

"That he is."

Rachel walked past us, moving from the stage to Deana in the drive-through. He leaned toward me. "You should know… Young Jonn is in therapy like you suggested."

My brows shot up to my forehead. "Really? How's he doing?"

"Good, I think." Big Jonn tapped the counter. "I'll go find a seat. Can't wait to see those little ones with the big, bouncy curls."

"They are super cute." My phone vibrated in my pocket with a text from Thomas.

THOMAS

Hey, my Irish Eyes. Meeting went well. OMW. No dancing without me. XO

Per his new custom, Thomas attached a song to the message. This one was Van Morrison's "Have I Told You Lately?" I sighed deeply as Deana approached. "Thomas is running late."

"Thomas is here," he declared behind me.

I turned around, my phone still up high. "That's weird. I just received this."

He shook his head and shrugged. "Remind me to put you on my plan. Your network stinks."

"It's—"

Deana's whistle cut me off. "Looking mighty fine, Professor." At her pause, I realized the whistle had been a full-blown catcall. "Is that a custom sports jacket?"

Thomas's gaze dropped from me to his front, then back up. He lifted a shoulder. "Good tailor's hard to find."

"What has you so fancy this morning? Most people wear jeans and T-shirts to this shindig."

"Early meeting with the boss's boss. They tried to re-woo me into staying at the university. I showed him around the lab and briefed him on our progress."

"Did it work?" I asked.

He gave a crooked grin. "I have to let him think there's hope. We're still finalizing the affiliation. Banger and I thought of a way to keep them as a partner."

"Your message said it went well."

"Very. They're coming around to my way of thinking." He leaned in to kiss my temple. It was like a brief meditation, letting my soul pause for a breath. "Let me change into my party clothes."

"Sure. Just change in Dee's office. Mine's already occupied. Oh, you should know…" I tipped my head toward the bistro table with Big Jonn.

"Fuck me." Thomas groaned. "Here I had a great day going too."

I tapped his arms. "The guards are watching him closely. Our interaction went well… enough. He's put his son in therapy."

Thomas lifted an eyebrow. "There's a wonder." He pinned Mateo with a look, and they did that silent macho talk thing.

Then Thomas squeezed my ass out of sight of the patrons and headed to the back, a duffel bag in his other hand.

"Remember to turn off the camera," I said, hoping I wasn't too loud.

"Shh." Deana scolded. "Don't take away my fun."

I clicked my tongue back at her. "Behave."

Her warm chuckle filled my ears. "Never and always."

STAR OF THE COUNTY DOWN

KICK

"The one out front reminds me of Rachel," my mother said to me from her perch at the bar. She'd come home in part to see the dancers. It always cheered her up to watch the kids go through their routines. I still didn't know why she didn't teach part-time. She obviously missed it. Then again, Bobby would despise not being the boss. I laughed at the thought, and Bobby's brows squished together, like she couldn't make sense of me. It was also her default face where I was concerned.

"She certainly can't dance like Rachel though. The child has no rhythm."

"Jaysus, Mother, can you be a little louder?" I whisper-yelled at her. "The baby's what... six?"

"Rachel knew her steps and felt the music at that age."

"Not every child will be a professional, but they can have fun."

"I think she's adorable." Rachel interrupted us. My peacemaker.

"You've always been too generous." Somewhere in there, I

believed Bobby said it as a declaration of love for her grand-daughter. Judging from the smile on her face, Rachel took it as one, so that's all that mattered.

"Where's Juan again?" I'd been determined to not mention his name, but Bobby's harsh criticisms could get out of hand. I took one for the sake of the tiny hearts on stage.

She smirked like she'd won something. "He's judging a competition in Ohio."

"How come you didn't go with him? You must enjoy watching the formal events too."

"I need to figure out what to do with my town house."

Rachel and I both stopped working and looked at her. "Are you selling it?" I asked.

She took a sip of her latte. "Probably. Juan lives in a high-rise, and I like being on one floor. I might rent my place or buy a beach property. I don't like the idea of having nothing of my own."

Bobby turned back around on the stool and watched the end of their current routine while rubbing her knee. I wondered if she'd ever noticed how mentioning anything that could aggravate her knee made her massage it for several minutes. That's what she implied with the one-floor comment—she'd complained for years about having a two-story condo. So much of her life seemed to be driven subliminally. It was a huge part of why I tried to do things with intention.

The music ended, and Bobby turned back to her latte while the dance teams transitioned.

"It's smart to have your own place," I said.

"Well, thanks for your permission," she snipped.

I raised my hands. "Just trying to say I think it's a good idea. The renting thing is too." I watched my reflection in the wood as I wiped the counter. "I appreciate you for taking a rideshare from the airport. We've been swamped around here."

"You're always swamped," she responded.

I sighed, about to give up. I kept thinking about Thomas's offer to cut her loose. Constantly dodging the lines she relentlessly tried to hook me with was exhausting.

Bobby added, "Juan showed me how the ride thing works. He couldn't drop me off, so he set it all up on my phone. It's easy. A nice Italian boy picked me up. Not too sure about the one who brought me home here." She leaned in and said, "I held on to my purse the whole time."

Jaysus. I rolled my eyes. How many times had the kids and I offered to set her up with the app? We thought it would be safer than her driving anywhere beyond Oakville, especially since her doctors were on the other side of the county. Why would her lack of independence be used as a means of love and attention from the family, but she made no demands on Juan? Was their relationship okay? Could it be that she wasn't compelled to manipulate him? Did it matter?

The only thing I really knew was how nice it had been with Bobby out of town. Thomas and the kids and me. I rolled my head, stretched my neck, and tried again. "Sounds like you're happier up there. Maybe you should buy a place when you go back. In his building, possibly."

Bobby held out her cup for me to refill it—another sign of my failings. This time it was for my lack of customer service. *Whatever.* There was something about Thomas's out that made these attempts to hook me fail. It empowered me. Stay or go... it was my choice now.

Bobby twisted her face again, like I was too stupid to be her blood. "I'm moving in with Juan when my house is settled. If it's good enough for you, it's good enough for me."

Wow. So if it goes South, I'm to blame? I let that one roll off my back and handed her the new latte. Decaf this time. "If it's what you want, sounds great. You don't have to answer to anyone anymore."

My words were the complete truth from where I stood.

Thanks to Thomas and this Felidae business, I'd become more intentional with what I wanted.

Bobby squinted and studied me for a moment. I raised my hands. "I'm serious. You worked hard. You didn't choose many of your life… situations." I shrugged. "You can now. Go for it."

Bobby nodded. "I'll look at beach property. We can winter there and live at Juan's in the warmer months."

I laughed, hoping this was the beginning of something good. "Living the American dream."

The music started again, offering a chance to decompress as Bobby turned around to critique the next set of littles. She'd been a miserable witch my whole life. If Juan floated her boat, it would be easier on my psyche all around.

"Please tell me the band is on schedule," Thomas whined, and Rachel laughed.

"The showcases do drag on."

"All the babies get a chance to shine," I defended. Thomas checked the watch I'd given him for Christmas.

Rachel tapped his shoulder. "It's almost over. Then Liam and I are dancing with the first band."

My youngest was changing in my office. Charley had watched the first showcase, then skedaddled to her meeting. Big Jonn also left without incident. I'd take the wins where I could get them.

Deana held her head in her hand, standing at the pastry display. Service always ground to a halt when the kids danced. "We could use some real tap dancing."

"Don't worry. You'll get that from Liam," Rachel said, loosely holding in a grin.

"You turned him into a monster with that old *Lord of the Dance* video." I scolded her. They watched it over and over when they were little, the way most children rewatch Disney movies.

"At least you're both dancing. I didn't come all this way to see other people's grandchildren on stage," Bobby said.

"That reminds me." Rachel snapped her fingers and pulled an

innocent face that immediately made me suspicious. "Fi can't come. She's miserable with allergies. Also, Arianne is spending the day at the pub, for her first Saint Patrick's Day since turning twenty-one." She batted her lashes at me. "Can you help a girl out?"

"Your step-dancing buddies ditched us?"

"They couldn't help it." She pouted. I knew the pout was for fun, but her eyes showed total disappointment. I was about to turn her down and tell her to bow out as well, but my mother rolled her eyes like it was a cure for her aging sight. I turned the other way and noted Thomas's lust-filled face. Did he want to see me make a fool of myself, dancing? It had been so long.

"I'd need shoes."

Rachel shuffled her feet like she was already on stage. "I stopped by the house and picked them up. They're in my car."

Like a Corleone lackey, I couldn't refuse. "I'd be glad to do it then, sweetheart."

Her eyes lit up, and she did a vertical leap. "Thanks, Mama. It'll be fun."

The more I thought about it, the more I warmed to the idea. I hadn't danced in front of Bobby since I'd quit. I taught my kids their basic steps before they'd taken a class, but we lived across the country from my parents back then. Like I'd just advised Bobby, this was my time to do what I wanted too.

A wide, kind of vicious grin spread across my face. "It will be fun." I ignored the gasp of disgust from my mother. My days of trying to please her were done.

"NO, NO, NO... DON'T YOU DARE GO ALL *LORD OF THE DANCE*, Lee," I scolded under my breath, trying in some way to will him into submission with "the Force." Instead, Liam tucked his chin like a toddler and let his dimples loose. Then out went the arms as if he was Jaysus Himself, pointing at the musicians, pointing to the lights. Not to mention, he wheeled his arms and pointed to his sister. I hung my head in embarrassment. This was why we pulled him from a formal program way back when. He never could contain himself in class. He was better suited to making music and performing with his guitar.

To my chagrin, he received enthusiastic applause when the band stopped playing. One song was left for the first band. Liam chatted with the lead singer, and before I knew it, they brought Thomas up on stage with his fiddle. Rachel jumped on the mic and pretended to coerce Bobby into dancing.

"Keep in mind my knees aren't what they used to be since my surgery," she told the audience. Her Irish lilt, which could turn on and off like a light switch, was at full strength. For some reason, it made me chuckle. The party put me in a celebratory mood, and her attention-seeking antics came across as quirky rather than weaponized.

"Ah Gran, you're the one who taught us," Rachel bantered with her on the second mic as the musicians checked in with Thomas and each other. "How about we stick with the basic eight?" She turned to the crowd to explain, "Those are the steps that are taught in a beginner class." My daughter pivoted to Bobby again. "Lee and I can take on the advanced moves."

I leaned into the first mic. "I'd appreciate that." The audience chortled at us.

Bobby raised her hands, soaking in the attention. She morphed into her version of an Irish lilt. "*Foine, foine.* Get on wi' it then."

The band began a lively, albeit slow version of "Star of the County Down," changing the name from Colleen to Kathleen in my honor. Refraining from the usual speed of the song allowed Bobby to keep up, and she came alive, leading the rest of us.

The song ended with a roar as Rachel called out, "A big hand for my Gran, Bobby Allen."

Thank heaven for my daughter. She allowed us all to have a

much-needed family bonding moment. Something in me had shifted. My mother's antics rolled off my back, and I was proud of myself. *This* was what I wanted.

"He plays like an Irishman," Bobby observed of Thomas's musicianship as we made our way back to the serving station.

Smiling at her, I said, "Why, Mother, are you complimenting my fiancé?"

"*Pffft.*" She waved a hand. Whether it was at my tease or my reference to Thomas's change in status, I didn't care. "I thought you said he plays the guitar, is all."

"He plays both, plus…" I caught myself and swallowed hard. "He learned the fiddle first." I bit my tongue and nearly drew blood. I'd almost told her that Thomas learned the old folk songs from his Irish miner friends—the ones from the California Gold Rush. My first near slip made my heart race. How the hell did he keep these secrets every day? I ambled behind the counter to take a minute.

With Jake as an apprentice to Liam and Thomas, they broke down the first band and quickly brought in the second one. Those of us behind the counter took care of the rush to order and resettle with equal efficiency. Before I knew it, I was back up on stage with both my kids, dancing to "Galway Girl" and wearing myself out. My face ached from smiling.

The fiddle player graciously gave Thomas time to feature, and an old, familiar feeling rushed through me—celebrating culture and ancestry as a family. I loved how well he fit in.

A flush of melancholy swept through me as we were supporting the band by clapping to "Whisky in the Jar." I wished my dad could have joined the party. He would have adored everything about this day. *Craic* like this, as he called it. He would have been down in front, doing a jig and bellowing every word of the traditional songs. I also wished he had met Thomas.

Deana came up to me and gave me a hug, pulling me out of myself. "That's the first time I've seen all y'all up there."

"And?"

The mirth in her eyes told me a joke was imminent. "Give me tap dancing any day."

"You mean like this?" I gave her a few skips and jump-overs while my arms did their best exaggeration of Savion Glover, side-eye added for effect. Then I finished with a time step and arms at my thighs, mixing both dance forms. "Neither sits right if you ask me."

Her warm chuckle rose through the area. "I guess not."

"Thanks for making me laugh though."

"You looked like you needed a distraction."

"I love the idea of featuring other dancing traditions. Let's talk to Jake about it. Maybe we can host more showcases."

At the end of their set, the lead singer brought the kids back up to accompany them on their version of "I'm Shipping Up to Boston." It was a guaranteed crowd-pleaser.

Somewhere in the middle of "whoa...," I spotted Mateo out of the corner of my eye as he exploded from his position, one of the other guards and Thomas fast on his heels. I couldn't tell what startled them, if someone had come in for them or if there was a text. They ran down the back hall as my heart pounded.

I was about to push through the crowd after them when Thomas appeared. He read the panic in my eyes and held his hands up to keep me behind the counter. They must have handled whatever happened in the back, but I was dying to find out what lit them up. Then I remembered the panicked stampede from Halloween. Desperate to communicate everything running through my head, I peered into his eyes. He mouthed, *it's handled* and gave me a discreet thumbs-up.

Thomas stood guard in the hallway, apparently taking Mateo's place as security until he received an all clear. *I should've known something would happen today.*

INTO THE MYSTIC

THOMAS

"Dammit, brother! You've lost your edge. Hell, you've chucked it off a cliff!" Banger slammed his hand on Kick's desk. He and I were conferencing in her office the evening after the Saint Patrick's Day party. "I don't blame Kick for this one. I blame your dick." He ran his hand over his buzz cut. "Swear to God… if you *ever* turn off the cameras in here again…" His beet-red face told me all about what he'd do.

"The security team worked." We'd tripled it to accommodate the crowd.

Banger's nostrils flared. "Mateo and his guys are good, but they're not you. I can't spare my top-tier associates for the daily shit. They're working behind the scenes. If the cameras had been on, we'd have this guy." He paced to the back door and returned, wringing his hands as he murmured to himself.

At least we were alone. Kick wouldn't handle the rebuke. My best friend laid it on thick like I was a juvenile delinquent, and I let him. I took every harsh, right word he spat out. Even the dick thing. The night before the party, I let myself get caught up in emotion. I'd spent several days at the lab and missed Kick. Finding her in her office afterhours, growling with frustration over the shitty service from the stage rental company, I distracted her with some desktop play. Convinced her it would ease our tensions.

"You're right, man. No more." Not until life's back to normal—whatever that looked like. I pinched the bridge of my nose. "The thing I don't get... it's like this kid knew the cameras were off."

"Yeah." Banger crossed his arms and ground his teeth. "This two-steps behind shit is..." He stopped and stared out the window, his jaw flexing. "I keep coming to one conclusion. It's unthinkable."

He didn't say anything else, just stewed as he gnawed on his lip. I could practically taste the anger emanating from him.

"What's going on?"

He spun around. "What if I have a mole?"

My eyes flashed wide. "Fuck."

Except it made sense. The working cameras picked up a male in a winter-weight hoodie who slipped into the hallway and disappeared into Kick's office. When he left through the back door, he tripped the silent alarm, which set off Mateo and me. "Kick's furious with herself for telling me to turn off the camera in Dee's office, but this guy didn't even touch the doorknob there. He came straight here." I slapped the desktop.

"He knew how to keep his face out of the cameras," Banger said. "Not to mention the size of the crowd." He settled into a club chair, though his posture stayed stiff. Now I knew the anger wasn't only about me. He vibrated with fury at himself too. "Listen, rein in your woman with these big nights. Not until I'm done. I don't know if she's planning an Easter bash. But it's off if she is."

"Don't worry. Remember Liam's senior trip? Angel's been

vetting it for us. It's over Easter—Spring Break." I sighed and stretched in her chair.

Banger's shoulders relaxed. "Thank fuck."

"The proposal party had gone so well we thought the system worked."

"Part of why I think there's a mole. But who? And why? It's just..." He rubbed his face.

"I don't understand why nothing's missing." Desk drawers were left half-open, and Kick's bags were dumped on the floor, but everything was accounted for. Kick, Deana, Jake, and I went through the contents with the police, and after they'd gone, Banger also swept for listening devices. Nothing. "What the fuck was he looking for?"

Banger's foot bounced along with his jaw. Hell, we had a jaw flex-off going on as we both seethed in our thoughts.

I drummed my fingers on the desk. "Let me guess... you're going out of town."

"More like underground. You don't understand."

Except I did. Angel Security wasn't just Banger's company, it was *him*. I'd been there when he fought with Alaric and Ellie over his vision and plans to protect the Society while also taking it into the twenty-first century. It required working with regular humans, but he developed a system that rewarded loyalty. The higher up and closer to Banger's inner circle someone went, the greater their reward. Like the rest of the Felidae, loyalty was personal. He couldn't abide a traitor.

His foot resumed bouncing. "Need you to hold down some shit for me now that Tess is dug in here."

"Damn." My hands raked through my hair. "What do you need?"

"First, Siobhan's taking over our real estate hunt. The woman I'm working with usually reports to her anyway." He lifted a shoulder and grinned. "There's only so much of me to go around. It's narrowed to four sites. You'll have to give final approval when they're ready to bring you in. Are you still on schedule with your end of things?"

"Yep. My lawyers should have the proposal for the university by the end of the week."

"And what's your timeline to start?"

"If we secure a building soon and get a clean construction crew on board… beginning of August. The dean will warm up to a partnership if I show them we'll be ready when the students are back."

"Siobhan's prioritizing facilities with minor modification needs," Banger assured me.

"Excellent."

"Also, Tess knows to call me if she needs anything, but she won't. Can you keep a close eye on her? She won't talk about it, but the Charley business rocked her."

"That's easy. Yeah, man. We've got her."

Banger almost grinned. "Kick's girl and her roommate are determined. They give Tess a taste of her own meddling medicine."

I lifted a shoulder. "Kick said something about spreading the love around. Anyway…" I stood and stretched my legs, letting the tension go. "Tess can stay at the farmhouse if she needs a break from the girls. I'll tell her."

"I don't know." Banger stood too. "We're testing the next upgrade at my place. I'd rather she stay where I can keep an eye on her from afar."

"Then I'll… schedule time with her."

We clasped forearms and said goodbye. "Thanks, brother."

"One last thing…" I rubbed my chin, hoping I wasn't about to overstep. "We've set a wedding date for Memorial Day weekend. Will this be over by then?"

"Fuck." Banger dropped his forehead against the door. "I hope so. Why can't you wait until we're sure?"

I forced air through my cheeks as I grabbed the back of my

neck. "Something's niggling at me. Telling me we should've done it yesterday. Can't explain it, but the sooner the better."

Banger tapped the doorframe. "Fine. I'll do my best. If you catch wind of anything, holler."

"Of course." Unfortunately, I was swamped at the lab. Many items on my to-do list had to be pushed until after the new lab was finished. I hated the idea of pushing Banger, especially now. He'd always been intense, but he balanced it with a play-hard attitude. I worried about what would happen if he didn't get to release it soon.

"I can hear you thinking," he said. "Don't worry about me. This became more than you and Kick today. I'm sure it all ties together. Whoever's behind it is taking advantage of our closeness. Since my eyes are open now, they're going to pay. Just hold tight. Yeah?"

I nodded. "Sure."

"Be in touch." He opened the door and turned back. "I have the last point now… When you speak with Siobhan, have her find you a damn event planner. You and Kick have too much to do to add in the running around for that. Don't make those guards taste cake samples, and don't play it shoddy. I'll only play this best man role once."

I laughed as I let my head hang. "Sure thing. And Rafa…" He lifted an eyebrow. I never called him by his given name, but this was vital. I walked over to him, looked in his eyes. "Stay smart. You're needed here. You listening?"

He grasped my shoulder. "Keep the faith."

"In you? Always." If I found out who'd betrayed Banger, I'd kill them myself. Still, I worried about how he'd take the information once he had it sorted. How bad would the fallout be?

Banger jerked his chin up and stalked out to his waiting Harley. I heard it rumble as he thundered out of the parking lot. A modern-day knight on a quest to protect his family and avenge his honor.

I sank down in a club chair and brooded over the day's events. As usual, my thoughts moved to Kick.

"It's too much, Thomas," she'd said when I explained about the silent alarm tripping. This time had been different. She'd spat the words through her teeth and added, "I want to wring his fecking neck."

"Let Banger and the team handle it. We're your secret weapon. It's the benefit of living life in the shadows. Graham thinks he's the one with the connections. He has no clue who Banger and I really are." At the time, I was convinced that Big Jonn was involved with what was essentially a break-in. My gut still believed it, but we needed proof.

"I appreciate it, cowboy. Honestly, I do. It's just… the damsel-in-distress thing? It's… I don't know." She shook her arms like something was crawling on her.

"Come here." I pulled her in for an embrace. "Much better." My hands ran up her sides, pushing her special edition Saint Patrick's Day T-shirt up to her breasts. It was a knee-jerk response to help us settle. Her eyes closed for a moment, lost in the feeling before Kick regained her senses and pulled the shirt down.

"You can't fix this with sex."

"Wasn't planning to. I'm sorry, baby. Touching you calms me. For the record, you're not a damsel in distress, unless I am too."

Kick's hands jerked up between us, making me step back. "The hell I'm not. I've been one before. I know how it feels."

"This is different," I insisted. I lifted my eyes to the ceiling, searching for the right words. "You've spent your life battling your family and your body. There are similarities here. Consider yourself like a warrior in training. Your instincts are fine."

She sighed a long breath and scoffed. "A warrior who can't focus with a weapon?"

"You're getting there." I bent my knees to make sure I had her attention. "I was supposed to be a career soldier, remember? My father made me train long before I enlisted. Hell, I understood a battlefield before I even knew how to use my cock properly."

Kick lifted an eyebrow, a glint of humor in her eyes. "I'm pissed."

"Good. So am I. And that's not the response of a damsel in distress. It's how a fighter feels when their ass is handed to them."

"If you say so."

"We'll figure out why we're always a step behind."

"Thanks, cowboy. I know what I need to do." Kick's face was resolute.

"What's that?"

"I need to figure this self-defense out the same way I did those others."

"Yeah?" I tilted my head, wondering what she'd decided.

Her eyes narrowed, like she could see through me. Then she tapped her heart. "It's in here. I need to hunker down and find it." Kick went up on her tiptoes and kissed my jaw. "I'll be at the range."

"Hang on, I can't go with you." I'd been neglecting my horse thanks to so many hours at the lab. Sure, he was an animal, but our rides cleared my head. It's where I did my best thinking, and my mind was swirling with too much shit. But first I needed to go over the papers my lawyers had drawn up for my proposal to Lord University. It was a healthy stack that I couldn't take for granted.

"I know," Kick said. "Mateo will come with me. I need to do this myself anyhow. I also know you need your trail time. Please don't make me wait till you get back."

I didn't protest. In fact, I was proud of her. She'd crashed through this mental block. As I walked through the empty coffee-house an hour later, my mind struggled to think of anything but Kick's progress. I pulled my phone out of my pocket and sent her a text.

Done here. On to Eddie. How're you doing?

Kick didn't answer, but after watching Mateo work these past weeks, I trusted them to have each other's backs. She had to be still on the range. I did, however, receive a text from the lab.

BETHANY

Call me ASAP.

CLOSER TO FINE

KICK

"Do you need anything else, Ms. Kick?" Mateo had helped me collect the weapons and set up the range on Thomas's property. The hardest part was bringing the bag down from Thomas's main office since no one else had access to it. Mateo scouted the property and made sure we were alone.

"Why don't you keep watch by the path on the high point? I know you like those. Maybe we can take turns, but no coaching, okay?"

Mateo chuckled as he held up his hands. "I heard you the first time and promise to zip it."

My first three tries were mediocre at best. One shot even ended up in a tree trunk again. I made a mental note to bring a tree surgeon out to the property. I didn't want to be the reason any of these beauties became sick.

I waved at Mateo. "Come at me."

He turned his head and chortled. "Pardon?"

"I need to loosen up. You know…" I waved at him again. "Pretend to attack me."

His brows rose. "Ah. Alrighty."

My muscle memory surprised me. It clicked in fast, letting me parry Mateo's first moves. He'd worked out with Thomas and me twice, so he knew where and how to push me.

"Let's try something different." Mateo taught me new moves from a slightly different discipline. Within a few minutes, my hands and knees were useless. He put me in a hold I didn't know how to escape. I kept testing joints to see if they had enough give to wiggle away. "Good," he said in my ear. "Remember this… your goal isn't winning a match. You want to live."

He squeezed me so tight it quickly became difficult to draw a breath. My heart rate soared through the roof as panic set in. I knew he wouldn't hurt me, truly, but the adrenaline spike almost made me pass out.

"Living to see another day might mean complying for a time. It's more important to stay calm. Keep your head."

"Can't… breathe."

"You can. Shallow breaths, Ms. Kick."

They were still coming too fast as my lungs longed to take a full inhale.

"Come on…," he ordered. "Mind over matter. Get your bearings. Look in each direction. See the path?"

I barely managed a head twitch, let alone nod, but he felt it.

"Good. Eyes on the pond. Now straight ahead."

It worked. My heart rate wasn't normal yet, but it stopped racing.

"Nice," Mateo said in my ear. "Stillness can be self-defense too."

He let me go, and I gasped the longest inhale in my memory. I felt like I'd been kicked in the stomach. I was furious with myself for falling for it, but Mateo smiled at me like a proud parent.

"Good work, Ms. Kick."

I chuckled as I held my head. The world still tilted a little. "What are you talking about? You made me into a chump."

"Self-defense starts here." He tapped his head. "There's always the possibility an opponent will be bigger, stronger, or hell, they might sneak up behind you. Panic kills. You stay alive with your mind first." He pointed at the range. "That's also what I see when you hold a weapon. Odds are, if you need a gun, you'll use it in close range. It's not the aim you have to perfect, it's having the balls to pull the trigger." He tapped his head again for emphasis.

I hated that this had become my life and wanted the madness to end. My tongue rolled around in my cheek as I thought through everything he'd said.

We'd talked the adrenaline down. Mateo had shown me a quick move to keep my bearings. Maybe I could do something similar with the Sig Sauer.

Multiple coils of curls had fallen out of my ponytail. Instead of fixing it, I tucked them behind my ears and picked up the weapon. I thought about finding my bearings. Looking around wouldn't help, since shooting required a focus on the target. What else had grounded me over the years?

As if summoned from deep inside me, the song "Closer to Fine" bubbled up. I began singing it from that place in my soul. I stopped relying on the gun to save my life. Like Mateo and Thomas had been telling me this whole time, the answers came from within. So did self-defense.

"Focus," Mateo called out.

He didn't understand, the song was my focus. I belted the hook as loud as my voice allowed and emptied the clip.

"Holy shit." I whispered hoarsely. It wasn't perfect, but it was pretty freaking close.

I changed out the magazines and sighted the second target as I sang the song again.

No more time spent as a victim.

No more time as the family scapegoat.

And no one knew my body better than me. It was up to me to protect it in all ways. Self-defense started in my mind. I took a deep breath and fired as I kept singing the song.

Mateo's whistle out-shrieked the weapon's reverb echoing off the pond. "Nice!"

The shot pattern rivaled Thomas's and Mateo's. My grin stayed plastered on my face as we switched out the targets. "Want to shoot side by side?" I asked him.

"Are you gonna keep singing?"

I shrugged. "Maybe."

"Good thing I have these." Mateo set his ear protection in place. Then he yelled, "Even if you do sing nice."

I bit my lip to keep from laughing and readied my weapon. I inhaled and found that deep place inside again. This time I sang the song inside. It wasn't the words that mattered. The magic came from revealing what had been waiting for release. After a nod at each other, we each emptied our magazines. My streak continued through two more rounds.

"Now you're just showing off," Mateo said, a smirk on his face.

"You're right." I didn't want to stop but hated the idea of wasting bullets.

"I was kidding, Ms. Kick. If you need more time, we can keep going."

"No, no. My goal's accomplished. Let's clean up." I picked up the rake we kept nearby and cleaned up the mess on the ground.

"Do you remember how to break these down?" Mateo asked.

"Good point." I thought so, but Thomas often did that work for me to make it go faster. "Let me take a picture of this last target, then you can quiz me."

After we cleaned the guns and secured them, I sent the photo of the target to Thomas. He had texted me about ten minutes earlier, but I hadn't noticed it until now.

ME

Going very well. Are you finished yet?

THOMAS

Knew you could do it.

The message included a kissy-face emoji. I smiled at it, thinking of how far Thomas had come from the serious man I'd met in September. Then came the second part.

THOMAS

Actually, had to head to the lab. Might take a while. Can you apologize to Eddie for me?

I laughed.

ME

Of course.

Thomas hated going more than a day without seeing his horse, and it had been a few already. He claimed Eddie pouted if Thomas became too busy to ride. I couldn't blame the horse. I felt the same. Still, I thought Thomas used the time the way I used my meditation pillow in my room.

"Hey Mateo…"

My bodyguard swung the bag of weapons over his shoulder and spun toward me.

"Want to go meet a horse?"

THE REST OF MARCH FLEW BY IN A BLUR EVEN IF IT WAS A QUIET one. No more weird break-ins happened at the coffeehouse or at home. The only thing I couldn't find was my lip balm, but I blamed Liam for its disappearance.

Banger had gone underground and, according to my fiancé, was hot on the heels of whoever wanted to harm me. All I knew was he'd gone to England. I couldn't keep the cities straight, but

Thomas had the details. The hush-hush-ness of it all made me antsy even if I trusted the men. They handled our current circumstances like danger was an everyday occurrence. Then again, it was sort of old hat for them.

Even the bodyguards stayed need-to-know. Thomas only allowed Tess and me into the inner circle that included Banger's right hand, Siobhan. The first time I met her, when she led the security installation at the Perked Cup, I saw her spiked, fire-engine-red hair and knew I liked her.

Since Thomas insisted on getting married on the Saturday of Memorial Day weekend, Siobhan hooked us up with a top-notch wedding planner. I knew what a crazy zoo planning a wedding could be, especially a fast one. I'd done it myself my last semester of college. Even though we wanted a family affair, getting someone else to do the heavy lifting was an immeasurable help.

Then the day before Liam's spring break arrived. The three of us were to join a group of families from Liam's high school on a cruise to the Bahamas. Thomas walked into the bedroom while I packed my suitcase.

He sat on the edge of the bed but wouldn't look me in the eye. "I have news."

I stopped rolling a T-shirt. "What's wrong?"

He cleared his throat. "*Grand-père* wants—"

"No." I dropped the shirt on the floor. "Don't tell me you can't go on our trip."

My chest tightened at the thought of breaking this to Liam. I couldn't see how we could go without Thomas. We'd have to bring a bodyguard or two. "We can't get another room. The ship is booked." Ironically, I knew someone in the group chat was on a waitlist for two rooms like ours. They'd been quite vocal in their disappointment over missing the booking window.

"Can't Alaric wait?"

His shoulders slumped. "It doesn't work that way, darlin'. The team and I caught a big break with Toni's project. That's why I've been at the lab so much. Plus he wants updates on you. Alaric doesn't want me sending updates online anymore even though it's encrypted." Thomas grabbed the back of his neck and stretched it. I bet mine was tighter. "The last time I updated Alaric, he guessed Banger's mole situation before I brought it up. Besides, I've stretched his patience as much as he'll take with our… circumstances. It'll go a long way to stay the good soldier this time."

"Our circumstances?" I squeaked. "You mean where we're engaged or where I'm one of you?"

Thomas's Adam's apple bobbed. "Both."

I picked up a pair of already packed shorts and threw them on the floor. "Here, I thought our engagement meant *I* was your priority."

He grabbed my wrist as I reached for a sandal. "You are. Look, I know the timing is bad, but finals are also fast approaching. I can't miss them. This is the only nonessential time on my calendar."

"Shit." I stared up at the ceiling while I bristled at his rightness. Liam's delivery had been induced during Shane's team's bi-week so that he could be there for it. My son's first five birthdays though? It had been me and the kids by ourselves. My eyes widened. This trip had been just as important to me as it was to Liam. The last senior trip. How would I fix this?

Thomas pulled me between his legs and wrapped his arms around my waist. "I'm sorry. I'll make it up to both of you."

I'd heard that before too. But Shane tried his best to come through. Why shouldn't Thomas be as beholden to the Felidae as my late husband had been to his team? Both entities basically owned the men.

I laid my head on top of his and hugged him back. "I'm still taking Lee somewhere. He'll probably pick a place with topless beaches to get back at me."

Thomas groaned and squeezed, pressing himself into me. I

stepped outside my hurt heart long enough to note his messy hair. He hadn't showered yet either. He needed time to relax as much as I did. "Mmm. You at a topless beach. You're killing me."

"Good." I kissed his head. "You get 'topless beach' me every night. What's the difference?"

"The sun. The sand. The water—"

"The burned skin. Besides, no nude beaches will be allowed."

"Your presence alone will keep your boy in line."

"Exactly." I moved back and stood with my hands on my hips, wondering where to begin first. "How many guards will we need?"

Thomas rubbed the bridge of his nose, considering. "Two should be fine, as long as it's a resort I know and you take a chartered plane."

"You know resorts?" I folded my arms and stared down at him. This was yet another of those moments where the reality of Thomas blindsided me. Somehow it still made sense.

He lifted a shoulder. "Some of my connections own resorts."

Of course they did.

And that's how Liam, Mateo, Wes, and I ended up spending five balmy days on a sunny beach in Barbados. It didn't diminish how hard it had been to break the news to my son. All his close friends went on that cruise, including Jax and her parents. The poor kid almost cried over it.

As a consolation, I arranged to fly in the Irish cousins for Liam's graduation, under the supervision of Shane's mother, Anna, and Uncle Billy, and I agreed to let Lee fly back with them for the summer. It turned out my nest would empty earlier than planned.

Then? I did cry.

ALL THE SMALL THINGS

KICK

"Will it be too much trouble to stop by a jewelry store on the way home?" I asked Mateo. We were standing in a parking lot in front of the restaurant I'd taken Rachel to for a birthday dinner. We'd had painfully little time alone and decided on a quiet evening without the boys. Dylan was buried by his school project. Liam's band had booked a paying gig. Rachel asked for a family dinner the following weekend too, when all three men could come. Thomas was due home later this evening and would join us for the second dinner. I loved how she included him in the ask.

The end of an era loomed heavy on my heart. Rachel had landed a role in a summer theater production in the Outer Banks. This was the first summer Rachel wouldn't work at the coffeehouse. I'd have to consider myself lucky to see her for the wedding and Liam's graduation. It took a lot of effort to keep my shit together during dinner. I spent the evening focusing on celebrating my girl and all she was about to become. It helped a little.

Despite how much my body had been physically changing—reversing, according to Thomas—these upcoming changes made me feel old. Even if I'd begged for the empty nest when the kids frustrated me. Even if I liked Thomas's promise of naked weekend every night. So I took advantage of the opportunity to celebrate Rachel one-on-one, afraid those times would become few and far between. Except with guards eating across the room from us, of course.

They were wonderful about it. Mateo and Wes—Rachel's detail today—gave us plenty of room for privacy and agreed to let me drive my Camaro while they tailed us in the Escalade Wes used to chauffeur Rachel. All of that was on the condition that I agree to stick to a preplanned route.

Fortunately, the Graham's were busy with Young Jonn's trial. It was set to start soon. According to the tail Banger had on him, the boy was faithful to his therapy appointments. I hoped we were nearing the end of this weird-ass year.

"You pay the bill, Ms. Kick. I go where you tell me," Mateo answered with his sheepish grin.

"Right. Let's head to this artisan market then. The jeweler promised to stay open for me. Mums the word to Thomas too. I'm picking up his ring." I shared the location of the store with Mateo.

"Promise." He held his fingers up, Boy Scout style. "The GPS report still goes to the office."

I waved him off. "Feel free to explain the stop to Siobhan. Just keep the stop from my guy."

"Of course. Everyone's expecting some of that, given the quickness of your wedding."

I shook my head. "Don't know why he's in such a hurry to make it official, but thanks."

A half hour later, I buckled back into the Camaro, giddy with excitement. The ring turned out better than I'd hoped. Southern oak set in tungsten. It was masculine and earthy.

The wood came from live oak in the park at the Center of Oakville. It inspired our town's name. The tree was thought to be around a thousand years old. When we first moved there, I often took the kids on picnics under its shade. The heavy branches bent to the ground, seeming to invite the kids to climb them. After Shane's funeral, I often escaped to those sturdy branches to clear my head. It became a sanctuary, a way to escape the pain, where I could just be.

As soon as the ring landed in my palm, it occurred to me I'd chosen the wood because Thomas was my sanctuary now. Plus that tree was one of the few things I knew of older than him. We speculated it was an ancestor of the tree at the edge of Thomas's property where we committed ourselves to each other. I couldn't wait to see this visual representation of that commitment on his finger.

"You had it inscribed?" Rachel asked, holding the ring up to the interior light. She turned on her flashlight app and read the Gaelic out loud. "*Mo chuisle, mo chroi.*"

Her face twisted into a frown. It wasn't the reaction I'd expected.

I placed the ring safely in my purse, then hit the road, checking the rearview mirror for our bodyguards. "Something wrong?"

Her chin quivered. "My heart's pulse, right?"

I spared her a glance as I watched the vehicles around us. "Pretty much."

Turning in her seat, she faced me and said, "But Daddy's ring had the Gaelic for *soul mate.*"

"It did." My chin dipped in agreement, not liking where this was heading.

She huffed at me, her hands reaching as high as the interior allowed. "How can someone have two soul mates, *Mother?*"

Mother? When did I land in the doghouse? "Thomas has always liked the meaning behind Macushla's name. It'll make him happy." I thought about her question and the answer hit me hard. "Besides, it's true. I have had two soul mates."

A quick head turn her way showed me no sign of a smile. She pressed her lips together as she stared out the window. Glared was more like it.

I took a deep breath and pressed the pedal to the floor, both literally—to enter the freeway—and figuratively—to make Rachel understand something I wasn't sure I did. "What if my soul is completely changed from when I married Daddy?"

Again with the scornful face. She looked like a raven-haired version of my mother. "That's impossible."

"I disagree. Your dad's death changed us all. I can't speak for you precisely, but I believe it transformed me in my deepest parts —you could call it my soul."

"So you think you're a fundamentally different person now than you were before his accident?"

A light bulb went off in my mind. "Do you think Thomas is my second choice? That's not fair either, Snow."

"Can you honestly tell me that if Daddy were alive, you'd marry Thomas?"

"You know we'd be together." I shrugged. "My point is… I'd also be different from who I am now." Her chin quivered harder. I had to think fast. "Do you think I'd have the Perked Cup if your father still lived? Do you think I'd have learned to stand up to your grandmother the way I do?"

Her mouth twisted as she thought. "You could."

I shook my head. "I'm certain I wouldn't. Back then, I just wanted to paint in peace and feel better. I never wanted to be an entrepreneur with the responsibilities that come with it. I wouldn't have needed to either. Nope." I shook my head with vigor. "I know I'd be different if he were here."

"So that's bad?"

"It's life." I reached for Rachel's hand. "It's neither good nor bad." From the corner of my eye, I saw her head stay down, eyeing my engagement ring. "What I mean is, Thomas fits exactly who I am now. He's not a consolation prize. He simply… fits." She lifted her head and stared out the windshield. "Tell me you understand," I pleaded.

"Can I think about it?"

I patted her hand. "Absolutely."

Music from Blink-182 filled our silence as we made our way down I-540. The skies opened up yet again and began a steady sprinkle. April had been one of those months with all the weather, especially rain. At least it wasn't pouring, and it washed the pollen away. As much as my eyes had improved, I still hated driving in the rain after dark. The days might be getting longer, but it wasn't summer yet. Not sure why, but squinting helped me keep my focus on the road.

I went over the schedule in my head to keep from being irritated by the road. Next we'd pick up food for Rachel, Isabella, and Tess. Then Wes would drive her home. Only a few more exits until the grocery store.

I shifted our conversation from me to my daughter. "So are you and Bella still doing well?"

A sarcastic smile returned to her face. At least she hadn't forgotten our native language. "Are you asking me if *I'm* getting any? Do you ask the boys if they are?"

"Dylan acts like I do. But noooo." I drew out the last word. "I'm asking how your household is faring in general. You were with Cody a long time, and the change to Bella seemed quick. You can't blame me for wanting to make sure my girl's happy. Then you two jumped into repairing Tess and Charley. Thank you for letting up on that, by the way."

Rachel flicked her wrist. "Absolutely. They're destined. They'll speak soon enough. I guarantee it." She tucked her foot under her thigh and turned toward me. "As far as Cody goes…" She sighed heavily, her posture easing in my periphery. "It's a relief to be free of him."

I quickly turned my head and smiled at her. Rachel was the most relaxed I'd seen her in a while.

Rachel lifted a shoulder. "Anyway, Bella's great. We're having a great time. It's all... great."

I reached over and squeezed her hand. "That's all I care about. How are you planning to handle summer theater and a new relationship?"

She perked up. "Oh, it couldn't have worked out better. Bella has an internship in Virginia Bea—"

Something pelted against the passenger-side window, spider-webbing it. A second burst made a hole, sending small shards across the front seat and who knew where else. Sharp drops of water hit my arm. Rachel's scream pierced my ears before it registered that we'd been shot at.

A few more bullets thudded into the rear quarter panel. My heart pounded as my head swung to the right. Mateo's words came to me—*get your bearings.*

I saw the spoiled rotten son of a bitch, gun still drawn, trying to steady his filthy hand. Jonn Graham. The piece of shit was in the back seat of a red BMW, just like the one from the snow-storm. The window was down, a buddy drove, one more cheered from the front passenger seat like he was at a Hurricanes game. For a split second, I watched the bastard gleefully bounce in the back.

Forget the shine on the road from the rain, I saw red. How the hell was this asshole out of his house? My chest pounded, but not from fear. I was enraged.

"Get down!" I grabbed Rachel's arm and practically threw her under the dash, causing the Camaro to swerve toward the Beemer.

I straightened the wheel as another bullet shattered the small back window. "Fucking hell!"

We had to get away. *Self-defense starts with your mind.*

I'd forgotten about the Escalade until I heard more shots,

ducked, and swerved, but no bullets hit the car. Wes was firing at the BMW.

I chanced a glance to the right. Graham's deadly stare stayed pegged on us, glimmering as much as the water droplets clinging to the bits of glass on the edges of my windows. He gnashed his teeth at us like a mistreated, starving beast. Another quick look and he aimed at the door where my daughter was curled up on the floor. I had to get her away from this monster.

An exit I knew like the back of my hand was fast approaching, so I slid my car from the left lane all the way to the right. The tires squealed from the maneuver as we cut off the Beemer and accidentally also lost Mateo and Wes.

A call came in over Bluetooth. I hit the button on my steering wheel.

"Kick! Where the hell did you go?"

"Shit. Sorry, Mateo. I had to get Rachel out of there. He was aiming for her. For my daughter!" I shrieked. Flying down the road, I nearly rear-ended a car stopping for a yellow light. My tires squealed again as we swerved around it and flew through the intersection.

"Where. Are. You?" Mateo repeated.

For an instant, I forgot, though instinct told me safety was close. Why were we here? Six Forks! "We're on Six Forks. There's a police station coming up." I had to think. "You still have eyes on Graham?"

"Yep. Call 911. Let them know what happened and you're coming."

"Gotcha."

"Fuck. Remember... keep your head. I'm gonna stay on these guys until we stop them. This ends tonight."

"Thanks, Mateo. Be safe." I hung up and watched the business parks and shopping centers roll by as I searched my memory for the location of the substation. "Rach..." My voice was shaky as hell, but I made it as commanding as I could. "You have your phone down there?"

"Yes," she whimpered.

"Call 911. Tell the operator about them shooting. Tell them we're going to the substation. We'll need cover when we pull in. Hell, ask them if one's handy for an escort." I watched my rearview mirror more than the front while I spoke. I couldn't help thinking they'd given the Escalade the slip. Every car I saw looked red to me.

"K-kay," Rachel said, dialing.

She handled the call well enough to tell her story. Unfortunately, the intersection where we were supposed to turn left had a red light. The logical part of my brain knew Mateo and Wes kept Graham and his buddies occupied, but the primitive side of it stayed in flight mode. I'd keep Rachel safe no matter what. I treated the intersection as a four-way stop, or really, as a yield, turning the wheel as I slammed on the brakes. An icy mist hit my face and fought with my lashes, blinking rapidly as I made the turn. The car's momentum pulled it into the new street more than the wheel did.

Thank goodness it was a Sunday evening, the road virtually empty. Another quick left and we were in the police parking lot, flying way too fast. We skidded to a stop, the rear end fishing, making one hell of a squeal on the wet pavement. It saved our asses when we stopped inches from smashing into two cruisers with the side of my Camaro. We were too close to open my door.

I took a moment to gasp for breath as I reached for Rachel. She whimpered in terror yet again as four officers cautiously approached us with their guns drawn.

"We need to see your hands. Are you the one who called in a drive-by?" A surprisingly kind face bent toward the open area of the passenger window. Rachel screamed anyway.

"Shh, Snowy... mama's here." I instinctively reverted to soothing her the way I had when she was little. As far as the police were concerned, obedience was no problem. I raised my hands up as far as they'd go. "Okay, okay," I called out. "We were shot at. C-can I pull forward a bit? I can't open my door."

The first officer shook his head. "You'll have to crawl out this side."

Over the glass? Maybe if I yanked off my jacket. It could be a buffer between my hands and the glass. "My daughter needs help getting out. Please."

"Sure, ma'am." He opened the door to lift Rachel out when I truly saw her. She reached for him, her right arm covered in blood. She was bleeding so much from her head I couldn't see her right eye.

To hell with keeping my mind clear. This mama turned into a full-on banshee.

THE SKY IS CRYING

THOMAS

I landed at the airport twenty minutes behind schedule and powered up my phone while waiting to deplane. My heart started pounding as I read a series of texts from Banger.

BANGER

Heard from Kick? No one's responding. Not her. Not the guards. Not Princess.

I was doing the penguin walk down the airplane aisle when another came through.

BANGER

Graham's on the loose. His tail never checked in. Sent a man to investigate. The tail's dead.

My pulse immediately pounded so hard I couldn't hear the woman behind me speaking.

When another came through saying, *Where the fuck are you????* I knew Banger had lost his cool.

The second I stepped onto the jetway, I bolted. Tried my best not to knock anyone over, but I couldn't be certain and apologized while passing each person. Finally able to run through the open airport, I turned on my Bluetooth and called Kick, hoping my shoes didn't slip on the slick floor as I kept up the sprint. The call went to voice mail. I needed to keep her away from the house, figuring that's where Graham would head. Unless he went after Rachel. Then I remembered Kick had taken Rachel out for her birthday. *Fuck!*

I thumbed my contacts for Mateo, but he called me first. My heart dropped into my stomach as I answered. "Tell me they're alright."

He sounded out of breath like he was running. "Have you landed?"

"Just." Thank Christ I'd parked in the airport deck and didn't have to wait for a shuttle to long-term parking. "Throwing my gear into the trunk now. Did Banger reach you?" I heard three sharp bangs—like gunshots—over the phone, then tires squealing. My heart simultaneously stopped and jumped out of my chest. *Not again.*

"Talk to me," I ordered. My Camaro roared to life, the growl mimicking my anger at feeling helpless.

"The fucker took a shot at Kick's ride. He unloaded on her passenger side."

Fuck! Kick.

She sat in the passenger seat when Mateo was on duty. Hell, she hadn't driven herself in weeks. "Where are you?" More squealing tires. "Why isn't everyone in the Escalade?"

At this point, I was maneuvering around the parking deck's circular exit tower way too fast to be safe, even for a Sunday evening.

"Um... Kick and Rachel took her Camaro and Wes and I followed behind. It should've—" Another gunshot shut him up.

I slowed enough to go through the gate, then I bolted the hell out of there. "Where are my girls? Talk to me!"

"Sorry, sir. We're uh… following Graham and… Kick got out of dodge like a pro, sir. She should be at the police station by now."

"You *lost* them?" My temper grew murderous in an instant.

"Technically… she lost us. We're keeping Graham's car occupied… till the cops intercept us. Wes is on the phone with RPD now. We're trying to lure them off the freeway and away from innocents."

Fuck. Find Kick or help the guards? I could help Wes and Mateo if the Escalade was nearby. That is, if the women were away from danger. Frankly, I was long past wanting to kill Jonn Graham. I needed it like I needed air. If either of my women had been hurt… I couldn't think about it.

"Which freeway?" As I approached the eastbound ramp that would take me home, two cars flew past the airport exit. "Was that you? Did you just pass the airport?" I pressed the brake and switched lanes to take the ramp going west, the decision made for me.

"Huh? Yeah! Guess we did."

"Don't exit yet. I'm coming up behind you. Keep them occupied. Be right there." I opened up my muscle car up on the entrance ramp. The wipers were on high to keep up with my speed. I'd never known a car that could beat mine in a flat quarter mile. I saw the two cars in no time. Made out one gunman sitting in the back seat. Saw the shadow of a head in the front passenger seat. I had to assume he was armed, but only the one shithead fired at Mateo and Wes. Thank Christ the Escalade had been bulletproofed.

"You driving, Mateo?"

"Yes, sir."

Another shot fired. Kid must've reloaded. Bastard must've snapped.

"I'm here. Inside lane." I patted the dashboard. My secret weapon. "Sorry for the next few minutes, Ginger." My Camaro wouldn't mind. If my plan worked, I'd still drive her home. I spoke to the guys again. "Listen. Keep them occupied till the straightaway. On my signal, slam on the brakes. I'll put the Beemer into a skid. Then I'll back off. You guys get back in and ram them. Understand?"

"Got it. Signal. Brake. Smash. We end it."

"Right." We took a curve to the right. The BMW either didn't notice me matching their speed or was too hyped to care. With their attention on the Escalade, I stayed two lanes over on purpose. I moved my car into the middle lane as we came out of the curve. Even with the SUV now, I called out, "Brake."

Mateo backed off as I cut the wheel and hit the gas. My faithful muscle car bolted for the rear bumper of the BMW and sent it into a sideways skid, like it was angry too. Then I pulled away and ordered, "Go, go, go!"

The Escalade rammed the passenger side of the BMW. Mateo pushed it into the grassy median. A loud "Take that, asshole!" echoed over my Bluetooth.

As well as the BMW was made, the car couldn't hold up against the heavy SUV. It was through. However, the driver's side stayed unscathed. We all stopped on the shoulder. No one was firing, but being behind Mateo and Wes blinded me to the action in the BMW. The rain at night didn't help either.

I'd had enough. I wanted that nightmare finished yesterday. Kick and Rachel flashed through my mind. They hadn't called yet, not that I could've answered. *Christ*, I hoped they were alright.

As I reached for the gun under my seat, the red and blue lights of multiple police cruisers flashed in my rearview mirror. "Mateo… still with me? What's happening?"

"So far… nothing, sir. We might've knocked them out."

Fuck! I wanted my piece of them. But fighting in three wars and then some had taught me the most important part of war—living to see another day. My leg bounced as I talked down my rage. "See the cops?" I asked Mateo.

"I do. About time."

"Let the police handle them now." I gnashed my teeth, wishing I could take back my words. Getting to my women came first.

"Roger that."

I beat on the steering wheel. What good would it do for Kick to get away from those idiots and lose me to the police? I didn't worry about being shot by the likes of Jonn Graham, though anyone can be lucky. The weather conditions and our circumstances primed the situation for confusion.

The flashing lights turned into no less than five cruisers. I rolled my window down as they skidded to a stop around us and exited their vehicles with guns drawn. I raised my hands as raindrops pelted my face, hoping my hands could be seen in their headlights. My heart pounded again, praying like hell that they figured out who was whom in this fucked-up scenario.

"Out of the car!" The gun pointed at me seemed to speak since the cop was shadowed by the night.

I kept my hands visible as I opened my door in obedience. Before I even took a step outside, gunshots opened up, sounding like a damn firing squad. On instinct, I yelled for Mateo since the earpiece was still on. "What's happening?" I couldn't see a fucking thing back behind the Escalade.

A hand came from nowhere and shoved me down. "Get on the fucking ground!" As gravel bit into my cheek, the gun that had been pointed at me fired.

"Not the Escalade! They're good guys. They're my security team." It was a stupid thing to say, but I wasn't thinking straight. For a minute, I was back in a war trench in France, laying helpless as my uncle bled out. What would I tell Kick if her guards died trying to end this madness?

Not daring to move my hands, I coughed away the wet dirt

sticking to my mouth. I figured the heat of the moment was the only reason I hadn't been cuffed. Better to make my hands as frozen as possible. The hard part was keeping them from shaking with the cold. I coughed as exhaust from the Escalade filled my nose.

In seconds, the shooting stopped. Police called for ambulances. The acrid scent of gunpowder replaced the exhaust. Risking turning my head toward the bottom of my car didn't diffuse the smell or the PTSD that sometimes followed. The muscles in my arms spasmed as I forced myself to stay calm. I despised the helplessness of the moment. Then more cruisers arrived and shut down the expressway.

Wes had been on the phone with a 911 operator during the start of the chase, so the police knew the situation of the BMW and the Escalade when they arrived. They didn't know what to make of me and the Camaro, but the bodyguards straightened it out once the scene abated.

I ended up with a bump on the head and small scrapes from the shove to the ground. It was a move to keep me out of the line of fire as much as it was to subdue me.

Mateo and Wes were fine, thank Christ. They'd been kneeling on the ground, their shields in their hands when Jonn Graham and the driver of the BMW tried to make a run for it. As soon as they realized they were surrounded, they fired on the police. The firing squad sound of the moment ended up being real. Those sick boys died anyway—suicide by cop.

Whatever. As long as my men were alright. My ladies too.

Then the real challenge started. While I sat on the side of the freeway in the pouring rain, with what seemed like all the police in the county milling around, I plotted how to get the hell out of there and find Kick.

. . .

I FOUGHT MY NERVES ALL THE WAY TO KICK AND RACHEL. IT WAS A new form of torture to keep my speed respectable while I kept dialing her phone. Since my Camaro was drivable, law enforcement let me follow a cruiser back to the station to give my statement. They knew about my women but wouldn't divulge any details.

She never picked up, which amped up my worry. I was going out of my mind. I heard an ambulance siren while exiting the freeway. My heart did a somersault. Had one of them been hit? Mateo never answered that question.

Every.

Damn.

Light.

Was.

Red.

Sweat poured down my temples and my back. I'd grabbed my drover coat from my car and slid it on to cut the chill once the police were satisfied I wasn't a threat. The horse smell on the coat, the wind whistling through the crumple in my front bumper. Everything grabbed my attention. The wipers still smacked at full speed from the earlier chase. I turned them down to appropriately handle a misty night at street speeds. At least I could fix something.

If anything was wrong with them—

Two more left turns and I was in the parking lot. Every available officer was in the damn parking lot. Most of them stood around Kick's car. A flashlight fixed on a bullet hole and my blood boiled.

I nodded to the officer who parked ahead of me, letting him know I was right behind him. As soon as I found my woman. Entering the vortex of activity, my eyes landed on her. Hard not to. She was yelling at an EMT attempting to wrap her hand in a bandage.

"It's fine... Why won't you tell me what's going on with my daughter?"

I wiped at my face to get any leftover dirt off. I hadn't checked myself in the mirror. Didn't want to scare her.

"Ma'am, I promise, your daughter's—"

"Kick!" I bellowed, relief rushing through me as she turned. Except for the bandage on her hand and shallow cuts across her cheeks, she looked alright.

The wind blew the sides of my coat apart as I stalked toward her. Kick flew at me full speed, slamming into my body, making me step back to recover. I wrapped her in my arms, the coat engulfing her, swallowing us both. I breathed in the lavender scent of her hair. Her heartbeat pounded against my chest like it sought mine. Proof I hadn't lost her. Then we both started shaking violently.

"Sir." A cautious officer approached. "Need to see your hands."

He held his gun on me, and I reluctantly lifted my hands as Kick yelled, "He's my fiancé!" She stuck her left hand straight up out of my coat. Her voice was hoarse, almost laryngitis bad. What the hell had she been through?

"This true?" the cop asked me.

"Yes." I nodded. "May I?" Pointing with my hands, I asked permission to place them back around Kick.

The officer who'd escorted me here told the one speaking, "He was at the shoot-out on the 540."

Kick's eyes flashed wide. "A shoot-out?"

The first officer lowered his weapon.

I squeezed Kick and drank in her life... her living, breathing, wellness. My worst fear hadn't come true. If I could have, I would've floated, but my lady wasn't ready to celebrate. To answer her, I gave her the important facts. "It's over, darlin'. Bodyguards are fine. Jonn Graham and his driver are dead. Third guy's on his way to the hospital. In custody."

Kick let her head fall into my chest and whimpered. I repeated "it's over" countless times as I rubbed her back.

Another officer came up to us. "Ms. McKenna? You can see your daughter now. The EMTs are finished. Good thing it was just a graze, huh?"

Kick started shaking like a chihuahua in an ice storm.

"Come on, baby. I've got you."

"Ms. McKenna?" the same officer called out as we walked to the rig. We turned toward him as one. No way was I letting her go. "We'll have to keep your car for the investigation. We want to make sure the bullet holes match the gun from the scene. It should be easy, honestly."

I caught Kick as her knees buckled. "My car." She buried her face in my chest. "I'm not sure I can drive it again, Thomas."

"Shh. We'll figure it out… I'm sorry, darlin'. So sorry." I kissed her temple over and over. There was no way I'd let her out of my sight again.

"I LOVED THAT SHIRT, MAMA." RACHEL'S SAD VOICE SOUNDED MILES away as we walked into the house in the middle of the night. We had more questions to answer, and it felt like we'd been at the station for a week. Kick's arms held her daughter and mine held them both.

She kissed Rachel's cheek. Despite the height difference, she kept her daughter close, expertly steering her through the first floor and up the stairs. Of the three of us, Rachel looked the worst. Her arm had been grazed, and a shard of glass had hit just above her hairline. She had multiple stitches from both injuries and an assortment of smaller cuts all over. A large bruise bloomed on her cheek from hitting the dash when Kick shoved her down.

I felt every one of those injuries, and I wasn't her father. Standing in the kitchen, I glared out the window into the dark until the reflection let me know they were upstairs and out of sight.

"I'll get you a shirt just like it, sweetheart. Are you sure you have to go to school tomorrow?" Kick's voice filtered down to me, answered softly by Rachel, poor kid sounded ready to drop.

"For my afternoon class… yes. I'm doing a scene with three others. If I don't go, I'll mess it up for everybody."

"Learning early that the show must go on, eh?"

"You've taught me that since I was two." Rachel laughed, but the tone wasn't right. The distance in her voice concerned me. They disappeared into the loft, and I made a fist, slamming it on the cold, hard granite counter.

Fuck me. Fuck Banger too. I was certain he was reeling from the loss of his man, but what the hell happened to the surveillance? How did an idiot like Graham slip through? The answer shouted loud in my head, and I hit the counter again.

Traitor.

I raked my hands through my hair, then turned to the kettle. I could make tea in case Kick or Rachel needed some. As the water heated, I turned on my laptop and checked on the university's policy regarding therapy. Rachel would get trauma counseling as soon as I could arrange it.

Whether out of practice or simply a macho clod, I should've also considered Kick. Her instincts, like most parents, went first to her daughter. She took care of Rachel with nerves of steel— settling her into bed. Brought her chamomile tea. Called Isabella and Tess.

I admired her pluck. Stood in awe of it. I was a fool.

SOMEWHERE ONLY WE KNOW

KICK

"There you are." The words bounced off my ears in slow motion, sounding like they were underwater. Or maybe it was me.

Thomas's gentle tone irritated me as he maneuvered to my side of the bed. He'd found me too soon. I'd planned to hold on to my secret for a while. For the first time, I welcomed the darkness that used to periodically envelop me. Instead of the scary monster who would frighten me with whispers of self-loathing, it nestled deep inside me like a warm retreat. It transformed into a friend offering escape from the discord all around me. Intrigued by its promise, I played with it, swam in it. I relished in the numbness—health and gene expressions be damned. I wanted more time with it.

"Wes texted. Rachel's safe at class. He's sitting in the back of the theater." Thomas's strong hand caressing my back scratched like sandpaper. "I also found a counselor for her. Appointment's tomorrow morning. Tess and Isabella promised to make sure she goes. Tess will tag along in case she needs someone to talk to afterward."

"Great." The dull, uninterested echo in my tone reached my ears. The irony of my not caring if Tess mothered my daughter through her trauma didn't escape me. Maybe that had been the takeaway message when Tess comforted Rachel after her breakup. I'd been doing this on my own for too long. Even when Shane lived. Too late, I added, "Thank you."

"Not feeling well?" Thomas pressed his lips to my forehead in that parental way that told me he checked for a fever as much as he expressed affection. My eyes squeezed shut, a long sigh stalling for time. How could I explain just enough to make him go away and leave me to linger in my black peace? All the versions I knew of "Somewhere Only We Know" played on a loop in my head, and it was the only thing I wanted to think about.

"My immune system's fine." A pretend smile. That quick lift to the corner of my mouth was all I could muster. "I'm taking a little nap after the long night." *Now go away!*

He brushed curls off my face, exposing me to the world. *Shit.* Then he ran his hand across my shoulders. "No… something's wrong."

My eyes opened just enough to see through my lashes. Thomas scrutinized my face, his eyes way too warm, way too caring. "You've unraveled." His shoulders fell as he exhaled. Then he moved around the bed and snuggled in behind me, pulling me into his chest. He murmured into my hair, "I'm so sorry, baby."

"You don't control the world, Thomas," I clipped. "Maybe this isn't about you." I felt the wince against my back and didn't care. I'd do anything to be alone. Blissfully alone.

"We should've figured out the mole. Doubled security. Those boys had to know you weren't in the Escalade. Someone told them you'd changed your routine."

I appreciated how he didn't blame Mateo and Wes for what had happened or me for thinking it was safe to spend alone time with my daughter. It didn't mean I wanted Thomas blaming himself either. "It's not that at all. Please… just go." I risked glancing over my shoulder. "I don't want to pull you into this. I promise… I'll be back soon." Where my body called out for the security of the darkness, his touch hurt.

"No." He shifted to look me in the eye. "Your messes are mine, and mine are yours. That's how we work. Tell me why you're sad. Please."

The word *sad* lit a fire in me. This wasn't about an unfair grade or a bully's tease. It wasn't PMS either. It made me want to scream, but the motivation had vanished. The peaceful darkness consumed my focus and dampened any fire that would have stoked my temper. I settled on leveling him with a glare.

"Don't patronize me and don't excuse my weakness. *I* fucked up last night. I'll pay the price. You shouldn't have to." Then I rolled away.

I didn't blame myself for the shooting, but I sure as hell despised falling apart. I was supposed to be the poster child for meditation, supposed to be beyond this by now.

Thomas took a deep, ragged breath. His patience had found its last leg. This was why I wanted to be alone. He didn't know how warm and soothing the liquid depths of the darkness were. Well, I could swim in here for a good long time. He might as well baptize himself in my world.

Welcome to the real me, cowboy. Maybe this was the beginning of the end? I was too far under to care. I deserved it.

"Sorry for patronizing," he responded softly, ignoring my efforts to push away. "Please talk to me." I chanced a quick glance at him without moving. Thomas stared at the ceiling and spoke to the room. "Forgot how much we steel ourselves for the sake of the children. Should've noticed you doing that." His lips brushed my neck. "Your demons don't frighten me, by the way. Mine are close friends."

I looked over my shoulder and was shocked by the compassion in his eyes. No one had ever offered to trudge through the trenches with me. Even Shane had his limits. He'd never left me over it, obviously, but he'd emotionally distance himself until I found my way back. At least he had never yelled at me to snap out of it, like other family members.

Since Shane's accident, I'd perfected "fake it till you make it" in public and sinking in the pool in private. Still, maybe Thomas told the truth. Maybe he was brave enough to offer a hand.

I sighed and confessed. "I had a panic attack in the bathroom after Rachel left." The sound of my voice made me recoil. "It kind of... came out of the blue. Only it didn't, you know? The sh-shooting wasn't the catalyst, I don't think. It was more of a last straw. Like a switch flipped, then I turned around and here I am. Again. I should've expected it. It's not so scary this time, so there's a plus."

I felt Thomas nod. He was such a good listener, but I wasn't ready for it. "Doesn't surprise me. You've been through a ton of shit recently. Hell, I'm an upheaval to your life. Just hope it's a positive one."

I couldn't laugh at his self-deprecation. I closed my eyes and imagined the deep waters caressing my skin.

"What do you mean, it's different this time?" he asked.

I attempted an explanation after taking forever to collect my thoughts. "The darkness used to terrify me. Like another kind of narcissist in my life, it chased me... clung to my skin... a cross between toxic sludge that wouldn't wash off and a seducer offering relief. The taunting and provoking scared the shit out of me because it came from within." It seemed to be proof that the doctors were right about everything being in my head. Until someone finally listened and diagnosed me. It turned out mental health symptoms were a part of my physical diseases.

"Anyway, this time feels different. I saw little clues here and there, but there's been so much to juggle." I rolled to my other side, placed my hand on Thomas's cheek and breathed him in— his sandalwood scent. "You've been an amazing surprise. Don't blame yourself."

The tenderness he expressed as he closed his eyes. *Jaysus*, he calmed me. Why didn't I want it? I continued, "The blackness doesn't frighten me now." I shrugged. "It's not healthy, I know. I just don't care right now."

A tear slowly slid down my cheek. In a dare to make Thomas flee, I didn't wipe it away. Not even when a few more followed. "Please," I begged. "Leave me alone. I'll be back to Miss Sassy Sunshine tomorrow."

He didn't go, and I remembered how he hadn't left any other time I'd pushed at his boundaries. Instead, Thomas kissed my forehead again. "No."

Irritation filled my voice. "Why the hell not?" I'd be damned if I would snap out of it like everyone always wanted me to do.

Thomas tilted his head. "Like attracts like, remember? My world's also been rocked. I need this *darkness*, as you call it, as much as you do."

"Really?"

"Damn straight. I won't be your fair-weather friend. Ever. I love all of you... even the demons." He squeezed me gently.

A shiver ran up my spine. "My shell might be cracking... a little." Thomas smiled as I touched his face, recognizing his melancholy. "I'm sorry I can't help you back."

He rolled me around until we were spooned again, and I gripped his arm with both hands as he asked, "Tell me, if you could go anywhere physically to escape, where would you go?"

"Muir Woods," I answered immediately. The national park north of San Francisco had been one of my favorite places during those early years in California.

"Tell me about it."

I turned toward Thomas, confused. "Haven't you been there before?"

He smiled and cocked an eyebrow. "Yes. Tell me your version."

My smile surprised me. "So you know where I'm talking about, right?"

"Of course."

My breath hitched. "I've been in countless churches, but Muir Woods was the first place that inspired my heart to worship. The light… was more reverent than stained glass windows. The smells… clean and spicy. If heaven has a smell, that's it."

Thomas nodded like he could smell it too. "Tell me more about the scents."

"The bay laurel and evergreen oils…" I closed my eyes and remembered sitting on a park bench. "Sunrays sliced through the layers of vegetation, but the area gets so much fog it was always damp at ground level. It made the essential oils spring from the plant life. You could breathe better just sitting there."

"Oh yeah." Thomas inhaled, like my memory had been a suggestion. "Mountain air's the best."

"I loved how the forest floor had trillium, rhododendron, and azalea, like we do here. But the little redwood sorrels were my favorite. The first time I noticed it, a small grouping opened after a light beam shifted away from it. They don't like direct sunlight, see." I almost giggled as a memory surfaced. "I once convinced toddler Dylan that his baby sister was a sorceress. I stood her in front of me as we shaded a patch of sorrel. He bent over them in awe as they opened and showed us their pretty color. Then I picked her up and stepped away, letting the sun shine back on them. And they closed. Dylan stopped complaining about Rachel's crying for a week. She was teething, so everyone in the house suffered along with her."

Thomas chuckled softly, like that, too, touched another old memory. Despite my heavy heart, the pleasure of reuniting Thomas with long-forgotten memories found me.

"Did you go there often?" he asked.

"As often as we could. Little Dylan pretended he was a dinosaur on our early walks. Then it morphed into acting out *Star Wars* scenes as he grew. It helped me relax during a time when that eluded me the most."

The clock caught my eye, and I gasped. "Your lunch with Charley—"

"Already canceled." Thomas squeezed me.

"Don't let me keep you from your cousin. You say like attracts like and all that, but it's a miracle you found her."

He kissed my neck and spoke into my shoulder. "Could've lost you yesterday. As I said, my soul's shaken."

We lay in silence, absorbing and reassuring each other. "You appeared from nowhere in the parking lot, like an avenging angel," I whispered. Is this what I needed—to decompress and process with him?

Thomas's deep chuckle rolled through me. "Rafa's the angel, darlin'. I'm the terrified man who probably knocked over a senior citizen, sprinting through the airport. Nearly ran innumerable cars off the road."

"I'm certain I won the crazed-driver award," I answered with a sigh. "There's a vague memory of running two red lights."

I shuddered at the thought and sent a word of thanks that no one had been hurt. I also remembered how Mateo's words stayed at the front of my mind. My reflexes and focus had felt like they'd heightened. Maybe that's why I had handled the car okay.

Somewhere deep inside, my soul lifted off the bottom of the black lake. It didn't equal surfacing, but I wasn't stuck in the depths.

"Liam will be back by two thirty," I said, afraid I wouldn't be ready by then.

Thomas rolled away and typed on his phone. "Liam has an AP study group after school. We have until five. Said he'd pick up dinner, but we can eat in here if we need." He rolled back, returning his hands to their former places on my body. "In the future, let's promise to take a retreat if either of us feels over-whelmed. We'll hole up here or get away to the woods. Something like that."

I pressed a kiss to Thomas's lips and felt the edges of my real smile. "I do love you to the moon and back."

"Same, baby." He raised a questioning eyebrow. "Think you could do a comedy?"

I bit my lip. "Maybe."

He patted my behind and added, "See if there's something you'll like. I'll get us food."

Twenty minutes later, Thomas carried in a tray of lettuce wraps with avocado and smoked salmon, plus tea. It still surprised me that my inner mess hadn't scared him away. He embraced it, nonplussed.

We ate in the window seat, then Thomas stripped to his boxers and crawled into bed behind me as I queued up *So I married an Axe Murderer*. My shell continued to crack each time his soft laugh rumbled against my back as I recited the lines.

"Funny you'd pick a film set in Northern California," he said as his fingers ran a gentle glide continuously along my side.

I squirmed away, taking it as a sign of friskiness. "Don't."

"I wasn't," he responded. "Promise."

"You're frustrated with me." I sighed with worry.

"Not at all." Thomas rolled me, forcing me to face him. "It works both ways." My brow pinched as I tried to catch his meaning. "What you said before about wanting... when you don't want, I don't want either. Just touching you reminds me you're alive." He lowered his forehead to mine and shuddered. "It was obvious something was wrong when I went looking for you."

"How?"

He touched my nose with his finger. "I usually feel you when you're nearby. Like your energy finds me." Thomas raised our entwined hands. "Our auras have started intermingling after this much time together, but they're not. Not worried though. They'll be back."

For emphasis, he repeated, "It kills me you've been there for everyone else but had to fight your demons by yourself. Thanks for opening up. Your demons are also mine now."

"Everyone has their own shit, Thomas. Why should I pile on my family and friends?" I huffed and sarcastically added, "It's not a polite way to friend."

"That's your mother talking." Thomas growled, like he rebuked her. "Remember… it takes strength to let someone in. You showed courage when you let me in." He brushed a curl out of my face and lifted the corner of his mouth. "Now you're stuck with me."

Overwhelmed, I returned to watching the movie. He'd touched a nerve with the reference to Bobby. Before I had a dark lake to sink into, I'd hide in my closet and work out my issues. The thing with years of gaslighting was, moving on didn't automatically make it easy to accept the "happy, happy" talk. Even from Thomas. It was easier to let hope build in small doses.

His laugh made the bed jump. We were at the wedding reception part of the film. "Can't wait to see you in your wedding dress," he whispered into my skin. Shivers tingled down my back. "Bet you'll look like an elf queen."

"Shut up." I smacked his hand, laughing, pleased to know I could handle goofy Thomas again. Seriously, though, how the hell did he know about my dress?

In a moment of pure serendipity, Rachel had hooked me up with a friend majoring in fashion. The centerpiece of her senior project had been accidentally ruined, putting her degree in jeopardy. The young lady jumped at the chance to make my wedding dress and have it double as the finale of her show. Her other dresses featured light silks and chiffons. The pieces reminded me of woodland royalty. It ended up being a win-win for both of us.

A memory from my first fitting made me smile, and I held on

to it. Not everything had gone haywire this year. I finally breached the surface of my moody lake. I was still far from shore, but I could see a clear blue sky.

I rolled into Thomas. "Hey, thank you for accepting me." My chin quivered and my voice caught. "I promise to walk in the darkness with you when it's your turn."

LOVESONG

THOMAS

"**R**eady, fam? I don't want to be late," Liam called out while bounding down the stairs, Dylan on his heels. "Do we have to do pictures in the park?"

Liam possessed steely nerves on a stage and now looked pasty enough to throw up. His hand tapped out a fast rhythm on his thigh as sweat dusted his freshly shaved upper lip.

"You mean miss the last prom photos under the big oak tree? Are you nuts? I'd crawl there if I had to." Kick adjusted the lapels on Liam's black tuxedo. Her chin subtly quivered as she adjusted the ends of curls around his ears. "You're so handsome and grown."

Liam's Adam's apple bobbed as he swallowed.

It occurred to me that Kick would need a distraction after the photos, or I'd have an overemotional fiancée on my hands.

"Load up, y'all." Liam twirled the keys to my '69 Camaro around his finger. Thanks to its unibody, the damage to Ginger—

my car's name—had been minimal. The shop had it back to mint in a week. Kick's car wasn't so lucky. Insurance totaled it, to our relief.

Was it a big deal to let an eighteen-year-old boy take the car that I'd driven off the lot decades earlier? Not when the boy was Liam. I already loved him like he was mine. Damn, my world had changed fast. I enjoyed seeing the grin on his face when I asked if he wanted to take it. Compared to the shit Kick and I had dealt with, it was an easy decision.

"Are you coming, Dyl?" Liam asked.

"Sorry, pretty boy. I'm still working here." Dylan pretended to wipe tears from his eyes. "You're so handsome, pretty boy. Now don't do anything I wouldn't do."

Liam punched his brother. "You did all the things."

Dylan waggled his brows. "Exactly."

"Dylan…," Kick began.

I cut her off with a hand to her back and a kiss to her temple. Dylan still had no sense of when to ease up on his family members, particularly with Kick.

"Let's go, clan," I said, checking to make sure I had the keys to my Land Rover. "Your mom and I will follow you to Oakville Square."

BANGER CALLED WHILE KICK PUT THE DINNER DISHES AWAY. WE'D taken Macushla along to the park and walked the trails after the kids left for prom. For a moment, it had taken Kick's mind off this next item in a lengthy list of parental lasts. We'd made it back to the parking lot as a quick spring storm popped up. Then we ate a quiet dinner with Dylan.

I hoped Banger had good news I could share with her. "What's new, man?" I moved into the office and shut the door in case he had bad news.

Banger breathed a long-suffering sigh through the phone. "I'm back and staying at the corporate apartment for now."

I sat behind Kick's desk. "Did you find the mole?"

"Several leads have converged. Just haven't found the linchpin, but I have an idea."

"Hit me."

"Let's shrink our circle of trust. You, me, Siobhan, the guards, and Kick. I want the guards to report directly to you. They're new, but they've proved themselves. The guy I had on Graham had pressed Siobhan for more responsibilities, so she gave him that assignment as a test."

"Who got to him?"

"I'm this close to nailing it down. That's why I need to tighten the trust."

"I'm not sure how Kick will take keeping the guards. She's eager for it to be over."

"Won't be long. Remember when I told you the bartender at Ducky's took a call from Oxford?"

"I do. Are you still looking at Nigel?"

Another sigh filled my ear. "I almost had the bartender. He slipped by me like he'd been tipped off."

"The mole."

"Right. Nigel has to be part of this. The problem is, he's known me my whole life. He knows my moves." I heard a thump, like a fist pounding. "The guy's a veritable Machiavelli."

I always pictured Ellie in that role, but I saw the comparison. "You need new moves."

"No kidding. Speak to no one about this except for the circle of trust. Understand?"

I drummed my fingers on the desk, ready to do anything. "What about the old man?"

"Bare minimum for now. What have you told him lately?"

"He knows about the shoot-out. I'd missed a check-in the day after. Alaric also knows between finals and the wedding, I don't have time for a summons no matter how important he deems it."

"Good. Keep conversations to nothing more than lab facts for now. I'm serious, brother. My plan depends on keeping the circle airtight."

I pinched the bridge of my nose, thinking of Kick. Hell, her entire clan had come to her side in the two weeks since the shooting. I'd almost overrode Kick's wishes and cut off Bobby on the spot over the way she had ripped into her daughter regarding Rachel's injuries. As if Kick didn't blame herself. As if she didn't have cuts and bruises too. Bobby then changed tack and blamed me for all the bad in Kick's life now. I wished it were that easy.

"I'll tell her," I said.

"Hit it hard, brother. I don't care about what's already happened. She stays tight with her movements. Force her to listen to you and Mateo. Rachel's situation is harder, but the end of a semester always shakes up a schedule. That works in our favor."

"It'll happen. You can count on it."

"Talk more tomorrow."

We finished the call, and I filled Kick in on the situation while helping her clean the kitchen. True to her nature, she saw the wisdom in Banger's plan. She'd come a long way since her first impressions of him.

"Jacklyn's dress was gorgeous, don't you think?" Kick and I had parked ourselves in the corner of the sectional sofa in her living room, me with my feet up, stretched down one side. She lay in the other direction, her head in my lap. A movie played, but I couldn't say which one, because my fiancée kept talking about the kids at the park as she thumbed through the photos on her phone. "I love this group shot. They've been an adorable bunch since they first met in kindergarten. Dylan's grade always had several assholes, but not Liam's."

A dried-off dog lay on my legs, snoring in between squirrel-chasing dreams. At the park, Macushla had bolted for a puddle as soon as the clouds opened up. The dog turned mischief into an artform.

"I'm so glad Jax's parents let her go with Lee."

"Did they buck on that too?"

Kick's nodding head rocked in my lap. "She already had a church prom with some boy from Raleigh. Jax really wanted to go to the school one, and fortunately for Liam, Regina Moore still trusts him."

"She should."

"Yeah, well, it's her father who looks at Lee and can't see anything but a penis."

"Typical." I'd forgotten many aspects of parenthood, but that stuck in my memory. Then again, my girls were married by eighteen, and modern society was night-and-day different. Not so much for Alton Moore. I also remembered how impossible it was to say no to my daughters' heart's desires.

A scene or two went by on the television.

"I'm going to miss them," Kick said softly.

There it was. I gently stroked her hair, making sure to not rake my fingers through it. "What's with the photo shoot though? You'd think the kids were in a fashion layout. I don't know how they put up with it." From my experience, parents had always fussed over the next generation, but the extent of this attention was new.

She sighed. "It's the end of an era."

"All finished, peeps." Dylan entered our space, two beers in his hands. He gave me one, lifted his mother's feet, and sat. "Can I pause this and show you how to connect the house computer to the outside world?"

"Absolutely."

Dylan gave us the gist of his upgrade. Since Banger was using his place to test Angel's latest tweak, Kick's house and mine were the betas for Dylan's project. The Felidae-related system always ran on a separate network. The upgrades allowed our computer to do the things smart homes did but with extra layers of security and no third-party data mining. No risk of a hacker taking over a camera and the like. Since Banger hadn't flushed out the mole, I welcomed the additional protection.

If the algorithm worked, it would be the launching point for Dylan's future business. This was his audition for Banger, so to speak. Everything with the medical clinic had progressed smoothly, so he planned to launch it on Mother's Day weekend as a surprise for Kick.

"Is this part of your thesis project?" Kick asked Dylan.

"Yeah. The initial use is almost ready to launch. This is a secondary system that my team's testing."

"I heard Banger's interested in implementing it too. Siobhan said you might work together after graduation."

"Banger wants to make Dylan a millionaire in his own right," I told her. Why not brag up her son's accomplishment? Kick might as well clue into the hell of a big deal he'd become.

"What?" She bolted upright.

"Yeah." Dylan blushed. He took a long drink from his beer, like he tried to hide behind the can. "We get to stay in the Triangle if we go with Banger's mentoring plan."

"Will you be the… what? CEO? How have I missed this?" She moved her head back and forth between us, murmuring as her brow furrowed. "My son's going to be a CEO."

"It's not that big of a deal." Dylan deflected. He pulled at his T-shirt and I almost laughed. Kick had the right reaction. He continued, "This has to work first. We haven't finalized anything yet. The only actual decision we've made so far is to partner with Banger and not the Silicon Valley companies."

"It's a *fecking huge* deal, lad. I'll make sure it works too." Kick's mouth parted a moment before she softly said, "You envisioned this and built it. I'm so…" Her voice caught. "Your father…" She reached out, grabbed his hand. "This beats any NFL gig to him. You know that, right? Never doubt your decision to leave the game."

Dylan nodded several times, keeping his head low. Kick's use of the present tense caught my attention. I wondered what she meant by it.

Dylan patted his stomach. "Might regret the growing belly not playing has created. A few hours on the field helped to counter the effects of sitting at a desk."

"I can help you with that," I told him. "Spending too much time in the lab makes me sluggish."

"Yeah? You have a gym?"

"Yep. I'll send you my schedule. We can meet there, and I'll show you around."

"That would be fabulous. Thanks, my dude."

Kick's eyes shone with tears as she grinned at us. I didn't need to ask her what moved her. These small steps with Dylan did my heart good. Now that he planned to stay local, we had years to develop our rapport. She brushed at her eyes as she padded into the kitchen.

"Where're you heading, Mom?"

"This calls for a toast. I'm getting a Bull City Cider from the fridge. Either of you want another?"

"I'm good." I checked Dylan's bottle. "Your boy could use a second."

"Great. Hey lad, since Thomas and I are restarting the movie, would you want to watch it with us?"

Dylan checked the time on his phone. "Can do."

With Kick out of earshot, I took a pull from my IPA and said,

"I'm glad you told your mother. She needed happy news, and the main surprise hasn't been spoiled."

Dylan finished his bottle. "Yeah, that's what I figured too."

"Any chance you can show me how to change the system's name?"

Dylan laughed. "You have a problem with Angel?"

"You know it's a reference to Banger's given name, right? I'd rather be like *Star Trek* and call it Computer than have to keep calling it Angel."

"Ooh, if you can make it have a Spanish accent, we could call it Alejandro." Kick handed her son his beer while I shook with laughter.

"You want to lust after the house computer?" I asked.

"No, but it'd be fun. Besides, Carmen would love it." She snuggled into my side. "Except let's not talk about lusting in front of the lad, okay?"

Dylan barked a laugh and almost choked on his drink. "Appreciate that, guys."

"How late do you think he'll stay out?" Dylan asked.

"Liam will have Jacklyn home by whatever time her father wants. He knows the merits of abiding by Alton's rules by now."

"I don't know." Dylan lifted an eyebrow my way. "I expect he'll be home earlier than requested."

"Why is that?" Kick sat up, refilling her small popcorn bowl from the big one on the coffee table.

I suspected the same as Dylan. Saw it coming. You couldn't miss the attraction between the kids when they sang together. Kick would've noticed it, too, but for everything else on her mind.

"While I helped him get ready, Lee told me he planned to declare his love to little Jaxie."

"What? No!" She stood up and planted her hands on her hips.

"They're just supposed to go as friends." She turned and paused in each direction, then flopped back down. "Oh hell."

"Don't blame yourself." I pulled her to my side and rubbed her arm. "Sometimes the heart needs to leap, or it'll break from the want."

"Fecking hell."

"Watch the movie, darlin'. Either way, it's a learning experience for him."

Kick turned to Dylan. "Not a word when he comes in, hear? When you broke up with Suzy, no one rubbed it in."

"I knew you never liked her."

"For Pete's sake, lad. It was never about her. The two of you simply didn't fit, but you had to learn for yourself." She adjusted her ponytail. "Jaysus, I hate this. For any of my kids."

I kissed her temple, wishing I could do more to help. "They'll be fine. Dylan has his software. Rachel's in counseling. Plus the summer theater gig will get her out of town. We'll visit her as much as you want." Taking her chin in hand, I tilted it toward me. "It'll be alright. Now let's finish this awful blockbuster."

THE FRONT DOOR SLAMMED, ROCKING THE HOUSE. KICK, ASLEEP IN my lap, jumped—catching air—and almost rolled off the sofa. Dylan had left an hour earlier when the movie ended.

"Liam," Kick called out from her groggy state. "How'd it go?" I could've laughed at her effort to sound nonchalant. Liam's anger vibrated through the room. Didn't take an empath to see his misery.

While the stairs boomed from his stomping, Liam growled, "Don't want to talk about it."

I bent my head and caught Kick's gaze. She looked like she was bracing for a crash. She pressed her lips together. "Shh." I wrapped my arms around her, whispering, "He's loved. He'll be alright. Not tonight. Not tomorrow. But we'll get him through it. For now… let it go."

"I won't sink away again, Thomas," she snapped.

"Maybe. Maybe not. If you did, I'd be there." I kissed her forehead. It was imperative she heard me. "Take care of you first. That's my priority from now on."

"HE WON'T OPEN HIS DOOR." KICK SLIPPED OFF HER YOGA PANTS and climbed into bed.

Raising my arm, I pulled her to me. "Hate to say told you so—"

"So don't."

I obeyed and squeezed her. "Let the boy process it his way. His ego needs time. Hell, the kid can have his pick of girls."

"Just not the one he wants." Since Liam refused to share, we were stuck speculating. Her breath made a hitching sound. "I'm angry with myself."

"Let it go for now." Out of ideas for what to do, I unbuttoned Kick's nightshirt.

"What are you doing?"

Like she needed to ask. I slipped it off and motioned with my hand. "Roll over."

She complied but added, "Why?"

"Hey Angel, shuffle and play the 'Well You Know' playlist at volume level three," I called out.

"Thomas—"

"Shh." I yanked on the warm quilt, pulling it high over my shoulders until it cocooned us.

Now playing.

The opening bars of "Lovesong" filled the room. *Perfect.* Kick had told me the song made her toes curl, whatever that meant. I liked the look it put on her face—like we'd become home for each other.

Reaching for the nightstand, I grabbed some oil and lubed my hands, then leaned down, my lips against her ear, her luscious backside stretched out under me. "I'm taking your mind off the children."

After enough time devoted to light-touch massage, with the appropriate amount of moans and sighs for my benefit, Kick smiled into her pillow and asked, "What children?"

THIN LINE BETWEEN LOVE
AND HATE

KICK

"Hey, cowboy. Mateo's mother had an emergency early this morning." I called Thomas with my cell phone while in my bathroom. He had spent the night in the lab, so my trusty bodyguard stayed over in the loft—part of Banger's plan to tighten security, except everything had gone dead quiet since the shooting.

"On Mother's Day morning? How awful."

"It's horrible any day, but yeah. I'm sending him home."

"No, Kick. I'll leave soon. He can wait."

This was why I'd taken the phone into the en suite. I knew Thomas would balk, but I could push back too. "I can handle an hour. Hell, Dylan's expected any minute."

I looked out the window over my tub at the beautiful May morning. A mockingbird trilled from its perch on the shrub outside. The little bugger had been waking me up before my alarm for a month. I longed to open the window and take in the fresh air, but it was against security protocol.

"Exactly. Mateo can wait."

Shit. "Come on, Thomas. His mother's in the emergency department right now. Mateo's father needs him."

My guard was his parents' firstborn. They depended on him for more than language translation. He was the family's rock.

A rustling of papers came through the line. "Dammit. I'm shutting down now. But check in with Siobhan. Wes too. Perhaps he and Rachel can leave now."

My daughter make herself ready before noon on a weekend? Hardly. But I'd take the win. "Will do. Then I'll send Mateo off with our best wishes."

"Sure."

"Thank you, cowboy."

I left the requisite messages and sent Mateo on his way with a thermos of coffee. He was too upset to eat but took a container of scones for his family. I was beginning our brunch preparations when Siobhan called.

"Hey Kick. I received your message. You good?"

"I'm peachy. Thank you." I wore my Bluetooth set so I could chop fennel and celery for a frittata. "Wes said he'd try to light a fire under my daughter. My oldest will be here soon too."

"Oh? When's that?"

He had texted about running late. "Probably an hour or so."

"You're sure you're fine?"

I looked out the kitchen window and waved at my neighbor. They were loading their kids into the van. "The quiet's actually nice for a change."

Siobhan chuckled into the phone. "I bet. Call me if you need anything. Any sign of trouble, hit the bat signal."

I laughed at her joke. My world felt a bit superhero adjacent, to be honest. "Will do."

"And Kick… Happy Mother's Day. I hope it's… relaxing."

"Thank you, Von. Now that you mention it, I think I'll hit my meditation spot as soon as I'm done cutting these veggies."

. . .

"Yo, Mom. Got your ginger beer and cupcakes." Dylan placed his contribution to our brunch on the island and kissed the cheek I offered. "Happy Mother's Day."

"Thanks, lad. I thought you were running late. Now you're early."

He lifted an eyebrow. "Are you complaining?"

"Of course not. Simply wondering what changed?"

"Oh." He gestured toward his shirt. "As you can see, I didn't take a shower after my good-boy workout at the gym. There was no way to shower and make it to the bakery before the gluten-free ones sold out. I figured the shower upstairs is worlds better than the locker room ones anyway. I practically threw my credit card at the cashier in the bakery."

I waved in front of my nose. "Whew! No kidding. Stand on the other side of the island, lad. You stink."

Dylan folded his arms… after he complied. "Why not just wait until after I shower?"

"I might forget what I want to say by then. So… well, I don't know. You're just… cheery this morning. Does this mean you had a date last night?"

Dylan leveled me with his devilish grin. He'd mastered it by age two, and I fell for it every time. "Does my mother want to know if her little boy got laid?"

I should've kept my mouth shut. Except he'd been understandably miserable these past months. "No. I just want—"

"One plus one equals—"

"None of my business. I just want—"

"Bingo." Dylan pointed at me.

I pointed back. "I can inquire about the state of my son's happiness without knowing about his"—I waved my hands in the air, butcher's knife still in one—"exploits."

He poured himself a cup of coffee. "My heart's good. Thanks

for asking." A huge smile graced his handsome face, saying he was proud of himself for getting a rise from me. Then he hid it inside the mug.

I turned back to the counter. "Pest." Then set down the knife while Dylan laughed at me. "Use the guest shower down here. Something's wrong with the one upstairs."

"Pretty boy and those curls again?"

"Hey." I hated when the kids razed at each other. The world was hard enough to deal with. "We have to wait until Banger says we're clear to let unvetted people back in the house. Then I'll call the plumber."

Please let that be soon. This way of living had worn out its welcome, not that I ever really welcomed it.

I picked up an avocado. "Please go wash the stink off, then help me chop this stuff."

"Right-o, Mama." Dylan laughed and headed toward the guest bath while I sliced into the avocado. My counter was filling up fast with bowls of cut veggies, which would make the cooking part go faster.

A split second later, he reentered the kitchen. "You're out of towels in the little bath. Mind if I use yours?"

"Huh? Shit." My head stayed occupied with my to-do list. I'd just remembered the steaks that were supposed to be placed in the refrigerator to thaw overnight last night. How the hell would I get them defrosted in time now? "Sure. Can you fix the towel situation in the guest bath when you finish? Help me keep my focus on brunch."

"Gotcha."

The steaks were in the chest freezer in the garage. I crossed the threshold and saw that Dylan had left the door up. He was always a stinker for that. It used to drive me nuts when he lived at home. The number of times I woke in the morning to find out he'd left it up all night... it would make me fume. Now it was a breach of security.

A hand clamped across my mouth as I reached for the garage door's button. An arm squeezed around my chest while a familiar, gruff voice spat in my ear. "Not a word, *Mrs.* McKenna. You bitch."

My first thought was that we'd left a stone unturned—Jonathon Graham, Senior. My second thought went to Dylan.

Now what.

TWO TRIBES

THOMAS

I accepted the incoming call with a laugh. In our short time together, I'd found Kick to be a perfectionist with her family gatherings. I chalked it up to what she called her "impending empty nest."

"Dylan. Let me guess… your mom forgot—"

"I think someone has a gun on Mom," he whispered, cutting me off. "Here. At the house."

An icy shiver ran up my spine. *What the hell?* "You know who?" If the mole was showing their face now, I wouldn't step off for the police this time.

"Mr. Graham, I think. Sh-she screamed. He yelled at her to shut up. S-sounded like him."

My heart beat a tattoo in my chest. *Ten minutes.* I was ten fucking minutes from her. I punched the pedal to the floor. "Where are you?"

"Your bathroom since our shower's broken. I heard boots

pound up the stairs. Don't know how long it'll be till someone checks here. Where's your gun?"

"My safe's under the extra pillows in our closet."

"Gotcha." I heard a quiet shuffling and gave him the combination. Dylan seemed to keep his head about him. Despite his terror, his voice stayed determined. "Oh, good. I know these," he added. Dylan had worked with Banger at my range. Banger had declared the kid a natural. I hoped he was right.

"Keep one by your side and hide the other in your waistband. Under your shirt," I advised. Then I heard a banging sound. "What was that?"

His voice choked. "I think he hit her. Sounds like someone else is out there. Should I just run out firing with both guns?"

"No, boy. You could hit her. Keep yourself as calm as you can. How many are there?"

"Can't tell. I saw a guy outside your window for a second, so... maybe three."

"Is Kick the lone woman?" It was an impossible hunch, but the icy shiver turned to artic steel as the thought washed over me. *Christ,* I hoped I was wrong about the mole, but it was the only thing that made sense after this. "Dylan..."

"Um... I-I think so... Not positive."

"Alright. Stay quiet. Assess the scene. You hear me? Kick's smart. She's come a long way with her training." *Fuck.* She'd stand in front of every weapon to keep it from her kid. Horns blared around me and tires screeched as I executed a fast right turn against the light at Main Street. I swerved to beat the left-turning cars with the right-of-way. "Almost home. Stay low and find out how many are with Graham. Then call the cops. I'm almost there. If you can, find a way to stall them."

Kick's house was second from the corner, and the neighbor's drive faced the side street. I parked near their mailbox and ran through their backyard, scanning for anyone who might work for Graham. From what I could tell, everyone was in the house.

The garage door was up, so I peeked around the corner and saw the shadow of a large man in the mudroom. If he'd been a few feet back or to the right, I could sneak up on him. He chose his position for its sight lines. He could see perfectly and be seen. If he checked back on the garage, I'd have to fire on him. Using the shadow of equipment attached to the walls, to sneak close, I turned the corner with my weapon on him and whispered, "Don't move, asshole."

The scene before me broke my heart. Kick was in Graham's hold in the kitchen, a gun to her temple. Her lip and cheek bled. A shiner bloomed around her left eye. Tears slid down her face, but her sneer told me she was more pissed than afraid. Or in pain. *Fuck.* Or both.

Dylan stood in the dining room with a gun in each hand, one pointed at Graham and the other at a second accomplice holding the kitchen island. Thanks to the many times I'd watched the footage of Kick's attempted kidnapping, I recognized this asshole as the bartender who'd spiked her drink—Graham's nephew. I held my guy's full attention while my focus stayed on Big Jonn. No idea what he'd told these idiots about the job, but none of them would be walking out of here. Like an old friend who'd been waiting on me, I flipped the switch. I wasn't Good Thomas anymore.

I reached around the wall behind me without taking eyes off the scene and pressed the button closing the garage door in case I was wrong about extras outside.

That's when Kick noticed me and started. Her eyes flashed with fear instead of relief and damn if I knew she was thinking of my safety over hers, ranking who took priority, as I had. I silently shushed her with pursed lips as another tear trailed down her cheek.

"Did you reach the cops, Dylan?" I asked, my eyes glued to my lady and Graham.

"Not before this one found me," he answered, referring to the guy I kept in my periphery. Dylan had a black eye of his own and cuts on his knuckles. He growled at the bartender.

"Doesn't matter. They're coming." It was half true. At the last minute, I sent a panic text to Banger. It should've been enough for him to alert everyone, including the authorities. Hell, he was the cavalry all by himself. Still, for all intents and purposes, we were on our own for a bit.

"Hang in there, baby." I tried to send Kick strength. I'd be damned if she lost any more loved ones, and I sure as hell wouldn't lose her.

Graham's sinister laugh betrayed his break from reality. His darting eyes shone with the maniacal lunacy of a man with nothing to lose. "Three guns are on you, young man. One wrong move and this goes off. Right… through… your Yankee *cunt's* temple." He pressed the muzzle into her skin. "A couple of bitches sleep their way to the top of a Fortune 500 company, and now they all think they can shake their asses and get whatever they demand. Isn't that right, whore?" He shook Kick's shoulder hard. She bit her lower lip and closed her eyes. I silently begged her to keep quiet. *Let him pontificate until backup arrived.*

"Need to learn your place." Big Jonn jolted Kick sharply with each word, and her eyes flew open, sparked with rage, on his last word.

No, no, no, baby. Keep your cool…

Dammit, why hadn't I developed telepathic powers? I'd heard rumors about them around the vineyard.

"What happens when you let bitches run amuck?" Graham yelled. "Why, they raise little bitches that bewitch fine young men."

"You've got to be—" Kick's face scrunched with indignation.

I cleared my throat to get her attention and shifted my chin to the side to keep her quiet. Needed to think of a way out.

"Haven't I been charming, attentive, polite… *whore*?" Graham kept shaking her violently. She pressed her lips together so hard they blanched. "Answer me! I gave you attention after your famous husband died. I welcomed you to the business community because I knew what you were going through. And what did you do? You ignored me! Then you hooked up with a... *boy toy*."

"Are you jealous?" She blinked, then flared her nose, her chin set in defiance.

"Kick...," I warned.

"No, Thomas. He doesn't get to throw threats around... tell me the reason he terrorized us is payback for not returning affection." Her eyes shifted up, like she tried to see Big Jonn. He kept too tight of a hold on her. "I'm sick of arrogant assholes thinking women owe them adoration only because they deem us worthy of their attention."

Graham's hand moved from a death grip on her arm to a clamp across her throat. The gag as she tried to breathe called my bluff and shortened my temper.

"Let her go, old man. Face it... you can't match me. Y'all are already dead men walking."

"Why the hell would I let her go? Damn straight, she owes me. The question is... who gets to pay? Should it be the son?" He quickly pointed his gun at Dylan. "Or you... boy toy?" Kick squealed in terror and flailed violently. Graham skillfully evaded a stomp to his foot. He moved his hand back to gripping her arm to regain control. At least she could breathe again.

He leaned to her ear and said, "She promised me endless years... like you and him." Graham tipped his head toward me. "Yeah... I know your secrets, asshole."

Kick gasped, then her gaze moved regimentally around the room. It helped to calm her. *Good.* Her eyes stopped on Dylan. His brows pinched with confusion. Not that I blamed him.

"What do you mean?" Kick asked innocently.

"Don't play dumb, you cunt." Graham cackled. The spit from it hit Kick's cheek. "I'm a descendant of the Marquis."

The Marquis?

Fuck.

My.

Life.

I swallowed audibly. "Do you mean the Marquis—"

Graham beamed like a son for a treasured father. "De Lafayette? Yep. That's what she said." He laughed and almost gave Kick an out. Then he caught himself and tightened his grip. "I made a joke."

"Big Jonn—"

"It's Mr. Graham to you, *boy*. Or should it be Mr. Lafayette? Or Mr. de Lafayette? I'll have to ask them. See… he had a son… when he served with Washington. He arranged for the mother to marry a man named Graham—thought he'd been my great-whatever grand-pappy. A good soldier. Gave them land right here."

Graham spoke to Kick again. "Why couldn't you be a good soldier? Just cooperated a little. Hell, I wanted to give you more… once I found out you have it too. See… I'm like you… or will be. Once the serum is perfected." He tapped the gun on her shoulder. "All they needed was your DNA. Had a hell of a time getting it. Thanks to your stupid muscle."

He stretched his chin toward me and stage-whispered, "That's you… boy."

"If you know my secret, you know I'm no boy. If you really knew me, you'd release my fiancée. You'd get down on your knees. You'd beg me for mercy." I tilted my head to the side, letting my eyes settle on each man. "Clearly you're misinformed."

"Naw," Big Jonn said. "I just have no desire for mercy. With no heir to pass a legacy on to, what's the point of money or immortality? Revenge is all that's left." His gaze shifted to Dylan, then back to Kick. "Too bad little whore junior isn't here. Your heir-apparent will do as a trade for mine, but I'd love to take them both out."

"What about me?" the bartender asked. "I'm your heir now, Uncle Jonn. You said so."

"Shut up, Jared! The offer was for me. Young Jonn and me." He tsked and shook his head. "If *you* knew what I did, you'd respect me."

Kick kept moving her eyes and taking regular breaths. I wanted her away from Graham, but for now she stayed calm. Banger should be here soon, and I wanted answers. Namely, who this woman was. I had a sinking feeling that I knew.

"What'd you do, Big Jonn? Impress me," I challenged.

"Call me Mr. Graham! You say you respect me... prove it. Don't think I don't know you're the one who threw my son out of Reynolds's shop."

Fuck. I closed my eyes and nodded. He could win this one. As much as Graham soaked up the attention, his nephew and muscle grew twitchy. The one on me sighed hard.

My small head bob was enough. Graham leaned down and spoke near Kick's ear. "It was me... the rumors. The newspaper articles. The crowd storming the stores. *I* stirred everyone into a tizzy." Kick closed her eyes and inhaled. I knew her enough to know she was counting through her breaths. "You know why?" She shook her head and Graham rattled her again. "Use words... *whore*. Or is your mouth good for just one thing?"

Kick took another long breath and set her chin. "No, Mr. Graham. I don't know why you sabotaged my reputation."

Graham's lips stretched in a cocky smile. "Because I *could*. See... when y'all were on the ropes, I planned to save the day. Get in y'all's good graces. Then I'd take you to her. That was the first plan, but you're too stubborn, aren't you? You wouldn't take advantage of my offers of affection. Then you wouldn't drink a damn drink with me. You stupid, stupid bitch. This could've been easy. No one would've been hurt. Not really. Now it's ruined."

Kick's eyes flashed wide as she turned her head in horror. My breath caught in my throat, afraid she'd lay into Graham. But she recovered, her face schooled again. "If I may... Mr. Graham...

wh-what about the graffiti? The way Rachel was tormented? Your son—"

"Kick...," I warned. It worked in our favor to keep Big Jonn going, sharing his "accomplishments" with us. Her submissive act also kept him calm.

Graham sighed. "Young Jonn always loved your *cunt* daughter. I tried to set him straight. Honestly, I did. Everyone saw she wasn't worth it. Flaunting her body... her uppity-ness... in his face." His nostrils flared as he looked my way. "I blame my late wife for spoiling him. He... he could make it hard for me. Sometimes. But your people interrupted my plans too. Took it from every side, didn't I?" Big Jonn whined the last bit, his damn chin quivering with self-pity.

I couldn't have the guy falling to pieces and escalating the scene before Banger arrived. The goons grew antsy, but they still paid attention. Dylan also did. It wasn't go-time yet. As far as I was concerned, there was one more thing to pry out of him.

"Tell me about the woman, Mr. Graham? Do I know her?"

3 9

ALIVE AND KICKING

KICK

A laugh stirred deep inside me as Big Jonn's grew frenetic. I winced, blinking from him spitting in my eye again. *"Does he know the woman?"* he asked me and no one.

"Well, Professor... I spoke to an uppity Englishman and your devious Siobhan. They actually work for... my *grand-mère*."

Well, there's the mole, or moles, I suppose. Shit. Banger.

For a split second, Thomas's posture fell, like he'd been punched in the stomach. He'd called Ellie—my ancestor—*grand-mère*. That made Big Jonn and I weird-ass cousins? My laugh grew. It wasn't a giggle or a chuckle. It was a cynical, barking, cackle starting in my toes and surging its way up, bursting out my throat. I surprised everyone in the room—Big Jonn the most.

My shoulders shook, and the gun pressed harder into my temple. It did nothing to stop me. I was pissed and terrified but couldn't get the picture of four teens and Great Dane out of my head. Or maybe I needed to fill my head with anything other than the madness of the Felidae and the past five months.

"Rut-roh," I said through the fits.

"Shut up, *whore!*" He jerked his arm so hard it stole my breath. As if nasty names would upset me when the asshole had already mangled my face and knocked the wind from me. Not to mention the guns pointed at my family. I'd been doing my utmost to follow my training.

Self-defense starts in the mind.

The strain of keeping it together, trying to stay three steps ahead, then hearing Big Jonn's defense for all this—some kind of promise from the Felidae Society—one I wasn't sure I wanted. It was too much. I switched to a mocking voice. "If it hadn't been for you meddling kids, my son and I would be mutant superhumans by now."

"Easy...," Thomas warned. Behind the macho gruff, I heard the fear. My entire house vibrated with it.

"If you'd taught your woman in her place, this could've been avoided, Professor."

"You've got to be... motherfucker." I lost the little cool I still held on to.

Anger flared in Big Jonn's eyes to the point they looked black. I didn't care. My temper woke, shaking me. "Everything about this catastrophe is on *you.* Not me or my kids. I was literally minding. My. Own. Businesses... When you and your half-witted son sighted my family in your crosshairs."

Graham growled, but Thomas cut him off. "Don't let the fact that I teach science fool you, old man. I can drop you right here. Right now."

"You'd chance my piece going off? On her?" Big Jonn took the gun he'd mostly kept pointed in my shoulder and shoved it into my jaw, making me choke. His laugh sounded demonic. "Didn't think so."

I forced myself to breathe, relying on the training to regain my calm and stay in the moment to think. *Keep my family alive.*

A cold determination passed over Thomas's face. We'd been

monitoring each other's cues this whole time. Reading each shift and twitch. Keeping each other calm. He kept Big Jonn talking as a stall tactic, I could tell. But the stalling was over.

With what appeared to be the flick of a wrist, Thomas shot the gunman closest to him and produced a second weapon from the back of his shirt. My sightline didn't allow me to see what warranted the response. All I could think was, where the hell did he get two guns?

When Thomas fired his shot, Big Jonn's gun hand jerked and I pushed as hard as I could. Before he regained control, I donkey kicked him in the balls. The gun tumbled to the floor without going off. We scrambled, and I grabbed hold first.

Thomas had a clear shot on Graham but didn't see that the nephew, Jared—the bartender who'd drugged me—had aimed at him. The lackey with the bullet wound recovered his weapon and trained it on Dylan.

Who to take out?

Who to save?

Don't leave me alone again.

Self-defense starts in the mind.

Noise faded away until I only heard my breaths. My heart-beat. The song "Closer to Fine" quietly surfaced in the back of my mind.

This was it.

My senses heightened. The smell of nervous sweat filled the air. The gun was warm in my hand, thanks to Big Jonn gripping it. It was usually cold when I'd pick one up. I never liked that. I liked them better warm. Funny, he carried a Sig. The gun I preferred.

I breathed in… out. In… out.

The answers are in me.

In… aim. Out… squeeze.

Seven shots fired in precision, as if we'd choreographed them. The bartender took a bullet in his firing shoulder.

I had to trust in my choice. "Drop!"

Dylan dove for the floor and shot the big guy shadowing Thomas. My fiancé fell backward, out of my periphery.

What had I done?

Don't leave me alone again.

In… aim. Out… squeeze.

The bartender took a second hit between the eyes and crumpled. The floor boomed an echo as he bounced on it. My first thought was *bull's-eye*.

A gurgling noise caught my attention. Big Jonn Graham, gasping his last breaths, lay at my feet. He'd taken Thomas's bullet in the heart.

Nice one, cowboy. I might have lost it.

"Fuck!" My head snapped at Thomas's exclamation. Blood soaked his shirt.

What did you do?

Wetness seeped into my underwear. No way. I seriously did not just… I looked down. Blood spread across the lower part of my shirt and out the leg of my shorts.

Fear blanched Thomas's face, but not for himself. I was covered in red warmth.

I'm sorry, cowboy.

40

SHE'S LEAVING HOME

Banger McHenry—his latest name and favorite one so far—growled at the perfect May morning sky. It beckoned him to enjoy a lazy morning on his back deck, sipping a black coffee while listening to the birds. His mood called for the thick fog of a highland afternoon. Dark and dreary.

He trudged through the entrance of his featureless corporate headquarters in North Raleigh, North Carolina, with one thought on his mind... *bitch better prove me wrong.*

He'd spent weeks traveling the globe, shoring up his offices and outposts. If he was right, he'd have to do it again. The phone calls from the bartender to an address in Oxford, UK, never sat right. Nigel worked at the university and considered it his hometown. But Banger knew all of the bastard's estates, safe houses, and hidey-holes, not that he couldn't add another. This flat was new and out of character.

Tess pressed her theory that Eleanor was the brains behind

everything going wrong with the Felidae, but Banger pegged Nigel for it. All the clues pointed to his weasel face. Through too many lives, the man played the role of kingmaker, the one with actual power. Since the time Nigel stood at Banger's monster father's side, acting as his right hand, they'd been rivals. Banger's sire saw to it.

At a certain point, men like Nigel grew tired of their invisibility... craved admiration... acknowledgment of their brilliant maneuvers... glory. Banger had watched it happen countless times in countless cultures. Humans were humans no matter where they lived. He figured the time was now for his old adversary.

However, Nigel never connected to the flat. Then, when he'd been about to call off the quest, in nearby Raleigh Park—he took the irony of the name as a big "fuck you" to the city he based out of—he met up with a witness who'd watched someone leave the flat on multiple occasions. It wasn't Ol' Nigel either, unless the man added cross-dressing to his list of talents. Banger wouldn't put it past him. The witness described a tall, nondescript woman, about thirty, dressed in black—sunglasses too despite the heavy clouds. Nothing to go on, except... her boots.

"The ones with those red bottoms," the fellow had said.

Banger had wanted to die.

He relocked his main office door and marched straight to Siobhan's room. It was in the corner opposite his, equal in space and importance. That's what she was to Angel Security. Banger was the head, Von the heart. This was the last step to proving his right hand had betrayed him. Idiot that he was, he held on to the thread of hope he was wrong.

Banger heard fingers typing on a keyboard in Siobhan's office at the same time his phone buzzed with a text. Probably Tess to pester him about their schedule—brunch at Kick's. Like he was in a mood to celebrate anything. Definitely *not* family.

Pulling the phone out of his pocket, Banger planned to blow

off his needy *maman.* He'd update Thomas with his suspicions too in case things went south in the next few minutes. But the message wasn't from Tess.

THOMAS

SOS. Graham and men @ Kick's. Guns on her and Dylan. Called cops. Siobhan or Wes? Only options for tip-off.

Banger swore under his breath.

Siobhan practically jumped four feet off the ground when he crashed through her door. He almost did the same.

"What are you doing here?" she asked.

"What the fuck have you done?" he said at the same time.

They shared a ten-second stare-down, Banger glaring at his protégé, arms folded, feet planted shoulder's-width apart. Even like this, he seethed with energy, ready to strike. The years with Siobhan flashed through his mind. When had she changed? Why wasn't he enough? She'd been like a sister—a daughter, really.

As the vignettes of their relationship played on, Banger's most trusted soldier transformed. He saw the moment she realized he'd discovered the betrayal. The familial affection usually showing in her eyes became cold, resolved. Siobhan flexed her hands at her hips.

Was he too late? As they faced off in her office, what had she set in motion at Kick's? He'd made vows to the McKenna's and his closest friend. Banger might be the sole man who considered that sacrosanct, but a vow meant something, dammit.

"No fucking around, Von. Answer me."

"Why should I? I'm not leaving here. Am I?"

True. "Do I mean nothing to you anymore?"

Von stared past Banger's shoulder, like a smart perp in an interrogation room.

He pressed. "Will you at least tell me when Nigel hired you?"

Siobhan pressed her lips together before chuckling like he

was a dumb shit. She let a long whistle blow past her lips. "How old is your resentment of him?" She relaxed her stance and added, "Fine, I'll help. There's nothing you can do anyway. The shit-show's doing what it's going to do. I'm guessing you know that." She ran her hand through her spiked red hair, breaking up some of the perfectly placed gel. Like him, Siobhan made herself stand out when she was at home in Raleigh, to keep the disguises effective when underground.

She put her hands in front of her. "It was supposed to be a simple side gig. Help some guy Nigel paid to nab a woman Eleanor had a beef with. You know the guy is Big Jonn Graham and Kick's the woman, obviously." She sighed heavily, like the thing had been an ordeal for her. "I rented a small warehouse and was supposed to sneak Nigel into the city under your nose once Graham set up the dinner date. Those assholes way overestimated Graham's wooing skills, but you ancient-ass men still think modern women will do anything for security and a few bucks, don't you?"

Banger took a step back, like he'd been shoved. Ellie was at the root of this? He didn't risk taking his eyes off Von as he processed the connections. The stories of Ellie's first life were as notorious as those of his own, but Banger had never known her that way. Ruthless and formal, sure. But... Eleanor. Edmund. Alaric. Kick. Power. *The woman behind the throne.* The queen.

"Have you finished your calculations?" Siobhan needled, folding her arms to match his stance.

Banger's jaw flexed as he ground his teeth, thinking.

"Careful..." She wiggled a finger at him. "If you people break a tooth... will another grow back? Or are they superstrong? Lord knows you should've pulverized your molars by now, the way you do that."

There it was. "You're fucking kidding me." She knew. Banger let his head drop, shaking it as he accepted the truth. He figured she hadn't taken the job for money; he paid Von enough to keep a vast collection of her precious Louboutin's for fuck's sake. Immortality though? *There* was a payoff. Made sense for Graham, too, however it was Nigel found the fucker.

"Do you have the variances?" he asked. Thomas had tested her. He would've said something. Anyone with variances was on a watch list.

"Still catching up, Boss?" She clicked her tongue several times.

Banger ran a hand over his bald head. He'd shaved it for his travels. "Nigel's project alters DNA, not enhances it."

Siobhan waggled her brows. "Still a risk, but… YOLO." She shrugged. "It's not like you offered."

YOLO… Not if you're Felidae. He threw his arms out and yelled, "What the bloody hell about my existence attracts you?"

Siobhan took a step toward her desk, her face twisted with rage. "You do, asshole!"

His jaw dropped. "After everything you know, you… want me?"

"Like the disposable girls do anything for you anymore. They haven't for years. Like my boy toys. Boring as fuck." She pointed at him. "I see your face after spending time with Kick and Thomas. You're either grouchy as hell or gloomy. You're lonely, Rafa."

"I'm skeptical." Thomas and Kick *thought* they were happy. For now. Banger knew better. He had watched. Hell, he'd begged the universe to show him a relationship that worked. If Banger was gloomy, he was preparing for Thomas's heartbreak, knowing it would fall to him to pick up the pieces.

Siobhan's arm dropped as she pushed a button on the desk. "We match in every way. I never could figure out why you held back when we'd be amazing together. Hell, I know more about you than Thomas does, considering you keep the really dark shit from him."

She reached inside the top drawer. "Last summer, Nigel sent me a secured message on behalf of Ellie. There's a visionary leader. She's gathering a new group—with a matriarchal line. Fuck the patriarchy shit." Von grabbed her gun, pointed it at Banger. "I planned to play along with that part. Figured they could do their thing in Europe. It wouldn't take much to convince them to let you and I be partners, here in the States. As equals."

"Von..." The word was a lament. If Siobhan had ever paid attention, she'd know the one thing Banger never tolerated was manipulation. He'd been raised in the thick of it, fought against it. Then again, she was right about keeping some things from Thomas.

He noted the gun but didn't care. Staring down the business end of a Glock was part of the work. "If you'd just come to me." They'd have taken out that fuck-face and wannabe-queen together. Murder between the Felidae was unheard of. Loyalty to each other above all else was central to their vows. But everyone knew it happened occasionally. Politics found its way into everything.

"You'd what? Make Thomas change me?"

"If it's possible. Sure. We'd have talked about it. Now?" He backed up to the door, needing the support. "Christ, lass... You were a young coed when I found you fighting off the attack behind your apartment."

"Draw your weapon, Boss. I've answered enough." Her face twisted, Banger hoped the memory pulled at her the way it did him. Siobhan had no skills back then, but she'd been fierce, as ruthless as... fuck.

He narrowed his eyes. "Taught you everything you know."

"That's why you should've figured me out as soon as that grad student turned up dead."

Thomas's lab assistant. That's why his internal alarm went off when he saw the police report. If he'd taken the job, it would've looked the same.

Banger shut down his emotions, used the cold from the solid

wood door holding him up to cauterize his heart. "What's going down at Kick's?" As much as he wanted to play cavalry, he trusted Thomas, Dylan, and Kick to handle it. Graham and his associates were idiots.

"Nothing surprising. Kick's guard had a 'family emergency,' so she relieved him early. I dropped the house surveillance. Was supposed to unlock the door, but someone left the garage door up." She inhaled deeply and exhaled arrogance. "There's nothing like the melding of stubbornness and a soft heart."

Dammit, Kick. Von was behind Mateo's emergency too. "Ellie and Nigel?"

"Show your gun, Rafa."

Right. They were in the wind. Those two invented the long game. Their best talent was survival. It's why they worked so well together. Banger reached behind his waist and paused. Siobhan set her feet, gave her shoulders a quick shift. Perfect.

Siobhan's favorite movies were Westerns. She loved a good gunfight but considered the standoffs before them even better. The drama of the pause between moments. She lived for them. They suited her natural sharp-shooting skills. Too bad for her.

With a fluidity coming from hundreds of years of practice, Banger pulled his *sgian dubh*—his trusty, old Scottish knife—from its waiting spot and threw. End over end, in an instant frozen in time, the little knife flew, landing square in the heart of its target with a crisp thud. Siobhan still managed two shots, as expected. She'd earned her spot at his side after all. Her movements shifted the knife more, tearing enough of the organ to ensure a quick death.

Von's first love had always been guns. She'd taken to them like a kid to sweets. Banger, though, had been throwing knives since he was a toddler. He'd grown up in a violent time, and the Felidae made his childhood more like a training camp, even when he was under Tess and Edmund's tutelage. As soon as the knife left his fingers, Banger dove to the right—he always went to his left. The bullets buzzed past, less than an inch from him, as they tore through the solid door behind him.

Despite his heavy heart, the first thought he had when he landed on his side was, *Not bad, lass*. Banger had taught Siobhan everything she knew, but not everything *he* knew.

41

MY HERO

THOMAS

"It's a scratch, dammit. Let me see my fiancée!" The poor emergency department intern working on my arm fetched the attending physician because I'd turned into the human equivalent of a rabid animal, seething and gnashing my teeth.

The woman with salt-and-pepper hair chided me like I was a petulant child. "Sir, there's a big enough tear in your deltoid muscle to justify stitches. We'll fix it and get you out of here as soon as we can. Just be patient. We're understaffed thanks to the holiday." She checked my bandage and tsked at me. "You're a lucky man, but it won't help your fiancée if you bleed all over my department. Now please… sit still. Let the medicine work, and we'll get those stitches in when the patients ahead of you are finished."

They didn't know my shoulder would be fine. Hell, the scar would fade in a few months, a year tops. If Kick hadn't been somewhere upstairs, having who-knows-whose hands inside her belly, I wouldn't have come in. With a skill borne of long years of practice, I played the good boy. I even let the nurse put unnecessary prophylactic antibiotics in my equally unnecessary IV. What I needed was an update on Kick, and the staff was too busy to check. A family in a boating accident on Falls Lake had come in minutes before our posse rolled up.

Finally my turn, I forced myself to relax and tipped my head back on the pillow, releasing my tension via a rumble in my throat. The intern did all the useless things to my shoulder. Each item checked off their list brought me closer to Kick. That's all that mattered. The door to my unit whooshed open. I figured the attending was coming back to check on my doctor's progress.

"You're a right noisy bastard today." Banger pulled up a squeaky chair, sitting by my head. "They're not supposed to let me back here, but I promised to make you shut your gob." He tossed the young doctor a flirty wink. "Hello there. Nasty-looking burn he's got."

"He's lucky," she answered back without lifting her eyes from her work.

"Kick's the reason it's a little graze."

"Finally hit her bull's-eye, did she?"

I laughed at the thought. She'd done well after her breakthrough but hadn't practiced since the freeway incident.

"Stunt driving and sharp-shooting. Your woman's solid under pressure."

"I'll take her fumbling with no pressure from now on, to be honest."

"Bet."

"As long as everything's over. And I keep my lady." I pinched the bridge of my nose with my good hand. Absolutely could not think of losing her. "Any updates?"

"That's why I came down. She's out of CT and was taken into surgery."

"Just now? What the hell? Why the wait? Why wasn't I told?" The paperwork had recently been filed, but I didn't know how long it took to go into effect. "Where the fuck is Dylan?"

Banger rubbed his head. "He's upstairs. Almost took a swipe at his grandmother. That woman's a piece of work. Got a bee up her arse about transferring Kick to the hospital at Lord University."

"An hour away? We're already at a Level 1 hospital, for fuck's sake." I shook my head and received a dirty look from the intern.

"Please stay still, sir."

"Sorry. I'll behave."

Banger motioned with his hands for me to relax. As if that was happening anytime soon. "Dylan tracked down their lawyer. He located the old legal next-of-kin documents. Smart lass, your Kick. According to Dylan, she'd done that as soon as her daddy died. When the old lady heard about it, she hit the ceiling and caused another delay until security escorted her out. Everything's good now. He also told the staff you're Kick's fiancé and will take responsibility from here. You should know, there hasn't been much communication between departments. He didn't know if you were conscious. That's why I came down."

"We're swamped right now." The young doctor defended her coworkers without looking up from her sutures.

Banger raised his hands again. "Didn't mean to offend."

"Everyone in the hospital is stressed. Goes with the territory," the young doctor said, still never stopping her task. She finished and pushed the instrument stand aside, assessing her results. "All done, Mr. Harrison. My attending will check in once more, and your nurse will be back to give you your shots. Shouldn't be long."

"Thank you, Doctor. My apologies for being an ass."

"I understand. I'll say a prayer for your fiancée. And rest assured, Dr. Jacobs is one of the best trauma surgeons in the Triangle."

Tried my best to give a smile but couldn't get my lips to behave. Probably looked like a psycho. "Appreciate it."

Once we were alone, the shakes started, but not from shock. I needed to get to Kick. The image of her in my lap, blood spilling out on the kitchen floor... so brave, so pale. I raked my hair with my good hand. "She did everything we asked of her, Banger. Everything. Now she's paying for it."

Banger bent down, his forearms on his knees. His head dropped.

"Hey man, I didn't mean you..."

"You should have."

"Siobhan?" I quietly asked, though I knew.

He stared at the floor. "Fuck."

"How'd you—"

"That's why it took me so long to get to you," he started. "I surprised her at the office." Banger stood, a restless ball of energy. He turned in circles on the tiny floor before dropping back into the chair. "Wes had already told me about Mateo's emergency while I was en route." He stretched, like the chair itself pained him, and kicked his feet out in front of him. His hands folded behind his head. Banger's face twisted, looking more vulnerable than I'd ever seen. "Von was there when I walked in, acting squirrely as fuck. Hadn't expected me, obviously. But I was playing a hunch. When your text came, I knew." He shot up and walked to the glass wall. "Fuuuck!"

"I'm sorry, man."

Banger didn't look at me. He practically vibrated as his clenched fist froze in the air with nowhere to land. "Worry about your woman. I'll deal with the fallout."

"Trying to think of anything besides her since I'm stuck down here."

Banger came back and sat. "Stay here as long as you can. Kick will be in surgery for a while. It's a madhouse in the waiting room."

"Who's here?" I exhaled, flopping my head back on the pillow. I didn't want to have to take care of anyone when my heart was on an operating table with an abdominal wound.

"There's been a steady migration since we arrived."

"Deana? She needs a call, but she doesn't have to—"

"She's here. Tess too. She rode with Rachel and Wes."

I imagined Deana, Gordon, and Tess taking care of the kids. Being with them would help me feel close to Kick.

I stared through the glass to make sure the staff stayed busy with other patients. There was more we needed to say in private. "Dylan say anything to you?"

The question granted me a knowing grin. "He gave me the basics before the police took him for questioning. He's the sole witness not needing medical care, so he's theirs for a while." Banger rubbed his head. "I told him to leave out the things that sounded weird and emphasize Graham's madness over losing his criminal son."

"Then he told you."

"He did." He huffed a quiet laugh. "Hold him off, yeah? Kick should be there if we have to let him in."

"Christ." What had Nigel and Ellie done? The Felidae secrets were on the verge of getting out. They were the team that protected us above all else—or so I thought. "What the hell was Ellie thinking? I can't..."

"Before I killed her, Siobhan filled in the details. It seems Nigel discovered the Edmund connection last summer. The convoluted plans revolved around getting samples from Kick, which they finally scored on Saint Patrick's Day." He shrugged. "I guess Ol' Ni-ni wanted to experiment on her at first, but he reluctantly settled for a lip balm and hair samples from her office."

"That son of a bitch. But... what about Kick's brother?"

Banger sighed. His eyelids were heavy with exhaustion. I could relate. "They broke into his house first. Without a surveillance system, he never realized it. You know since they don't take anything obvious. There was also something about Ellie targeting women—making matriarchal lines, specifically. The bastard and Ellie are both in the wind now. If I ever get a team I can believe in again, they're my first priority."

Shit. What a clusterfuck. "Did Siobhan say why? I mean... I have a theory. Why did Kick matter so much? Hell, I thought Ellie would be thrilled." Alaric sure as hell was, and I knew it wasn't an act.

Banger pressed his lips together as he shook his head. "Long story, brother. Fuck all, everything with the old ones is. Edmund's death never sat right with me. Tess is convinced Ellie arranged his accident. That woman plays a mean long game." Banger scooted his chair closer to the bed and grabbed my forearm. "I promise you... my house will be purified. Wes is already going through the rest of my personnel... finding out if Siobhan had turned anyone else, like she did the tail on Young Jonn." Banger shook his head, his nostrils flaring. "I might fly out and see the old man if... if you don't need me."

If Kick survives, he meant. I swallowed hard, wanting to curl in on myself, but she didn't deserve my fear. The memory of the morning she'd discovered my secret flashed through my mind. I had prepared myself to let Kick walk away, and my heart felt like it was imploding—as it currently did. She fought her way through every unbelievable explanation I threw at her then. Damn if she didn't up and choose me regardless. "She has to come through."

"Listen... the trauma team wouldn't tell us anything specific about Kick's condition, but you and I know how abdominal shit goes. A shot to the gut can fly right through and hit nothing, or it could be the worst way to... yeah." He scrubbed his hands over his face, swallowed hard. "She'll fight, brother. She wouldn't want to let us all down. Count on her fighting for you."

If Kick survived this—when... dammit—Banger would end up

the one who'd lost. He'd need us whether he'd want it or not. I grabbed his arm. "You're not alone either. Whatever we need to do."

We sat in an awkward silence, both of us reeling.

"Where the hell is the attending?"

42

ZOMBIE

KICK

*N*oise.

So many sounds.

Please… make it stop. Holes pounded in my head and colors filled my vision. Too colorful. My eyes refused to open.

Turn the lights off. They hurt.

"She's tacky…"

The hell? That was mean.

And the pain—like fire all over.

The noise again. Thumping, pounding in my head.

Stop it please. It hurts. *JaysusMaryandJoseph*, I hurt.

"…still Kick… you better… Go, go, go!"

Yesss, *at last.* The pain stopped.

WARM BREEZES TICKLED THE TENDRILS FALLING FROM MY ponytail. My gaze fell to recycled wooden floorboards under my feet. Salt permeated the air. The ocean. A deep breath was a welcomed relief from the pain of a tight chest. Gratitude filled me for the absence of that pain. Atlantic waves crashed on the beach in front of the house. I was on Emerald Isle.

We'd done it. Shane and I had built the beach house—our dream home.

Filled with glee, I spun and hopped, eager to explore the inside.

Pain sliced from my knee to my hip, chinking my step before I reached the screen door.

Where the hell had that come from?

A cane leaned against the clapboards. I grabbed it to stay upright.

How odd. I hadn't used a cane since the worst days of my diagnosis.

The interior of the house was exactly as I remembered, but how could it? I hadn't been here before. Not only did I know where we'd placed everything, I held hazy memories of purchases, decorating, even small tiffs about what would come with us and what went to charity.

A thick, driftwood mantel ran the length of the wall facing the door. The fireplace below was stunning, but photos on the dark-stained wood beckoned. I limped over to them, wondering why the hell my leg refused to cooperate.

Fatigue lived in my bones the way it had in the old days. It made no sense. I lifted weights, did yoga, occasionally ran. Didn't I?

Frustration grew. A voice in the back of my head told me it was naptime, like I was a damn baby.

Damn... Damn it all.

I knew someone who said that word. Often. Someone I loved. He called me "baby"—our private joke. The word rumbled at my ear in his velvety baritone turning my insides to liquid. That honeyed Southern accent. Gray-blue eyes that sparkled with his smile. I wanted desperately to see *him*, except he was gone.

Dylan's bright silver eyes looked at me from a hand-cut frame, and I picked it up. Why was he wearing a Michigan State University football uniform? He turned down the offer to play and stayed close to home for some reason. Hadn't he? Despite the grin, my son's eyes were sad. My brow furrowed, wondering what happened. Several images of him with concussions flashed through my mind. Doctors' offices and tests. *Were these memories?*

A picture of Rachel as Elphaba Thropp from the musical *Wicked* brightened my spirit, as did one of her holding a toddler. Her smile didn't reach her eyes either. Her face held that hidden concern that mothers carry for a sick child. Something was wrong with the baby. More vague memories of worrying about him flooded me. For both of them, really.

I turned and found his *Fisher Price* toys in the corner. We often kept him.

The football-themed office in the Northwest corner irritated me. I'd wanted Shane to put his office upstairs and let me set up my studio down here. But his knee replacement made stairs difficult, and I'd become too sick to paint.

Too sick to paint? What the hell?

Memories of coffee filled my mind so crisp I could almost smell it. And cigars.

And guns.

No!

Where was everybody? I ached to see the gray-blue eyes. But... Shane's eyes were the color of the sky on a Carolina morning.

No... they were silver when *he* smiled. And navy when aroused.

My heart raced. Breath caught in my throat. *Where was he?*

Something didn't sit right about the house.

I didn't belong there. The light was wrong.

Light?

We had a light… blue and purple. If I could find it, I'd feel better.

I bolted for the door and tripped when my joints wouldn't behave. I slid through the threshold, scraping my side. *Is that why it hurts?* "Hurt" didn't begin to describe the furious pain. I crawled to the porch railing and pulled myself up as I called for *him*. Words wouldn't come. Air moved through my throat, but no sound projected from it. Dread made me shake.

I hated the house. I hated the pain, the fatigue. I'd lost something.

Me.

All that work on my health.

I'd lost someone.

Him.

I wanted him back.

A song reached my ears… "Maybe I'm Amazed." We danced to it. I sang it when he… proposed?

But Shane didn't dance.

Tears spilled down my face.

Down.

My gaze dropped to my stomach. Pain, fire… a hole.

I needed *him*. Where are you?

43

AIN'T NO SUNSHINE

THOMAS

"**S**he's taking too long to wake up."

The nurse, Joy, patted my shoulder. She'd come in to check Kick's fluid output and lines. Until she woke, there wasn't much else to do.

She patiently reiterated the facts I already knew, like I was a child. "Her surgery was long. Most of the damage was in her liver. Her son told me she's sensitive to medicines too?" I nodded and triple-checked that they had the list of antibiotics she couldn't take. "Put those things together, and it means it'll take a while for the drugs to clear her system." She checked the IV bag. "The pain medicine Ms. McKenna's on keeps her sedated. It shouldn't be much longer. Just... don't expect much when she wakes, okay, sugar?"

"Kick."

Joy blinked at me. "Pardon?"

"Please call her Kick. It'll help. Right?" Again, I didn't resent her last name, but I ached for her to have mine. I hated that I hadn't been able to talk her into eloping. As if I wasn't equally busy. I didn't care. Fear made me irrational. Not to mention irritable.

"Of course. Kick." The nurse nodded and turned to leave.

"Thank you, Joy."

"That's what I'm here for."

When she left, Banger slipped into the room. "How's our girl?"

I sighed. "See for yourself."

I needed her to dance with me, tell me to shut up, or ask me if I'd checked on the hospital cafeteria's cross-contamination precautions. Her tight, curly coils had even loosened, thanks to shuffling between beds. Rachel pulled most of them into a high bun, but the stragglers hardly bent anymore. They lacked energy too, I guessed.

The bright overhead lights made the purple bruises on her face look nothing like the pretty color of her aura. These contrasted with her paler-than-normal complexion, turning her into something like an extra in a zombie movie. My beautiful lady, my strong fairy queen, my heart... blown apart and stitched back together into colors she was never meant to show. For the thousandth time, I reminded myself they were signs of her healing, just like her unconscious state. Kick was gone.

Her chest rose and fell like a metronome. At least she was off the machinery. As I breathed along with her, my fists clenched in the blanket covering her. I should've taken comfort in her audible heartbeats, but I needed her voice, not her vitals. The antiseptic bite in the air held my nose hostage. The stale air blowing on us didn't help. It all disrupted any peace I could draw upon.

"She saved me and Dylan. And I can't do anything for her." I laid my cheek on her thigh and said, "If I could kill Jonathon Graham a thousand times over, I'd do it for her."

"It's not your job to help her yet. She's still in the hospital staff's hands. Your turn will come." Banger sat on Kick's other side and squeezed her hand. "Isn't that right, purple lady?"

I wished I could laugh with him. Each blooming bruise made me want to punch the wall. I'd been born into a world of bruises and scars. No one felt sorry for them. They were a testament to the life you'd lived. My Kick came from a different time. The stitches and colors screamed at me about how much I'd let her down.

"I keep playing her songs, hoping they'll wake her up. Except, will she be alright when she does? The doctors say one step at a time. They won't predict anything. I don't know how to handle the wait. It's so… new. Feels like the worst of my memories wrapping the past and the present together. What have I done?"

Banger ran his hands over the back of his neck. "Based on what I witnessed last fall, you had no choice with Kick. Now? I'll tell you this… your woman is no fragile flower. Her body gives her hell, but her will is made of iron. She'll wake. She'll recover. She loves you something fierce."

I dipped my chin in acknowledgment.

"Use your energy when she wakes. A birdie told me it helps."

My head knew Banger was right, but my heart still beat with fear.

"Are you family?" Joy, the nurse, poked her head in and stared straight at Banger.

"Sorry, ma'am. I brought Thomas here a coffee. I'll be going."

"Her daughter's waiting in the hall."

My abused bladder, the one I'd been ignoring most of the night, screamed loud enough to catch my attention. With Rachel here, I could step out for a minute. Reluctantly, I said, "I'll come with you."

I kissed Kick's head. "Love you, baby. I'll only be a minute."

Beeps mocked our one-sided conversation.

Banger held the door open for Rachel, who hugged me like a

koala. "Hey, pretty lady." I lifted her chin with my finger. "The nurse said she could wake any minute."

Her voice cracked. "I-is it over? Are we safe now?" Tears sat at the ready on her lower lids. They'd been that way ever since she arrived at the hospital yesterday. We'd had this same conversation a handful of times already. If she needed it one more time to believe, so be it.

"Yeah, darlin'. All the bad guys are in jail or dead." I couldn't tell her about the Felidae part, but they'd never been after her. Her terror was all Young Jonn's obsession. "You're safe, Rachel."

"I'm sorry. It's… still hard to accept."

I gave her shoulders a gentle squeeze. "You three kids went through hell this year. I'll answer every question whenever you need, got it?" *The ones I could.*

"Sure." She cracked a small, sweet smile. "Thanks."

"Go sing to your mama. Bet it'll wake her." I winked at her and gave a small wave.

Banger grabbed my arm and pulled me away from Kick's room. "You want a reason to be strong? It's those kids. They're one loud beep machine going awry from being orphans, and their next closest relative is a looney bird."

"Fuck you, man. I'm doing the best I can."

"You can do better. For Kick's sake, her kids accepted you into their hearts. They need you now. I walked in on you on the verge of giving up. Then Rachel came in and you gave her hope. Stop blaming yourself and go be with them."

Banger tipped his head toward the waiting room. "Liam's climbing the walls back there, but he's too scared to go into her room. You can talk him back to earth. For some reason, the boy's almost as fond of you as Kick is."

The picture he painted in my mind did its job. He was right. Kick would want me to step up. I grabbed my neck and stretched it, preparing myself for Liam. "Thanks for scolding me, man."

"Anytime. Listen… if the nurse doesn't mind, I'll stay with Rachel until you get back. She shouldn't be alone."

"Right again." We grabbed forearms as I nodded. "Thanks." After my pit stop, I entered the waiting room. "How long have you been here?"

Liam sat with his head in his hands, looking like a giant little boy. "Colin dropped me off last night."

I sat beside him and stretched my arm around his shoulders. "Why didn't you come back? I know your mom wants to see you."

"I peeked in." When Liam sat up, the dark shadows under his eyes were almost the same color as Kick's bruises. My anger flared for his sake this time. "She can't see us right now. You know that."

"Ahh, Lee." I pinched the bridge of my nose. Was I really up for this? "The nurse believes she hears us." I stood and took him with me. "First let's freshen up and get a bite to eat. We can't help your mom if we're on the ragged edge, can we?"

He let out a shaky laugh. "Guess not."

My phone buzzed with a text from the ICU and my heart leaped. "Finish fast, gang. She's awake!"

Dylan and Banger had joined Liam and me in the cafeteria while Rachel and Bobby sat with Kick. Dylan was still incensed with his grandmother and couldn't stay in the same room as her. I hated how Rachel played peacemaker between them. From what Kick had told me, she'd been the self-appointed go-between for her mother and grandmother since she was little. Now she stepped in for her brother—the golden boy.

A cheer rose from the table, and we dumped our trays. I stayed twitchy during the ride up to Kick's floor. What—or who —would we find in her room? I'd been so excited by the summons I hadn't asked the staff anything. What did "awake" mean? *Christ, I hope she tells me to shut up. Or strokes my chin.* Last night, I had held Kick's thumb and made her do it, hoping it would stir something in her. Without her intention, the desperate, empty gesture brought me to tears.

"THERE'S MY LADY." I SAT IN THE SEAT RACHEL HAD OCCUPIED. SHE hovered in the corner while the boys shuffled an obstinate Bobby out of the room. The kids honored and humbled me by insisting I was immediate family.

Kick's hazel eyes turned at my words. Her head slowly followed the movement. I attributed the fuzziness in the green of her irises to the drugs. The brown barely showed. I watched her fog turn to recognition as she perused my face. Her chin quivered.

"Hey," I soothed, caressing her cheek with my hand. Tears streamed from the corner of her eyes. "Please don't cry." I smiled at her and cried too.

"I l-lost… you. Looked for… you… didn't like it there. Not without you."

I stretched across the space between us and kissed her temple, her nose, her quivering bottom lip. "I've been here… waiting for you to come back. So were the kids."

Kick squinted to focus and found the trio on the opposite side of the bed. "My babies." A sweet smile stretched across her face in recognition. Her voice sounded distant and scratchy. Her vulnerability sent my protective mode into overdrive. I'd make sure she received the best of everything while she was here.

Kick's eyes landed on Dylan, and I watched her eyes clear. I guessed memories returned from the shooting. Graham had threatened to kill Dylan with his warped life-for-a-life sense of justice. Her head moved up and down, checking every inch of him the way a parent does when they meet their newborn.

"Dylan? You doubled over." A new tear trailed down her cheek.

He stepped forward, taking her other hand. "Something about Thomas's face told me to duck. Then you yelled 'drop.'" He gave her a coy smile and squeezed her hand. "You should follow your own advice."

"Really, Dyl?" Liam snapped.

"Not funny, twat waffle," Rachel said as she smacked her brother in the abs.

Their frail jokes and tenuous laughter broke the tension. It also gave away how much stress the kids carried. It filled the room every time they crossed the threshold, because children shouldn't be made to watch their parents suffer like this. Kick once told me that after Shane's accident, the kids would freak out whenever she had a bad day. Like they were waiting to lose her. Now she was in a hospital recovering from a gunshot wound. *Recover* being the takeaway.

Kick brought her gaze back to me and saw my sling. "He aimed at your heart."

"It's a small graze. Your bullet hit the bastard aiming at me, and he hit my shoulder instead." I ran my hand over her hair. "You saved my life."

"You thought I was dying." My throat dried up at her words. I couldn't respond, just kept swallowing. "S-sorry I scared you," she said.

"Christ, Kick." I'd been furious at her heroics at first. The truth was each of us would've gone down for the other. I brought her hand to my lips and kissed it.

"I'm tired." She yawned and winced from the pain it caused. She did her best to not moan from it but failed.

The kids gasped, like they'd been waiting for signs of Kick's fragility. Dylan ran his hand through his hair. "I'll go get the nurse."

Liam slipped into the chair opposite mine. He leaned toward his mom. "Sh-should we go?"

Kick squeezed his hand and gave him a pained smile. I

answered for her. "Give her a minute. You're more of a balm than you think."

Joy arrived and added medicine to the IV. "Why don't y'all give mama an hour? Patients only have about ten minutes of energy at the beginning. Don't worry, it grows. Before you know it, all y'all will be out of our hair."

I walked toward the door with the kids. Joy followed, leaving us with hope. "It doesn't look like it to you, but she's doing great."

Kick quietly called after us, "Can Thomas lie with me? I'm a-afraid to sleep without him."

Joy turned around, her hand on her hip. "We need to order bigger beds around here. Everybody wants to crawl in with the patient." She walked back to the IV stand. "Let's see if we can scoot you over without pinching the lines. You've got two hours until the shift changes. I can give you that much."

"Thank you." I hugged each kid and told them I'd text when Kick woke again. I promised this was a nap and nothing to be frightened of. Climbing into the bed alongside her, I encouraged her to rest while I watched over her. My eyes continuously scanned her monitors and her body for signs of change. I held her free hand under the blanket, willing my energy to come out and help her heal.

It was a shock when Joy shook my knee to get me to leave the bed at the end of her shift. I'd been up almost two days and had fallen into a deep sleep with Kick safe in my arms.

4 4

THEY

KICK

"Ow! Don't make me laugh, Liam. Especially when my belly pillow's missing. One of you bozos stole it, and I want it back."

"*Must you* with the Oscar-worthy performance? You don't hear me griping about my knee." Bobby indignantly folded her arms and turned away, smiling at the room, like she was scanning it for allies. Even now, the competition she'd built between us from the day I was born continued. The one-way one-upping would never quit with her.

"I was *shot*, Mother. A chunk of my fucking shitty-to-begin-with liver is gone. Besides, you gripe about your knee every chance you get. You're the one who turned pain into an Olympic competition I never signed on to." I sighed and closed my eyes to her performance. "I can't care anymore."

Bobby clicked her tongue. I couldn't see her eyes rolling, but I practically heard them rattle around in her head. I supposed the chance to recruit more fans to her side of our mother-daughter war had energized her. The hospital staff was fresh meat where she was concerned.

"You've always been a hypochondriac and never took care of me. You hate when the spotlight's off you."

Funny how my memories were the exact opposite. Thomas's offer from back in January roared in my head every single minute of Bobby's visits this past week.

"There's my cue to leave," Liam said.

Of my three, he'd been the hardest on himself for being out of town while everything went down. How did he not see my immense gratitude for the band's gig? But he'd always been sensitive to my ups and downs. As a toddler, before the diagnosis, he'd go out of his way to snuggle close or entertain me on bad days.

"Okay, Wee Man. Promise me you'll go to practice. The café's doing fine." When he leaned down for a hug, I whispered in his ear, "Keep the gig in Chapel Hill this weekend. Last-minute bookings like this don't come around often."

His shoulders dropped as he sighed. "Yeah, gotcha. We've got a new girl to get up to speed anyway."

"So Jax won't sing with you at all?"

Liam's brows pinched as his fingers beat a rhythm on his thigh. "Chill, fam. We need…" He lifted a shoulder. "Space." Dark shadows still sat under his eyes, where everyone else's had faded since I was officially recovering. My poor baby had lost his best friend, and we'd never talked about it. He still refused to open up.

"Sure, sweetheart. What's your new singer's name? Do I get to meet her soon?"

"Her name's Mary Lawrence. You can meet her the next time you come to practice."

"Mary Lawrence? Is she studying to become a nun? Does anyone call her Mary Larry?" Bobby chuckled, but Liam looked embarrassed by my flippant remark. *Shit.* I'd let Bobby's critical nature rub off on me again. "I'm sorry. That was rude."

"It's the South, fam. Girls get men's names all the time down here."

"True. I forgot. Name them after Grandpa, but don't let them have their own opinions."

He laughed at my joke and said, "Like we're better." I childishly smirked at the dig at Bobby, who'd named both her daughter and son after her, in her never-ending need for validation.

Liam turned and waved. "Bye, Gran."

"Yeah, yeah." Bobby flicked a hand in his direction.

I called after him, "Tell Macushla I miss her."

"Gotcha." He blew me a kiss and left the door ajar as he disappeared down the hall.

Once he was out of sight, I glared at Bobby for a long time. If this Felidae business could develop the power to shoot lasers from my eyes, I would have gleefully toasted her.

She shuffled in her chair, as if she'd been on a radiator instead. She knew I judged her for the way she treated Liam. This ancient fight between us had become so predictable.

Bobby was spot-on too. I judged her for a hell of a lot. She was lucky we were in a hospital. Biting my tongue kept me from screaming at her. I'd spent my life biting my tongue around her. It's a wonder it wasn't pierced.

"Are you ever going to forgive and forget?" Bobby demanded. She reminded me of an adulterer who blamed their spouse for their destructive behavior. *Then again, she'd done that too.*

The truth was, I'd forgiven her years ago. It didn't mean we were resolved, though, or ever would be. Resolution required penance from the offending party. Or at least acknowledgment and honest reflection. Bobby was so busy hiding from herself I suspected true contemplation would cause a breakdown.

I needed that resolution.

Bobby wanted permission to fly her mean flag as high as she wanted whenever she wanted. Especially at my expense. If I continued to allow it, I would end up unable to look at myself in the mirror. Time for this to come to a head.

"Forgive what exactly, Bobby?" My words spilled out more clipped than planned. "You've never apologized for anything. How am I supposed to forgive someone who—according to you—has done nothing wrong?" My voice rose with bitter sarcasm, and Joy stuck her head in my room. "Sorry," I said, though I didn't mean it. Our timing stunk. What was new? Joy nodded and ducked back out.

"I apologized for the sweater I shrank."

From high school. *Seriously?* "No you didn't. You put me in charge of everyone's laundry as punishment for being upset with you." I gritted through my teeth. "All you do is make excuses for your mean streak."

"You know how my family treated me," she shot back. Her chin quivered as bitterness instantly dissolved into self-pity.

"Intimately. Instead of taking responsibility for yourself, you responded in kind. You could've done better, but you turned love into a weapon. That's on you, not your parents. For my self-preservation, I can't care anymore with you." Sighing, I turned my head away, refusing to see her someone-just-made-a-rank-fart face anymore. An icy shiver skated up my spine, doing a quadruple something-or-the-other jump, landing hard on my heart. Numbness replaced all the years of hurt and bitterness. Numbness was all I could hope for with Bobby.

"I built my school from the ground up. Who helped me? No one." Bobby fretted, refusing to let go of the pity party she was hosting.

True. She worked her arse off to run the best school in the metro area. But, uh... Daddy worked his ass off between shifts playing single parent.

I said nothing, so she continued, "You and your father made me give it all up!"

*You sold it for a fecking mint after the orthopedist told you to retire.
Then Daddy did his money magic and set you up for life.*

"It's called retirement." I hissed. "The doctor warned you that
your knee couldn't take the daily punishment. Daddy had to get
away from the cold, and Raleigh reminded him of home. You've
never given life here a chance."

"You took me away from Robert."

I'd heard this at least a million times. My field of fucks was
harvested. There weren't even any left for gleaning. Numbness
was a welcome relief to the pain of her accusations. I made my
decision. If only Thomas had been here to witness it.

"We're done." I exhaled a long, quiet breath. The peace that I
usually required meditation to achieve washed over me. "I'll have
Thomas's assistant arrange a mover for you. You'll have a nurse
to oversee your health issues if you need it. Hell, anything you
want, you can call her. But never call me again." I swiped away a
tear. "Move in with Juan. Do the things you've always wanted to
do, whatever lights your fire. I don't care. From here on, we're
dead to each other."

Bobby's voice rose above acceptable hospital volume. "I never
know how to act or what to say around you. My words get twisted." She fussed with an invisible piece of lint on her shirt before
spitting, "I'm damned if I do and damned if I don't."

No surprise she didn't know what to make of my decision.
Except this fish was done swinging from her hook. I cut the
fecking line. "Right back at you, Mother." I tucked a wavy tendril
behind my ear. "Now neither of us needs to worry about it…
anymore."

Bobby clenched her fists as if she were restraining herself
from hitting me. In my hospital bed. I lifted my eyes to the ceiling
tiles, wishing I could walk away from her. I contemplated
pressing the nurse's button and having her thrown out.

I swallowed and said the words I'd known my whole life but

never admitted. "Listen, I know if given a choice, you would have never picked me to be your kid."

"I wouldn't go—"

"It's the same for me." I interrupted, and hearing the words shut her mouth tight. "We're never going to be one of those mother-daughter bestie duos. It was never in our cards."

Her brow pinched in anger. The truth hurt, I guess. It didn't matter anymore.

Bobby loudly exhaled several times, sounding like a horse after a long carriage ride. "I wish... well, I wish..." She never finished her sentiment. Instead, she sat in her chair, staring out the window, her cowardice shouting louder than her temper ever could.

"Yeah. Me too." And that was the closest to an apology I'd ever receive from her.

"I'll be going then." She stood, smoothing her clothes, checking her purse, anything to avoid eye contact.

I channeled the speech Thomas had given me in the bathtub as I called after Bobby. "You'll want for nothing. Money, medical care, a shopper, a companion. You can have it. You just won't have me."

After she slammed the door, the tears let loose. Overwhelming relief and crushing pain mingled together. The judgment of friends who'd lost good mothers raced to the front of my mind. *You'll regret it when she's gone,* they always said. The thing was, I'd been mourning the mother I'd never had since I was a girl.

I pulled the blanket to my mouth as a sob escaped. The pain wracking through my chest didn't register. I didn't even press the button on the medicine dispenser. Emotions took front and center, and no button existed for them. I felt good and bad, guilt and relief all rolled into one. Moreover, I was proud of myself for finally sticking up for the little girl who'd been treated like shit for so long.

45

SOWING THE SEEDS OF LOVE

KICK

"You cut your hair." I inhaled Deana's shea butter and vanilla scent as she leaned down to hug me. "It's so Anita Baker."

She laughed, her deep rumble, taking my mind off the post-op pain. After my cry over everything with Bobby, the physical pain came back with a vengeance.

She touched her short, wispy hairdo. "Gordon calls me Halle Berry."

"Your cheekbones stand out like hers for sure. It's beautiful, Dee. Not that you weren't before." Exhausted from talk of recovery and therapy and my family drama, I took full advantage of mindless beauty experiments.

She laughed and patted my shin. "No worries. I know what you're saying. Thank you. Now tell me… y'ight?"

My shoulders shrugged with ease, thanks to the meds. "Distract me please. What's new at the Perked Cup?"

Thomas had told me about the vigil she'd kept during my

surgery. This was our first time alone, and we both buzzed with pent-up energy. I wanted to thank her for holding the kids together. She wanted to chew my ass out. I didn't need to read her mind to know that.

"Jake bumped up his hours. You'll be proud of him." She slid the visitor's chair closer to me and fell into it.

One more restless day in this bed and I could go home. Thomas, the kids, and Cyndi helped me make slow laps around the unit each morning and night. The infection was minimal, and a new antibiotic didn't cause any reactions. The nurses regularly commented on my quick recovery. Little did they know. Every night Thomas spent with me, he ran his energy over my skin until mine woke up to it. He promised to study what it was all about when he took his work over to the private sector.

"How's Dex doing with Hugh? Have they started the expansion into the space next door?"

Deana swiped her thumb over my palm several times and wouldn't lift her gaze. "They have."

"I can't wait to peek at what Charley's crew came up with." I grabbed her hand and squeezed it. "There's something you're not saying. Are the men getting along?" I didn't know what I'd do if there was a problem. Despite my resolve to say goodbye to Bobby, I was still drained. Constantly fighting pain made it harder for me to give the way I was used to.

"They get on great, shug. I didn't know Hugh made him a partner though," she said.

Thomas had mentioned it in passing, but I had other things on my mind. I shrugged. "It's a great idea." I tilted my head. "What am I missing?"

"You were supposed to be Hugh's partner. I feel like we've taken something away from you. Your future security. Your kids..."

"Are you talking about money?"

Deana's normally spot-on posture fell as she looked away.

"Hey…" I shook her hand to get her attention back. "The kids and I are fine. We'll stay fine. My involvement had been a favor to Hugh—to honor my dad. The kids plan to do their own things. So why shouldn't the Douglases have a stake in the success of this venture? It makes more sense anyhow."

"We're employees."

Talk about pain. Her words felt like a slap. To my heart. Then again, Gordon and Deana had been burned by promises from employers before. In our part of the country, it was difficult for true friendship to cross racial lines. Rudely and brutally so. Like me with my mother's side, there was always a part of them that expected the worst so they wouldn't be disappointed.

"Tell me you know you're more than my morning manager."

When Deana said nothing, I swore to keep from crying.

"Thomas likes to say you're part of my clan. Dee, you're more my family than my mother's people have ever been. Who's managed her all these years for me? My dad?" I waved my hand. "*Pffft*. We both know it's been you… propping me up when she hit me with a zinger. You were the first one I could count on after Shane… You're family."

Deana's face dissolved into a visage of tears and fury. "What the *fuck* were you thinking… shooting a gun like a *damn* cowgirl? Getting shot." She jumped out of her chair and paced the little space in my room, lecturing. "You expect me to pick up these kids' pieces because you went off half-cocked? Like Superwoman?"

Her emotions opened my floodgates. My hands shook as the memories rushed back. "I was so terrified. He said he'd kill Dylan. Then Thomas." I don't remember Deana moving, but we ended up holding each other for a long time.

"You're the one we almost lost," she muttered into my neck. "Stupid girl. G agrees with me."

"Does he now?" I pushed her back and wiped away her tears with my thumbs. "I thought Gordon always agreed with *me*."

She sniffled and reached for a tissue. "I tell you that to make you feel better."

"Appreciate it," I said, laughing as I dabbed my eyes with the blanket.

Deana picked up a scrunchie that Rachel had left on the windowsill. She finger-combed my hair, creating elaborate twists with an eased skillfulness that awed me. She fashioned everything into a high ponytail.

I began to giggle as she worked. It had been the first real laughing fit since the attack. It felt so good to release this way that I didn't mind the pain. I welcomed it.

"Hold still, you mess," she commanded through the bobby pins she seemed to have magically conjured and held in her teeth. "What's so funny?"

"I made you swear, Deana Douglas."

"Shut up." She pulled a little tighter on my hair because she could. "You'd make my *Grandmama* swear."

"THERE'S MY BEAUTIFUL LADY." THOMAS HAD SPENT A NIGHT AWAY from the hospital because Banger required his help with something. It had to do with the betrayal and putting Angel Security back together, but I didn't have the mental bandwidth to get into the details with them. My heart ached for Banger though, and I encouraged Thomas to help his friend however he could. I wouldn't hog all his energy when Banger was wounded too.

"You should consider glasses, cowboy. My face is doing an impression of a failed stained glass project."

He leaned over and kissed me in greeting. "Your eyes are bright today. The doctor must be tapering off your pain meds." His fingers lightly swept over my cheeks. "Swelling's going down. Your hair's damp from a shower. All clues that you'll be out of here soon."

Thomas swiveled his hips on the side of the bed, making

room for him to lie next to me. He pulled me against him, wrapped his arms around me, and buried his nose in my hair.

"Did you sniff me?" I smiled at the memory of him asking me that same question after I sprained my ankle and he had to carry me home. It felt so long ago.

"Damn straight." He continued inhaling as he paved a trail of kisses along my jaw, down my neck. "I missed you last night. It's too cold in our bed without you."

My favorite nurse opened the door, a clipboard in her hand. "It's official. Since you pooped this morning, you get to go home today. You can start on these papers while I do my magic at the desk."

Thomas turned to me with a wide grin. "You did?" He laughed into my shoulder, bouncing me up against him, getting more than a twinge from me.

"Um, careful. One BM doesn't equal an all clear." My skin heated with its red flush of embarrassment. Then again, Thomas had helped change many bandages and one nurse showed him how to give me a sponge bath on a night when the staff was short a nurse. We had no mysteries between us anymore. Though I'd still insist on doing my business in private when we went home. Some things are sacrosanct.

"Wish I could've been here to celebrate."

I clicked my tongue. "I'm not potty-training, you knothead. If I were, Joy would've given me ice cream for breakfast. Well, dairy-free ice cream."

"You gave your kids ice cream for breakfast for pooping in the potty?" Joy asked. "That's genius. We can't motivate my three-year-old to stay on it long enough to do anything, but that might work."

"Instant rewards get the best returns. Oh, right…" I tapped my thigh. "A successful week earned the boys a Thomas the Tank Engine." I turned to Thomas and held my hand flat. "I'll take Lady, thank you very much. She's my favorite engine."

"*You're* my lady." He kissed my palm. "This Lady character must be amazing if you remember her."

"She shoots magic gold dust out her stack, or something like that. And she gets kids to believe in themselves."

"Sounds just like you."

I laughed and winced. "I wish you guys would stop doing that. How can I heal if you keep making me hurt?"

"Hate to tell you, honey, but you have many more weeks of hurting until everything's considered healed," Joy said. "Which reminds me... I can tell you two will need to see this in writing." She flipped the pages on the clipboard to the fourth in her stack of what looked like twenty papers. "No orgasms until you can walk a mile or three flights of stairs."

"You're making this up, right?" I asked, annoyance saturating my voice while my cheeks flared with heat.

"The doctor will explain everything when he visits. Just keep in mind, you were basically fileted. Those muscles need time, and orgasms are intense contractions."

No shit. Lovely, mind-blowing, intense contractions. Now I wanted one... no, many. It had been too long.

Joy must've read the discouragement on my face. "No need to pout." She folded her arms over her chest. "Keep up with your walks and follow your discharge orders to a T. You'll be up to speed before you know it. Just remember... if something hurts, stop it immediately. Okay?"

Thomas scoffed at her orders. "Better keep her here."

"Hey!"

Joy tapped my compression-hose-covered calf. The cankles were going down. "I have all my faith in a full recovery. Shoot, I thought they wrote the wrong number when your chart said you're forty-seven. Then I saw those two huge boys of yours and couldn't believe you didn't have a surrogate. You'll be fine." She gave me a wink and left us to do the paperwork.

"Thomas?" I held the clipboard up, bringing my hand toward

my face, then pulling it away. "Speaking of glasses, I can read this without specs."

"It's all part of the reverse order of healing."

"But I thought getting shot would override any reversing."

He twisted his lips as he pondered my question. "My scientific guess is, you're in mega-healing mode. It could be a bonus side effect."

"Mega-healing mode? This a scientific term?"

He smirked. "I never dealt with aging eyes, but I had a stubborn ankle wound from the war. Also, I'd occasionally deal with muscle pain after contracting a bad illness as a kid. Both mysteriously improved in the first few years after my aura manifested. I guessed at a correlation but wasn't certain until I found the Felidae."

"Well, shit. Is there a hand mirror around here? I want to see if I can apply mascara without my x10 magnification mirror. Now *that* would be something."

46

REACH OUT, I'LL BE THERE

THOMAS

*N*ot teaching a spring semester class allowed me to help with Kick's recovery. My team also hit a road-block in the lab, so a step back benefited everyone. We held off on the next push until after moving into the new facility in Research Triangle Park.

A couple of weeks later I came home early, expecting Kick to be at the desk in her office. She'd taken on work she could do from home while the rest of the staff had her hours. Plus Liam was graduating in a few days. His party was pushed back to allow for more recovery time, but she still went all in with the planning.

We'd also pushed the wedding out. In fact, Liam's party would be the last weekend in June, then the guests would drive to the mountains for our wedding. It allowed the family members from Ireland to attend both events. After hearing about the shooting, Kick promised to check in with her former in-laws regularly. It helped ease the pain of breaking ties with her mother. It stung her deeply to make the hard call, but I couldn't have been prouder of her. Her near-death experience gave Kick a clarity that Bobby would never comprehend.

I looked forward to meeting her former mother-in-law and uncle. We spoke on the phone, and their support meant a lot.

Joe and Toni planned to attend the wedding. They spent very little time off our estate in Virginia, so I hoped they'd like the surprise I planned for everyone, especially my fiancée.

I'd bought a mountain retreat between Asheville and Lake Lure in western North Carolina. Since it was a vacation spot, most of the houses on the mountain were rentals. I secured them all for our guests to stay in. Kick did her damnedest to pry the details from me, but my lips stayed sealed. The surprise would be worth it.

Unfortunately, my lips felt stifled in other ways. Not so much my lips, but my cock sure missed her. Kick acted crankier than me. She'd picked a fight that morning over her cereal. When the dust had settled, I knew she was bored with her rehabilitation. And horny.

There was no sign of the dog as I entered the house. A sense of dread spread over me because of the quiet. Then I figured Kick was napping. The low hum of the dishwasher suggested Carmen was around. Probably had taken the dog for a walk on the greenway.

I peeked in the bedroom, surprised to find it empty, except for Macushla. Upon seeing me, she wrapped herself around my leg and sat at my feet, asking for a head pat. Once satisfied, she woofed low and bounced from me to the door, doing a perfect Lassie impersonation to make me go upstairs.

The whooshing hum of the treadmill gave away her human's location. It sounded too fast, and my brow furrowed with irritation.

"What are you doing?" I growled at the sight of her red, sweaty face.

Her smile beamed back at me. "Koosh and I did three flights of stairs, took a break, and now I'm at three-quarters of a mile." She could speak. Breathing steady, not too hard. "What're you doing home?"

"Gave my team the afternoon off. Picked up burgers for lunch."

Her eyes lit up. "With the good fries?"

To Kick, that meant a dedicated fryer, making them gluten-free. "Of course." The glee on her face was comical. Ever since we'd been involved and I drove near the joint on my way home, they'd become her guilty pleasure. Mine was watching her moan as she ate them. "The curry Dijon dipping sauce included."

Her squeal zinged straight to my neglected cock, but it didn't derail my annoyance with her so-called workout. It was too early for her to push like this. What if it messed up the wedding plans again? "Step on the side rails."

"But—"

"Do it," I ordered. She rolled her eyes and complied, making the machine cut off.

Before I could chastise her, Kick whined her defense. "I'm bored. Carmen won't let me clean because I can't bend over yet."

"She's a good woman."

"Thomas." She swatted my hand resting on the handrail. "I'm listening to a book and going at a slow pace." Her eyes saddened. "I wanted to walk the dog, but it'll hurt if she pulls on her leash."

"Macushla isn't neglected. She has Liam and me. Carmen also takes her on a short loop around the neighborhood when she's here." I bobbed my hands in front of her. "Pull up your shirt please."

"Seriously?"

I folded my arms, spread my feet in a commanding stance, and waited.

"Fine." She removed her tank, showing me a clean bandage.

"May I?"

"Do I have a choice?"

"Nope." I chuckled and eased the tape away from her stomach. No seepage. "Looks good. Did you change this before coming up here?"

"Yes, doctor."

"Don't forget it." I gently smacked her ass. I swear the contact made us both gasp.

"A *fud* doesn't count."

"Fud?"

She folded her arms, but the zipper on her workout bra had slid down. "PhD."

The move put her perfect breasts on display for me. I nearly swallowed my tongue. *Right.*

I remembered what I'd been trying to do and made a circle with my index finger. "Turn around. I'll check the exit." It was the harder site for Kick to clean, and she usually waited for me to do it. I pulled this bandage away. "Have to admit... you're healing like a champ."

"Told you."

"Sorry for snapping."

"You're forgiven for worrying. But I'm bored, cowboy. I can't work at the Perked Cup. I'm all caught up on paperwork. I've always done laundry, and Carmen's taken that too. She said I couldn't carry the baskets."

"She's right."

"I know!" She sighed and slapped her hands on the rests. "We have a gazillion relatives coming here in three weeks for three important events. And everyone tells me I can't do anything for them. Cyndi even banned me from making centerpieces. She said I needed to stick with fine art and leave the crafting to her. But I think she's upset about being out of town visiting her mom when shit went down. She feels like she has to do all this herself."

"I was here when shit went down. I'm still helping. Make a list of what's left, and we'll divvy it up." I took her hand, helped her off the treadmill, and pulled her into my arms. I did this every chance I had now. Each time, gratitude over what I still had versus what I almost lost swept through me. "Your clan wants to help, darlin'. Let us." I gave her my best seductive smile and kissed her neck.

"Stop with the smirk. Plus they already have enough to do. Deana and Jake are working around the clock."

"I'll hire an assistant, and you can promote Tina for the summer."

"Thomas…"

My lips stifled her complaint. "I almost lost you. Hell, we all almost lost you. We were in a tailspin over the what-ifs, even after you made it through surgery. Helping you helps us heal."

Her chin quivered a moment before she set her shoulders back. Then her hitching tells started. "His gun was on you… you didn't see it. I could've been alone again instead."

My forehead dropped to hers. "I saw it. I know. Believe me… I know. When I wake from nightmares, I hear you in the middle of yours."

"Then let's celebrate being alive." Kick ran her hand up my biceps to my neck and pulled my lips to hers. "Focus on the good."

Her rusty attempt at seduction made me smile against her lips. "All this fussing is about your empty 'O' tank."

She breathed in my ear. "My sugar bowl's empty, cowboy."

I pulled her body tight to mine, letting her feel we were on the same page. Except for one thing.

"Your pain concerns me. What if one of your incisions opens when you come?"

"Jaysus." She laughed. "You make me sound like a wild animal." Her brows raised.

"If you'd ever watched yourself orgasm, you'd understand. It's erotic as hell. Makes me feel like a king when you come multiple times. And now? With you asking like this… knowing you need me? I want to lock the door, take you right here. Against the wall, on the mat, on the ball. Anywhere. I want to slam into you, hear you cry out for me."

"The ball?" Her tongue worried her cheek as a grin grew. "I did promise you a backbend on it, didn't I? Once the wounds heal. But you know, good sex is more than the freaky-deaky, right? It's always eating steak."

She laughed at what I assumed looked like a confused expression on my face, then tapped my chest. I had a feeling of what it was like to be mansplained. "I love a juicy filet as much as anybody. But sometimes I'd kill for an authentic, grass-fed burger with hand-cut fries. The bottom line?" She went up on her tiptoes, kissed my lips.

"It's…" Kiss.

"About…" Kiss.

"Having a happy fiancée."

She spun around and wiggled her lush ass against my cock, getting the groan she sought. For Kick, I was a sure thing. Couldn't say no. She took advantage.

My head tipped back as I barked a laugh. "Mission accomplished, you minx. On these conditions—toys in your sweet pussy. We'll take it slow." I unzipped her workout bra and cupped her tits in each hand, teasing her nipples with my thumbs. "My mouth works these lush nipples till you come." Her sharp intake of breath hit my heart and turned my cock into a rod.

She tilted her head and traced a finger from my pecs to my cock. "What if I want to play with you?" She popped her lips for emphasis and went down in a Twist dance move as if she were Chubby Checker's backup dancer.

"Ow." Kick thumped on her ass when it became clear she couldn't twist her way back to standing.

"Yep." I crouched down to her level and stroked her ear. "A for effort, but I'm in charge now." Before her fluttering eyes could change my mind, I had an idea. "You'll stretch out on the bed on your back, your head will hang off the side—just a touch—and I'll take your mouth. If you can handle the stretch, you can reach around and hang on to my ass. But only if it doesn't hurt."

"You'd let me do that?"

My shoulders shook as I laughed. She killed me more with love than with her reckless behavior. I ran my thumb over her bottom lip. "How can I refuse your mouth when it's offered so sweetly? Know this though… if you're in pain and say nothing, I'll figure it out. And I'll be pissed. Feel something, you say something. If we need to change up, we do it. If we have to stop, we stop."

"I love you." She sighed, her eyelashes fluttering at half-mast.

I stood and swept her up in my arms, carrying her downstairs to our room and locking the door behind us. To hell with the burger and fries for the moment. I was her pleasure. Without the guilt.

ROAD TO NOWHERE

KICK

The sound of sixties mod music reached my ears as soon as I closed the front door. After a few hours back at the Perked Cup, I channeled a cast member from a zombie film, mindlessly kicking my shoes in their cubby. My first shift back hit me like a Mack truck in the past hour. By the time I'd dropped my gear off in the office, the music perked me up. I'd even done a couple of easy steps of the Pony along with the soundtrack.

"Wee hoo! Wee hoo! Woo pah!"

A pair of baritone voices complemented each other as they floated down from the loft.

"My dude. That was big."

"Good one, pal."

Ah, the telltale sounds of male bonding over the crazy adventures of Mario and his brother.

"Oh Lucy… I'm home," I called up.

"We're upstairs," two deep voices yelled back.

"I heard."

After crouching low to let Macushla sniff my new smells, followed by a vigorous butt rub, the two of us padded up the steps. She kept turning her head as she led me toward the action.

"I know, Koosh. I heard them." The sound lifted my heart. Thomas had held the kids together when I was in the hospital, and it further bonded him and Liam. I'd be forever grateful.

"Hey, guys." I sat and watched them collect coins for a few minutes before saying to Thomas, "Thought you were working late."

A huge grin turned my way. "My dishes are marinating. So I came home."

In my mind, we had two homes, and I loved that he thought the same. My attention turned to Liam. His eyes were bright and posture engaged, like he was moving on from heartbreak. "You look better, Wee Man."

He lifted a shoulder. "Meh. I'm vibin'."

Thomas and I exchanged a secret smile. "Good to hear, sweetheart."

"Anyway…" He paused the game and set his controller down. "Thomas has something to show you."

I turned to my fiancé. "Really?"

Thomas dropped his controller and stood. "Indeed."

"What's this mystery?" I asked as we descended the stairs.

"Patience, darlin'." Whatever it was, it couldn't top seeing Liam's buzz of excitement.

The two of them hit the wood floor and went straight to the mudroom. "Where is the magical joy-giving entity? I didn't see anything when I came in." I'd parked Thomas's Land Rover outside on the driveway. It was a tight squeeze to park it in the garage next to Liam's Jeep. After the police finished with it, my car ended up going to Camaro heaven. Besides the insurance company declaring it totaled, I knew I couldn't drive it without seeing Rachel's terrified face every time I slid in it.

Thomas stopped in front of the garage door. "Open it."

I hadn't opened the door to the garage since Big Jonn surprised me. Most of my nightmares involved me standing in this very spot, my hand hovering above the knob. I swallowed hard. "Thomas, I don't…"

He reached around me and opened the door. The shadowed shape I was accustomed to filled my parking space, only the gray shape the red car made was lighter. The motion detector switched on the light when I hit the first step. I turned back, my brows drawn together in question. Thomas shooed me forward with his hands.

I stated the obvious. "This is new. And a Z." It was fresh off the line, had a leather interior, a sunroof, and was white with orange stripes. My favorite design.

"When a rider gets back on the horse, it doesn't have to be the same horse. It helps if it's a better horse," Thomas said lightly.

I ran my hand along the plate at the back, touched the rally stripes on the spoiler, and giggled. "It's the opposite of yours." Thomas's was orange with white striping—the reason he'd named it Ginger.

"When we met, you said this was your favorite design. It took longer to arrive than I planned, but…" The silly man looked apologetic.

With my hands on my head, I stared at the car, uncertain what to think or how to feel, a bit like deciding to adopt a puppy right after losing the best dog ever. Was I ready to do this again?

Thomas came up behind me and leaned his head down to my ear. "Is it alright?"

His hesitancy made up my mind. I spun and circled my arms around him. "It's fantastic. Thank you." I lifted on my toes and kissed him. "I was waiting for the insurance to finalize before deciding what to do."

Thomas closed his eyes and inhaled, as if he was taking a moment to let the little kiss sink in. He'd been doing that a lot since the shooting. "It's an early wedding present. I was concerned you'd end up in an übersafe SUV." He tipped back his head and sighed. "These aren't made with a unibody anymore. Hell, I almost gave you Ginger for that reason, but you'd said this had been the one you always wanted. Hope it's different enough and familiar at the same time. Besides, now that we know about your stunt-driving skills, you'll be fine."

I buried my forehead in his shoulder. "What exactly have you heard?"

He murmured, "There's camera footage." Then he barked a laugh when I whined. I hadn't thought about that. "If Hollywood calls, I'll be your agent."

My hand sounded like it played on a bongo drum as I tapped his tight abs. "Shut up."

Liam pressed the garage door opener. "Does anyone plan to get in?"

"Yeah, darlin'," Thomas encouraged. "Slide in. Give her a test drive."

"Um… my car is a him. He has a Spanish accent." I patted Thomas's jaw. "You still have the best accent, but that'd be weird if my muscle car sounded like you."

"Christ." His eyes lifted to the ceiling, the muscles in his face fighting a smile. "Get in." Thomas opened the door and gave me a nudge into the driver's seat. Then he let Liam in the back on the passenger side before settling next to me.

The engine purred to life without bringing back memories of my nightmare drive. It made my stomach flutter… deliciously. Perhaps my new car did have Thomas's accent. It growled in a way that reminded me of him. I felt it flow through my core. A grin of delight spread across my face. I tilted my head toward my fiancé.

Thomas looked back at me with the smug expression of a guy who knew he would get lucky later. I bit my lip, and he barked another laugh. We needed this minute of pure happiness.

I checked over my shoulder at Liam. His hands explored the

soft suede inserts of the gray seats. My hands did the same on the steering wheel. The lack of worn spots on the soft surface called for future adventures together. Good ones, where no one chased us or shot up the body.

I raised my eyebrows, grinned at Thomas, and said, "Where should we go?"

He opened his hands out wide. "Anywhere you want, darlin'. How do you want to celebrate?"

"Liam?" I called out to the back, though I already knew his answer.

"Food, of course. I'm a growing boy."

Thomas and I laughed. He turned around and said, "You mean you're a bottomless pit."

"Same thing, fam."

I shook my head at my son as I made the final adjustments to the seat and mirrors. "Ready?"

"Impress me, Mama." Liam stretched his arms across the top of the rear seats.

I put the car in drive and eased out of the driveway. "I thought the current year didn't feature rally stripes," I said.

Thomas squeezed my hand as I navigated the neighborhood. "That's why it took longer to deliver than I'd planned."

As suspected, he'd commissioned them for me. To give me the vehicle of my dreams. Except I'd already had my dreams come true in the form of him.

Going against traffic on the expressway allowed me to open up this new car, and "he" didn't disappoint. The new coupe leaped to speed on the ramp.

My son yelled, "Woo-hoo!" from the back, competing with the ten-speed engine for volume.

"We need to take our two cars out to a test track," I told Thomas as we raced to our favorite sushi place in Brier Creek. It wasn't the closest, but I wanted time to enjoy the ride, revel in this new feeling of freedom. Not only from the joy of new transportation but from the lift of the ominous weight of danger that hung over us for months.

"Don't get cocky," Thomas warned. "No one beats Ginger in a quarter-mile. Ever."

I breathed deep the new car smell—more of a new life smell—and shrugged. "You do you. I'll do me."

"Will you park my car on the street before you leave tomorrow morning?"

I was safely tucked under Thomas's arm, snuggling under the covers and catching up on local news. We could watch it again now that the station stopped using us as their lead story.

He pulled back, staring down at me with a furrowed brow. "Whatever for?"

I scrunched my nose. Wasn't it obvious? "Did you see me shaking when we entered the garage this afternoon? The second the white shape of the freezer landed in my periphery, I jumped. And you were there. What will happen when I'm alone? I'm not ready."

"When will you be ready?"

I made a frustrated growl sound. I hadn't considered the ask a big deal and wondered why Thomas couldn't just say *no problem*. "I don't know. One day at a time, right?"

"Not always." Thomas climbed out of bed and slid his arms through his robe. He reached for me. "Come on."

I sat up and wrapped my arms around my legs. "Not the back on the horse thing. Isn't it enough that I drove the new car?"

"This is different. Trust me." He grabbed his tumbler of whiskey from the nightstand.

Like I wouldn't trust him. Thomas had asked me that since the beginning of our relationship. Whether it was remembering dance steps, learning to shoot, or giving my heart away again, he never let me down. I slipped out of bed and put my robe on.

Tying it shut as I walked to him. "Are we going to dance in the garage?" I didn't want to be loud, if for no other reason than Liam's mental health. He and the dog were sleeping safely up in his room, but I wasn't the only family member with nightmares.

"Something like that." Thomas tapped my ass before giving me a little push.

I made sure to end up behind him by the time we entered the mudroom. He opened the door, activated the motion-detection light, and my heart started racing. I might have to sell this place now. Ironic since we stayed after Shane's accident. But every corner of the first floor held fresh nightmares threatening the good memories.

Quick flashbacks stopped me in my tracks several times a day. If it weren't for meditation and deep breathing—not to mention my promise to Liam to stay through graduation—I'd have moved to the farmhouse already. Maybe that was it. Maybe Thomas wanted to meditate out here.

I crossed over the threshold, and a frigid chill slithered up my spine. My eyes landed on the chest freezer, and it held me prisoner.

Thomas's voice sounded like it was a block away. "Are you back there? Mother's Day morning?"

I whipped my head around. "You know I am. It's all bad memories around here." The warm light in the center of the garage prevented the space from looking garish, but it also deepened the shadows. At least the fumes from a fixative spray lingered faintly. Weird as it sounded, and as health conscious as I was, the artist in me loved the smell. I had used it on an art project the day before the attack.

"What if I gave you happy memories to override what happened?" The sudden closeness of his voice next to my ear made me jump. Thomas's arms wrapped around me from behind. "Hey now… Easy."

I hated how Big Jonn had done that—taken away the comfort of the velvety voice I loved.

Thomas spun me around. "Eyes on me." He lifted me and set me on top of the freezer. He cradled my face in his hands and kissed me thoroughly, banishing all other thoughts. His tongue swept into my mouth, dancing with mine in the way I craved. Slow and tender. Worshipful.

He pulled away and grinned as his thumb rubbed my lower lip. I bet it was as swollen as his. "Better, but not quite there."

I shook my head, laughing. "Is your plan to kiss away the old memories or something?"

"Or something… First…" His eyes sparked as he looked up. A hank of nylon rope hung from a hook above the chest freezer. My brows rose to my hairline when he removed it and snapped it, testing its strength.

"What are you—?" We'd played this way at the farmhouse but with silks. I loved it. This though…

Thomas winked at me before writing a quick note with the pad and pen in his pocket—he kept them everywhere for when research ideas popped into his head. He took a piece of packing tape from the next hook and stuck the note to the mudroom side of the door. Then he looped the rope around the handle and secured it back on the first hook, testing the door to see if it would open. He nodded approvingly at his work and said, "In case the boy hears something and gets concerned."

I tilted my head. Guess I'd been half right. I didn't know what turned me on more, Thomas's obvious plans for me or how he thought of my kid's feelings. My voice caught. "Here?"

He opened my robe and started unbuttoning my nightshirt.

His eyes darkened with each inch of skin he exposed. "My nightmares are in here." He stepped between my legs and palmed my thighs, his gaze following the path they took as he stroked up toward my core. The hum started under my skin.

"First time I saw his arm wrapped around you, I stood in the shadows back here. Felt your terror and pain." He turned and picked up the tumbler of whiskey from the top step. I hadn't noticed that he put it down.

"Then I saw the gun pressed into your shoulder." Thomas took a long pull of the whiskey, closed his eyes as the liquid went down. I didn't need my own glass to know that feeling, the burning away of the visual. "I need this too. New memories. Victories."

He returned to his place in front of me. Thomas kissed me again and pushed me back with his free hand. I hummed at the taste of his lips, licking the smooth, spicy flavor of Defiant whiskey off my own as he proceeded to kiss his way down my stomach. The local single malt was serendipitous. We were defying the ghosts living in the shadows of the house and our hearts.

Thomas paused, assessing me. Then he dribbled the remaining liquor over my breasts and stomach. My breath caught as the chilly spirit fired up a round of goose bumps, making my nipples stand on end. The corner of his mouth ticked up in approval.

Just then, the light went out, throwing us into darkness. Thomas hummed, I think to keep my focus on him. My eyes quickly adjusted to the moonlight pouring in through the narrow window on the opposite wall. All the distracting, unromantic household items in the space disappeared, but I wasn't afraid. It reminded me of our first night together during the storm. Like then, the world melted away to only Thomas and me.

He pulled a vibrator out of his other pocket and shoved it into my hand before placing another slow kiss on my lips. "Take your pleasure back. In here and everywhere. You decide."

A quiet moan escaped my throat as the tip of his tongue traveled around my nipple before flicking it. "What else is in this robe of yours?" I giggled and teased. "Got a steak in there too?"

Thomas grabbed his cock, pressing it into my thigh. "There's a juicy T-bone right here. Whenever you're ready." He lapped the whiskey from my stomach. "Mmm. My two favorite flavors."

Well, shit, let's do this. I pressed the button, bringing the vibrator to life.

"That's it," Thomas encouraged, grinning as he descended on me, licking up the rest of the Defiant with long strokes, still humming his pleasure. This turned into quick flicks and hard pulls on my other nipple. That was all I needed to put the toy at my pussy, letting it tickle the edges of my lips until I shivered with need. The connection between my breasts and my clit grew into a fevered pitch. Still, the climax evaded me. My mind clung to thoughts instead of feeling.

"Thomas…"

"I got you." He reached down, adding his fingers to the vibration, letting one of them breach the tight rosette of nerves at my ass.

It was everything. I gave in to the sensations and let everything go. At the last minute, I remembered we weren't technically alone in the house and closed my mouth, biting my lip to keep from crying out. The sensations flowing through me ran in Thomas too. He struggled to keep his volume down as we growled through our bliss. The moment when time stood still, like I could come forever. He continued sucking on me and twisting his fingers until the waves subsided. Then he stretched over me and dropped his forehead to mine.

"The bastards couldn't take our lives or our love. We won't let them live in our heads."

"Thomas…" I gasped, writhing on the fecking freezer. It wasn't enough.

He raised up on his elbows. "What do you need?"

"Your T-bone. Now. The car." I pulled at the tie on his waistband.

"You have the best ideas." Thomas scooped me up. His

pajamas inched down as we moved into my new Camaro, but he didn't miss a step.

The overhead light flashed back on from our movements, letting just enough atmosphere through the tinted windows for me to see the soft sheen of sweat on his chiseled face. Panting and dizzy with need, I clung to him as we settled in the driver's seat with me straddling his lap. I caught my breath as he palmed my breasts. "Up for more?"

"Don't you dare stop."

He'd never forgotten what I'd told him about missing this and always took his time with my breasts. I stroked my pussy against Thomas's hard cock as he worked my nipples. The buzzing quickly returned. The victory of leaving our trauma behind hummed through us until we giggled with joy.

By the time I reared up and settled down on Thomas's thick length, we glowed. Our energy healed our physical bodies and our hearts as I eased onto him.

His eyes virtually sparkled with awe. "Damn, I love you."

Within minutes, my hands were gripping the headrest as Thomas buried his face in my cleavage—his preferred spot. We grunted and moaned as our strokes built to a frenzy until the waves went off again. I slid my body along his, pushing down with each ripple as Thomas pushed up. He pulled me down and captured my cries of ecstasy with his mouth as I rode him pedal to the metal like we were crossing the finish line—breaking in my new car in our own way.

All fears of this space, this house, disappeared as our heartbeats slowed, in sync. Thomas stroked my back as I collapsed against him, still attached. Always one.

"Wherever you are, wherever you go... remember this. Remember I love you." He pushed me back to meet my gaze. "I'll take it with me too."

WONDERWALL

KICK

"*W*hatcha reading, chica?" Cyndi asked, sliding onto her preferred barstool at the counter. She lifted the front of my book before I could answer. "A car manual? Only you would read an owner's manual."

"Hey." I grabbed it back. "It's good to know what's different in my new—"

"Wait a minute. Is that smoking new supercar out there yours?" I nodded as she whistled. "I was ready to make you introduce me to the hot customer it belongs to." Her mouth turned into a pout. "But it's just you. How's it drive?"

"Like a dream," I said with a sigh.

"You're good with the same model car, huh? I figured you drove your man's Land Rover now."

I tucked away the manual on the shelf under the counter since I wouldn't be reading it anytime soon. I didn't need to think about my answer. A true peace had settled over me. "Thomas suggested I get back on the horse and he was right." In all the ways. "It also helps knowing the bad guys are dealt with."

Cyndi's brows drew together, and I braced myself against the counter. We'd done the hug-and-cry thing as soon as she returned from her Mother's Day visit to Michigan. Then we jumped straight into wedding prep mode. We hadn't talked about the details of that day, not that I could say much.

I made her preferred drink as she talked over the espresso machine.

"I read the write-up in the paper, but I still don't understand."

My elation over surviving felt stunted since I couldn't tell my closest friend the whole truth. Like it or not, the Felidae Society had sucked me in even though I wasn't an official member. I struggled to look Cyndi in the eye. With my trusty rag in hand, I wiped down the counter as I relayed the acceptable explanation Thomas, Banger, and I had pieced together.

I called over my shoulder. "Big Jonn's obsession with me went as deep as his son's for Rachel. He'd been willing to wait for me to notice him, but I committed the cardinal sin of falling for another man." I'd shared this version enough times now I almost believed it. "Their delusions fed off each other until both men were crazed with jealousy." I handed her a flat white with a heart on top.

"I'm sorry, Kicky." Cyndi reached across the counter and stilled my busy hand. "I can't imagine. Those two turned your life upside down over their delusions."

"Not to mention because they could." The power-crazed never considered the consequences of their actions. I squeezed her hand back. "They didn't count on my friends and family. In fact, if they hadn't paid off Siobhan, I'm sure everything would've resolved sooner... before the bodyguards and such."

Banger's right-hand's role was another aspect of the story we had to manipulate. We told the authorities that she'd been working for Big Jonn and not the other way around. True to form, Banger had planted information to that effect.

Cyndi rested her chin on her hand. "The guards made fabulous eye candy though. What's Mateo up to anyway?" She sighed. "I miss that sweet dish of flan."

I chuckled at her version of looking on the bright side. "He's helping Banger put Angel Security back together. It was a stroke of luck that Jake hooked us up. Mateo and Wes weren't corrupted by Siobhan."

Enough with the reminiscing. I'd come a long way since Thomas fucked the fear out of me the previous night. I didn't want to risk it coming back and threatening my recovery. I thought about my orgasm in the car and sighed. Then, naturally, I changed the subject.

I touched the ends of her silky hair. "Can't believe you come in here, talking smack about cars and boys, and nothing about your sparkling hair. You did it."

"I did." Cyndi gave me an uncharacteristically shy smile. "What do you think?"

"Are you kidding? It's stunning." The way the glowing front contrasted with the dark back reminded me of the model Caroline Labouchere. After Cyndi mentioned her plan to transition to her natural hair color, I started following a few silver models on social media. I wondered if I'd get the chance to look like them. Still hadn't gone in for my color service and still didn't need it.

"Thanks, Kicky. I didn't expect so many people to act weird about it."

"Like how?"

She took a sip of her drink. "One client told me it's ridiculous."

"To your face or in an email?"

"Oh, to my face." She spread her hands wide. "Does something about me compel people to just… blurt their opinions?"

My brow furrowed in fury for her. "Fuck him."

"Her."

"That explains it." I reached for my ice tea and took a pull. "Seriously though… your hair complements your gray eyes. It's even more exotic than you were before. Screw anyone who gives you shit." I patted her hand. "Did you come in for a pep talk? I kind of like talking about other people again." Every fecking hour, someone walked in and expected me to recount the events of the past year.

"Ha, ha. I wanted my flat. Plus…" She slid a card across the counter. "Debra's desperate to finish the bridesmaid dresses. I made a long appointment and hoped we could make a girls' afternoon of it? Unless there's too much on your plate."

"Are you kidding? I'd love to help with something. All I hear is 'everything's taken care of, darlin'.'" I did a shitty imitation of Thomas's baritone and made Cyn smirk. We could use girl time, except… "What about Snow?" Rachel had been performing in the summer theater in the Outer Banks since the beginning of June. She wanted to pull out of her contract, but the shadows under her eyes had never lifted. Not even when I came home from the hospital. I insisted she go, knowing my girl needed a change of scenery. What better way to move on with her life than doing what she loved?

"I'll speak with Deb at the shop, see if she can fit us in on the morning of Liam's party. I can take her since you'll be swamped. Unless Isabella will be with her. I wouldn't want to be a third wheel."

I shook my head. "Bella's busy with her internship. Rachel will love to get time with her Aunt Cyn."

Cyndi tapped her chin. "Are you sure that's all?"

"It's what Snow told me, but I've been a bit distracted." I tucked a curl behind my ear. "Why do you ask?"

"It's a feeling I had after a hospital visit." Cyndi waved her hand like she was erasing the question. "Don't mind me."

I shrugged. "Ask her about it during the fitting."

She gave me a sympathetic, twisted-lip smile. "You can count on me. Snowy and I can commiserate over asshole men. I'll pass on my 'sing-gal' wisdom."

I laughed as she waggled her brows. "Considering I took two seconds to renege on my vow to never marry again, you mean?"

She winked at me and smirked. "Something like that." As much as Cyndi championed my relationship with Thomas, she still took advantage of any opportunity to give me shit over the impending nuptials I'd sworn to never take again.

"I still can't believe Thomas is getting married," Tess said as she approached us. She took the stool next to Cyndi and greeted us with hugs and cheek kisses.

I chuckled. "I bet." *Talk about swearing to never marry.*

Tess didn't just shake her head, her whole body joined in. "You two do not know how much he's changed this year."

"Pretty sure I do." I scrunched my nose, a bit insecure considering they'd known each other twice as long as I'd been alive. "I take it you consider this a good thing?"

"The best, my dear. Don't worry. I didn't mean to sound negative."

My oldest and newest friends chatted together while I made their lunches, then fixed a third one for myself. It was time for me to clock out anyway. I wouldn't be back to a full schedule until after the wedding.

"See you before the wedding," Tess said to Cyndi.

"What's this?" I placed the dishes and cups in front of each woman. I collected my meal and sat on the other side of Tess, keeping an eye on the door. Apparently, I lived a new normal now.

"I told Cyndi that Rafa and I are leaving for France tomorrow."

"Thomas said something about that. He didn't mention you're going," I responded after taking a drink of tea. I'd become an afternoon, unsweet ice tea woman, thanks to my doctor's dietary changes. "I'm sure Rafa appreciates your support." I almost said "your son," and bit my tongue to remind myself to keep the brother-sister ruse. How did these people do it?

When the girls left for their summer jobs, Banger moved back home with Tess. From what I could tell, he leaned on her now. I took her traveling with him to the vineyard to mean she was finally stepping up.

Tess gave me a small smile and nervously brushed wisps of hair off her forehead. Her clothes often said "going to the yoga studio," but the slightly disheveled braid and dampness around her hairline told me she'd been teaching a class. In the colder months, a sweater had hid her activities, but June temperatures made it too warm to cover up. "I hope you're right."

"You're coming back, aren't you?" Cyndi asked.

"Of course." She took a moment to chew her bite of the veggie wrap, then set it down like a dining ritual. "Rafa must meet with someone important. Like Kick said, he can use some… what's the word?" She tapped the counter. "Oh, yes… Backup."

Cyndi smiled approvingly. "Will you tell him I hope it all works out?"

I loved how my new friends were blending in with my old ones—as much as they could anyway.

"I will. Thank you." Tess reached an arm around Cyndi and hugged her. "This is why I'll come back with Rafa. His friends are so sweet it makes my heart happy too."

I played with the lettuce in my salad, but my appetite wasn't there. My bed called out to me. Despite the fatigue, my heart was happy too. Small steps in the right direction still equaled progress. "Speaking of a happy heart…"

Tess uncharacteristically froze with her sandwich in midair. "Please, Kick."

I shrugged in my defense, my hands raised in submission. "I only wanted to know if you and Charley have talked."

"We have." Tess sighed as she stared out the window across from us. "That's all I will say."

Cyndi touched Tess's shoulder. "Don't mind Kicky. She wants to match-make everyone now that she's found her person."

Tess scoffed.

"I'm sorry. I didn't mean to make you uncomfortable."

"It's nothing." Tess waved off my apology, adding in a little French. Still, I felt horrible. Rachel and Bella made it sound like there was hope between the women, but maybe not. Cyndi was right about me too. I wanted Tess's smile to reach her eyes.

KICK

"'Waterfalls,' Mama? Must you? You're so embarrassing." Rachel set her hand on the back of my chair, glaring. She didn't bother to acknowledge Shane's mother or anyone else sitting at the "old people's table" for Liam's graduation party. The Perked Cup was closed for the family party but also shut down for the week for vacation. Most of my staff were coming out to the wedding after this anyway.

I tried hard to stay positive through Rachel's obviously bad mood. *My* mother aired her dirty laundry at my graduation party to guarantee herself the center of the day's attention. There was a chasm between getting silly while celebrating your last child's graduation and making a fool of yourself because of unyielding jealousy.

"You know... Lee offered to accompany me on 'Sweet Child O' Mine' but..." I sarcastically raised a glass of sipping rum. "Thomas, here, pointed out it might look odd."

Thomas tipped his head, acknowledging his role in the

exchange. Shane's Uncle Billy wrapped the table in his hearty chuckle.

"At least someone has a sense of dignity." Rachel folded her arms on a long-suffering sigh.

What more could I expect? Bobby had called Rachel on the way home from our last interchange at the hospital, to put it lightly. She hadn't heard my side of the rift because I couldn't handle involving my children in our shit show. My daughter was grown and should've asked me for clarification, but she'd been through hell too. I couldn't pile on that. It felt like it would be cruel and manipulative on my part. Bobby, on the other hand, started collecting allies against me as soon as she'd left my hospital room.

"Liam never noticed my singing." I gestured to my son across the dining room. "He's in his own world with his friends." Minus his best friend, Jax, but Lee had assured me he'd made peace with it. I picked up my napkin and dabbed a stray tear.

"'Forever Young' and 'I Hope You Dance' were bad enough at my graduation. You made a trifecta of drunk-mom-sappy karaoke with the TLC song."

A warm, rough hand engulfed mine and squeezed. "You sounded lovely, Katie. I thought it was grand." I'd forgotten how much I'd missed that hand.

"Thank you, Uncle Billy." I held up my glass to his, letting them clink.

My late husband's mother, Anna, and Uncle Billy had arrived safely from Ireland the previous afternoon. They came with two of Billy's grandsons in tow to celebrate the youngest McKenna's entry into the big world.

Billy clinked his glass edge to mine. *"Sláinte."* I returned the sentiment and sipped my drink. "How about taking a turn at 'Danny Boy' next?" he asked.

"Uncle Billy..." Rachel stomped her foot as jammed her hands onto her hips. "Help me make her stop. Mama and drunk karaoke at our parties shouldn't be allowed." A definitely drunk neighbor currently sang his rendition of "Born to Run." I didn't see where I'd made it worse.

"I'm tipsy, not drunk." I shifted my gaze back to Uncle Billy. "I'll give the song a whirl when the crowd thins." I knew that song in my sleep, thanks to my father, but I didn't trust myself to not cry and actually make a spectacle of myself, considering.

I raised my glass again and flashed a cheesy grin at my daughter. At her scowl, my brows mirrored her pinched stare. "Oh hell, Snow... Ease up. I'm an empty nester now. I'm entitled to celebrate in style."

"Whose party is this again?" She wouldn't quit. Bobby blamed both shootings on Thomas since we met the same night everything with the Grahams had started. Except now we knew it hadn't. They'd been pulling shit without us realizing it for a while before that night. Not to mention they would've succeeded if it hadn't been for Thomas and Banger.

I also knew my daughter suffered from PTSD. I suspected the crowd triggered her, but bringing it up would set her off more. That's what had happened the night before.

Rachel had a therapist where she stayed in Manteo for the summer, but I didn't know if she went to the appointments. You mix privacy laws with how long it took for the insurance company to pay anything, and I guessed I'd find out by the end of the year. For now, the cues pointed to my daughter having taken Bobby's bait about her version of the truth. She'd been on my case since arriving with Cyndi.

I tapped my chin. There was an idea. Maybe Rachel could drive with Aunt Cyn to the mountains tomorrow. As much as my bestie loved being Liam's godmother, she had a special bond with my daughter. If anyone could unhook Rachel from Bobby's line, my money was on my bestie.

I pointed at Liam's table. "They don't care. Think of it as cohabitating parties, sweetheart."

Rachel shook her head and fled back to her table with Jake and the Perked Cup part-timers.

"You have a brilliant idea there—the cohabitating parties," Uncle Billy said, bumping my shoulder. From the moment I'd met Shane, the McKennas were my examples of a family's happy insanity compared to my spitefully dysfunctional one.

"I bet you like it." I waggled my eyebrows at him. It was a well-known secret he and Anna—Billy's widowed sister-in-law and his first love—had started shacking up a year or so back. We even gave them the use of Thomas's farmhouse until it was time to leave for the mountains.

"Easy now. Perhaps you've had more than a nip." He reached for my tumbler. "Better take this before you end up pissed, darlin' niece." He toasted me and swallowed the last of my Raleigh Rum. Billy's face scrunched in a way that reminded me of my mother, albeit comical. "Ugh. How do you drink this swill?"

"Hey!" I'd planned to keep it to two drinks, spaced hours apart. "The doctor says whiskey has too many parts per million to be Celiac safe, so I abide." I pretended to elbow Uncle Billy. "Besides, a birdie told me you were supposed to cut back." I wiggled a finger at his tumbler. "I don't see it."

Billy sighed and narrowed his eyes at Anna. "Listen... I'm a good patient."

Anna clicked her tongue and shook her head.

"I am." He tilted his head toward me like he was sharing a secret. "First I had a wee cry. Then I switched from Jamison's to Redbreast. In fact, I'll go get another one to wash down the burned piss you poured in your glass." Billy scooched his chair back and went to the bar we'd set up next to the stage.

"Not fair—"

"Now who sounds like one of the children?" Anna gently chided. "You're not on any of those opioids, are you, dear?"

"Heavens no." I counted off three fingers. "Herbal anti-inflammatories, Aleve if it's bad, cannabis if it's superbad. Today's good so far." I held up my empty glass. "One more and I'm done."

"Or… tea." Thomas's buttery voice melted the prickliness left over from Rachel. I instinctively leaned back in my chair to connect with him, inhaling his calm. He reached over me and placed the cup on our table. Then he kissed my temple.

Uncle Billy returned and smiled approvingly at us.

"Is she behaving, Billy?" Thomas asked.

"God, I hope not." Billy howled, his bright blue eyes twinkling and his belly shaking like Santa's.

"Sounds like my kind of uncle," Cyndi drawled while the rest of us females rolled our eyes. Uncle Billy turned a beet red and danced his eyebrows in her direction.

He leaned toward her and stage-whispered, "I'm secretly taken, love."

She stretched her arm across his wide shoulders and stage-whispered back, "It's not a secret, Uncle B, but my lips are sealed." She mimed locking them with her fingers as I shook my head.

Voices rose from the table where Rachel sat, and she stormed off to the restroom area.

Cyndi leaned around Billy and whispered, "Our girl's in a mood."

No shit. "Any idea why?" I had mine but wondered if they had spoken during the fitting.

Cyn's mouth twisted. "The dress needed the tiniest taking out in a couple of places. A cloud descended over her afterward." Her eyes lit up, and she tapped the table. "I'll get her to do some karaoke. Does she know '50 Ways to Leave Your Lover'? When I saw it on the song list, I thought of our talk in the car. Why didn't we think of it earlier?"

"She was too busy criticizing me… but you're right. Rachel knows it."

I moved to stand, but Cyndi patted my hand. "Let me." I blew out a loud sigh and agreed, too tired to risk going another round with my daughter.

This had been my first bone-tiring day since the shooting. However, exhaustion couldn't defeat me when I was surrounded by people I loved. Family was as much who you picked as who the universe saddled you with. The only faces I missed were those of my brother and nephews. He couldn't score enough time off for both events, so Bert and the boys were meeting us in the mountains. It meant the world since Bobby had tried her best to sabotage that too.

Tears threatened to fall as I took a long pull from the ice tea.

No more meets, games, or matches... Ever. My baby graduated from high school.

No more getting up to make sure he caught the bus. Had all his supplies. No more stopping by the ATM to give him lunch money. No more... mommy. Not that any of my kids had called me that recently.

I'd cried for hours on Liam's last day of school. I'd been in too much pain to make his breakfast and Thomas had to cover for me. He even took the last-day-of-school picture for me as Lee stood by his Jeep. It hadn't come close to what I'd imagined. I lamented what else the Graham's had taken from me. Though small, it was significant to me.

Today I vowed to keep my shit together for the party. Despite Rachel's disapproval over my song choices, I'd smiled at the back of Liam's head as I sang the songs about him. I wouldn't make the day about me.

"Be right back, darlin'." When Thomas walked away, Anna leaned in and said, "I love his accent." The irony of her declaration made me bark with laughter.

"It's as smooth as a fine Bourbon, isn't it?"

"I was thinking a whiskey, but good enough."

"Come now, Mama A, Uncle Billy's accent has the soft whiskey tones."

"Sin an fhírinne."

It took me a minute to remember she'd said something akin to "True, that." Since my dad died, no one spoke Irish around me anymore. I missed it. I kissed her on the cheek, grateful to know some things never changed—and it was a good thing.

She squeezed my hand. "Sorry your mother couldn't be here."

"No, you're not." I snort-laughed. My mother had always been jealous of Anna's amiable nature, no surprise there. "Seriously, it's all good. If she's happy with her one true love, I'm thrilled for her. I would love to see her happy, but I guess love isn't always enough."

Anna tsked and shook her head. "I'll never understand her. Her only daughter and youngest grandchild. It's not right."

Billy leaned across me and added, "I agree with Katie. Good riddance to the hag." He pressed a whiskey kiss to my cheek in support. It meant everything to have Shane's family with us, not to mention supporting my new relationship.

"Don't worry, you two. I've learned there's a difference between a mama and a relative. A 'cessation of hostilities' is the best we'll ever have." They stared at me with sympathetic eyes full of disbelief. I'd already dealt with pity looks like this from Cyndi and Deana. Both women had the kind of mothers girls like me used to dream about. They wouldn't understand the peace that had settled on me when I admitted the truth and let her go.

I tried one more time. "I promise I'm good. You're here when it counts. Bert and the boys will be at the wedding. My kids are great. My friends are better than I deserve. And then there's Thomas…"

"I like him." Billy's voice cracked. He reached across my shoulder and shook it. "You did well, Katie."

I laid my head on his shoulder. "Thanks, Uncle Billy."

Life *was* good. Finally.

My fingers tingled under the table.

GIVING YOU THE BEST THAT I'VE GOT

KICK

"Hey sleepyhead." Thomas pulled my hand across the center console and kissed my palm.

I stretched into the ceiling of the Land Rover, all the way to my toes under the dash. After blinking several times, the scenery took me by surprise. We were climbing a narrow asphalt road at a steep incline. I did a double take at Thomas. "You drove the whole time? You were supposed to wake me at the halfway point."

He reached over and chucked my chin. "But you looked so cute I couldn't bring myself to wake you. Figured the extra rest to be necessary after your long week."

We took a hairpin turn, and the ascent grew steeper. "Should we be in five-point harnesses?"

"We're fine. Almost there."

"Oh, this is *the* mountain?" I watched the rhododendron blooms fill out the undergrowth as far up as I could see from my window. "How high are we going?"

Thomas navigated an interior curve. "To the top."

I hated taking these roads in the passenger seat. In fact, it surprised me to know I'd slept the whole way. I never slept in a moving car. Something wet annoyed my shoulder. I pulled my shirt away to investigate. "Oh hell, did I drool?"

Thomas flashed me his middle school grin. "Like I said… adorable."

"Ugh."

We crossed under a stone archway and ended up in a court-yard of a modern palace. Really, it was a five-thousand-square-foot stone-and-log lodge sitting on a plateau just below the mountain peak. A manicured cottage garden occupied the side of the entrance, adding to the atmosphere. I imagined taking our vows in the center of it.

Thomas drove through a portico and parked in back by a four-bay garage.

"Only four bays?" I muttered sarcastically.

"We can add more."

On a rental? Huh?

He killed the engine and pressed the button for the tailgate.

A young man appeared out of thin air and opened my door. "Good afternoon, Ms. Kick. I hope your drive was pleasant."

"Apparently it was amusing," I answered, thinking of Thomas laughing at me sleeping with my mouth open. Shit, had I snored? *From now on, I drive.*

Thomas gave the key fob to another young man and chatted him up a bit as I gathered my bearings.

Past the covered area, a walled veranda edged the back of the property until it met more rhododendrons traveling up. The property appeared to fall away beyond that.

My fiancé wrapped his arms around me from behind, making me jump. I'd become jumpy again after the attack. I hated that. For the thousandth time, I reminded myself of little steps. "What do you think?" he asked me.

"It's..." I tugged at the curls whipping around my head and into my eyes. The winds were brisk this high up. "I'm speechless." The view was breathtaking. I wanted to hurry and settle in so I could sit on the veranda and stare out at the neighboring peaks.

"Happy wedding surprise."

I patted his arms around my waist. "You did good with the rental. If I owned it, I wouldn't rent it to just anyone."

"I'll keep that in mind, since you do own it." Thomas jerked back—that grin back on his face—as I spun around.

"You own... this? Since when?"

"I said *you* own it. I bought it while you were in the hospital. My lawyer's working to transfer the title to you as we speak. We'll sign the papers when we go back." He held out his hand like it was no big deal. "Let's check the place out."

I stayed in my spot. "Who the hell are you?"

"Your fiancé, remember?" Thomas glanced over his shoulder and back to me. "Don't you like it? Was the surprise a bad idea? Tess warned me—"

"It's not the lodge, per se." I shook my head. "Sometimes you still surprise me."

He walked back to me, pulled my hand to his lips, and kissed them. "Keep these two words in your memory bank whenever you wonder how I do these things... compounded interest."

An inelegant snort escaped my nose as I remembered Banger's explanation for the questions I'd thrown at him.

I SAT ON OUR NEW LOUNGE CHAIR IN FRONT OF OUR NEW FIRE PIT in the middle of our new, spacious patio, attached to our new mountain home. Like everything else Thomas did, the man had gone all out. At forty-seven-hundred feet of elevation in the Blue Ridge range, the house didn't have a typical view of the mountains. It *was* the mountain view. The ground-floor veranda in the back looked over the tops of the closest trees except for the ones to the front of the house.

From the second and third levels, the view lasted for miles. I swore I could see all the major peaks in the range. Thomas said he'd bought it so we could do naked weekends out here without worrying about another human seeing us. He was right there. The only hint of neighbors came from that cottage garden in the front. From there, you could see down the mountain road and catch sight of our three closest neighbors. Well, I saw the mailboxes. The houses were mostly in the trees.

Since the Blue Ridge Mountains were a major vacation area, most of those houses around us were also second homes. Thomas had rented as many as he could for our guests. This would leave us alone at night despite the lodge's ability to sleep sixteen. We could've easily housed most of the guests. Maybe another time when we weren't about to celebrate our wedding night.

Thomas walked out to join me, two glasses of water in his hands. He gave one to me, then settled in the next lounge. "It's amazing out here." He stretched his legs, crossing them at the ankles. For as packed a schedule as we had, I couldn't remember the last time he relaxed like this. Not since before Mother's Day. "An associate of mine owned the house and needed quick cash. The sale had been serendipitous, to be honest. I told him about my amazing, brave fiancée and how I wanted to give her a majestic present, not that it could equal her grace and majesty." He squeezed my hand. "You're my lucky charm."

Considering how quickly he'd set up Liam and me in the lap of luxury for spring break, courtesy of "an acquaintance," this shouldn't have surprised me. He could have bought an island. I scoffed at the label *lucky charm* though. "Doesn't Banger call me a menace?"

Thomas shook his head. "He's a grumpy old man. Don't listen to what he says."

"Speak for your damn self," Banger called out. He spread his hands as he approached, Tess and another man following behind. "Nicely done, brother." He bent over and gave me a hug. "Good to see you doing well… Menace." He sat on the end of Thomas's chair. "It's not my castle in the highlands, but…"

Thomas tipped his head back and laughed. I'd never seen him more in his element. He did a double take as his eyes caught our new visitors. Then he shot off the lounge chair. "*Grand-père?* Holy shit. What are you doing off the vineyard?"

Banger quietly said, "Surprise," as Thomas dashed off. While the men greeted each other with hugs and cheek kisses, Banger leaned toward me. "This is a big fucking deal. The old man hasn't left his chateau grounds since the late forties." He tipped his head in their direction. "Go say hello."

I slowly stood, suddenly scared to death of what this man would think of me. This man—who had been built up in my mind as the most important man on the planet—left the security of his estate to see me? What if I disappointed him?

Thomas turned Alaric around, their arms around each other's shoulders as they spotted me. The deceptively older gentlemen stepped away from my fiancé and toward me. Tess stood back, her arms folded, as she observed the scene. How I'd thought she was Rachel's age, I'd never know now. Tess relied on her outward presentation to fool most, but the wisdom in her eyes couldn't be missed. I smiled at her and received back a motherly twinkle. Maybe it was a sign she and Banger had resolved their differences.

Thomas moved to me, his arms stretched between me and Alaric, like a bridge. "Alaric, meet my fiancée, Kathleen Allen McKenna. Kick, this is Alaric Kraus, the man I call *Grand-père.* Patriarch of the Felidae Society."

"My dear." Alaric took my hands in his and brought them to his heart, like meeting me was an honor. He tipped his head from side to side as he studied me. I suppose I did the same.

Thomas had cut off our budding romance because he believed

this man had posed a threat to me. Banger and Tess clearly held grudges against him, yet here we all stood. They'd brought him with them. Thomas's face lit up when he saw the man. Those two things convinced me all would be okay. What family didn't have its issues? Look at mine.

Banger and Tess joined our trio, standing a step back. Banger set his feet wide and folded his arms, like a bouncer protecting... me?

"Don't worry yourself, Rafael," Alaric said without taking his eyes off me. "Thomas is right about her." He kissed me on both cheeks, European style, smelling of fresh air and old spices—not the grandfather's aftershave, actual ancient spices. Though salt-and-pepper, Alaric's hair was darker than I expected for a man of his... experience. He wasn't particularly tall, but he stood straight, shoulders back, like he knew exactly who he was. And accepted everything.

THE FIVE OF US ATE LUNCH AND SETTLED IN BEFORE THE REST OF the guests arrived. In that time, I found out my man had pulled off this surprise because he was a real estate mogul long before he'd become a scientist. That's what happened when you lived an abnormally long time. He had holdings across the East Coast and Europe. The assets Thomas had fully liquidated upon leaving them had been the ones in San Francisco when he left to serve in World War I.

Soon our table grew as Thomas's blood family arrived. It was easier to think of them this way than as grandchildren, considering they appeared older than him. My brother and nephews arrived twenty minutes later, allowing me a reprieve from the tension between Joe and the other Felidae members. He didn't believe things would change. Not yet.

I gladly showed my family around the lodge, discovering the lower-level rooms for the first time with them. Thomas told me the house came furnished and only needed minor remodeling for now, though he had revamped the owner's suite on the top floor. It boasted a new, two-person jetted tub with a view, and a shower that could have been its own room. One side had a love seat sized bench installed underneath a waterfall shower. Thomas called it a "make love" seat.

Three other bedroom suites were on the main level, so the kids each had their space when they visited. He claimed the house would rent better with multiple masters. I'd met the realtor and the couple who handled the property management while exploring the first-floor gaming room and bunk area. My nephews wanted to spend their entire time down there, of course. I couldn't get over the idea of having a game room and theater.

Presently, I found myself in time-out, wrapped in a blanket, in front of the fire after the rehearsal. Stupid, wobbly knees. I shouldn't have worn platform sandals out in the garden. Good thing my wedding shoes were hand-painted sandals with a tiny wedge heel.

I itched to stand in the kitted-out kitchen and run my hand over the solid oak, live-edged bar. It was one hell of a focal piece, indicative of the regal yet comfortable decor in the lodge. But the catering company had charge of the space for the next two days. I didn't mind my lounging spot too much either.

A stage area was already set up under the main-level balcony. Everybody took turns playing. Liam surprised me by singing Anita Baker's "Giving You the Best That I've Got" with his cousins accompanying. He continued his quest to put his spin on my favorite songs. Lee used his raspy baritone to full effect, creating a haunting, soulful version of some of my all-time favorite lyrics. Then my other two kids joined in. Dylan never caught the performing bug like his siblings. But he played the bass, claiming it helped him think through mental blocks in his work.

Rachel's practice performance of Kelly Sweet's "We Are One" brought me to tears. It was the song I'd asked her to sing for the reception, and she learned it on the drive up with Cyndi.

When Thomas plugged in his guitar and performed Stevie Ray Vaughan's "Pride and Joy," my ovaries flipped. I physically couldn't stay in the chair any longer, knowing my man played and sang his heart out for me. Grabbing Cyndi, Deana, and Tess, we shook our tail feathers on the veranda in front of the fire. Thomas's relative, Toni, joined in too. He had explained to me how her transition, as he called it, was the official focus of his research. Her life had been challenging for the past two years. I couldn't imagine being in Toni's shoes, her body stopping aging while losing family and friends at the same time. It could happen to me eventually, but Thomas promised to help me prepare for it.

As the evening wore on, Toni engaged in a long chat with Alaric, Banger, and Tess. After an urging from Thomas, Joe joined the group too. If we could help heal the broken trusts in the Felidae, I'd consider the torments of the past year worth it. Even the shootings. Where we went from here, though, I figured none of us knew.

The music continued for hours, thanks to the number of musicians in our group. Banger even produced a keyboard from the music room and played boogie-woogie through Elton John, ending with Chopin as the night wound down. Thomas moved off his position on the wall and came to me. He'd spent the past half hour watching me work the crowd from the shadows. Friends would stop by and chat him up, but every time I looked his way, Thomas's gaze had been on me.

He wrapped an arm around my shoulders and said, "Time for you to head up, don't you think?"

"As if you'd settle for no," I said coyly. Thomas didn't have to worry about me putting up a fight. He left his perch as soon as I yawned.

"Maybe I'm also tired." He pulled me close and ran his hands up and down my arms, warming them. "What happened to the blanket I gave you?"

"Is there anything you miss?" Nights on top of a mountain chilled quickly. I couldn't wait to use the jetted tub. "Deana was shivering. Our management couple left before I thought to ask where the extras are kept, and I didn't want to miss this." I waved my arm in the direction of our guests. "Not that you'd let me."

Thomas pulled me into him and murmured, "After the third time almost losing you, I hate letting you out of my sight."

True to that, my man had observed me like an artist—or a scientist, I guess—since I'd woken up from surgery. I had to remember my recovery was as much for Thomas as it was for me.

I waggled my eyebrows. "Maybe we should work on your PTSD, like we did with me and the garage."

He bent and murmured in my ear. "No excuses needed to fuck you. Ever."

I tilted my head back and grinned, trying to keep the guests from knowing my fiancé's growly ways had started my engine purring. Like they couldn't tell. Everyone I hugged good night to wore the same, knowing smile on their face.

Not for the first time, the mechanics of hosting our wedding frustrated me. All my important people came to witness our vows, but I couldn't spend quality time with anyone individually. We didn't have enough days. I wished we could convince Joe—he offered to officiate in a show of support—to marry Thomas and me right there and be done with it. Then we could turn our wedding into a big vacation.

At the same time, I knew Thomas ticked down the minutes until he could declare naked weekend for just us. He bought the lodge for getaways, but I hoped we could host big events like this often as well. A vision of our future settled over me—family and friends celebrating life's moments out here for years to come. I longed to stay up into the wee hours talking, singing, goofing around.

"I can hear you thinking," Thomas complained as we stepped inside the great room. "Tomorrow's a big day, then you're not getting out of bed the day after."

I caught up to him and bumped his hip. "I'm not complaining about naked weekend, it's just—"

"Let me finish…" We started up the stairs to our suite. "The Matthews—you remember the property managers, right?" Considering the sea of fresh faces swimming in my brain was rather small, I nodded. "Well, the Matthews have a schedule of activities planned for our guests the day after tomorrow. Dining and shopping in Asheville, caves, waterfall tours… you name it."

I sighed at the mention of waterfalls.

"Another time, darlin'. My point is… whoever is still here the day after that is invited to hang with us here." Thomas stopped in the middle of the steps and kissed my temple. "You have more than tonight to enjoy your clan."

This man. He knew me so well. He lifted my heart from promises alone. All my emotions swirled together and hummed beneath my skin. I glowed by the time we entered our room.

THE BEST IS YET TO COME

THOMAS

*S*he stood in our bedroom beside the french doors to the balcony, studying our guests mingling below. My elfin queen observing her clan from her royal perch.

My sexy wife.

Kick had disappeared after lunch. The bright smile she wore hadn't fooled me. With a quick kiss, she feigned interest in checking on the children gaming in the media room. Her tell was the crease between her brows. *Fatigue.*

She healed faster than even I expected, but we'd packed a lot into the past week. I kept everyone occupied for thirty minutes, giving her a break from hosting. Then I sought her out to make sure everything was fine. I also hated being away from her for more than a few minutes since the shooting. I'd work on it when we returned to Oakville.

I selfishly stood in the hallway's shadow to our suite and dwelled on the vision Kick made as she stared at the distant mountains. Despite my attempts to trick her into telling me about her dress, the sole hint she'd given me about it mentioned vintage Halston as the inspiration. The clue didn't do justice to the dress or her in it. When I laid eyes on Kick in the garden where we married, she paused with her sons on each arm and smiled. The world and everyone in it boiled down to the simper she privately shared with me.

She captured the epitome of my fantasies of her since the day we'd met. Rachel's friend had nailed the dress design. As the boys escorted Kick down the pebbled path, I memorized each square inch of the layers of silk caressing her curves. The end product—my fairy queen—had been all for me.

As if the dress wasn't enough, Kick's soft curves had returned to my prurient delight, thanks to her forced rest and recovery. Material flowed around her with each step like it was intended to optimize her shape. She took my breath away. While Kick stayed lost in her thoughts, I reveled in the memory.

The halter neckline plunged enough for a peek at her spectacular cleavage. Delicate crystals and garden-inspired embroidery caressed her décolletage, complemented her ivory skin. At lunch, she'd told me the delicate pinkish-peach color of the fabric was called "blush." I called it perfect. I'd never seen a color favor her more. A few pleats falling from an empire waist lightly shadowed those lip-biting curves, teasing my eyes with the subtlest movement.

I took in her elegant back. Like a magnet, I felt compelled to touch, to run my fingertips over the angles of her perfect posture. The halter tied in a bow at her neck, daring me to walk up and pull the ends. The bodice disappeared around her sides, returning in another deep V at her sacrum. Here's where the material turned fantastical. From behind, it fell over her perfect ass, simulating a waterfall as she walked.

Drop earrings mingled with curls falling from her sexy updo. Pink and amber stones in the earrings matched the ones at her neckline. The best detail for me came in the form of a Celtic-inspired tiara, her curls artfully woven around it, instead of a veil.

Maybe I'm amazed.

I thought of the song we loved so much we asked Rachel to sing it for us during the ceremony. I was amazed that Kick loved me. Amazed and overwhelmed.

Two things about this view stood out. One, Kick hadn't covered up the scar on her back with makeup or material. Two, the deep back allowed a butterfly wing of her tattoo to peek out. Since the dress was almost finished when Kick was shot, not much could've been done about the scar, but the tattoo had to have been deliberate. She had hid it for years, fearful of judgment from people like her mother. That wing waving across her hip told those people to go fuck themselves. Hell, the material was sheer enough to also catch the essence of the rest of the artwork.

A choked laugh escaped as Kick tipped her head. I thought she might be crying until I caught the ends of a smile at the slight turn to her profile. Her body and spirit continued to call to me, so I stalked over to her—my magnet. My compass.

In an instant, touching her became a matter of life and death. My hands slid inside the dress, around her waist, then up, caressing each breast, savoring the softness and the weight of them. "Hello wife."

Kick's smiling cheek touched my own as she turned in to me. Her body pressed into mine and hummed, like I knew it would.

"You didn't flinch." I moved an errant curl with my nose and kissed her neck. Her exotic floral-mixed-with-lavender scent filled my nose with each press of my lips.

"I wanted you to come to me."

I settled my arms across her stomach, kissing her neck above the bow. "Are you tired? Has today been too much?"

She shook her head. "I took a moment to think." Settling back against me, Kick exhaled. "When... after the sun came out during our pictures... I required a few minutes."

For the past week, while all eyes were on Liam and Kick, something had needled me deep inside. I couldn't put my finger on it until my insecurity bubbled to the surface right before the ceremony. I pulled away and took a guess. "Shane?"

"Yup. But not what you think."

What I thought? Down in my soul, I'd been afraid she secretly wished I could be Shane. Like women I'd been with before, I feared she'd settled for me. She'd told me how awful the NFL spotlight had been, but it was nothing compared to the screwball life I lived. Or so I thought. "Tell me."

"When the clouds parted—during the shot of us with the rhododendrons in the background—the sky was his blue. The color of his eyes." She continued to stare off as she spoke. "Sounds silly, but Shane used to show up when the sky was that color. I'd feel his presence and know I could make it through another day."

"Did he show up during the photo shoot?"

"No. That's the thing. But it's okay."

"You sure?" I started. "You don't… wish this was about him instead of me?"

"No." Kick's chin quivered as she pivoted around fully and embraced me.

She tipped her head back and studied me. Her eyes bore straight through to my secrets. She'd already proved that. "I choose you today and every day. Don't doubt that."

I still tended to wake in the middle of the night—sweaty and at a loss for breath—thinking I'd lost her. "It's ridiculous. Sorry." I kissed Kick's forehead, letting my lips linger as I breathed her in. "You know I don't mind that you think about him, right?"

"You're never ridiculous… except when you give me your middle school smirk. And yes, I know how you feel. It's another reason I love you." She pulled our hands together and brought them to her heart. "I thought about something Rachel said when she saw the inscription on your ring."

"It's inscribed?" I shifted my hands to pull the ring off, but she squeezed tight and said, "Check it later, cowboy. Anyway, we fell into an exchange on whether someone can have two soul mates. I made the case I was fundamentally transformed when Shane died, even at a soul level."

I nodded, contemplating her argument, remembering Alicia's death. "I can see that."

"The sky color startled me. It reminded me of beach skies. Soon I was contrasting the original plan to retire at the beach with this mountain-top retreat you bought us."

I lifted an eyebrow, a little lost, and she shrugged. "I mean, both settings bring me peace. They fit me equally."

I scratched my head. "Would you rather have a beach house?" Shit, what an idiot, surprising her like I knew her deepest desires. That's not how marriages worked. From what I could tell. What did I know anymore?

"Not at all. Will you stop?" She went up on her toes and whispered, "You're supposed to be the confident one in our relationship, Professor."

I rolled my eyes. "Ha." Hardly.

"Emotions are hard to explain. I'm sorry. What I mean is… I feel like my soul's had two lives. You could call the first a beach one. Now it's a mountain one. I'm as thrilled with this as I was with the first."

Like a lightning strike, it hit me. I nuzzled her neck again, peppering her shoulder with kisses, and remembered what she'd said when she woke up in the hospital. I whispered, "You went there, didn't you?"

"Pardon?"

"To the other side. With Shane. We know someone who can do that at will."

"You're kidding?" She started. "Who?"

I lifted an eyebrow. "Alaric. To him, it's like moving into another room. He claims he can stand on the threshold, making it possible to be in both at the same time. In the hospital, you said you were looking for me. Did you see Shane when you were unconscious?"

I knew I'd hit the right nerve when Kick bit her lip. "Shane didn't show. I did go to the beach house we'd started building though. It was finished and furnished. Everything about it was wrong, like what life would have been had he lived. Except my body was a mess. The kids… it was very wrong." A tear came to her eye, and I squeezed her tight. "I wanted to escape it and called for you."

A lump formed in my throat. "I held your hand and demanded you come back to me, as soon as the staff let me."

A pair of eagles circled in the sky, saving us from our thoughts as we watched them hunt prey in a distant meadow. We became lost in their precise teamwork, as if we were spectators at a sporting event. The way they worked together reminded me of Kick asking me to fight her battles with her and not for her. I'd repeated the promise as part of my wedding vows. The events of the past six months had shown me how to do just that for her, made me a better man for it.

My hands lowered to her belly, covering the softness below her navel. "Mmm. Your curves are back." Earlier in the year, as Kick lost weight, her body tightened. She didn't know what to make of the changes then. I loved each manifestation of the process because it was hers. But this…

She shifted her gaze to watch the path my hands traced along her skin. "I hate to admit it, but it's from meditating more than resting. I guess my body and I made peace."

"Are you saying…?"

"You were right about my body obeying what I wanted," she reluctantly said as the corner of her mouth lifted.

I tapped my ear in jest. "Come again? Think I'm hearing things."

Giggling now—the sound went straight through my heart…

and down to my cock—Kick repeated, "You were right, Professor Thomas Butler Theodore Harrison. I discovered I liked my body the way it was."

I squeezed her middle. "Wow. I must be a genius."

"You're something."

She leaned back into me and sighed, letting me support her full weight. She laughed again when my cock stiffened. "My admission turns you on?"

"My sexy-as-hell wife turns me on." I pressed into her. "I've had this situation since I saw you standing here. What if I eased up this skirt and played with you right now, make you come? With our guests below us?" My hand pushed up the hidden side of the dress, seeking my desire.

Kick reached for my chin, her thumb stroking the cleft before she licked it. I closed my eyes and let the sensation fill me.

"You... want to fuuuck." She drew out the *u*, and I almost canceled our reception on the spot. We hadn't gone full-tilt since the night in the garage. Even then, her wounds stayed at the front of my mind. "You better give me that big, juicy T-bone later... *husband*."

I growled at the possession of the word, enjoying each sylla ble. "What about an appetizer now?" I slipped my finger under the silk panel of her little bikini pants. "Christ, these are already wet."

"Thom... as..." Kick purred my name, reminding me of the day we met.

I lost my senses and gave in to desire. My fingers took over, playing with her pussy, easing around her folds, working her bud. Her hips encouraged my actions until the hum under my skin began. I felt Kick's too. Fuck, we were so close.

Then a group of people laughed from below, breaking our spell.

"No appetizer for you, baby. Should've kept my wits." I slowly removed my fingers and let my head fall into the doorframe. "We have to work on this aura business." I pulled my hand to my mouth and licked my fingers, savoring her sweetness.

Her eyes sparked with desire as she watched me. "It is hella hard to hold it in now."

There was an understatement. In order to help her heal faster, every evening we'd been putting all our effort into joining auras, starting with meditation and ending with mind-blowing orgasms. We had inadvertently caused a new problem. The energy now tickled under my skin constantly, like it begged to be released.

"Glowing in front of the guests is not a good look?"

She scrunched her nose. "It's the idea of answering those questions. Hell, I can't explain it. Add in the Felidae knowing why it happens and the word *embarrassing* also comes to mind. Unless you want to hide up here the rest of the day. Lock the door and draw the drapes. Our guests might understand."

Laughter from the veranda floated up again, breaking our bubble for good.

I sighed in resolution. "Sorry, wifey. The next time you call my name, I want you yelling it. Besides, the caterers cleared away our meal and the fire pit's almost ready to make the gluten-free s'mores you requested instead of cake. I, for one, plan to eat a marshmallow off your nose."

Kick brushed her fingertips down the front of my waistcoat. I'd removed the jacket when we ate. "What the hell is it about you in a vested suit?" She inhaled slowly, like she savored me as I had done to her. "Just does it for me. Watching you work the crowd in your dark linen…" She touched my bare forearms. "Cyndi calls this arm porn."

Kick bit her lip, I guess to keep from laughing at the face I made. "I adore your friend, but she can be weird." Who the hell cared about forearms? As long as they worked.

.   .   .

I SNIFFED THE AIR, CONFIRMING MY SUSPICIONS THE FIRE PIT WAS ready, then grabbed her hand and maneuvered us through the doors to the balcony. "We need to get back. Besides, you also owe me a foxtrot. Oh, and no one else gets to dance with you in this dress." I adjusted my trousers. "I can't handle it."

Her laughter tickled my ears and other areas. "What about my boys, my brother, and Uncle Billy?"

"Alright, they get a pass. One dance each."

Kick squeezed my arm and shook her head.

I pulled a remote from my pocket and pressed a button. The opening bars to Tony Bennett's "The Best is Yet to Come" floated up from the outdoor speakers. Several people turned and began clapping as we descended the steps. Pulling her hand to my mouth, I kissed Kick's knuckles and winked. "Come on, Mrs. Harrison. I have a feeling the party's just begun."

*****

Turn the page to read the cut scenes from the original edition of *Kick Home*.

5 2

BONUS CUT SCENES

These scenes takes place after the Poker night, when Thomas, Banger, and Dylan interrupt an interchange between Big Jonn and Kick. They have a small fight in the book, but there may have been some unresolved issues the following morning. (Also, the location has changed from Kick's house to the farmhouse, but I can call artistic license on that one. ☺)

THE BIG FIGHT

THOMAS

The toasty warmth and clean-scented air of my kitchen welcomed me after a hard workout with Eddie. The space was devoid of signs of lunch. Considering Kick's strict schedule had played a key role in bringing her health back in balance so quickly, I was concerned she might not have been feeling well.

The silence in the house was another clue something was off. Was she sleeping or had she left? An emergency, perhaps? I pulled my phone from my pocket—no missed texts.

The downstairs was empty, along with the second floor, leaving my third-floor office. Since we'd blended our lives, Kick had informally taken the first-floor office, while I worked in the third-floor one—my inner sanctum, as she called it. I heard the faint tune of a song from the eighties as I approached the stair. Another quiet sound of sobs made a chill race down my spine.

Oh no.

I sprinted up the steps. I'd meant to tell her about the damn videos, but the time never seemed right to bring it up.

I spotted Kick at my desk. A stone-cold mask shifted into place when she noticed me. My head dropped in shame. I squeezed my eyes shut, pinching the bridge of my nose as I listened to her click through files, knowing exactly what they were—security footage that I'd kept of her from the fall. I should have thrown them out, but I couldn't bring myself to do it.

Her face turned back to my monitor. In a quiet, detached voice, she stated, "Some over-my-head router issue is happening with my laptop. It wouldn't let me log in, so I came up here. I suppose... it's my fault, really." She double-clicked the mouse. "This file had my name on it. Nosey me wondered if you were working on a surprise." She looked up. Her cool smile refused to reach her eyes, breaking my heart.

"No part of me thought you'd been spying."

The air was acrid from anxiety—mine—and anger—hers. I ran a frantic hand through my hair.

"Swear to Christ, darlin'... meant to tell you about these, but hadn't figured out how to bring it up."

"You spied. On me." Kick's voice stayed deadly calm. I

would've given anything for her furious temper right then. "This is all kinds of fucked up."

All my senses woke, but that was my reality now when it came to her. The air in the room seemed to solidify as I struggled to inhale. I shook my head. After all the impossibilities we'd already shared, this couldn't be the uncrossable line. I started cautiously, pleading, "From the first night we met, I had to make sure you were safe. Somehow, I needed it. No matter what happened between us, I knew I always would."

"You needed footage of me falling apart? This feels like something Big Jonn would do."

She was looking at footage from the afternoon of our fight in Mick & Hugh's, when I tossed Young Jonn out of the store, then Kick threw me out a few minutes later. My spine stiffened and my fists clenched. Did she really believe her words, or were they from shock? How dare she put that man and me in the same category. "I've never disrespected you. Graham, on the other hand…"

"Disrespect? Nice," she scoffed, waving her hand in dismissal of me. "Big Jonn's arrogant, but also harmless. Okay, you two almost came to loggerheads last night. But he cleared up the gossip articles."

"You can't seriously believe him." She was damn lucky Graham backed off as easily as he had. "The man doesn't care about you or your boundaries. He behaved because of Jake and Mateo."

"Do you care about them?" She swept her hand in front of the screen. "This looks like disrespecting my boundaries. I've never seen shots from this angle. How are they possible? You crossed a big line here."

I opened my mouth to add to my defense, but she cut me off. "Especially with this one." Kick clicked on the video I'd heard on the walk up. A tear slid from her hazel eyes. "This… I can't abide."

It was footage of her and Macushla on the patio dancing. She forwarded to the part where she collapsed into a sob on her bench.

She stared at the screen, sounding detached as she watched. "I had no idea there were mics on the cameras. My files don't have sound."

My fingers slammed through my hair again, making it stand on end. That whole day would forever stay imprinted in my mind. From finding Young Jonn Graham threatening Kick to her throwing me out of the store and possibly out of her life to seeing this and running a search on her. I'd finally understood her and lost her at the same time. But the video... it haunted me.

"This...this is so..." Kick's jaw had set, but her eyes held her vulnerability, revealing a heart broken.

I'd done that. Again. "I split in half that night."

"You weren't the only one," I mumbled. Damn her for not seeing it, seeing me. I'd been ready to walk away, then I saw this and had to stay.

She leveled a pissed-off glare at me. She had me to rights. The bright afternoon light warming the room mocked the darkness settling in my heart. Deep down, I believed we could work past this, though it would hurt like hell.

"Did you notice that's the last video in the folder?" I asked through gritted teeth. "That night shattered me as much as it did you—"

"I seriously doubt that."

I raised my hands in surrender. "Fine. It shook me to my core, though. I knew then—"

"Knew what?"

"That I'd do anything to keep you safe. That I was falling for you."

Kick jumped up and paced the room. Finally, her fury showed, giving me hope. Kick's temper meant she still cared. Lord help anyone she went cold rock on. "You were falling for me, so you could, what? Stalk me? Do you think having feelings makes this okay?"

"Yes, but no, too. I told Banger to take me out of the surveillance loop the next morning. I had to trust Banger's protection would be enough for the both of us."

She spun on her heel with fury filling her eyes. "Jaysus Thomas! Do you know how this makes me feel? Like I've been handled. Or manipulated. I sure as hell never expected it from you."

Her last comment whipped my head back like I'd been slapped. My temper flared in response. "Of course you were handled, dammit. No one targets a barista for shits and giggles. My instincts were on alert from the first night with the graffiti. Don't be naïve."

"Argh!" Kick slammed her hands on the desktop before jumping up. I cut off any more protests. I'd had enough. "Banger has an entire security team on you. Do you think only Siobhan monitors your feed?"

Kick jammed her hand on her hip. "Are there cameras I don't know about? Inside my house, maybe? Did you watch me in my bedroom?"

Breath shot through my nose like a bull about to charge. "Tell me you're fucking kidding right now."

I took a step toward her and made myself stop. I was too angry. "Your temper's doing the talking, not you. You know me better than that. Banger walked you through each camera's location. He told me so."

Kick stopped moving and became like a statue with her arms folded tightly across her chest. I couldn't tell if I'd gotten through. I moved a few steps again. She did know me. She knew I'd never purposefully violate her. Didn't she? She dropped her arms and took off, charging for the stairs. A sharp spark shot between us when I reached for her arm, to keep her near, to keep her talking. Suddenly, I was terrified she'd leave the house and never return. Kick shouted at the sting, pulling her hand into her abdomen. "Don't follow me!"

I bent down to pet a shaking Macushla as her mama stormed down the steps. "She'll be fine, girl. Won't she?" The dog answered by licking my hand hesitantly. I didn't know if it was to reassure or

console me.

THE MAKE-UP

KICK

The back door slammed shut after I stomped over the threshold into the chilly March afternoon, without a jacket and shoes. Cold usually made my joints hurt, so I tried to avoid it at all costs. Furious to my marrow, the chill had no effect on me at the moment. Or I just didn't care.

I pounded my way through the backyard, down the path to the clearing. Roots and slick debris on the ground nearly stopped my progress. The pond seemed to call to me, and pride kept me moving that way.

I'd heard gunshots earlier and figured Banger was on the range. Part of me hoped he was still hanging around, so I could give him a piece of my mind. Another part of me wanted him to be long gone. I wasn't about to get into a battle over semantics with him or Thomas. They were dead wrong for spying on my most intimate moment—the night I broke apart only to have Shane knit me back together.

I halted at the water's edge. Thomas had hurt me, but I'd also hurt him. Did embarrassment over knowing Banger's people and Thomas watched my breakdown fire my temper? Or did guilt?

Thomas had been right about the footage in the garden being the last file. I hadn't noticed anything from inside my house, even though I'd accused him of it. I also didn't tell him about the impossible encounter with Shane. Is that what set me off? He'd come close to a secret I didn't understand myself. I sure as hell couldn't explain it to Thomas. And how silly did that sound, considering everything I knew about the Felidae?

I growled in frustration at a couple of Canada geese doing laps around the pond. Thomas was right.

I'd given an entire security team permission to see those files. If Banger's people could see those moments, why wouldn't I let the man I love in on it? That was easy to answer. Thomas took an advantage I hadn't given him. My cluelessness about the extent of my troubles back then didn't matter.

Anger at the situation spread up my spine again. The truth stared me straight in the face. Like picking at a scab on a wound, I had to admit my family needed help to stay safe. Even with the security improvements, I kept trying to fix everything on my own. The bottom line was I could be vulnerable to the people set on hurting us or to those protecting us. But vulnerability was unavoidable either way.

I squatted down and wrapped my maxi skirt tight to my ankles, then vigorously rubbed my calves.

The chill finally penetrated my adrenaline-fueled state, sparking some sense in me. Pain set in with an unmatched quickness. Mud seeping through my socks, squished between my toes. I dropped my head to my knees in frustration. I'd been an idiot. I hadn't listened to Thomas's defense or trusted his motives. He deserved the benefit of the doubt, not the presumed evil intention.

I had reacted... like my mother would. Fuck. Forty-seven years old and I still defaulted to behavior that I'd learned under her tutelage. Being like Bobby was the worst kind of insult and completely true in this instance. I'd treated Thomas as an enemy instead of an ally, thanks to my embarrassment over the night itself.

I remembered all times Bobby had been her most lethal. The meanness came out when she felt she had an advantage. She was deadly when she'd viewed herself as weak. I had to kill that part of me immediately or Thomas and I wouldn't last.

Tears streamed down my cheeks. I brushed a few away, then let the rest slide unimpeded, as they cleansed the shame.

The first sensations to hit me when I opened the mudroom door were the smell of brewed coffee, then the heat. Pain sliced through my nose on the inhale, thanks to the contrast in temperatures between outside and in. Briskly rubbing my hands together and holding them over my face, I exhaled, hoping to thaw out quicker. The socks came off next, dropping them straight into the garbage can. My nerves turned into sharp knives as my body warmed.

Still amped with adrenaline, I didn't dare touch the coffee. I heard the light tapping of computer keys from the first-floor office and was pulled toward Thomas. The need to make this right was foremost. My body would have to come up to temperature without any help.

Heading straight for the doorway without thinking of cleaning up, I found Thomas at the desk with my laptop. His furrowed brow stirred my shame again. I'd put that concerned and hurt expression on his handsome face.

"Your log-in problem is fixed." He didn't bother to look at me as he clipped his words.

"Thanks, but—"

Thomas looked up at me. What I saw cut off my next thought. His silver eyes had darkened to a cold charcoal, like he was gearing up for war. My chest lifted in self-defense, but I owed it to him to make the first move.

I inhaled and finished my thought. "I screwed up. I was surprised and hurt that you took liberties before they'd been given. I was so mad, I wanted to spit… or kick you. However, you were right too. I never considered how many eyes are on my security footage every day. In the end, you've always been on my side, my champion. I shouldn't have treated you as if you're one of those who have harassed me. I don't like being vulnerable, and I took it out on you."

Thomas looked shocked at my change in direction. Didn't that convict me more? I bit my lip, wondering what he'd do now.

Trying his best to stifle a smirk, Thomas swiveled the desk chair toward me, spread his knees wide and held his hands out. "If you're that mad, just go for the balls."

"What?" Scrunching my nose at his lunacy, I tittered at the comment. "No way. No one gets to hurt them. Not even me."

"You still want them, then?" He challenged me with a lifted eyebrow. I matched his brow lift, adding a curt nod. I had more to say though. "I'm upset over the timing. Call me naïve, I don't care, but I didn't know Banger had given you access to my files. One of you should've said something."

Thomas rolled his shoulders and raked his fingers through his shaggy hair. "I'd do it all over again."

I threw my hands in the air in frustration. How could he not see my perspective?

"You weren't supposed to happen." Thomas spat out, his hand slapping his thigh. "You've upended me from the beginning."

I folded my arms across my chest. "Are we having a pissing contest about whose life changed more? Hello? Felidae, anyone?"

His expression moved from defensiveness to doubt to surrender as he stared at me. "You know you're my heartbeat and the air I breathe?" I knew and trusted in the depth of his feelings for me, but I'd never considered how quickly they might have developed before he said anything.

I rolled my eyes, instantly regretting the move when Thomas winced. "Sue me for the cheesy words, but they fit." He continued, "You've got to admit your life's been in danger since the day we met. When I was overseas, it drove me crazy being so far away, not knowing if you were safe. You'd already made these…

in-roads into my locked-up heart. It exposed me to vulnerability again. I didn't know what to do about it. So, yeah, I had Banger loop me into the feed reports. The alternative was a constant stream of phone calls, making sure he did everything possible to protect you."

Thomas let out a shaky breath. "It wasn't about stalking you, darlin'. My soul needed easing. Don't you get it? Your safety has never been optional for me." His head dropped. Since he'd never displayed

shame over his emotions, I interpreted his posture as conflict.

"Yes. I get it." I moved to the desk, leaning my hip on the end.

He lifted his gaze. "You do?" His eyes lighted with surprise and a dash of hope. The desperation and defensive set to his jaw vanished.

My heart eased as a grin raised the corner of my mouth. "Did I let you off the hook too easily?"

Thomas reached for my hips and shifted me between his legs. "Christ no. For a while, I thought I'd done the unforgivable."

"People do a lot of fucked up stuff when they're in love." I leaned on my hands and tilted my head to the side. "I can't fathom you doing anything I couldn't forgive, though. Never. Sometimes, I will need a moment to clear my thoughts."

He ran his hands up my back and down my thighs. "Christ, you're freezing. Didn't you grab a coat?"

Thomas's hand traveled down my leg, lifting my foot. His eyes widened in surprise at the dirt and scrapes on my soles. "Or shoes?"

"Case in point to what I just said?" I sat on top of the desk, closed the laptop, and slid it out of the way.

Thomas rucked up my skirt to where it was clean, or at least good enough to wipe my feet. A wisp of air from the floor register caught in the open space and fluttered the rest of the material up.

"Mmm." His eyes hooded as his hands reached farther up.

The differences in our body heat caused more stabbing pain in my legs as the circulation returned.

Placing a foot against his chest, I pushed Thomas back in the chair. The air blew my hem higher, but I didn't care. "Listen, pal, there are some things I need to be certain you understand." One of those cursed jolts that happened whenever we were angry shot through me at our touch. It ran up my leg and beyond.

"Shit!" My foot lifted for a brief second of its own accord, until I set it hesitantly back in his lap. "What the hell?"

"I've never minded the sting." A devilish grin spread across Thomas's face as he examined my muddy legs. The only recognition he'd felt the charge too came from a flex in his jaw. "Not where you're concerned." A molten gaze lifted to mine as his hand moved to his balls. He didn't adjust himself, though.

He grabbed my ankle and rubbed it against him, letting me know where the jolt landed.

"Stop lusting and listen. Please." I leaned in, snapping my fingers in front of him. I'd forgotten I wasn't wearing a bra. Well, it was a Sunday. The scoop-necked tee impeded my efforts to make a point.

That lust-filled glare moved from my chest up to my face. Love softened both the blue in his eyes and the cold steel in his voice. "I'm listening. Say everything you need to."

My foot stayed on his tight abs while the other leg rested on the seat along his thigh. I clasped my hands in my lap. "I was a bitch. I admit to needing physical protection, even if I didn't understand it before. But…" I pressed harder into him. "I'm also no longer the wilting flower who cowed in the shadow of a big, strong man. I fight my battles now. Hell, I've fought the wicked witch my whole life. Honestly, the boogeyman doesn't frighten as much as he pisses me off."

"You think you cowed behind Shane?" Interesting. That was what Thomas picked up from my speech.

"Yes. Him and Dad. I felt safe in their shadows." A shiver ran through me. "Don't know if I'd be as far along in my recovery if I hadn't been forced to face life out in the open though."

Thomas shook his head. "I seriously doubt it." He pulled his chair up to the desk and scooted my ass closer to him. His eyes followed his hands as they rhythmically rubbed up and back. "They gave you what you needed. I'm trying to do the same. Or do you question that?"

"Not at all. Only… you need to hear this, Cowboy. I… I'm done being patronized. And I won't be owned." My foot moved south, rubbing his hardening cock through his jeans.

"Patronizing? Darlin', I respect no one more than you. I hang on to your opinions. I have since we first met." His eyes darkened. "As for owning…" He lurched forward, reaching all the way up my skirt. With the tips of his fingers and a little help from me, Thomas slid my underwear off and threw it on the floor somewhere, leaving me exposed in the good way. "Damn right. I claim ownership of you." He laid his head between my legs, spent a moment nuzzling. Those dark irises glazed over as they lifted back to mine. "What I've been trying to tell you is… you own me too."

The tip of Thomas's straight Roman nose tickled as it softly stroked along one thigh, then the other. Caressing, as he breathed me in. Watching him, as those criminally long, black lashes touched his cheek, he took my breath away. Yeah, I understood why he had those videos. And I probably would've done the same, if I were in his shoes.

The truth of the thought struck deep and quick in my heart. Thomas did own it and my body, not because of some outdated social order, but because I needed him too. Own me? Hell, I wanted him to inhabit me.

My muscles twitch with the need to give him more, to give him everything. But he wrapped his hands around me, holding me in place. His nose slid into my exposed folds, and he gently blew on my clit. A better jolt shot through me—the kind that hummed and set my aura free.

Thomas groaned as he licked along my seam. The sensation mixed with his love set my body aflame.

"Damnitall, you own me. All of me." He placed each of my ankles on his shoulders, forcing me to lean on my elbows. "So beautiful." Then Thomas grabbed my hips and pulled me toward his mouth. "I accept your apology, Baby. Now watch me give you mine."

*****

The End!

THANK YOU FOR READING KICK AND THOMAS'S STORY. I HOPE YOU LOVE these characters as much as I do. What's next, you ask? Sign up for my newsletter by scanning the QR code. You'll find the sign-up there, along with all my social media links.

MY WEBSITE ALSO HAS THE SALES INFORMATION ON CYNDI Sendaydiego's book, *Love You Better*. That's right, Kick's bestie has a standalone book in the same world. She gets a second chance with an ex you haven't met yet. Blake is a successful restaurateur and single dad. So, why does he scare the pants off her... literally?

- If scanning QR codes isn't your thing, you can also get on the newsletter list by going to www.kallynjones.com. Letters are sent monthly except in the run-up to a book release. You can unsubscribe at any time.
- **You can make a difference in an author's career by leaving a review.** Seriously. Writing a short review helps readers like you find their next favorite book. If composing a review makes you uncomfortable, a rating is a wonderful gift too.
- Like with the first two books, *Kick Home* has a playlist on Spotify, called *Kick Home Tunes*. A link is also on my website.

AUTHOR'S NOTE

Thank you so much for taking this journey into Kick and Thomas's world. Early scenes between these two popped into my head nine years ago. Back then, I was sure the cannabis part of the story wouldn't be speculative when published. Alas, it helped me imagine what the scenario might look like in my state when it finally happens (including how the opposition to legalization might play out). This is a reminder, however, that cannabis products are still illegal in real-world North Carolina at the time of publishing.

The secret society of humans with anti-aging genetic variances? Well... ;-)

ACKNOWLEDGMENTS

- To my beloved Jones crew: Unending gratitude for your support with this new venture. Thank you for your advice with story ideas. Thank you for cooking for yourselves most nights, now that you're 'big boys.'
- To my editors, D.A. and Lisa: Thank you for fixing all the words. Your enthusiasm for Kick and Thomas's story means so much.
- Hugs go out to Mom, Linda, Joye, Shannon, Jenn M., Bethany, Jeanne, Laura, Annie, Renae, and Jamie. Your evangelism for my work is humbling. Your friendship and support are essential to my spirit.
- To my budding ARC team: I'm indebted to you for helping spread the word about my little series.
- To my first readers: Undying gratitude to you for taking a chance on an unknown author with little "social proof" and a big idea. There are endless books to choose from, and I'm honored you picked mine. You have brought smiles and encouragement to my first year in this publishing venture. Hugs to all of you. XO KJ

ABOUT THE AUTHOR

Kallyn Jones returned to her roots as an author after a successful career as a brand specialist. She brings the same passion for diving into unique stories as she writes about her sexy, down-to-earth characters and their offbeat families. She delights in finding heroes and heroines in unusual places and believes hard-fought happily ever afters are the sweetest.

Kallyn lives in her adopted hometown of Raleigh, North Carolina, with her own hero, their three sons, and their dog. In her spare time, she enjoys trail walks, digital painting, and testing out new, "healthy" recipes. She's proud to say her fellas usually like her experimental dishes. *Usually.*

Follow Kallyn Here:

Website: www.kallynjones.com
Facebook: KallynJonesAuthor
Instagram: KallynJonesWriteNow
Goodreads: Kallyn Jones
BookBub: Kallyn Jones